Changeling Press, LLC

ChangelingPress.com

Darkling

Torri Heat

Darkling
Torri Heat

ISBN: 978-1-60521-829-8

Publisher:
Changeling Press LLC
315 N. Centre St.
Martinsburg, WV 25404
ChangelingPress.com

Printed in the U.S.A.

Editor: Margaret Riley, Crystal Esau
Cover Artist: Bryan Keller

The individual stories in this anthology have been previously released in E-Book format.

Table of Contents

Nyctophilia (Darkling 1)
Torri Heat

Ava Green is doing her best to live her life quietly and stay out of her small town's gossip -- until Jasper Knight, a dark private investigator who seems to keep popping up at the worst moments, comes to town.

Ava can't deny the pull she feels around Jasper, but the more time she spends around him, the more she has memories of a past that surely can't be real. Jasper finally lets her in on his secret -- he's a werewolf. But he's not what she should be afraid of.

Someone -- or something -- in her quaint little town is hunting local werewolves, and picking them off one by one.

Chapter 1

The first time Jasper showed up at the coffee shop, I didn't even notice him. Not because he wasn't worth noticing, but because my attention was focused on Mollie, my best friend, who was, as usual, regaling me with stories of her exciting Saturday night. I, as usual, had stayed home, despite her pleas for me to come out with them.

It was a Monday morning, and I sat at my small table in the back corner of our small coffee shop. I always worked here for two reasons. One, the coffee shop was one of the few places in Merrillan, Wisconsin that offered free Wi-Fi, and two, everyone knew this table was mine. I sipped my tea as Mollie stopped mid-sentence, and her mouth dropped open.

I waved my hand in front of her face. "Earth to Mollie!" I was teasing, but she knew it made me uncomfortable when she was so blatant in checking people out. I would much rather blend into the background.

She ignored me, her voice dropping to a whisper. "That is the hottest guy I have ever seen."

I should have known Mollie was man-watching. I really wished she wouldn't draw so much attention towards us, but Mollie didn't care what anyone thought of her. She didn't need to. A tiny, perfect blonde, and a force of nature, she was loved by the whole town. That was the price to pay to have her as my best friend -- a small price.

"Ava, seriously, turn around. And then I'll drop it, I swear."

I rolled my eyes, trying to be as subtle as possible. Merrillan was small, and we knew all the guys here, so someone must have gotten a haircut or something to catch her eye. I turned to look around the coffee shop. Fortunately for me, I found the subject of Mollie's scrutiny. Unfortunately for me, familiar looking bright brown eyes had caught my gaze. I blushed and flung myself back around in my chair.

Mollie was right -- he *was* hot, with dark, messy hair

and a complexion Mollie would've spent weeks in a tanning bed to achieve. Tattoos peeked out from under the collar of a dark leather jacket. Definitely not my type, but hotter than I'd expected. And he had 100% seen me checking him out. Hopefully no one else had.

"Are you sure we don't know him already?" I asked. I was having a major case of *déjà vu*, like I had met him before.

Mollie shook her head. "Definitely not. I would remember that body anywhere. So hot."

"He's okay." I downplayed the newcomer's looks, hoping to disperse some of the embarrassment I was feeling.

Mollie sighed. "Sometimes I don't understand what you're looking for, Ava." Before I could respond, she was back to the story she had been telling me before the stranger walked into the coffee shop.

* * *

After that first morning, I watched him every day. I should say, I watched him get his coffee every day, from my small table. I couldn't shake the feeling I knew him from somewhere. He came in every morning, just like I did. Ordered his coffee. Large. Black. No frills. At least not with his beverage order.

His mannerism when he ordered said coffee was a different story. A smile for the middle-aged cashier who took his order, asking how her son in high school was. A wink for the college-aged barista who responded with blushes and smiley faces on his to-go cup next to his name -- Jasper. He moved through these interactions with an ease I envied. Of course, the smouldering smile and effortless way he pushed his dark hair off his forehead definitely helped. It surprised me. I never considered myself to be the judgmental sort, but I guess I had pictured a scowl more fitting on his face. I'd probably be tempted to draw smiley faces on his cup too with a smile like that.

Tempted for sure, but I wouldn't. "Ava Green" and "flirting" typically weren't heard in the same sentence. They weren't in the same book, for that matter. And with Merrillan being so tiny, it was hard to break free of whatever box you got shoved into growing up. My box happened to have a giant label of "Socially Awkward," written in permanent marker. Don't get me wrong, it's gotten a lot better since I left town. By left town I mean attended college the next town over. My small group of friends didn't judge me when I stuck my foot in my mouth, I have my own little apartment, and my job is great, but college doesn't perform miracles. I wasn't about to sprint over to Jasper and throw him my number. I was happy to admire the new guy from afar. Leslie, the gossipy clerk at the local grocery store, told me Jasper was in town as a private investigator, working on some big case out of Chicago. He was a temporary fixture. But a handsome enough one to churn up the Merrillan rumour mill.

"Excuse me." Someone brushed against my arm, moving past. I muttered something noncommittally, not looking up from my computer. For the most part, I tried to stay out of the way of the gossip-crazy locals. The cute stranger from the big city was the biggest news since local teenagers were caught trying to tip cows on one of the surrounding farms. I would know. I edited the newspaper's blog post about it. The clueless teens mistook a bull for a cow. Needless to say, the cops were waiting for them when they got out of the hospital.

That was the reason I worked at this table every day. It was secluded, tucked away in the back corner, and barely visible from the front door. Even with the community style seating, no one ever tried to sit here. Compared to the long tables, the table for two I sat at seemed too intimate. It was the perfect place for me to get my work done and to people watch without anyone trying to socialize.

"Pardon me." Someone else bumped my chair, squeezing behind me. I gave a brief smile, not paying attention. My spot was the perfect place to daydream about Jasper, the mysterious new guy with his charm and his black coffee and his full lips. His sultry smile revealed teeth that were bright against his tanned skin, and his shirts always stretched tight across his chest. I could understand the appeal for everyone else, but Jasper's brooding eyes and his bad boy looks were usually not what I found attractive in a man. But I could still fantasize. I could imagine his soft lips covering my own, his kisses on my neck, his lips on my...

"Is this seat taken?"

I glanced up from my stupor, expecting to see another hapless customer squeezing past. But I was sorely mistaken. I was looking at my daydream come to life. Jasper in his leather jacket with his tattooed knuckles curled around the paper cup of his black coffee, standing in front of my table. The one that people brushed past on their way to the restroom. Why was he here? "No. Well yes -- I mean no," I stammered.

He smirked, obviously finding humour in my flustering. "Is that a yes or a no? The coffee shop's pretty busy today, and I'd really rather not drink my coffee in the rain." His accent washed over me, too warm for a Chicago accent. Looking around I realized while I was busy narrating my love story with a guy I didn't know, the coffee shop had gotten crowded with people trying to avoid the cold rain. Fall in Merrillan comes quick and hits hard.

I could do this. I could talk to a handsome man. Right? I collected myself and started again. "No, that seat isn't taken. I was trying to say there might not be a lot of space because of my laptop." I gestured towards my gear sprawled out over the tabletop.

His smile grew wider, his bright eyes flashing with amusement. "I'm sure I can squeeze in." Jasper's smile was so beautifully imperfect. There was a quality about it I couldn't place, but it drew me in. Regardless of whatever it was, I found myself unable to say no to him. But before I could respond he was already making room for himself, sitting down at the small table. While I wasn't going to refuse, Jasper's assumption that I was going to move my laptop for him grated me the wrong way. Who did he think he was?

I locked my computer. "I guess I'm done working for now then." I couldn't keep the edge out of my voice. I had known this guy for all of two seconds and I was already aggravated.

He seemed impervious to the ice in my voice, because his smile seemed to get even bigger. "Guess so." He sounded pleased with himself. Jasper might have been the most handsome guy I'd seen in a while, but he was also pretty full of himself.

As I started to pack away my computer, he spoke up again. "I'm Jasper Knight." I glanced up and saw his hand stretched out in my peripheral vision. *I know*, I thought to myself. But score one for me, because I managed to not blurt that out loud. Although the way Jasper looked like he was trying not to laugh I had a feeling it didn't matter that I hadn't spoken. He knew without me saying a word.

I weakly offered him my hand in return. "Ava. I feel like we've met somewhere before. Did you go to the community college in Easton?"

Jasper's smooth voice sounded off. "No, I didn't."

I sounded crazy. Perfect.

He stretched out his long legs under the table. I hadn't noticed how tall he was before. "So, Ava, what do you do on that computer of yours all the time? I've noticed you working here almost every day."

Jasper had noticed me? He must have been teasing. We weren't just on different playing fields. We were on different planets. I brushed a lock of unruly hair behind my ears. "I'm a social media consultant. I keep businesses up to date on all the popular social apps when they're too busy to do it for themselves."

He twisted his full lips, and took a sip of his coffee. "Don't you need to be working out of their office for that?"

I tried my best to not roll my eyes. I had my career options planned out before I even started applying to colleges. The less personal contact the better. Less chances for me to make a fool out of myself. The fact that this conversation was flowing so well was a surprise to me. "No, I freelance for several different companies so I can work from home. The coffee shop keeps me from having only my cat as a critic…" I trailed off. I couldn't believe I had brought up the fact that I live alone with my cat to a guy who was hot enough to model. It screamed desperate. Or crazy. Or both? Probably both.

Jasper rolled with it. "Cat person, huh? I'm not too fond of cats myself." No wonder we weren't getting along. Moral differences, right there. "You're lucky though. Sometimes I wish I could work from home. Of course, it's kind of difficult to conduct investigations from my couch."

He didn't elaborate, likely assuming I knew what he was in town for. Which I did. But I wasn't about to let him know that. I put on a blank expression. "Oh? What line of work are you in?"

His gaze shot to mine. His eyes were such a bright brown. Almost rust in their colouring. And full of mischief. He knew what I was playing at, but I wasn't sure if he would play along.

"I'm a private investigator. But you already knew that, the same as I already knew you were a social media consultant, Ava Green. This town does not mess around when it comes to telling stories."

I blushed as Jasper flashed me another award-winning smile. There were many reasons I didn't try to flirt, my tomato coloured giveaway being one of them. "Okay. You caught me." I looked away from him, pretending to check out the muffin display to avoid his piercing stare. "So how long will you be in town?"

He ran one large hand over his face, looking frustrated. "I'm not too sure yet." For the first time since Jasper approached me, he seemed uneasy. "This case I'm working seems to be tougher than I originally expected."

My ears perked up. In a town this small, everyone knew everything. Why was a private investigator here? "What's the case?"

And just like that, his grin was back. "Ava, you strike me as an intelligent woman. I'm sure you understand the whole idea of a private investigation is it's, well, private."

He was teasing me, but I would have been lying if I'd

said I didn't like it. I understood what had all the women in town talking. Jasper Knight had more than just the looks. The way he spoke to me made me feel like I was the only person in the room worth talking to. "I figured it was worth a shot." I smiled back, confidence boosted. Adrenaline or something had to be pumping through my veins. My inner self was much less confident, and I had no idea who I was. It normally took me weeks to crack a joke with someone new -- after I had carefully planned it of course.

Jasper coughed and took a sip of his coffee. "Tell me what you do when you're not hard at work."

Daydream about you. I squashed the intrusive thought. "I hike. I like to be outside."

His eyes lit up. "Oh yeah? I'm pretty outdoorsy myself. Are there any good places to hike around here?"

Of course he was outdoorsy. "I usually head over to Harvest Falls, which is about a half hour drive from here. It's got the best views." I couldn't believe it. Here I was making easy, natural conversation with a guy. And not just any guy, Jasper Knight.

Jasper nodded. "What about closer in town, any good trails the locals frequent?"

His phrasing was weird, but I was sure that was me picking him apart. I chewed my lip as I considered my answer. It might have been my imagination, but I was pretty sure he was staring at my lips. "There's an older trail I use for my morning run. It's beautiful, but it's in pretty rough shape if you don't know where you're going."

Jasper finished his coffee and pushed his hair out of his eyes, his gaze unexpectedly serious. "Hey, Ava? Do me a favour."

If he smiled at me again, I would do a thousand favours for him. "Okay. What's up?"

"Stay out of the deep woods. At least until this investigation is over."

I burst out laughing. Whatever I was expecting, it wasn't that. I had grown up in Merrillan, playing hide and go seek with all the other kids my age in the thick woods surrounding the town's borders. This was before boys and popularity divided us. The scariest thing we ever saw out there was maybe a bear trail or two.

The laugh didn't stop a chill from racing up my spine. I had felt things in the woods before, could've sworn I heard voices calling for me. But I had been a child, and those were just childish fantasies.

He reached out and gently took my wrist, staring into my eyes as he did so. I drew back at the sudden contact, but didn't break away. "I'm serious. Promise me you'll stay out of the woods. It's not safe for you."

I frowned at him, my brow creasing in displeasure. He couldn't know what I had imagined as child, could he? I gently pulled my wrist away. "I don't know you. I'm not going to make a promise to a stranger. But if it makes you feel any better, I haven't been off the trails since I was sixteen."

Jasper's eyes flashed with annoyance and he stood. "Good. Keep it that way."

He turned and tossed his coffee cup in the recycling bin. When he looked back at me over his shoulder, amusement danced in his eyes once again, like there was some joke I was missing. "You're right though, you don't know me. But you will."

I sat in my chair wondering if that was a promise or a threat -- and which I wanted it to be. I doubted I would be able to work again after our encounter, but I pulled my laptop back out all the same. My computer had almost booted up when I realized what the confusing quality in his smile was that put me on edge. If I was being honest, it compelled me, too.

Hunger.

Chapter 2

I stopped at the grocery store on my way home to grab some food so I could at least try to pretend to cook. Grabbing a basket I headed to the fruit section -- luckily that didn't require any preparation. I snagged a bag of perfect looking oranges, feeling the fabric rip as I moved it to my basket. I watched in dismay as my bright oranges spilled all over the oatmeal coloured floors. It would be my luck I would make this kind of mess today. Hopefully no one had seen me. I bent over to stuff the fallen oranges back into my basket.

A deep voice rang out next to me. "Here. I can help you with that."

Jasper. Of course he would be here to see my giant mess in the middle of the store. Wonderful. I was still annoyed with him thinking he could order me about, and I definitely did not want his help. "It's fine. I've got it. Thanks."

Jasper chuckled. "I'm sure you do. But I'm still here, and I can help."

I continued to pick fruit up off the floor, trying to pretend like I didn't notice how close his body was to me. He passed me an orange, his fingers lightly brushing against mine. Abruptly, I stood up and turned to walk away.

Unfortunately, he followed. "You come here often?"

Rolling my eyes, I headed into the cereal aisle. "It's the only grocery store in town. So yes."

Jasper pretended to look at the cereal. "You don't like me." It was a statement, not a question. But it wasn't like it mattered to him. He didn't even know me.

"I never said that," I sighed. "I don't know you. I don't like people telling me what to do."

He grasped my shoulder lightly and I pulled away.

"You won't though, right? Go into the woods I mean." His voice was serious. I didn't get what the big deal was, but he could go bother someone else.

"You're not asking me, you're telling me," I informed him, and strode away.

"Next time I'll make sure I ask nicely!" His humour filled voice loudly followed me into the next aisle, but it held a note of truth underneath it. So much for not wanting to make a scene at the grocery store. I would have to do my best to make sure there wasn't a next time.

Managing to evade him for the rest of my shopping, I juggled a large bag of cat food to try and find my car keys. But Jasper's cheerful voice found me again. "That's a lot of cat food!" I groaned. Was he following me again? I ignored him, and kept digging in my purse for my keys.

"Let me give you a hand." He tried to take the bag, but I whirled around before he could. First the oranges, now he was here to watch me as I struggled with my giant bag of cat food. This was not shaping up to be a good look for me.

I finally managed to fish my keys out of my bag. "Got it!" I opened my car door and stowed the bag on the backseat. Jasper was leaning against the driver's door. "Why are you still here?"

"You don't mince words, do you?" He seemed amused by my irritation, which irritated me more. To top it off, how good he looked leaning against my car also annoyed me. My body was betraying my mind. "I thought this is what people who live in small towns do. You know, have polite conversation."

"Uh huh. Well someone told you wrong. For the most part, we just talk shit about each other behind everyone's backs," I said, hoping to move the conversation along.

Jasper smiled at me, but it didn't quite meet his eyes. "Don't I know it. Well, Ava, don't believe everything you hear." He touched my hand, looking like he wanted to say more, but I pulled away, eyeing the clerk watching us from the store. Last thing I needed was people talking about me.

"I don't." I rubbed my hand gently, still feeling his touch. But that was crazy. "I should go." Jasper nodded, like he had remembered where he was. He stuffed his hands into his pockets and strolled away, leaving me remembering the feeling of his skin on mine.

I got home still reeling from my interactions with

Jasper. My head was filled with questions. Why was he asking about me? What was he investigating? When would I see him again? Did I want to see him again? I was simultaneously annoyed at his presumptuous tone and desperate to get to know him better.

Guys like Jasper didn't think about girls like me. My parents, Jim and Monica, were a college professor and an artist respectively. They had tried to teach me my value wasn't based on my physical appearance, or my partners, or the labels on my clothes, but rather on what was in my mind. Of course, this value, combined with my talent for consistently putting my foot in my mouth, never won me any popularity points. On the other hand, I never seemed to be good enough at it to please my parents. I always felt like my personality was an affront to them in some way.

Really, if Jasper was that desperate for someone to pass the time with in Merrillan he was better off with Rose McDermott. Rose was the local beauty queen with the perfect blonde locks and large enough chest to secure her bombshell title. I was happy to let her have that spot. My newest flirting experience alone left me feeling exhausted.

Brushing off my racing thoughts, I wandered into my kitchen to put some food in Betty's dish. Upon hearing the food hitting the bowl, my large tabby came trotting into the room, winding herself around my feet. I gave her a few absentminded pats and moved towards the fridge, noticing my answering machine blinking angrily at me.

Shoot, I thought, my cell must have died again. There were some blessings to not being a member of the small town's inner circle, like not being glued to my phone. I was the worst for keeping it charged, and Mollie never let me live it down. Mollie worked as a hygienist for the local dentist, and kept me from living under a rock like I was prone to doing. She also called me on her lunch break every day to fill me in on the latest gossip, and was not impressed when she couldn't reach me.

Sure enough, as I pressed the play button her energetic voice filled the room. "Can you tell me what the point in you having a cell phone is if you never keep it charged?"

With my head in the fridge trying to find something edible I mentally spoke her next words along with her. "What if something happened to you? What if something happened to *me*?" As I sniffed some leftover Chinese takeout, her message wrapped up. "I'm buying you another phone charger to keep in your backpack. Call me. I have a story for you!"

For once in our friendship, I had a story for her as well. I wasn't sure if I was ready to share it yet. I sat down at my kitchen island and started eating the cold chow mein. I didn't pretend to be a chef. It's just me and Betty, and thankfully she never complains about what we eat. I grabbed my phone and called Mollie's cell as I ate.

She picked up on the first ring, huffing into the phone. "Hello. Nice of you to finally get back to me."

I smiled. Leave it to Mollie's dramatics to break me out of any mood. "I'm sorry my phone died. I promise to charge it tonight."

Mollie sighed. "No, you won't. You're so lucky I love you. Not everyone would put up with their best friend ghosting them nearly every day of their life!"

I attempted to sound contrite. "I know. I don't deserve you. Now what's the story you wanted to tell me earlier?"

Appeased, Mollie launched into a story about one of the locals whose teeth she cleaned today. Apparently, we went to school with the client's daughter, and her niece, who lived out in L.A., had been offered a television role on a major network. I would never say it to Mollie's face, but I couldn't care less about people I barely knew or who was getting married next spring. But it made her happy, and it kept me from being a complete outcast so I listened to her chatter contentedly. I wondered if she had heard anything new about Jasper. I wondered what he was doing right now. Thanks to this town's never-ending stream of gossip I knew where he was staying. He was probably eating something better than cold chow mein, and still wearing his leather jacket. Or maybe he had changed into pyjamas in his motel room, a tight white tee shirt stretching over his muscular chest, a pair of soft black bottoms slung low over his hips... that is, if he even wore pyjamas.

"Are you even listening to me?" For the second time today, I was shaken out of a daydream about this man. It was for the best. Regardless of how good he looked in his fictional sweatpants, he still had tried to tell me what to do without even knowing me.

"Of course, I'm listening," I placated her. "Go on."

"No, you weren't." Mollie lightly complained. "What was the last thing I said?"

"Umm..." I was caught.

Mollie sighed. "What has you so distracted tonight? Not that you normally love hearing these stories, but usually you at least pretend to have appropriate responses. Hold on a sec." I heard static as she muffled the speaker with her hand. "It's just Ava. I'll be right there."

Ben, Mollie's boyfriend of five years, must have been over at her house. Ben was a sweet guy, an accountant. He kept her grounded, and was the perfect balance to her contagious enthusiasm. They had met in college, and I was happy she had found someone so perfect for her. Mollie and Ben were my standards for relationships, but I doubted I would ever find something comparable. That would mean having to actually talk to a guy and not immediately put my guard up. My thoughts drifted towards Jasper again... what the hell was this guy doing to me? We had spoken for all of five minutes and here I was planning our future. I mean, there was no denying the guy would probably rock a tux.

"Sorry, where were we? Oh, yeah. You being distracted."

Now it was my turn to sigh. "It's nothing. Work stuff. You should go hang out with Ben. You can talk to me later."

She wasn't buying it. "You don't have 'work stuff,' Ava, you work off your computer. What is it?"

I could practically hear the gears of her mind churning as she worked over all the possibilities. "Ohmygod did you meet someone?"

I stood up, put my empty container in the sink, and walked to the living room. "No, Mollie, I did not meet anyone. Like really, do you even remember who you are talking to?"

"No. You can't fool me. I know those drawn out pauses, the feeling like you can't concentrate on anything else. That's how I was when I first met Ben. You met someone! Spill."

I started closing the curtains in the living room and wondered how I could get her to back off. I hadn't met anyone. Technically. It was nothing to tell her about though. Was it? "Mollie. I'm an independent woman. I do not need a guy to distract me. I'm pretty sure I do that well enough on my own. I promise you the second there is a potential man in my life, you will be the first to know. Now go pay attention to Ben before he thinks you like me more than him."

"Fine. Keep your secrets." She huffed. "I'll get them out eventually."

I walked over my sliding doors that opened onto my balcony. I had signed the lease for my apartment based on the balcony. The large sliding doors looked out onto the most perfect view of the edge of the woods, which always filled me with a sense of peace. Once I realized all the things I had been hearing and seeing were in my head, it became my happy place. My father was a passionate camper and the scoutmaster for the local boy scouts troop, and always brought me along on their weekend excursions. It was what had begun my love of hiking, and left me feeling capable out in the woods. "I know you will." I started to pull the curtains across the glass doors and stopped.

Mollie continued talking. "Are we still on for our lunch on Wednesday? At the diner?" The lunch she was referring to was our weekly date we had started in high school. But I was frozen with my hand gripping the curtain, looking out into the woods. The woods always brought me a sense of calm, the woods Jasper had annoyingly warned me to be cautious of. Looking back at me out of the bushes I could've sworn was a bright pair of animal eyes that definitely did not belong to a raccoon. Every hair on the back of my neck stood straight up, my nerves shot to hell.

"Ava? Lunch?"

I shook my head and blinked. Should I mention what I thought I'd seen to Mollie? When I looked again, the eyes weren't there anymore. She wouldn't understand anyway. Even when we were kids she thought my imagination was over the top. No, I must have spent too much time on my computer today. Or dreaming about a certain private investigator... "Sorry. Yes. Lunch. I'll see you Wednesday."

"Are you sure you're okay?"

I could hear the concern laced in her voice, and felt bad for making my best friend worry about me. Guilt for not telling her about Jasper spread through my chest. "I'm sorry, I'm honestly just tired. I'm okay. I'll see you Wednesday for lunch." I tried to sound as upbeat as possible. I didn't want her stressing about me all night.

"If you're sure... I'll let you get some rest. But make sure your phone stays charged! Love you." With that, she hung up before I even had the chance to say goodbye.

I triple checked the locks before I went into my room -- just in case. It seemed silly. Jasper had made me paranoid, nothing more. As I sat on my bed, I turned my laptop on and flicked through shows until an old episode I knew by heart popped up. Betty curled up on my lap, purring. I still felt unsettled. The whole thing with Jasper, the eyes I thought I saw looking out from the woods... Something wasn't adding up, and it left me feeling uneasy. I was missing something. I knew I had to be.

I left the show I was streaming running overnight. The few dreams I had were filled with images of Jasper, and eyes in the forest. After tossing and turning most of the night, I decided sleep was a lost cause and got ready to go for a run instead.

Running cleared my head. It was a habit I had started when I was younger and was difficult to break now. I jammed earphones in and turned on some upbeat music as I set off into the still dark morning. Jasper's warning echoing in my head, I avoided my usual shortcut through the woods, sticking to the main roads. I would never admit it to him, but something wasn't sitting right with me about the woods right now. I hadn't felt afraid of them since I was a child, but the last few days had brought it all back. I tried to let go of all the thoughts plaguing me, focusing on work instead. Unfortunately, Jasper's bright eyes kept coming into view instead of my current projects. I debated calling my mom, but our uncomfortable relationship had never included talking about boys, and now didn't seem like a good time to start.

I eventually found myself making my way to the old park on the outskirts of town. No one really came out this way anymore since the new playground had been built around the corner from the elementary school. But it was still nice to come out to, and was a perfect midpoint for my route. I took my earphones out and sat down on the low hill, watching the fog dissipate over the tree line. The trees had only just started to turn colour, and the sight was truly beautiful. Too beautiful to be dangerous.

"Am I interrupting something?" A deep voice, thick with humour. One I recognized.

I turned to see Jasper walking towards me, looking only slightly dishevelled. "No," I answered him truthfully. "But what are you doing here?" What *was* he doing out here this early? I came to this place because it was deserted and I could be alone with my thoughts, not plagued by them.

"Out for a run, same as you, I imagine." He gestured towards my athletic clothes and smiled at me, brushing the dark locks from his eyes.

"Uh huh. Out for a run. In that?" I pointed to his black leather jacket, which seemed pretty impractical for a morning jog.

Jasper sat down next to me, casually lounging back on his forearms. "Maybe I'm in better shape than you are."

I scoffed. But it was probably true. His arm was as thick as my waist. I decided to not make a snide comment, ignoring him and turning my face back towards the pinkish sky over the forest instead.

"It's really something, isn't it?" he asked me, his voice softer than I had heard it before. My heart jumped. After all his annoying appearances, the fact we were on the same page about something so pure really hit me.

It was like he had read my mind. I turned towards him to agree, finding him not staring at the beginnings of the sunrise, but at my face. It made me uncomfortable, and I felt myself flush.

Jasper shuffled closer towards me, and I could have kicked myself for being so aware of his proximity. His shoulder brushed against mine, and I could feel his breath close to my ear.

I opened my mouth to protest but he cut me off. "Shh. Don't worry, I won't interrupt anymore. The sun will be coming up soon, and you don't want to miss it," He whispered into my ear, and my stomach tightened with every low word. Jasper faced the horizon again, and together we watched the sun break over the trees. I was preoccupied as I noticed Jasper's hand subconsciously crawl towards mine until our pinkies touched. This time I didn't pull away. I embraced the small touch in such a beautiful situation.

It felt like we had shared more than just an everyday moment together, and we sat there quietly for a few minutes after. I didn't know what to say to him, or even how to say it if I knew. I opened my mouth to speak, but no words came out.

He jumped to his feet. "I should go. You probably have to get back and get ready for work. I'll see you around, Ava Green." One last devastatingly beautiful grin, and he was gone.

After a moment I stood up, too. I wasn't sure where to go from here. I wasn't sure how I felt anymore. There was only one way to figure out what was going on. I had to talk to Jasper again.

Chapter 3

"Come on, girl! It'll be fun, I swear!"

Mollie was trying to persuade me, once again, to go out with her and Ben to the bar in Easton. "I don't think so Mol. I'm pretty tired." I *was* tired. I also didn't like the bar. It was noisy. And busy. And dark. Did I mention noisy? And I didn't enjoy being the third wheel.

"Pleeease?" Mollie wheedled. "I feel like you haven't come out in ages. I'll even lend you a dress."

I felt my resolve caving. What she said was true. I hadn't been out with her in ages. "Okay, fine. But you're buying me a drink. And I want to be home by midnight." My voice was stern, but I smiled at Mollie's excitement over the other end.

"You won't regret it! Come over now so we can get ready together."

I hung up the phone and headed back out the door, hoping she was right and I wouldn't end up regretting my decision. My bed was sounding awfully tempting right now.

Mollie met me at the door in full makeup, a drink in hand, before I could even get my shoes off. "We are going to have so much fun!" she said. "Babe, stay out here," she called over her shoulder to Ben. "We have girl stuff to do." She dragged me down the hall to her room and shoved the cocktail glass into my hands. "First things first. Drink."

I obliged, taking a big gulp of the cocktail. I coughed and sputtered as it hit the back of my throat, warming my belly on the way down. "Shit, Mol, what is this? Are you trying to get me trashed?"

Mollie laughed from inside her closet. "You've been so uptight lately! It'll be good for you to relax for one night." She came back out holding a tight black dress. "What do you think? Drink."

I took another swallow of the deadly concoction, the alcohol already racing through my bloodstream. "I think you'll look great in that."

She shook her head. "No, this is for you to wear." I took

a second glance at the dress. Mollie was a good four inches shorter than me, and this dress would emphasize every extra inch of skin. I took another sip before she even asked.

"You aren't going to take no for an answer, are you?" This dress would be my enemy tonight. And I doubted she would let me wear my sneakers.

"Nope." She tossed the dress at me, and walked out the door. "Get dressed. There's a pair of wedges in the closet you can wear. We're leaving here in ten minutes."

Shit. I finished the last of my drink, definitely feeling buzzed. Hopefully it would give me the confidence to pull off this dress. I slid the silky material over my head, and checked myself out in Mollie's full length mirror. It didn't look half bad. But I needed another drink to not be concerned about its length. I strapped on the wedges and carefully made my way out to Mollie's living room.

"Well? What's the verdict?" I twirled in front of Mollie's eagle eyes. She carefully looked me over, walking around me in a circle.

"Almost perfect." She pulled my hair out of its elastic, ruffling my curls to give them more volume. From some hidden pocket on her dress she pulled out a tube of mascara, and expertly swiped it on my lashes. "There. Beautiful. Don't you think, Ben?"

I had always liked Ben. He was sweet and genuine, and he loved Mollie to death. He came up behind her now and wrapped his arms around her tightly. "I think I'll be the envy of the bar with two beautiful women on my arms tonight."

The drive to the bar was quick, but as soon as we got in the doorway I realized this had been a mistake. The place was packed, with people jammed on too few barstools, the dance floor crowded with too many sweaty bodies. I sighed. This was going to be a long night.

"We need shots!" Mollie announced, and wiggled her way through the crowd to get to the bartender. By the time I made my way next to her, she already had two full shot glasses in front of her. "Drink this!" She slid one of the glasses down to me.

I put my lips to the glass and took a cautious sip. "What was that?" Whatever it was, it was strong. Thank God Ben was the designated driver tonight.

Mollie's smile was sly. "Tequila! And we need two more!"

I didn't fight her. The alcohol was loosening my body, turning off the thoughts that kept cycling in my mind. Another shot and a drink later, I was almost sure I couldn't feel my fingers anymore and I was definitely sure I was going to have a hangover in the morning. The lights were disorienting, and the bass was pounding so loudly I could feel it in my belly.

"Let's go dance!" Mollie had to yell to be heard over the music, but she grabbed both of us, dragging us out on the dance floor. Mollie immediately began moving her body against Ben, shifting easily in time to the music. I stood there, trying to decide what to do. Maybe if I was awkward enough we could leave.

"Ava! Close your eyes! Dance!" Mollie called out to me, raising her arms and swaying to the beat.

Thankfully, I was drunk enough that what she said made sense. So I did. Closing my eyes, I let my body sway to the music, feeling the beat take over my body. When I opened them again, Mollie was smiling encouragingly at me. "Now you've got it!"

It was fun. Being young, feeling carefree. We danced for an endless amount of time before Mollie shouted at me that she and Ben were going to get some air.

"Do you want to come?"

I surprised myself. I was having a good time dancing.

I shook my head, and she raised her eyebrows. "Will you be okay?"

I nodded, and she took Ben's hand and they headed out. I felt good. Confident. I closed my eyes and let go. Just for one night.

Hands held my hips. "Dance with me." I stopped dancing and whirled around. Jasper stood uncomfortably close to me. Here. In this bar. His hands still rested on my hips, but we weren't moving. My skin was tingling from where we touched, but that had to be the alcohol.

"What are you doing here?" I shouted at him. I couldn't say I was disappointed. If anything, I was the opposite. His dark hair was pushed back away from his face, his skin flushed with the heat of the bar.

"It's a bar. Am I not allowed to be here?"

I shrugged. I didn't know how to explain everything I was feeling. The pull he had over me. The space he was occupying in my mind.

"You look beautiful tonight," he said into my ear.

Right now, I felt beautiful. Jasper's hands slid back over my hips, pulling me closer against him.

"Is this okay?"

I nodded. His proximity, mixed with the alcohol I had consumed, was a heady mix.

"Come on. Dance with me."

I wasn't sure I even knew how to dance with a guy, but I wasn't about to say no. Jasper started moving his body in perfect tempo with the music, pulling me closer against him. I didn't notice the people around me, losing myself in the moment. Nothing else mattered. Our bodies pressed together in every possible way, and he spun me around. Jasper's face was so close I could feel his breath in my ear. "Why do you keep running away?"

I frowned, the moment feeling over. "I'm not."

"You know what I mean, Ava."

Even over the deafening music I could hear his words perfectly. I couldn't deny it, I did know exactly what he meant. In another situation, I would have lied. But the alcohol made me brazen. "You scare me."

Whatever Jasper was expecting me to say, it wasn't that. He froze. "I scare you?"

I nodded, continuing. "I feel like I've known you my whole life. Or maybe in a different life." I realized the utter insanity of what I had said and I pushed myself away from him. "I'm sorry, I don't know why I said that. I should find my friends." I ran off the dance floor before I could see his face. Before I could regret my decision to leave.

In my haste to get away, I nearly ran into Mollie. "Whoa, careful girl. Are you okay?" Mollie held me at arm's length, looking me over.

"I'm fine, a little tired. Can we go?"

Mollie pressed her lips together, but nodded. She wrapped her arms around me reassuringly and led me back to Ben's car.

* * *

There was enough alcohol in my system that by the time I made it home I fell asleep immediately. But my sleep was far from restful. Moonlight flooded my room. My dreams tormented me that night. Dreams of his voice in my ear, like silk.

"Why do you keep running away?"

Jasper. His strong hands were on me, sliding my dress over my hips, baring my pale skin. "Do I scare you now?"

Yes. I wasn't aware I had spoken aloud. I wasn't aware of anything other than the feeling of Jasper's skin on mine. My inhibitions were gone, released under the shadow of the dream.

He kissed his way down my neck, his full lips hot against my skin. "Good." I gasped. He had my dress over my hips now, nothing between us but my thin panties. I had never felt anything as good as his lips on my skin. Would his lips feel this good in real life? There was no doubt I was scared, but I knew I needed him. "More."

His eyes flashed to mine, dark with lust. His voice dropped an octave. "I want you to be scared. Scared you'll never feel my touch on your body. Scared I'll never give you what you want." Jasper's fingers dipped beneath the waistband of my underwear, dancing across my pussy. I knew exactly what I wanted. It was exactly what I shouldn't want. "Show me how you touch yourself."

I was shocked. I couldn't do that. Except. This was a dream. It wasn't real. And since it was a dream I could be as bold as I wanted. I pressed my lips against his, feeling my mouth sink into the motion as if I'd kissed him a thousand times before. I slipped my fingers down my body, replacing his on my clit. I didn't look away as I started to rub small circles on my sensitive skin. He watched my eyes, not the motions of my hands and I realized Dream Jasper only wanted to see the pleasure reflected in my gaze.

I stopped touching myself, turned on beyond belief, and crushed my lips to his. I needed to feel his touch, wanted him to take over. He responded exactly the way I hoped he would. One finger slipped inside of me, pulsing, in and out. It wasn't enough. I needed more of him, all of him. He knew. Another finger joined the first, stroking me. His other hand tangled in my hair, tugging tightly. "I'll give you what you want. But are you going to give yourself to me?" Jasper's voice was quiet, raspy. Desperate.

I had wanted to give myself up to him the first time I'd seen him. I kept running because I knew once I gave in to the craving, I wouldn't be able to stop. I arched my back in response, pulsing my hips to meet his fingers. He cupped my clit, putting pressure on me in the most delicious way. "I want all of you."

Jasper groaned, the sound tortured and low in the night. "I shouldn't be doing this. We shouldn't. But I can't stop." His fingers didn't stop, bringing me closer and closer to the edge.

He was right. But temptation just made it that much sweeter. "Oh... Jasper," I moaned into his mouth. There was nothing else in this world except him. His gaze locked onto mine, warring emotions showing in his eyes. Coaxing, but demanding. Gentle, but forceful. I couldn't focus. I was too close to orgasm.

And then he stopped. My body felt cold from the loss of his touch. Lost.

"I'm sorry, they're calling me. I can't." Jasper's gaze looked nervous. I wanted to protest, but he wasn't there anymore.

"Jasper?" I called, whirling around. But Jasper was gone, and I was alone in the forest. A young girl in a white dress was running ahead of me. Dark figures dressed all in black stood a distance away from her. But she wasn't trying to get away, she was running towards them.

"Wait up!" she kept calling, but every time it looked like she was about to catch up they would slip through her fingers like they were no more than air.

* * *

I dragged myself out of bed with a pounding hangover. I wasn't sure what to make of my life anymore, let alone this guy who I was now dreaming about. At least I was pretty sure it was only a dream. I started mindlessly tracing my hands up the soft skin of my hip, travelling the same path Dream Jasper had taken last night. It had felt almost real. The feeling of loss certainly still reverberated through my chest. Could you miss someone you barely knew?

The dream left me nervous. I was sick of not understanding what was going on. Fuck. I needed answers. Thankfully, working on my own schedule had its perks. I skipped my run. By the time I managed to wake myself up and get ready for the day it was an hour later than normal. I made my way out to my clunker of a car, but today I wasn't on my way to the coffee shop. I had other priorities. Heading downtown, I swung into the parking lot of the small motel I knew Jasper was using as his headquarters, thanks to this town's never-ending stream of gossip. I swung my backpack over my shoulder and opened the front door to the office, nearly knocking down Merrillan's chief of police as I did so.

"Oof, sorry about that Ms. Green." Sheriff Kelly grabbed my arm and steadied me as I struggled to regain my balance. Tom Kelly had been our chief of police for as long as I could remember, and while he was respected by the whole town, something about him always kept me on edge. His smile never seemed to quite reach his eyes. "You all right?"

I took my arm back, and brushed myself off. "I'm fine. No harm done."

Why was Merrillan's chief of police hanging around at nine in the morning? It wasn't exactly like our motel was a hot spot for illicit activity. Not that I knew of, anyway. I wasn't given much time to dwell on it because he was moving out to his squad car, tipping his hat to me as he did so. "Have a good day then, Ms. Green. Stay safe."

Shrugging off the odd encounter, I made my way to the front counter, where the motel owner, Deidra, was reading the newspaper. She set her paper down. "Why, Ava Green, long time no see. How are your folks enjoying their time in the sun?"

I smiled. "Hi Deidra. They're well." I knew Deidra didn't mean anything by it, but I wish some things could be kept to our family. Everyone knew everything here, including that my father had started teaching only in the summer semester, meaning my parents had time to take an extended trip to Florida over the winter.

"That's good to hear. What can I do for you so early this morning?"

I hadn't gotten this far in my plans when I was scheming to find Jasper. I was pretty sure it was a thing to not give out motel client's information. But I was here, so I had to try. I hoped my schmoozing wouldn't be the talk of the town tomorrow. "Well hopefully you can help me, Deidra. See, that new guy, Jasper? He left something at the table in the coffee shop the other day and I was hoping to return it."

Her eyebrows nearly shot to her hairline. "Uh huh."

"If I could have his room number, I'll swing by really quick and drop it off."

The eyebrows had all but disappeared by this point. "Ava Green, are you asking me to direct you to a single young man's room at nine o'clock in the morning so you can... drop something off?"

Shit. Definitely going to be the talk of the town. Why couldn't I have inherited my mom's ability to make small talk? Being honest, a small part of myself was also offended. I know it was unusual for me to be seen, for all intents and purposes this morning, chasing after a guy, but come on. My casual oversized sweater and leggings didn't exactly scream "booty call." To top it off, it *was* nine in the morning.

Thankfully, I was saved any further embarrassment by the chiming of the bell over the door. Before I could turn to see who it was, Deidra announced the arrival. "Mr. Knight, what a coincidence. Ava here was looking for you." I turned to face the only person who could possibly make this entire encounter more uncomfortable.

After whatever you could call our experience in the park, I found myself less annoyed than usual by his appearance at yet another awkward moment in my life. This time, it actually involved him. Jasper's hair was damp from the shower, and he was without his signature leather jacket, so I could see more of his extensive tribal looking tattoos working their way from his collarbone to his wrist. I couldn't help the thought that I'd like to trace those tattoos from start to finish from coming to my mind. Who the hell was I?

Almost as if he could hear what I was thinking, the smile Jasper gave me could've melted an iceberg. "Was she now." He probably had girls showing up to motel rooms for him all the time. *Jerk*.

I tried to maintain my composure. "Uh, yeah. I was looking for you to drop off that thing you forgot at the coffee shop the other day." I crossed my fingers subtly, hoping he would play along.

When his smile grew broader, I knew I was in trouble. "Oh yeah? Remind me what I forgot again?" Double shit.

I couldn't play it cool under the best of circumstances, and Jasper's amused eyes and his bone melting smile were not helping the situation. I dug into my laptop bag trying to find something I could claim he had left behind. "You forgot your... oh your..." I triumphantly held out a pair of sunglasses. "Your sunglasses!"

Jasper burst out laughing. It was an absolutely delicious sound. "How could I have forgotten? Walk me back to my room, so we can drop them off there."

Now my palms started to sweat. My body kept rebelling against me. I had functioned fine on my limited contact with men before, and yet this stranger was occupying every inch of my mind. Regardless, I followed him out the door.

"Listen… about last night…"

Jasper waved his hand, dismissing it. "We were both drinking."

I knew that wasn't it, but I gratefully accepted the excuse he had given me. We stopped outside room 103, and Jasper leaned his long frame against the door jam. "Would you like to come in?"

I hesitated. "Oh, um…" In a typical scenario I would not be caught dead going into a motel room with a strange man, but his tight black tee shirt was distracting me, and I couldn't think straight…

He felt my hesitation, and his grin was back. God, his teeth were perfect. I wondered if he'd worn braces as a kid. "Why, Ms. Green, do you really think I'm inviting you into my room to do improper things to you?"

The way he said Ms. Green made me think he was mocking the way Sheriff Kelly had said my name earlier that morning. But he couldn't be, because the only other person in earshot of our conversation had been Deidra. It was impossible for him to have heard that. Right?

Jasper interrupted my train of thought to continue his assurances he was not, in fact, thinking of any inappropriate behaviour towards me. "I simply thought you would like to talk in a more private place, Ms. Green."

"Okay, first of all, no more Ms. Green. I'm not my mother."

His mouth twitched, almost in annoyance. "Noted. Just Green it is then."

I rolled my eyes but let it slide. Green was about the same, if not worse, but I didn't think we'd be spending enough time together for that to bother me. "Second of all, how do you know I wasn't here to drop off your sunglasses?"

He pointed to the top of his damp hair, where a pair of aviators sat. *Oh.* I could already feel myself blushing again. I should never have come. This had been so embarrassing from start to finish. I bet this kind of stuff never happened to other girls.

Jasper didn't seem weirded out that I had showed up at his motel to speak with him. He smiled and held the door open for me. "So then, Green, are you coming in or are you going to give Deidra more gossip to tell her knitting circle?"

Glancing over my shoulder I saw Deidra watching us from the office window. "Actually, I don't think that's the greatest idea. We're already going to be the talk of the town tomorrow."

"Doesn't it ever get tiring?"

"Doesn't what get tiring?" I wasn't sure what he was getting at.

He waved his hands in the air. "Hiding. Not doing what you want. Making sure everyone isn't talking about you."

I shrugged. "Of course it does. But it's the only town I know and I don't want people to judge me any more than they already do."

I couldn't be certain, but I swore his face fell when I said that. I ran through what I had said in my head, realizing he might have thought I meant people would judge me for being seen with him.

I tried to recover. "I do have some questions for you. Obviously. That's why I'm here. But maybe we could meet at the coffee shop to talk?"

Jasper had ducked into the room as I was speaking and was shrugging into his leather jacket as he considered his response. My eyes widened at how hot he looked in it, and I tried to regain my cool before he could notice.

His gaze met mine. "Dinner."

I frowned, my question unanswered. "I'm sorry, what?"

His eyes darkened. "You heard me. Dinner. You have questions, and I'll do my best to answer them if you have dinner with me."

Jasper was asking me out to dinner. I weighed my

options. Getting answers to the weird things happening to me, and possibly (okay, definitely) making a fool out of myself in the process *and* getting to have dinner with a man hot enough to be a model to boot, or eating leftovers again with Betty. It seemed like an easy choice, even with the high probability of embarrassment. My only confusion was what he was getting out of the bargain. But before I could respond, Jasper was already speaking.

"Vincenzo's. Tonight. Seven o'clock."

Vincenzo's was the nicest restaurant in town. Mollie was going to freak. I wasn't even sure how I could explain all of this to her. I responded with the only word I seemed capable of saying. "Okay."

Jasper seemed pleased with my response and we exchanged numbers. He busied himself with locking his door, and when he looked up at me again his eyes seemed to get even darker. "Green."

I couldn't move. Forget icebergs, that look was melting me to my core. "Yeah?"

He leaned into me, his breath touching my ear. "Next time I invite you into my room, I hope you won't say no."

Chapter 4

"Okay, who are you and what have you done with my best friend?" Mollie's voice rang out over my cell phone. She had called me on her dinner break, and I finally filled her in on everything that had been happening the past few days. Understandably upset at first, she also was used to my need to process things myself first. I had to grovel, but eventually she forgave me, turning her energy towards my dinner plans instead.

"Mollie, it's not a big deal. I'm sure he has dinner with lots of girls." I was driving home, since working at the coffee shop was an impossibility with dinner taking over any available space in my mind. I would have to focus hard tonight to make sure I got my questions answered. But I couldn't help but wonder what he would be wearing.

"He might have dinner with a lot of girls, but you definitely do not have dinner with a lot of guys. And his idea of dessert probably involves a lot more nudity than yours."

I started to choke and tried to cough to cover it up. I hadn't considered that. While I wasn't a virgin by any means, my sexual history was, well, limited. And awkward. The guys I had dated in college were usually sweet and geeky, and equally as uncomfortable in the bedroom as I was. I was fairly certain Jasper had no such difficulties in this respect. His hair was probably perpetually tousled from all the sex he had. Women probably took one look at his dangerous smile and automatically found themselves undressed. But none of that mattered because I had questions Jasper needed to answer. And that wouldn't happen if I was ogling his butt in his tight pants.

"What are you going to wear?" Mollie asked impatiently. It was probably killing her that she was stuck at work until seven and wouldn't be able to help me choose an outfit in person.

"I don't know. My navy blue dress pants?" Clothes were not the first thing on my mind. Although to be fair, neither was my concern about what I had seen in the woods last night.

Mollie was aghast. "Dress pants? You have a date with the hottest guy in town and you want to wear dress pants?"

I knew a losing battle when I saw one and I was quick to forfeit. "Okay. What do you recommend?"

"Let's see." The line went quiet while she mentally ran through my closet in her head. "Your black dress?"

"The one I wear to funerals?"

I heard Mollie's laugh on the other end of the phone. "Okay, maybe not. What about your pink dress? The backless one."

Of course that's the one she would choose. "I haven't worn that dress since college. I doubt it even still fits. I'm sure I have a skirt or something I could wear."

I heard Mollie's name being called across the phone and I knew her dinner break was coming to an end. Sure enough, she came back on. "Hey, sorry, Ava but I have to go. But call me when you get home so I can hear the whole story about your hot date. And keep your phone charged!"

She hung up as I pulled into my unit's parking lot. I looked out into the woods before I got out of my car, cautiously searching for anything out of the ordinary. Just in case. Nothing seemed out of place, but I was realizing this meant nothing. I headed up to my apartment, chastising myself for being paranoid. With a quick pet for Betty, I began the process of trying to find something suitable to wear for my date/not-a-date. I wondered what Jasper thought it was. I started pulling different options out of my closet and trying outfits on.

Two hours later I stood in front of my mirror wearing the backless pink dress. While it definitely wasn't too formal, it was safe to say it didn't exactly spell out platonic friendship, either. The dusky rose colour always made me feel confident though. That was the reason I had bought this dress in the first place. But the hem seemed to hit a lot higher on the thighs than I remembered, and it felt like a lot more back was showing than the last time I had worn it.

Unfortunately, it was either this or the navy dress pants, and I didn't want to face the wrath of Mollie. I finger combed my hair until the unruly waves seemed deliberate and swiped some mascara on my lashes -- my extent of a beauty routine. I stood back to look at my reflection. I was nothing compared to the girls Jasper was probably used to, but I looked pretty damn good. Besides, this wasn't a date.

I dropped some dinner in Betty's dish and walked back out to my car. When I pulled up outside of Vincenzo's, Jasper was already waiting out front. He was dressed to kill in tight black dress pants and a white button-up shirt with the edges of his tattoos peeking out under the rolled sleeves. He also wasn't alone. Rose McDermott stood exceptionally close to him, running one manicured finger down his exposed forearm. I couldn't make out what she was saying, but I had a feeling she wasn't asking him for directions. What I had said before was true. I hadn't ever been bothered by Rose's status. Until now. A new feeling in me awakened, eager to prove something to myself. I straightened my dress and made my way over to where they stood. My mind was telling me to run in the other direction, but I forced myself to stand tall.

Don't trip, don't trip, don't trip, was the mantra running through my head. I had to admit, they were a good match for one another. But things were so comfortable with Jasper I was jealous. As I got closer, I felt rather than saw when Jasper noticed me. He spotted me with barely concealed desire, and I gave myself a pat on the back for pulling the dress off. It was worth all the effort it had taken me not to trip. Rose also looked me up and down, obviously wondering what I was doing here. Her look of superiority turned to one of shock when I approached the two of them.

"Hope you weren't waiting too long." *Take that, Rose.*

Jasper carefully removed himself from Rose's clutches. He ran an appreciative gaze down my body before offering his hand, his tattooed knuckles curling softly around my fingers. "Not long at all. Rose, it was nice to talk to you." Rose merely nodded, her jaw still on the ground. I knew I looked good, but his intense scrutiny seemed more than the dress warranted. Why was he staring at me like that? A nagging thought pinged in the back of my head. *Didn't you say at the club you felt like you had known him for ages?* Maybe he felt the same way. But that was crazy. You weren't supposed to feel like this about someone you just met. Jasper Knight was turning down Rose's charms to go for dinner with me? Maybe this *was* a date.

I twined my fingers with his and immediately relished the electricity flowing from his warm skin to mine. We left Rose gawking at us as we walked into the restaurant and quietly waited together until a host seated us at a secluded booth in the back.

Jasper slid in the booth close to me, and our thighs pressed together. I contemplated protesting. I shouldn't have been okay with being this close to a man, any man, on a first date. But something made me feel like Jasper and I had been going out for dinners forever. And I wasn't about to complain about feeling this good. Being this close to Jasper, in the back of a dark room, was almost too much for my senses.

"Um, so…" I started to ask him a question when I noticed his gaze drifting down to my chest, then snapping back to my eyes with a guilty blush. I gulped audibly. I could feel myself drawn to him, so I had to get things back on track.

I tried again. "Why did you invite me for dinner?" I traced a ring around my water glass.

When he finally spoke, he sounded surprised. "Why wouldn't I have invited you?"

It was a direct question and I found myself nervous to give him an honest answer. I couldn't meet his gaze. "Because you could have answered any questions I had over coffee, and been here with someone like Rose." I hated how quiet my voice got, and I pulled my hands into my lap.

"What do you see when you look at yourself?" Jasper asked me.

"I'm sorry, what?" This evening was already way off

track from whatever I had planned in my head.

"When you look in the mirror, what do you see?"

"I'm not sure." I didn't know whether I should be honest or bluff my way out of this line of questioning. It didn't matter because my decision was made for me.

"How about I tell you what I see?" Jasper said. "I see a beautiful woman. I see a woman who pretends she's shy, but isn't. I see a woman with a world full of potential."

My heart skipped a beat. Did he actually think all of this about me? Maybe I had read him entirely wrong.

Jasper took my fingers in one large calloused hand and forced my eyes to meet his. "Do you want to know a secret?"

"O… okay," I managed to stutter out.

Jasper dipped his head close to mine, his full lips dangerously close to my own. If I turned my head a micrometer our lips would be touching. His voice was quiet, yet his words managed to reverberate through my entire body. "I didn't think you'd ever say yes to dinner with someone like me, so when I saw my opportunity to force your hand, I took it."

Before I had time to think he closed the distance between our mouths. I was pretty sure my heart was going to explode. Jasper's lips were on mine. He was kissing me. It was better than any fantasy I had come up with, any dream I had envisioned. His lips were soft, and moved against mine gently, like he was afraid he was going to scare me off. I didn't know what else to do, so I kissed him back with everything I had. He started to part my lips with his tongue, before breaking away with a groan.

His sweet words contradicted his kiss, sending a shiver down my spine. I debated if I was more shocked he had been paying so much attention to me, or that we had kissed. Or how good his touch felt. "Oh. Well. I don't think that's a good idea." That wasn't what I had wanted to say to him. It had accidentally come out. I shook my head, hoping to correct my words.

His mouth tightened and he pushed his dark hair off his forehead. I immediately ached at the loss of contact from both his hand and his lips. But he brought his hand back to mine. Jasper's voice was hoarse as he looked deep into my eyes. "Are you really going to pretend you didn't want to have dinner with me after that kiss, Green? Don't tell me you don't feel this when I touch you." He drew lazy circles on my wrist with his index finger. My stomach tightened with every rotation he made.

I couldn't think. Not when he looked the way he did, admitting what he was feeling, doing what he was doing with his hands. I hesitated. I had no idea what to do in this situation. My previous first dates had been chaste movie nights with some awkward getting to know you talk. Kisses like that before dinner were out of the question.

Jasper's voice dropped an octave, and he ran his finger softly up and down my forearm. "Don't tell me you haven't been thinking about all the things I could do to you with these hands since the first time you saw me."

This was definitely how all those girls ended up in his bed. But I had to concentrate. I had questions. Sex hadn't led me astray so far in life, and I could withstand Jasper's games now to get what I needed. Shaking my head, I tried to brush off Jasper's advances the best I could. "I didn't realize this is why you invited me here."

He stalled, and his smile was slow and dangerous. "Green, are you telling me you're going to try to interrogate me before I even have a drink?" Raising his other hand, he flagged down the waiter. We ordered our meals and Jasper requested two whiskeys, neat.

I didn't know how much longer I wanted to keep avoiding his advances. "How did you know I drank whiskey?" Most of the guys who had taken me out before had ordered me a drink with an umbrella in it, or was some ghastly shade of pink.

Jasper winked. "Consider it a lucky guess. Now let me ask you a question. What do you want, Ava?"

"What do you mean?" The question threw me for a loop, and I didn't know what kind of answer he was looking for. At the present, I wanted a lot. A lot I wasn't comfortable admitting.

He cocked an eyebrow at me, gesturing around the restaurant. "I mean, what do you want out of life? I'm assuming you don't want to spend your entire life making sure people aren't talking about you."

"I want..." What did I want? No one had asked me before, and I wasn't expecting Jasper of all people to ask me these questions tonight. I thought for a moment. "I want to be taken seriously. I want to be strong enough to stand on my own feet."

Our drinks arrived, and Jasper swirled his lazily. He nodded, looking solemn. "Good answer." Jasper threw his drink back in one quick shot.

I felt my chest tighten, and knew I was in trouble. Flirty Jasper who acted interested was attractive. This Jasper who was looking at me with eyes like liquid caramel could be dangerous. Very dangerous.

He met my gaze and grinned. "Okay. Before you explode, shoot."

Here was my chance. Putting the image of Jasper swallowing his drink out of my mind, I began with, "Why are the woods dangerous?"

He seemed to be carefully constructing his response in his head. I wanted honesty, not a run-around answer. When he responded, his words were slow and measured. "There are dangerous things in those woods right now. But I'm taking care of it. It shouldn't be too much longer."

A half answer. "What is so scary?"

His eyes seemed to speak for him, pleading with me to accept what he had given me. "You don't need to worry about it. I will take care of it."

Few things got on my nerves like being placated. I huffed. "I'm really not sure what a private investigator would be able to do about such a dangerous problem. And I was also promised answers if I came to dinner with you."

Jasper grinned. "Actually, I recall promising to try to answer your questions. And I did try."

He was so frustrating. I had been more annoyed with

him in a few days than I had ever been with anyone else. As good as his hands did feel on me, I wasn't about to sit around and be made a fool of. "I'm sorry, maybe this really wasn't a good idea. I had a long day and I think I should be getting home."

Jasper took both of my hands in his before I could get up. His gaze didn't move from mine. "No. Stay. Please."

"You're treating me like a child. I'm capable of hearing whatever it is you're hiding from me. And if you don't want to tell me, that's fine. But don't expect me to stick around while you laugh about it," I told him, my anger rising to the surface.

"I'm sorry." He sounded sincere. "Please, stay. I'll try."

My head was telling me to leave, but my heart was saying stay. I slowly sat back down, and looked up at him expectantly.

Jasper ran both his hands through his hair, causing it to look even more tousled than usual. I urged myself to pay attention to his words, not his looks. He seemed to be battling with himself about something, and I waited patiently for the result. Finally, he stopped, and when he met my gaze his eyes were bright. "What I'm going to tell you will not sound believable. But I'm asking you to trust me."

Did I trust him? I had known Jasper for all of a few days. And yet every bone in me knew the answer to that question. "Okay."

With a brisk nod he began. "Many years ago, before Merrillan was a town, there were animals that used to live here in the area. As the people came and the town grew, the animals spread out, becoming stories instead of something people knew and understood."

I was confused. "Like, a mountain lion?" There had been talk of one in the area a few years ago, but no one I knew had actually seen it.

"No." Jasper's voice was tight. "Less believable."

I was trying to add up everything he was telling me, and kept coming up blank.

He tried again. "Do you believe in myths?"

"Like, unicorns and stuff?" I shrugged. "Some of it I guess, if I had proof..." I trailed off, wondering where this was going.

Jasper made a dismissive gesture with his hand. "Think more serious."

"Jasper, if you tell me there's a ghost haunting my apartment building, I'm leaving right now." I smiled, trying to make a joke. In reality, my stomach was in knots, and I wasn't sure if I wanted to hear what he had to say anymore. But I had fought for the truth, so I was going to hear him out.

He slowly shook his head, not cracking a smile. "No, Green. I'm talking about a predator that hunts werewolves."

Chapter 5

I couldn't believe what Jasper was saying. All those times in the woods I thought I'd felt something watching me, I hadn't been crazy. Things that weren't human were out there. I had sensed it before my mind even allowed me to believe it. How? "So you're telling me werewolves exist, and there are some in my woods." I paused, taking a deep breath. "But they aren't the bad guys. There's something even worse out there."

Jasper simply nodded. His whole body was tense, waiting for my reaction. I had definitely changed my mind -- I didn't want to hear any of this. I wanted to go back to my whiskey and his hands on mine. But my curiosity was also getting the best of me, and I could always play along. Until I got some answers at least. I couldn't help the excitement I felt. Maybe this was all a big joke. But there was a taste of a memory on my tongue. Somehow I knew what he was saying was true. I leaned forward. "Start at the beginning."

Jasper laughed. "You sure you're not a private investigator, Green?"

I ignored him. "How does one become a werewolf?"

Jasper mimicked my posture, leaning forward. "You're born with it. Most of the ones I know actually started phasing when they were teenagers."

"Phasing." I turned the word over in my mouth. "You mean like changing into a wolf?"

"Exactly."

"Do they howl at the moon? Change under the light of the full moon?" My mouth was working faster than my brain.

"I've definitely heard some howling. But I'm pretty sure the full moon thing is an old wives' tale."

"Why do you know so much about all of this?"

Jasper's expression became closed off, for once looking like what I had originally expected. "Some of my closest friends happen to be wolves. That makes me a concerned bystander. But it's also my job to investigate what I'm hired to do."

It was a lot to comprehend. But I had promised my trust. He was watching me cautiously, probably expecting me to run out the door. I closed my eyes to stop the noise. Werewolves. *Werewolves.* Really, was it that much of a stretch? I believed in spirits and Ouija boards. Why not werewolves and evil creatures? And I had *felt* things. Things I couldn't explain. "Okay."

Jasper looked surprised at my response. "Okay?"

"Okay. You told me to trust you, and for some insane reason I can't possibly explain, I do. But I have other questions."

He smiled, looking instantly more relaxed. "Of course. Anything. Within reason."

"So what is this big bad monster that's hurting werewolves? Why doesn't everyone know monsters exist? And why aren't werewolves the bad guys?"

Jasper started ticking off my responses on his fingers. "I'm not entirely certain what's doing the hunting. The characteristics of the attacks don't add up, but I'm getting closer. And it's a pack thing. Most werewolves are sworn to secrecy. And werewolves are really... misunderstood creatures."

I still felt like there was more he wasn't telling me but also... *werewolves?* What alternate universe had I woken up in this morning? I sat, quietly processing all the new information.

We were interrupted by the waiter bringing our meals. After an awkward silence while we waited for him to leave, Jasper turned to me with heat in his eyes.

He brought his hand to my bare thigh under the table, sending waves of electric through me. "This is a lot to take in. And you're right, you barely know me. Are you sure you're okay?"

Oddly enough, I felt fine. I should have been more afraid, but maybe I was in shock. Or maybe I had known my entire life that things like this existed and just hadn't wanted to acknowledge it. Regardless, the one thing I was sure about was that with Jasper, I felt safe.

I met his gaze and placed my hands gently on top of his. "Really. I'm okay. I know I should be more shaken up by this, but for right now, I'm fine."

He grabbed my hands with a ferocity that took my breath away. "God, do you have any idea how beautiful you are?"

I looked down, uncomfortable. None of my boyfriends had spoken to me this way before, let alone on a first date.

"Ava. Look at me."

I looked into his eyes when he spoke my first name and could have melted with the heat in there alone. "I'm serious. You were already one of the most stunning women I've met. But you took some seriously crazy information and absorbed it like it was nothing. That is badass."

I pulled my hands away and tried to deflect the compliment. "Our food is getting cold." I picked up my fork and started absentmindedly toying with my meal.

Unfortunately, pulling my hands away left his palms flush against my skin. His fingers gently inched their way up to the hem of my dress. I knew I should stop him, push him away. But I was frozen by how good it felt to be desired by Jasper. All I could think about was how his kiss made me feel, and how much better his hands would be.

He brushed his fingers over the lace trim of my short dress. I could hear a growl in the back of his throat as he played his fingers across my legs. "I don't give a damn about the food."

Shocked, I dropped my fork onto my plate with a clatter. "Jasper... people are watching." I cast a furtive glance over my shoulders at the other patrons.

This time Jasper rolled his eyes. "For one night, stop worrying about what everyone in the town thinks. They're going to talk regardless."

I opened my mouth to speak and closed it again.

Jasper's shoulders were tense again, like he was afraid I was going to turn him down. I couldn't believe he was looking at me the way he was. His gaze poured over me and he slowly pushed my dress up. I felt like someone who did this all the time, someone who let guys feel them up under the table at a fancy restaurant. Someone worth desiring.

"Green."

Shit, forget dinner. His hand was now fully under my dress. Any higher and they'd be toying with the edges of my underwear. I didn't know how far I wanted to take this. I stilled Jasper's hand with my own. "Jasper. What if someone sees?"

He started to gently stroke the skin on my inner thigh. "If you don't like this, say the word and I'll stop. I swear. But from your lack of response to my question, I'm going to guess what you want is... me?"

God yes. I did. He was cocky and annoying and I wanted him more than I had wanted anything in a long time. I merely nodded, unable to lie.

His voice was pure sex as he continued his gentle touch on my skin. "No one can see us, baby. No one has to know how good I'm making you feel. And believe me, no one has made you feel as good as I can. So tell me, do you want me as badly as I want you?"

This was why bad boys were so dangerous. I wasn't even bothered by his forward use of "baby." In fact, I was surprised to find it turned me on. So I nodded again, the briefest tilt of my chin. It was all I could force my body to do.

His fingers dipped up to brush against the edges of my panties. "I need to hear the words, baby."

I shivered at his touch. Was this what attraction was actually supposed to feel like? His face was a breath away from my face again, and I was sure Jasper could hear my heart beating out of my chest.

"I want you, Jasper." It didn't even sound like my voice, it was so raspy with need. But it wasn't a lie. I did want him. No, I needed him. His eyes darkened so much with my response, they looked black as they stared into my own. His lips closed over mine again, this time with so much passion I was sure everyone in the restaurant was staring at us. I had to force myself not to care.

Pulling away, he put his lips to my ear. "Good." He took his hands out from under my dress, but before I could protest he pulled me to my feet. "Let's get out of here. Your place is close, right?"

Was I really going to bring Jasper back to my place on a first date? Stupid question. Of course I was. "But wait, don't we need to pay the bill?" I protested weakly.

Jasper pulled out his wallet and threw a mess of bills down on the table. "That should cover it." Then, pulling me close, he led me outside. We reached my car and Jasper turned to me. "I'd say we should take my bike, but that dress looks so beautiful on you I'd rather not ruin it."

My heart couldn't possibly beat any faster, so it settled for beating harder. "I think I'd rather you not ruin it, too. Are you okay riding with me then? Or did you want to drive separately?"

He pulled me so close I could feel his lips against mine, our bodies touching at every possible point. "I'd rather not be apart from you any more than I have to tonight."

As much as I wanted to stay in this spot all night, locked in Jasper's tight embrace, this was still Merrillan, and I was still worried people would talk. I disentangled myself, and got my keys out from my bag. "Hop in."

Jasper slid into the passenger seat, smoothly putting his hand back on my thigh. "I hope you don't mind this. It's much more comfortable here."

I didn't mind. But... "Can I ask you a question?"

Jasper grinned. "Haven't you been doing that all night?"

I couldn't help but smile too. "Yes. But no. I meant a personal question. I mean, I barely know anything about you and your hand is on my leg. I know this sounds crazy, but I don't normally do this kind of thing."

Jasper started gently massaging my thigh with the hand in question. "I don't usually either. It doesn't feel wrong though, does it?"

I was surprised. Jasper's persona had me pegging him for a playboy, sleeping with hordes of busty blondes.

"I know what you're thinking, Green. I'm not that person anymore. I haven't been for a long time."

I played dumb. "I wasn't thinking anything like that!" But I was.

He shot me a look that said he didn't believe me. "Shoot. What would you like to know?"

"Your accent. It isn't from Chicago." I tried to not think about what he said -- he wasn't that person *anymore*.

"It's not. I was born in Louisiana."

"How the hell did you end up here?" Merrillan was pretty far off the beaten track.

"We moved to a small village a few miles away when I was younger. My parents split up, and my mom moved to Chicago, so I never really saw any point in going back. Never lost the accent though." No, he definitely had not. I didn't mind one bit.

It was addicting, finding out who he was underneath it all. I needed to know more. "Do you like your job?" I asked him.

"I love being an investigator. I travel a lot, so it can be lonely at times, but it's such a rush I don't think I could ever do anything else."

The whole time he watched my face, trailing light fingertips down my bare arm and by the time I pulled into my building I needed more. Jasper must have been as bad as I was, because as soon as we were out of the car, he was kissing me hard, his fingers tangling through my hair. I brought my own hands to either side of his face, trying to bring him impossibly closer. We stumbled towards the main door, and for once I actually didn't care who saw us. There was a sense of freedom, being this person. It gave me a bigger rush than running. I raced up the stairs to unlock my front door, giggling, Jasper hot on my heels. I paused to kiss him again, and then turned back to unlock the door, fumbling with my keys.

This whole thing was crazy. I must have lost my mind. And yet, there was no way in hell I was going to stop now.

I pulled Jasper into my small entryway by his shirt

collar, and he pushed me back against the door, grabbing my wrists with one hand. He pulled them over my head, pinning them there, never losing the contact between our mouths. God, he was strong. I could feel him holding back and I wanted to tell him not to. He pulled away for a moment, to ask, "Are you sure you are okay with this?"

I was sure. But before I could tell him, Betty came around the corner. My normally docile cat went berserk at the sight of Jasper. Back arched, she hissed and slashed at him.

I knew it was too good to be true. Of course my cat had to ruin the moment. I was burning with embarrassment. "Oh, my God, I'm so sorry. She's never like this. I don't know what got into her."

Jasper was frozen to the spot. He looked like he was about to have a heart attack. I knew he wasn't a cat person, but surely he wasn't afraid of them. Right? I grabbed my insane cat and started to rush out of the room. "I'm so sorry. I'll lock her in the bathroom. Hold on."

Jasper seemed to shake himself out of his trance, and cursed under his breath. When he spoke, his voice was strained. "Actually, I should go. I forgot I have an early morning tomorrow. I'm sorry." He started backing towards the door. "I'll see you soon. Sorry."

And before I could say anything, he was out the door, leaving me in the same spot wondering what the hell had just happened.

* * *

I passed through the next couple days in a stupor, wondering exactly what had taken place that night with Jasper. He hadn't come into the coffee shop the next day, and I found him taking up more space in my brain than I would have liked. Had he just been using me, and magically developed a conscience? Not that I had tons of experience, but we'd had some pretty honest conversations, so that one didn't seem likely. Was he afraid I was going to freak out over all the crazy things he had told me, and didn't want to stick around for the fall out?

I had no idea.

I met Mollie on Wednesday for our weekly date at our favourite diner downtown. After we sat down and ordered our usual meals, she turned to me with eager eyes. "Okay, spill. You told me it didn't go well, but that was all I got out of you. What the hell happened?"

My question exactly. I filled Mollie in on the disastrous date (minus the werewolves -- I didn't think she'd take too kindly to that lunchtime topic), and Jasper's sudden departure. Her eyes steadily grew wider, and when I finished she sat back, mulling over my story.

"I knew he looked like a jerk! No one looks that good in a leather jacket and isn't an asshole."

I shook my head. "I don't know, Mollie. Maybe I'm naive, but something about the whole situation doesn't add up to me. Maybe something was wrong, and he had to leave. Maybe he left his oven on."

Her mouth dropped open. "So you're telling me you aren't even a little bit pissed off? No offence, but you don't normally let guys get up close and personal, period. This guy did, and then took off."

I *was* hurt, and angry too. But I also felt the need to defend Jasper from Mollie's wrath. I toyed with the straw in my drink. "I think there's more going on than what I know."

Mollie looked past me. "Well if you need closure or whatever the hell you think would make you feel better, now's your chance." She poked her fork towards the window. "Your brooding bad boy just showed up, and he's staring at you."

Jasper was here? I slowly turned to look over my shoulder, and sure enough, there was Jasper outside the window. If anything, he looked hotter than he had at dinner. His white shirt curved across his shoulders, with his black tattoos peeking out around his collarbone. I wasn't the only one admiring his strong build. Outside, a woman walking by on the sidewalk overtly checked him out as she passed. Must have been a coincidence. Jasper wouldn't search me out like this. He'd practically run out of my house.

But as my gaze met his, a hopeful smile spread across his tanned skin. He curved up one finger in a "come here" gesture. I was angry, but I was also more than eager to be near him again. Frazzled, I whipped my head back to Mollie. "What do I do?"

Mollie nonchalantly popped another fry in her mouth and shrugged. "Looks to me like he wants you to go out and meet him."

Very helpful. I sighed at her. "Obviously. But do I go?"

Mollie shrugged again. "Honestly, girl, it's up to you. But if I were you, I'd go give him a piece of my mind."

Gathering my courage, I pushed back from my chair and tried to look confident as I walked outside to meet Jasper. Mollie was right. I should give him a piece of my mind. When I finally stood in front of him, I crossed my arms and forced myself to look him in the eye. "What do you want?"

He at least had the courtesy to look ashamed. He shoved his hands into the pockets of his black jeans. "I'm sorry, Green. Really."

My anger had been simmering until this point, but now it boiled over. He'd left me, embarrassed me, and all I got was a *sorry*? "What the hell? I told you I don't do stuff like that, ever. So imagine my shock when I trust you for some crazy reason and then you proceed to run out on me like my house was on fire. To be honest, I don't even know why I'm out here talking to you. I already got the answers I needed." I started to turn away.

He grabbed my wrist so fast I didn't even see him move his hand. "Ava, wait. I can explain everything. I swear. There's… there are things you don't understand yet."

I felt instant sparks from where his hand grasped my wrist and did my best to ignore the desire stirring in my body. "So explain, but I don't have all day. Mollie is waiting."

This time, I was sure he felt the sparks too, his eyes getting a shade darker. "Not here. It's something I have to show you, not tell you."

We were still going in circles and I found myself getting frustrated. "Forget it, Jasper. It was a mistake going to dinner with you in the first place, let alone bringing you home."

He took his free hand and pulled my chin up to face him. "Then make one more mistake. Please. Go for a drive with me? I'm working right now, and Mollie is waiting on you but I'll pick you up tomorrow night, at seven. Give me one more chance."

I only saw honesty reflected in his eyes. Even though I knew I should make him work for it, what came out of my mouth was simple. "Okay."

He breathed out in one huge gust, like he had been holding himself tight. "Okay." He gave me another slow smile. "I don't think your friend is too happy with me."

I looked over my shoulder and saw Molly's gaze shooting daggers at Jasper from the table. "Don't mind her. She's a little overprotective of me."

His voice grew raspy, and I knew where he was going. "Well then, how about we give her a show?" He pulled my face closer to his, bringing my mouth a second away from his. "What do you say, baby?"

I wanted nothing more than to press my lips against his own, and feel every ounce of passion we had felt the other night. But he had left me last time, so he would need to earn that this time. I brought my hand to his chest and pushed him back gently. "I'm sorry, Jasper. I need to understand what happened the other night before this can happen."

He looked crestfallen, but nodded. "I understand. But you'll come with me?"

"Of course I will." I turned to go back into the restaurant. "You know, for such a tough looking guy, you really are a total marshmallow."

Jasper grinned at me, but his eyes narrowed. "We'll see who's the marshmallow later, Green." He waited for me to walk back to the table, and then turned and headed down the sidewalk.

I ducked back inside and sat down with Mollie, who

was eagerly awaiting my report. "So what was all that about? I saw him go in for a kiss and you totally rejected him. Good for you, girl. Did you give him a piece of your mind?"

I looked at my hands. "Actually, I'm seeing him again tomorrow."

Mollie looked outraged, but waited for my explanation.

"He said he wanted to show me something. I don't know Mollie, but I think he's worth a second chance."

Slowly she picked her fork back up and continued eating. "Whatever you say. Just remember I'll be here to pick up the pieces when he runs out on you again."

Ouch. But I didn't feel like I was making a mistake. My gut was telling me to trust Jasper. The rest of our lunch passed with Mollie telling me stories of her clients, both of us careful not to mention my date the next night.

* * *

After another night filled with dreams of werewolves and Jasper, I got myself out of bed and immediately plugged my cell phone in to charge while I made coffee. When I checked the phone again, there was a text from Mollie. *Love you. Be safe.*

I hadn't spoken to her since our lunch, and her message was appreciated. Smiling, I tried to figure out what to wear. Jasper hadn't mentioned where he was taking me, but I already knew a dress wouldn't work on a motorcycle, so I threw on jeans and a cute sweater and tried to get some work done.

At 6:55 pm I shooed Betty into the bathroom. I didn't want a repeat of the other night, just in case. At 7:00 pm on the dot my doorbell rang. "Coming!" I shouted as I forced myself to walk slowly. I swung the door open to reveal Jasper's grinning face.

He looked perfect as ever, his jeans and T-shirt showing off all his delicious muscles. But while he was smiling, his eyes looked tight. He looked nervous. "You ready, Green?"

I hoped so. He took my hand and I didn't pull away. Our hands fit perfectly together, which only reaffirmed to my inner self I was making the right decision. He pulled me out the door and across the parking lot. We stopped in front of his ride.

"Nope. No way. Jasper, I am not getting on that death machine." Jasper had stopped in front of a motorcycle, and was handing me a helmet.

He smirked. "What was that earlier about you calling me a marshmallow? You aren't really afraid of a little bike, are you?"

I was, but hell if I was going to admit that to him. I snatched the helmet out of his hands and shoved it on my head. My hair was going to be a real treat after this. Jasper laughed at me, and I loved the sound so much I couldn't help but smile too. He straddled the bike, and I had to admit he looked really good. He patted the seat behind him. "Hop on."

I tried to get on as gracefully as I could, which is to say not at all. Something occurred to me as I tried to get comfortable. "But wait, don't you need a helmet?"

Jasper gently tapped on his head with his fist. "Don't worry about me. My head is tough. Now wrap your arms around my waist."

I took him up on the opportunity to get closer and wrapped my arms tightly around him, feeling his chest rise and fall with each breath. He touched my hands briefly, and then kicked the bike into action. "Hold tight, baby."

Chapter 6

The ride wasn't as bad as I expected. In fact, it was pretty exhilarating riding in the cool autumn air, not caring how my hair looked blowing about. Also a perk was Jasper's hand gently squeezing my thigh at every red light. Apparently wearing jeans was not a deterrent for him, but I found myself hoping we would get stuck at more stop lights.

Jasper turned the bike onto an unmarked road, a little outside of the town limits. He drove cautiously down the narrow lane, the moonlight filtering in between the thinning branches. After a couple minutes, he pulled up at a small cabin and stopped the bike.

I got off as carefully as I could, and walked around, trying to get used to moving on my own two legs again. I looked around the clearing. "I didn't even know this was here."

Jasper walked up the stairs to the small porch and sat down on the steps. "Not many people do." He patted the space beside him.

I sat down next to him, enjoying the warmth radiating from his hard, muscular body. "I thought the woods were dangerous. Should we really be out here?" I tried to make it sound like a joke, but nerves were evident in my voice.

"We're safe here. For whatever reason, what's happening seems to be staying within the town boundaries right now." He turned to me, and placed a hand on either side of my face. He was so close to me I thought he might kiss me. His bright eyes stared into me, and I couldn't tell if they were alive with excitement or fear. "I want you to know you are in no danger tonight. You will never be in any danger with me. Do you understand, Ava?"

"I'm not afraid of you, Jasper. But I can handle myself, you know."

He smiled, brushing my lips with his thumb. "I know you can."

I smiled back, his genuine emotions so refreshing. "Okay, but back to business. You said you wanted to explain, so start talking." He confused me by standing up and slowly taking off his jacket. "Not that I'm minding the show, but don't think you can distract me from the truth with your gorgeous body."

He ignored my jab and looked at me seriously, his eyes tight with unspoken emotion. "I'm not going to talk to you, I'm going to show you something, so you need to watch carefully. And remember what I said." He peeled off his shirt and it was all I could do not to run my hands up and over his chiselled abs. He looked like he was made out of stone, for God's sakes. I really needed to start doing something other than running.

"Green. Are you watching closely?"

Was I ever. Jasper was undoing his belt buckle and sliding his black jeans over his hips, until he stood before me in nothing but a pair of black boxer briefs. I couldn't see too much in the filtered moonlight, but I could imagine...

"Ava."

"Yes, Jasper, I'm watching. But what exactly am I supposed to be watching besides your striptease?"

Jasper turned and walked out a few meters into a small clearing, throwing me a smouldering smile over one shoulder. "Don't blink -- and remember I told you you'll never be in any danger from me."

What the hell was going on?

Jasper stood with his back to me in the clearing, his back muscles rippling under the moonlight. He stood there so long I was about to call out to him, but before I could he raised his head to face the sky and his whole body shuddered. A piercing howl escaped his mouth, and his body began to twist grotesquely. I didn't know what was going on, but I clung desperately to the fact that he'd told me I wasn't in danger. I wasn't sure why he had told me not to blink, because I wouldn't have been able to look away from the scene in front of me if I tried.

I pulled my knees up tight to my chest and watched as his body elongated, and fur started appearing from his skin. The night air was loud with Jasper's deep moans and the sounds of bones popping. I was no longer sure how much time had passed. It could've been a minute or an hour. But as the moon came up overhead full and bright, a massive grey wolf turned to face me. It stood, unmoving, staring at me with Jasper's brown eyes. I found myself moving towards the beast. "Jasper?" My voice was barely more than a whisper.

The wolf tipped its head, and I knew instantly it was Jasper. *I'm not in any danger. I'm not in any danger*, I repeated to myself. Hopefully. I gently reached my hand up to stroke the soft fur on his neck, as if to prove to myself this was really happening. Jasper leaned into my touch, allowing me to take the time I needed to grasp this new reality. He had told me werewolves were real, and I adjusted. But for your crush to actually be one? That was a different story.

"Is this why you couldn't tell me? Because of the pack thing?"

He nodded his large head. At least he wasn't lying for the hell of it. After a few more minutes, Jasper shifted back. The transformation back to human was quieter, and less shocking.

When he was human again, he pulled his jeans back on leaving them slung low on his hips. I tried to tell myself the tingles I felt must have been the adrenaline coursing through my veins, but from the look on Jasper's face it was definitely something more than simple adrenaline.

He made his way back to me, never breaking eye contact. When he was close enough to touch me, he brought his hands to either side of my face again. "Ava, are you okay?"

I nodded, afraid if I spoke I would say something incriminating or embarrassing. Jasper looked at me, his gaze heavy. Calculating. My body clenched under his scrutiny, and I managed to choke out, "What?"

He skimmed his hands down my sides and clutched my hips tighter to him, his eyes full of wonder. "You really aren't afraid, are you?"

His bare skin was so close to mine I couldn't breathe.

His woodsy scent was overwhelming my senses, and I wanted to rake my hands down his muscular back. "I'm not afraid of you. It's a lot to take in, but I'm not scared. I don't think you would hurt me."

He breathed out heavily and bent so he could rest his forehead on mine. "Thank God. I was so worried you would run away." He dipped his head further so he could kiss me, but for the second time that day I stopped him.

He looked at me, a question in his beautiful eyes. I tried to ignore his overwhelming presence and asked him the most important question on my mind. "You aren't going to run away again, are you? I don't think I could take that embarrassment twice."

Jasper looked bewildered. "I'm not going to run away again, baby. I left last time because I didn't think it was fair to go any further if you didn't know about this side of me. And I'm pretty sure your cat sensed something was off about me."

Oh. Well that made sense. And was oddly charming? Could a werewolf be charming? Could a cat be a mood killer?

He opened his mouth to say something else but I stood up on my tiptoes and kissed him before he could. He stood still at first, and then crushed my body to his, groaning into my mouth. When we broke apart, his eyes were dark with lust. "The phasing, it affects me. It doesn't make me *want*, it makes me *need*. I won't have a lot of control around you, so you need to tell me now. Are you sure you're okay with this? With me?"

I wound my arms around his neck and looked at him. "I'm not gonna lie, I still have a lot of questions. But I'm not going to question how right it feels when your hands are on my body."

Jasper closed his eyes and cursed under his breath. His whole body was tense as he struggled to control himself. When he opened his eyes, I saw the wolf in them, and when he brought his lips to my neck I nearly melted right then and there. He nipped at the tender skin under my jaw and growled low. "Fuck it."

* * *

I couldn't believe this was real life. Jasper was actually in front of me, holding me so tight I could barely breathe. He swung me up into his arms as if I weighed no more than air and moved us both into the small cottage. He gently put me down on my feet in front of him on a faded rug.

"Not to ruin the moment or anything, but are we breaking and entering? I don't really want to end up in jail tonight."

He barked out a laugh and closed the distance between us. "No, Green. It's a friend's place. I have a key."

That made me feel better. I mean, I was still about to hook up with a guy I barely knew. But at least I wasn't breaking the law. I licked my lips in anticipation, and Jasper's eyes narrowed. His voice was dangerously low. "Goddamn, Ava, you have no idea what you do to me." His head dipped to my neck, licking and biting. His hands slid up under my sweater, raising it up over my breasts.

I could barely get a full sentence out. "Wha… what do I do to you?"

I still couldn't believe I could have the same effect over him as he had over me. It didn't seem possible. It was too soon. And yet, when he whispered in my ear, "How about I show you instead," I knew he was telling the truth. His voice trembled with honesty.

I took my sweater off the rest of the way and wrapped my arms around him, kissing him hard. He met me with a passionate groan as our bodies desperately tried to get closer. Jasper reached behind my back and in one deft move undid my bra.

He pushed back far enough to admire my breasts, with something close to worship in his eyes. "So beautiful." And then he was kissing me again, one hand toying with my nipples, the other tangling in my hair. He brought his mouth to my breast, alternating sucking and biting.

We had only begun, and yet I wasn't sure how much more of this teasing I could take. All I could think about was how much I wanted all of Jasper. I brought my hand down his sculpted abs to cup the length of his hard cock through his jeans, and I heard him suck in a breath through his teeth. "Fuck."

He stood frozen in place, panting. I moved my hands to the top of his waistband, and unbuttoned his jeans. But before I could get any further Jasper snatched my hands in one of his own, pushing me back to the couch. He undid my jeans, and I helped him push them over my hips. "I told you I didn't have a lot of control around you Ava, and I think it's close to maxed out."

I gave a small nod, lying in front of him in nothing more than my panties. His hand was dipping lower beneath the thin fabric with every word he spoke, and I felt myself getting more turned on with every small movement. "Do you understand me?" A brush of his fingers against my core and my hips jerked off the couch.

His fingers hooked into either side of my underwear, and pulled them off smoothly. I watched as his delirious gaze trailed over my body, coming back to focus on my eyes. He wanted to watch me. Jasper's hand was back, his finger grazing over my now slick pussy, teasing me. "Ava, do you understand me?"

"Yes," I stuttered.

He thrust two fingers into me, with his thumb coming up to rub circles around my clit. I moaned with pleasure, bringing my hips up to meet his touch. "Jasper, that feels so good."

He grinned hungrily. His smile undid my intentions, as usual. I gave in to the pleasure of his fingers working my body, sliding in and out, his thumb making smaller, quicker rotations. I couldn't control the small sounds escaping from the back of my throat. This was better than any dream. "Those noises you make. God." His mouth pressed on top of mine, swallowing any cries I made.

I could feel the pleasure building, and I cried out. "Oh fuck, Jasper!" I was close, so close. And just as quickly as they were there, his fingers were gone. I made a small note of displeasure, but stopped when I noticed Jasper standing in front of me.

His eyes were black with lust, and he was undoing his zipper, sliding his jeans down over his toned legs until he stood before me, bare. "I'm sorry for being selfish. I want to feel you come around my cock, not my fingers. I want to feel you give yourself over to me."

Fine by me. As long as I got release one way or another. I ran my gaze over his body longingly, pausing at his erection. *Oh.* I didn't know how that was even going to fit. But as if I were someone else, I reached out to touch him. I took his cock in my hand and began to stroke it. "God, you're so hard."

He brought himself down to kneel between my legs on the couch. "How about we do something about that."

I heard the crinkling of a condom wrapper, and I had enough sense left to stutter out, "I'm on the pill. Are you clean?"

"I'm safe." I nodded, and then I felt the broad tip of him nudging me. I tried to relax to take the size of him in. He slowed, resting his forehead on mine. "I'll be as gentle as I can. I just don't know what that's going to look like." I tilted my hips and he groaned deeply. "Fuck, you're so tight."

Jasper moved his hips and in one slick move thrust the length of his cock deep into my pussy. "Oh!" I cried out, feeling stretched in the most delicious way.

Jasper froze, letting me get used to his size. When he looked at me, his eyes were unfocused. "Are you okay now? I can't hold back any longer."

I wanted, no, I *needed* the friction. When I nodded, he began to move. His powerful thrusts bordered on pain, but I'd take the ache in exchange for the pleasure. It called to something primal in me, something I didn't know was there. I needed to be connected to his in a way I couldn't comprehend. Every cell in my body strained to be closer to his, to possess and be possessed. I reached behind him to grab his buttocks, willing my body to take him in further. Until we could move as one instead of two. "Oh, Jasper."

He growled in response, moving quicker. "I have wanted to fuck you since the first time I saw you." He took my wrists and pinned them above my head, and I knew with how tightly he was holding me I would have bruises there in the morning. Worth it. Worth it all.

It didn't take long until I felt myself riding the edge of an orgasm again, and I tried to tell him. "Oh God..."

This time Jasper didn't, or couldn't stop. He drove deep into me with each thrust. "Ava. Let go." The tone of Jasper's voice didn't leave any room for argument.

I let go, moaning as I came around him while he continued to pound into me. Wave after wave of pleasure enveloped me as I kissed him softly.

Jasper wasn't far behind me. He swore and I felt him come inside of me. He said my name like a prayer as he shook and trembled, before collapsing next to me.

We lay quietly like that for several minutes, embracing the silence after what could mostly definitely not be described as just a hookup. Would I have let a hookup fuck me without a condom? Probably not. Definitely not. Quietly, Jasper got up and left the room, coming back to hand me a warm washcloth. I raised one eyebrow at him. Either he knew what I was thinking, or he was just thoughtful.

"Don't tell me you're shy now!" Jasper laughed, breaking any doubts I might have had. I smiled and gratefully took the wash cloth as he lay back down next to me. Jasper sighed softly and threw his arm over his eyes, giving me some semblance of privacy as I cleaned up. "Jesus, I knew you were something special, but you might just kill me."

I turned away and smiled shyly to myself. "I'm sure you say that to all the girls."

He rolled me back towards him, hooking his finger under my chin to turn my face to look at him. He shook his head. "No, Ava. You will be my downfall."

I wasn't sure how to tell him I felt the same way. Because I knew after tonight Jasper Knight was dangerous in ways I could have never imagined.

I thought it would have been awkward. The after. But I found myself at ease to ask him what was weighing on me. "What did you mean the other night? When you said you weren't that person anymore."

Jasper laughed. "Anyone else probably would've asked that question before we had sex."

I rested my head on his chest, rolling my eyes. "Throw me a bone."

He was quiet, running his hands up and down my back. "I've done things I'm not proud of. I was angry for a long time, and I fell in with the wrong crowd for a while. My friends, my real friends, made me see who I was becoming."

"Have you..." I hesitated. "Have you..." My unspoken sentence hung in the air. *Killed someone.*

"No. No, I haven't." He answered without me having to say it out loud. "But there are other things I've had to make amends for. I took different girls home every night. I've hurt people badly."

"Did they deserve it? The people you hurt?" So many questions were racing through my mind, I couldn't believe this was the one I decided to voice. But right now, it was the only one that mattered.

"Yes." His voice was quiet. Resolved.

I nodded against his skin. I was sad for people I had never met, for a younger Jasper I hadn't known. I needed to change the topic. "What do they mean?" I asked him, tracing one of the large tattoos across his chest.

Jasper sat up a bit. "Some are for the pack." He gestured to the larger circular one spanning his shoulder. "Some are for my family." He pointed to the roses sprawling across his chest. "Some are for me." He splayed his fingers across my hands so I could clearly see the animal skulls outlined on them for the first time.

"*Memento Mori.* Reminders that I'm still capable of death," he told me, as I turned his fingers around, examining them. The tattoos were delicate and beautiful, contradicting their dark meaning.

But I didn't say that. I said, "Boy, you're really

committed to the whole bad boy image, aren't you?" I also left out the part where the whole "bad boy image thing" was really doing it for me.

"What's that supposed to mean?"

I shook my head. "Nothing."

Jasper put two fingers on my jaw, stopping my head from moving. "No, I'd really like to hear what Ava Green thinks about me and my image." He drawled the last word, and I knew he was teasing me.

I was game. "Well, let's see. The mussed up hair -- check. The leather jacket -- check. The tattoos -- check. The whole air about you screams *bad boy*. You're nearly the perfect specimen."

One eyebrow shot up. "Nearly?"

"I'm not too sure about the whole personality. Underneath it all, you seem like a pretty sweet guy." My voice still had a joking note, but I meant what I was saying. Despite my misgivings, Jasper *was* sweet.

"I'm only sweet when a pretty girl makes me want to be." He kissed me, making me forget our conversation entirely.

After a while he kissed my forehead and disentangled himself from me. He helped me to my feet, and I started the awkward task of finding my clothes. But Jasper shook his head and tugged me down a narrow hallway.

"I should get dressed," I protested, although the truth was, I'd go anywhere he asked. Especially if it meant I got to look at his stunning body without clothes on a bit longer. I was going to have to do something about my weakening self-control, and quick.

"I need a shower before we head back. I thought you might like one too."

Oh. The rest of my self-control officially exited the building. I let him lead me to a small bathroom, and waited as he turned the squeaky knobs to hot. I stepped into the shower, and let the steam envelop me. I was going to shower with a guy I had just met. Who I had just had sex with. Who was also a werewolf. Pretty sure a shower was the least of the moral codes I was breaking tonight. Jasper joined me, tucking my hair around my shoulder so he could kiss my neck. "Mmm…" I leaned back into his firm body, letting my ass grind against his growing erection.

He chuckled darkly. "I thought we were taking a shower to clean up."

"I'd be impressed if your intentions were actually that pure."

Jasper let his hand wrap around my slick body, cupping one breast. One rebellious nipple rose up to meet his touch. He pinched it gently, and it sent a shock of desire right through me. "Nothing about me is pure."

Fuck. I needed him. "Show me," I gasped, arching my back into him again.

With a growl that sounded desperate and primal, Jasper spun me round so I was facing him. "Don't say I didn't warn you." He picked me up as if I weighed nothing, resting my back against the wet sides of the shower. I tried to find purchase, something to maintain my balance with, but everything was too slick. "Hold on to me," he commanded. I wrapped my arms tightly around his neck as he drove into me.

This time Jasper didn't give me a moment to adjust. He sucked and bit at my breast, his hands holding me by my ass. It was an assault on my senses as he lowered me up and down. I closed my eyes and let his touch overwhelm me. I wanted him to wreck me in the best way possible. The fullness of his thick cock inside of me, his wild pace, and his not so gentle bites quickly built the pleasure rising inside of me. I had lost control of my body, to a man I wasn't sure had any control at all.

Need consumed my every thought. He hitched one of my legs higher on his legs, driving deeper into me. "Whether you accept it or not, your body is already mine." I arched my back again, looking for release. Jasper gave me what I wanted, sucking firmly on my breast and never stopping his firm thrusts. Ecstasy exploded from inside of me. I cried out, hearing him call my name and feeling his body shaking inside of me only moments later.

I rested my head on his, breathing heavily. "I'm not sure if I'm coming out of this shower cleaner or dirtier."

He grinned. "I'd apologize, but I'm not sorry."

We stepped out of the shower and Jasper passed me a towel. I dried off before heading back to the front room where my clothes were, not bothering to wait for him. I was in a daze from the hard sex and the warm shower, and got dressed slowly.

"Ava," Jasper called from across the room.

"Yeah?" I turned to look at him, still in a sex fog. His hair was damp from the shower, and his dark clothes were no worse for the wear from our evening.

He hesitated as if he were making a decision, then crossed the space in two sure strides. "There's something else." Jasper handed me a small framed photo. I rolled my eyes. I didn't really need to see a family photo of whosever's house we had just violated. But then I looked at the photo. And then I looked again. *It couldn't be.*

"I wanted to tell you. Really. But I had to figure out a way to get around the rules. When I found the picture..." Jasper watched me warily as I studied the photo.

I drew in a breath to steady myself. "What the hell is this?"

The blood drained from Jasper's face as he watched my reaction. *Shock. Anger. Betrayal.* I held a group photo, taken a few years back from the looks of things. Jasper's arms were slung around another young man's shoulders, their contagious grins frozen in time. And in the back corner, smiling widely at the photographer, stood my parents. I had no idea what the hell was going on.

Chapter 7

I began making a mental pros and cons list. Con -- Jasper was a liar. And a big one. Pro -- I had just had the best sex of my life with that liar. Somewhere in the middle ground, Jasper was a werewolf. I'd classify that situation based on how this conversation went down. The tension in the room was so thick it practically suffocated me. I could see Jasper trying to decide how best to handle the situation. The *situation* being me. To be fair, I was set to go off like a bomb if he didn't have a damn good explanation for how he knew my parents, and why he hadn't told me in the first place.

Jasper kept looking from me to the photo, running his fingers through his dark hair. If I hadn't been so livid, his perfectly dishevelled appearance would be sexy as hell.

Finally, he walked towards me, looking like he was about to speak.

I took a step back. I needed space until I understood everything. Frustration flashed across his features. "Goddamn Alpha's orders. Goddamn Jim and Monica, keeping you in the dark."

What?

Jasper must have read the confusion on my face. "Look, you have to believe me. It wasn't my choice to leave you out of the loop. Your parents made that call and I had to respect their decision. It was a command by the leader of the pack, the Alpha. I had to figure out a way around the order without directly disobeying him."

His tone was pleading, his eyes begging me to believe him. But I had to hold my ground. I ignored all the crazy Alpha wolf bullshit and went right to the point. "*What* didn't they want to tell me?" My voice came out sharper than I ever thought possible.

His hands were pulling at his hair again and he sat down on the couch. "Look, Green -- Ava -- would you please sit down?"

I folded my arms over my chest. "I think I'm fine here."

Jasper sighed. "Okay, fine, have it your way. But you have to know this isn't my secret to tell. I wanted to tell you everything. Truly."

I gritted my teeth. "Get to the point, Jasper."

He held his hands up in defeat. "Okay. Okay. Look. I've known your parents for a long time. They've helped the pack out with a lot of different problems."

The wheels were turning in my head, but I couldn't figure out how everything fell into place. "What would my parents possibly help werewolves with? Was my dad teaching you Latin? My mom is an artist, for Christ's sake."

Jasper looked away, uncomfortable. "Your parents are special people. They are a part of a group of people we know as Venators."

My mouth dropped open. "I'm sorry, what?"

"Venators." He continued, as if reading a textbook. "Descended from Romans. Bred to fight dangerous creatures, or so history goes. History conveniently leaves out the part about what they hunted."

I narrowed my eyes. "Venators. Uh-huh. Sure. What did they hunt?" I kept expecting him to laugh at me, tell me he was messing with me. But it never came.

Instead, he looked even more serious. "They hunt supernatural creatures, Ava. Evil ones. And your parents are some of the best."

This couldn't be happening. This kind of stuff being real was one thing. But my parents knowing about it my entire life was another issue altogether. Not to mention them *lying* to me about it. My mind flashed back to a vivid dream I had as a child, of hurting myself on a funny looking knife I had found in my dad's study. I had gone back after I had woken up the next morning but the knife wasn't there.

What if that hadn't been a dream after all? What if I had talked myself out of believing in other things too?

I kept trying to speak, but no words came out. Eventually I sat down on the couch next to Jasper. He turned to me, reaching his arm out to touch my shoulder but stopping himself before he did. I was torn between wanting him to hold me until I forgot this whole thing, and wanting to bitch him out for not being honest in the first place, screw my parent's wishes. They had lied to me. Jasper's instincts won out and he gently touched my shoulder. "Are you okay? Talk to me."

"I just don't know what to think. My parents lied to me. My parents are some kind of weird monster hunters and I never suspected anything." I rested my head in my hands, trying not to let the panic overwhelm me.

His hand took my shoulder more firmly and pulled me to him, enveloping me into his strong arms. I tried to pull away, still angry with him, but he just held me tighter. "Ava, please believe me. I wanted to tell you. I brought you out here tonight, to show you who I really am. Why would I show you that if I wanted to lie to you?"

I knew he was telling me the truth. He wouldn't have shown me his wolf side if there hadn't been some semblance of trust between us. But I was so angry at my parents, that fury had to filter somewhere. I couldn't believe they hadn't trusted me enough to tell me such an integral part of their lives, of who they were. I let Jasper hold me until I felt ready to talk. "Can I ask you a question?"

He chuckled gently, and it lifted my soul a little to hear it. "I think we're beyond asking if you can ask me a question or not."

"Why didn't my parents tell me?"

He sighed, the disappointment echoing around us. "You'll have to ask them for the whole answer. But I think they were hoping it would protect you, if you didn't want to live this life. Obviously, that backfired."

I sat up, curiosity getting the better of me. "What exactly do Venators do now?"

He stiffened, his tattooed skin taut over his arm muscles. "Are you sure you want to know?"

"Yes." And I *was* sure. I was tired of the lies. I needed to know the truth. The whole truth, for once. I wasn't going to be complacent with the easy answers anymore.

"It's a calling that usually passes down in families, so

very few outsiders are aware supernaturals exist. Venators hunt down bad creatures, like the one I'm tracking in your woods right now -- the ones that are dangerous, deadly. Not just to my kind, but to everyone. And they kill them so they can't hurt anyone else."

Shock flooded my body. I couldn't imagine my parents tracking things, let alone killing them. And yet, memories of my father's survival lessons came flooding back. "How?"

"They're trained in different weapons, taken from different cultures over the years. Let's be honest, Roman weapons aren't exactly known for being discreet." He smiled tightly, trying to lighten the situation. "Most are usually well versed in hand to hand combat as well."

I wasn't sure my brain had room to fit all of this, let alone figure out where I fit into this whole new world. "Are they expecting me to be one of these... hunters?"

He held me tighter. "I think the only person who can answer that is you. This is a lot to take in, even compared to what I've told the past couple days. I think you should get a good night's sleep and speak to your parents about all of this."

I nodded, dumbfounded by all the new information. "Yeah, that's probably best."

Jasper released me to hold me at arm's length. "Are you okay? If you don't feel like riding we can stay here tonight."

Sleep was an impossibility at this point. I shook myself off and stood up. "No, I'm good. I just want to go home. Let's go."

Letting him take my hand, we walked out to his bike. He got on and then helped me on, and I found even though his touch still sent shivers through me, I was slightly numb. I just needed to get home, sleep in my own bed.

The ride home was uneventful, and before too long we were in my parking lot. I hobbled off the bike, nearly falling flat on my face. My emotions were running high. "I shouldn't be okay with all of this. I shouldn't."

He nodded, stepping closer to touch my arms gently. "Green. At least let me text you to make sure you're okay tonight. Please."

I turned to go, but paused and looked at him. "Thank you for telling me about my parents." I placed a soft hand on his face, unable to keep myself from touching him. Deep down, I knew it wasn't his fault. It made me uncomfortable how many secrets I had already pried out from him, but I knew they weren't all his to share to begin with.

He bent to kiss me. "Text me tonight. Just to tell me you're okay."

I kissed him back, my body responding regardless of my anger and disappointment. I wasn't even sure who I was angry with anymore. Myself? My parents? Jasper? But my body ignored all of that even as my mind warred with itself. I channelled my frustration and hurt into the kiss, wanting him to understand my emotions. The air between us was heavy when we broke apart, our bodies expressing unspoken longing. I stepped away and walked to the front door without saying anything. Jasper knew I would text him. How could I not? I seemed compelled to be close to him, despite the strange circumstances. When I turned back, he was still in the lot, watching me. Predator or protector, I couldn't be sure.

* * *

I walked into my apartment in a daze, ignoring absolutely everything to go lie down on my bed fully dressed. My emotions were the worst kind of roller coaster. The connection I felt with Jasper was electric, and I knew I was becoming attached to him. The evening we had spent together had been incredible. Goose bumps rose up on my skin as I thought about the way he had touched me. And yet, all of that felt tainted by the knowledge that my parents weren't who I thought they were. My life wasn't what I thought it was. This wasn't a small thing they had kept from me and I wasn't sure I could ever trust them again. I was so confused about everything.

Before I could get my thoughts together enough to make any decisions, my cell phone vibrated in my pocket, stirring me from my thoughts. I pulled it out to find a text message from Jasper and my heart soared.

Hey. It's Jasper. Checking in.

For someone who looked the way he did, and was a terrifying werewolf to top it off, he sure was a whole lot gentler and sweeter than he let on. Oddly enough, Jasper was definitely a comfort in this new world I had found myself thrust into. I messaged him back, letting him know I was confused, but okay. Then I deleted the whole thing to send him one that said I was fine. I threw a quick message to Mollie too, so she knew I had gotten home in one piece so they wouldn't stay up worrying I had been buried alive in the woods somewhere.

It wasn't quite midnight, meaning my parents would still be awake in Florida. *If that's even where they actually were.*

* * *

Sighing heavily, I called the number of the one person I really didn't want to talk to. But I would get my answers, one way or another. It rang once before she picked up. "Ava? Everything okay?"

No. Everything isn't okay. I felt my resolve cracking.

"Ava?"

I had a flashback to Jasper, grasping my body. *"Are you sure you're okay with this? With me?"* But I wasn't with Jasper now, and his hands weren't teasing me. I was on the phone with my mom. "Mom. How could you not tell me?" My voice cracked midway through, but I refused to cry. Not now.

"Tell you what?"

"Are you even *in* Florida?"

"Of course we're in Florida!" She already sounded defensive.

"Mom. Jasper Knight is in town. He told me about the Venators. And now you need to tell me the truth."

A sharp intake of breath, then a disappointed sigh. "When I told the Goddamn pack to send someone to watch you, I meant anyone other than Jasper Knight. How did he manage to tell you about us? I thought the Alpha had forbidden it."

"I worked it out for myself. I'm not stupid." And what vendetta did her parents have against Jasper? "What do you mean you sent someone from the pack to watch me?"

"Just because you didn't know about this world doesn't mean you don't need protection from it. We asked the pack to send someone to keep an eye on you while we were gone..." Her voice trailed off, the unspoken words hanging. *Because you couldn't do it yourself.* "I guess I always knew you'd find out about the Venators eventually. But what the hell are you doing hanging out with Knight? He's no good for you, Ava."

I couldn't believe her. I had always looked up to my parents. They had always seemed so powerful. But they had not only hidden the truth of my heritage from me, but now that I knew, she was showing no remorse. And her dislike of Jasper was far from subtle. Her defence was ridiculous. "Jasper has been good to me, Mom, and he's been as truthful as he can be. Which is more than I can say for you." My body felt like a spring tightly coiled, unspoken anger bubbling up in my throat.

"Ava, we were truly trying to protect you. This is a dangerous life, and you've struggled enough with the non-supernatural side of things."

Now I was angry and offended. A dangerous combination. "You never even gave me the option. Now I've been thrown into this crazy world -- something's hunting werewolves in town -- and I've had zero preparation. How do you expect me to pick up our supposed *family* business if you never even told me about us?"

Mom scoffed, clearly annoyed. "You aren't going to take over for us. Your father and I discussed that a long time ago, and it was decided you weren't cut out to take on this role. And nothing is going to hurt you. We still taught you important life skills. Your father tried to make sure you were as prepared as possible for a non-member."

My anger was no longer veiled, and I was close to screaming into the phone. "How dare you? How dare you decide what I'm capable of or not capable of? You and Dad *lied* to me. You lied to me my entire life. No. Not telling me is worse than a lie. You *decided* for me. You decided I was weak without even knowing what I could do. There's a whole other world out there that Jasper had to tell me about because my own parents wouldn't."

Her voice cut over the phone, sharp and to the point. "We chose because we are your parents, and sometimes that involves making difficult decisions. And I'm sure Jasper didn't tell you everything. He has secrets of his own. Did he tell you what Venators could truly do? What you will never do?"

I couldn't figure out why she was so cold towards Jasper. In the photo I had seen, they looked like they were friends. She obviously doubted how much I knew. "He told me everything."

"Knight needs to learn how to keep quiet. Did he happen to tell you about werewolf mates then, Ava?"

Werewolf mates? Mom's voice insinuated I should know something I didn't. But I wasn't about to tell her that. "I know everything, Mom."

She sighed. "Ava, look. It's been a long day for both of us. Your father and I truly have your best interests at heart and I'm sure you'll see that in the morning, after a good night's sleep. But Ava?"

I was still riled up, but I was done talking and wanted to get her off the phone. "What now?"

"Stay away from Knight. I mean it when I say he's no good for you."

I hung up on her before she could say goodbye and lay on my bed, staring at my phone like it could answer all of life's questions. How could they think I wasn't cut out to be a Venator? How could Mom not trust Jasper?

I was sure I wouldn't be able to sleep. I lay in that same position for a few minutes, trying to decide what to do with my pent-up anger. My phone vibrated again, and I eyed it cautiously, anticipating another guilt fuelled conversation with my mother. Instead, Jasper's name popped up on the screen for the second time that night. Had it really been only a few hours since I watched him transform? It felt like years.

"Hello?" I answered cautiously. The argument with my mother had left me feeling worn out and wrung dry.

Jasper's raspy voice was instantly soothing as it washed over me. "Hey. It's me. I know you seemed like you wanted space, but I needed to make sure you were actually okay. If you don't want to talk that's all right. I thought I'd check in."

All the tears I had held back on the phone with my mom came flooding out. Great. Here I was bawling on the phone with him less than three hours after we had sex for the first time.

Jasper sounded worried. "Hey, Green, seriously. If talking to me upsets you, I'll go."

He thought I was crying because he upset me? "It's not you Jasper. I just got off the phone with my mom."

He breathed out heavily. "Oh, I get it. I take it the conversation didn't go well then."

I laughed bitterly. "You could say that." I filled Jasper in on our short conversation, leaving out the part about werewolf mates.

Jasper stayed quiet while I ranted, making sympathetic noises when it was appropriate. Finally, he sighed. "I'm sorry Green. I dragged you into a world you never asked for. It wasn't fair of me."

It wasn't fair of *him*? Whether I liked it or not, this world had always been a part of me, I just hadn't known about it. Jasper was the first thing in a long time that felt right in my life. "Jasper, it's not your fault. It's my parents' fault for not being honest with me, and for not believing in me enough to trust me with the truth. I can't believe they think I'm not Venator material. Who do they think they are?"

"Obviously they can't see the kickass woman in front of their own eyes." Jasper's voice was warm with amusement.

This time my laugh was a bit more genuine. "Can you tell me more about the Venators?"

"What do you want to know?"

"How do they become so... powerful?" It was the only

word I could think of to describe the image I had constructed in my mind.

"They aren't born differently, if that's what you mean. It comes more naturally to them -- the fighting. They train endlessly. Always learning, always adapting." His voice was admiring, but I was tired just thinking about it.

"So, nothing is… wrong with me?" I asked quietly. It had been weighing on me since speaking with my mother.

"No! There is absolutely nothing wrong with you."

I sighed. "I've always felt like I was letting them down in some way. That I wasn't good enough. I never understood it -- now, I get it."

"Ava, don't let them get to you. You're stronger than you know, and you could do anything you put your mind to. I'd put money on it."

Anything I put my mind to? A thought occurred to me, and before I could talk myself out of it, I asked him. "Would you do me a favour if I asked?"

I could hear Jasper's smile over the phone. "Well, Green, you already got all of my secrets out of me, turned me into the kind of guy who talks to girls on the phone late at night, and got your parents pissed at me. I'm not sure what favours are left, but okay. Doubt I could say no anyway. What's the favour?"

I sucked in a breath. "I want you to train me to be a Venator."

Silence. Either he was seriously considering it, or contemplating the best way to reject me without hurting my feelings. The wait was excruciating. Maybe this was a stupid idea. Maybe Jasper didn't think I could do it either.

"You sure about this, Green? It's not a small undertaking. It doesn't make for an easy, picture perfect life, either."

I'd never seen my life as perfect. I pictured myself living alone, working alone, eating alone in my same old routine until I died. Or I could take a huge risk, and possibly find what I was really meant to do on this earth. Maybe I could make a difference.

My heart soared with hope. "I'm certain, Jasper. This is what I was meant to do."

"Okay. I don't know everything they teach, but I can do my best. We start next weekend."

A pit grew in my stomach, and my voice was dangerously close to a whine. "Next weekend? Why not tomorrow?" I was sure whining wasn't a quality held in high regard by the Venators.

Jasper let out a low chuckle, one that made me smile like a fool. "First of all, I think you've dealt with enough the last couple days. Secondly, I'm out of town this week. Friday, you already have plans."

I couldn't remember making any plans. I racked my brains trying to figure out what I had forgotten when Jasper spoke over my train of thought. "Friday, Green, I'm taking you out on a date."

Chapter 8

I looked down at my phone for the fifteenth time, willing a message to appear. Something. Anything. But not even my deadliest glare produced a text message. I huffed in frustration and shoved my phone into the bottom of my bag where I wouldn't think about it. I turned back to my computer and tried to throw myself into my work. I was exhausted. I had spent every night since last Saturday pushing myself harder in my workouts. I needed to be better. Stronger. I could be a Venator. I could prove my parents wrong. My muscles hurt in places I didn't even know I had, but it was worth it.

Jasper and I had stayed on the phone late last night, talking about everything, and nothing. It had never felt so right with someone. It wasn't only last night either. We had spent every night this week talking. He talked about growing up in Louisiana. About his mom, who was still in Chicago.

"Did your mom join a different pack?" I asked him.

"No. My mom isn't a wolf."

"What? How does that work?" There was so much I didn't understand. But I wanted to know everything about him.

I could hear his amusement over the phone. "Being a werewolf is a dominant trait, Green. My dad is a werewolf. Mom let me grow up with him so I could get the pack life."

I told him about Merrillan, and how I felt like I could never shake the labels put on me as a kid. So instead I hid from people, from stories they could tell about me. "That's probably why I don't date a whole lot. The guys I went out with after college all knew me from high school and I felt like I couldn't redefine myself," I whispered to him one night, my eyes already closed from exhaustion.

"I still can't believe that," Jasper responded, his voice husky with sleep. "You should have guys knocking down your door, begging to take you out. On that note, remind me not to take you to Chicago. I might have some serious competition." I had fallen asleep letting his voice wash over me, my whole body warm with the feeling of being desired.

Last night before Jasper had reluctantly hung up, he had told me he would text me the next day. So now, here I was. Sitting at my usual table at the coffee shop, and I was becoming one of those girls who stare at their phones until a boy messages. Because it was now 3:00 pm and I hadn't heard a word from him.

Mollie had texted several times, and I had sent her back some brief messages, but I wasn't ready to talk about everything with her. To top it off, I wasn't even sure how much of my new life I could actually share. I had to get my story straight in my head first.

I felt a faint buzzing from my bag and lunged for my phone like it was on fire. I couldn't stop the smile spreading across my face when I saw Jasper's name on the screen. But my smile froze when I read his message. *Sorry but I gotta take a rain check on our date. Something came up. Call you later.*

My stomach sank. It sure sounded like he was blowing me off. Jasper hadn't messaged me all day, and now he was sending a text cancelling our plans tonight. I felt irrationally upset. After all, Jasper wasn't my boyfriend. Yeah, we had really hot sex but it didn't mean anything. I had stupidly thought maybe it had been going somewhere. Obviously, he was a little too good at playing the game. Except… except for the fact he was also a werewolf. And a private investigator. Except for the fact he might not be blowing me off, something might actually be wrong. And he was hiding it from me.

I messaged him back quickly, *Do you need help?*

Nothing. Silence. Now I at least felt justifiably upset. Either I was being ghosted, or he was on some wolf mission I wasn't a part of.

The afternoon dragged by. Jasper hadn't messaged me back, and I found myself becoming increasingly annoyed. I forced myself to go to the gym, running until my legs hurt and my lungs felt like they were going to cave in. The endorphins didn't help my mood any, and I sent Jasper another quick text. *Are you okay?*

No surprise, I didn't get a text back. By the time I got home it was after sunset. I unlocked my door in the darkened stairwell, my thoughts spiralling, my chest tight. What if Jasper wasn't blowing me off, and something was seriously wrong? What if he was hurt? I had no way to find him. I didn't know where he had gone, what he had been doing today. Next time I needed to make sure I knew where he was going. I rolled my eyes. Bet my parents would know. But that wasn't an option I wanted to explore.

Fuck. How had I ended up in this situation? To top it off, I was starving and my fridge was depressingly empty. I switched on my computer to play some angsty music, poured myself a large glass of whiskey and tried to think.

Betty came over to my hibernation spot on the couch and plunked herself down on my stomach, which was usually comforting. But not tonight. I tried to remember if Jasper had said where he was working this week, but nothing was coming up to mind. I was scrolling through old messages, hoping to find a clue when my phone rang. Only a few people ever called me and I didn't really feel like talking to any of them. But I knew I couldn't ignore my life forever, so I answered it. "Hello?"

"Oh my God, girl! I have been waiting all week to hear this great excuse Mr. Brooding came up with, so it better be a good one." It was Mollie's chipper voice on the other end of the line.

I sighed. "I don't really want to talk about it right now, Mollie." Either Jasper had dumped me after screwing me, or he was screwed. Neither was an option I wanted to explore with my perfect best friend at this point.

Mollie immediately went into guilt trip mode. "Come on, tell me the big, elaborate excuse for why he ran away from your apartment…" She stopped mid-sentence. "Ava Green. Are you listening to Death Cab for Cutie?"

Shit. I tried to turn off the music, fumbling off the couch as I did so. "No?"

"Girl. Did you sleep with him?"

I didn't want to have this conversation. I wanted to have my drink, figure out what the hell Jasper had been doing today, and scold myself for not being better prepared. "Mol, can we not do this right now?"

Mollie was immediately sympathetic. "God, Ava. I'm sorry. Men are assholes. Do you need me to come over?"

Luckily, her empathy gave me an out. I felt bad, but I really needed to make sure Jasper was okay. "No, I'm okay." It wasn't the truth. But as I said it, I realized I had said those words way too many times the last few days. Pretty soon they were going to be meaningless. "Really. I'm gonna mope around a bit. Maybe clean my kitchen." Mollie couldn't come over. If she came over, I couldn't get to the bottom of this.

She sighed. "If you're sure. But call me if you need anything, okay?"

"Will do." We made plans for our usual lunch next week and I hung up, turning up my music even louder. Fuck. Where the hell was he? I tried to call his phone again, but it went right to voicemail. Maybe he *was* blowing me off. Was this what my life was going to look like? Never knowing if Jasper was ditching me or was in trouble? *Ugh.*

I took another large swig of my whiskey. I'd give him five more minutes, and then I was going to head out and start looking for him. I wasn't sure where to begin, and I was pretty sure it wasn't safe, but I had to start acting like a Venator at some point.

I didn't know why I was so hung up about his safety and his whereabouts. At the end of the day he was just another guy who didn't call. But I knew deep down it was more than that. We had connected, and I had spoken truths to him about my life I hadn't even admitted to myself. I thought he had done the same. I took another drink, finishing my glass. Okay, no more drinking. I had shit to take care of.

My cell phone vibrated from my pocket. Probably Mollie again. I pulled it out to turn it off, but the name on it made me stop. *Jasper.* Finally. I released the breath I wasn't aware I had been holding in. I didn't even want to know where he had been anymore. But I knew that was a lie so I opened his message. *Hey. Just got back to the motel. Sorry. Again.*

That's it? I huffed. I had been about ready to go out searching for this man in the dead of the night, and all I got was a *sorry?* This was ridiculous. If he thought he could just brush off my messages, he was in for a rude awakening. Fuelled by alcohol and embarrassment, and messaged back. *Don't worry about it. I didn't expect too much from you anyway.*

Now I was a liar, too. I had expected a lot from him. But I shouldn't have.

Jasper's response pinged up almost immediately. *What's that supposed to mean?*

I rolled my eyes and stuffed my phone back into my pocket. *Asshole.* As if he didn't know. Whatever. I had more important things to do -- like drink. And be pissed at him. Now I knew he was at least safe, I could drink in peace. I wasn't sure why I didn't drink more often. It made me forget all my insecurities, all my anxieties.

I pulled Betty closer and closed my eyes, imagining my future as a kick ass Venator. Next time, I'd be prepared. I'd know better. I wondered if they made leather pants that were both badass looking and comfortable. In my pocket, my phone started ringing. I ignored it without looking. I didn't know who it was, and I didn't really care. It immediately started ringing again. I picked it up, but didn't say anything. Maybe they would go away if they thought the line was dead.

"What the hell did that message mean, Green?" Jasper's angry voice flooded my ear. Loud. Too loud.

Ugh. "Nothing. It meant nothing. Why are you calling me now? You didn't seem too concerned about keeping me in the loop earlier."

Jasper didn't sound any less angry. "I was busy. I told you I would call you later. So now I'm calling you. Later."

The booze was blurring his words, and I couldn't focus on what he was saying. I was angry I had spent an entire evening worrying about someone who was fine the whole time. "You didn't trust me enough to tell me what you were actually doing," I accused.

Jasper sounded exasperated. "I trust you. Of course I trust you."

I rolled my eyes again, even though he couldn't see me. "Sure, okay."

"Are you drunk?"

I didn't think I was. But I couldn't remember how much I had drunk or what I was actually mad about anymore. Except Jasper was a jerk. "Noooo way," I said. "You didn't bother telling me the truth about tonight. You don't need to update me on your schedule since you already screwed me."

The line was silent. It was quiet for one moment, then two.

Then, so quietly I had to strain to hear him. "Say it to my face, Green."

Was I hearing him right? "What?"

His voice was low and dangerous. "You heard me. You want to be a big bad Venator. Turn off your whiny music and come say that to my face."

My feelings were hurt, but I felt like I was going to spontaneously combust. Every word he said sent flares straight to my body. It was hard to remember I was angry with him. But, I needed to show him I wasn't a girl he could blow off. So instead of responding, I hung up the phone. I put my shoes on like I was on autopilot, on a mission. The motel was only a couple blocks down the road, I could walk there easily. Maybe not in a straight line, but I could. I probably should have thought about transportation before I started drinking. Next time.

I left my building and started walking down the street towards Jasper's motel, sorting out what I would say to him in my head. I had gone maybe a block before I heard the growl of an engine coming towards me.

It sounded a lot like Jasper's bike. Sure enough, Jasper came flying around the corner on his motorbike. He pulled up next to me and took his helmet off, glaring.

"What are you doing here?" I asked him.

"What the hell are you doing out here, Green?" he responded angrily, his eyes flashing.

I couldn't cave. Not yet. "You told me to come say it to your face so that's what I was going to do. Now, your turn."

He rolled his eyes at me and the gesture made him look years younger. "You were drunk and hung up on me. Did you think I wouldn't worry? I was coming to check on you. Make sure you hadn't done anything stupid, like trying to walk to the motel by yourself in the dark."

He was worried about me? I was at a loss for words. This whole thing was a big gigantic mess.

Jasper shoved a helmet into my hands. "Get on."

I climbed onto the back of the bike as steadily as I could. "Where are we going?"

"Motel." He still sounded pissed, but he grabbed my hands and pulled them around his waist tightly. I settled against his back, blaming the whiskey for the easy way my body fit into his.

He kicked off, and we were at the motel in no time at all. When he pulled up to the spot outside his room, I couldn't help but steal a furtive glance around to make sure Deidra wasn't snooping this late at night. Jasper waited for me to get off, then swung off the bike, assuming I would follow. I trailed him towards the door he was holding open. Once we were both inside, he shut the door.

He exhaled slowly, but didn't turn to face me. "Did you honestly think I was going to blow you off after fucking you a few times?"

Well yeah, I had. Bad boys usually didn't hang around, and they most definitely didn't hang around for girls like me. But none of this translated to a sentence, so instead it came out as an "Mmpphh…"

Jasper finally whirled around to look at me, and I gasped when I saw his face clearly. His smooth skin was mottled with bruises, and a deep gash ran along one cheek. My anger immediately dissipated. He looked exhausted, and once he saw I had noticed his appearance he spoke, his voice low. "I wasn't trying to blow you off Ava. I ran into some trouble."

I instinctively took a step towards him. "What happened?"

"Can we talk about this later?"

I nodded, and reached my hand out towards his face. "I'm sorry."

He caught my wrist before I could touch him, something unreadable in his eyes. "Don't worry about it. Wolves heal quickly. I believe there was something else you wanted to say to my face."

Jasper's touch incited an immediate response in my body. The ride over had sobered me up, and I all too eagerly melted into his touch. "Hmm?" I couldn't think of what I had wanted to say to him. I was too busy imagining his hands crawling under my shirt.

He stroked the inside of my wrist gently with his finger, his voice as soft as his feather-light touch. "You said something to me on the phone. Something about not caring about you because I already screwed you?" Jasper's eyes were dark, and held my gaze with intensity.

"Oh. Yeah. About that…"

Jasper brought my wrist to his lips, sucking on the delicate skin there. His gaze never strayed from mine as he spoke. "You should understand by now that once could never be enough." But his eyes only held need. "Tell me, Ava, was it enough for you?"

I closed my eyes and let his voice run over me like honey. When I opened them again, he was watching, waiting for an answer. Apparently his question wasn't rhetorical.

"No. Of course it wasn't. It will never be enough."

Jasper tugged me closer to him and I rested in his arms. He brought his mouth to mine, taking my lip gently between his teeth. I sighed into him, comfort washing over me. Everything felt so right with him. His voice in my ear was taunting. "You sure? Because I can always take you home if you're still angry."

I took his face in my hands, careful not to press too hard on any of the bruises. "Jasper Knight, if you take me home, you'd better be taking me to bed."

His mouth was on mine immediately, possessive and dominating. I pressed my body into his, needing to be closer, to feel no space between us. Jasper's strong arms swung under my thighs, lifting me. He covered the distance to the bed in a matter of two quick strides, and when he looked down at me I saw the wolf within him. "I could fuck you a thousand times and it would never be enough."

He didn't smile as he laid me down on the bed. I writhed under his kisses, his touch, his words. And from the way he was watching me, he knew.

"You like when I talk like that, don't you?" he asked me, trailing his fingers down my curves. "When I tell you how much I love watching you moan underneath me."

His fingers scooped under the waistband of my pants, moving steadily lower until they reached the heat of my pussy, exactly where I wanted him to be. "Oh, Jasper," I moaned.

He closed his eyes as he slid one finger across my slick opening. "Fuck, baby. It's been a hell of a day, and now you're here, and I need you. I don't think I can go slow."

Jasper turned his dark eyes to me, looking for consent. I nodded once. He pulled my pants and underwear off in one swoop. I unbuttoned his jeans, and he desperately yanked them off the rest of the way. I needed him, and I needed him now.

"Open your legs," he commanded. The demanding side of Jasper always spoke to something inside me, and I did what he asked without question. He lay down on top of me, holding his body weight up on strong arms. I felt the broad tip of his cock, not quite entering me. I shifted uncomfortably with the idea of being this close, but not close enough. Every nerve in my body was on overdrive. I dragged my nails down his back, grinding my body against his, and he cursed again. "Fuck. I'd like to take my time, worship every inch of your body...but I can't." He breathed and swiftly fitted himself inside of me. "One day I'll learn to control my need for you."

"Oh!" I cried out, feeling whole again. But I didn't have time to gather my thoughts before Jasper was thrusting into me hard and fast. I let him dictate the pace, darkness flooding his eyes as he watched me.

"You are so beautiful, underneath me like this. Letting go of control." Every thrust brought me closer to the edge. I gave myself over to him, knowing I had done so in more ways than just the physical. He grabbed me by my hips, angling me higher, driving in deeper. His thumb rested on my clit, swirling lazy circles. Each stroke pushed me closer and closer to bliss. Each circling of his thumb edged me towards pleasure, and I cried out his name. Jasper kissed me firmly, and I felt all the unspoken emotions from tonight flooding my veins.

He spoke, controlled, in contrast to his desperate pace. "I want to ruin you for any other man." He kissed me again. "Hold on baby, I'm almost there too. Come with me."

I let myself unravel as Jasper growled over me, giving over to the wolf within him. My mind was gone, focused on one goal only. I could feel the pressure mounting, and I needed release. "Harder," I cried.

He complied, thrusting faster and deeper. Pleasure exploded from inside and I felt myself coming, felt my body pulsing around his cock. At the same time Jasper cried out my name, collapsing to his forearms as he shook and shuddered inside of me.

We lay next to each other as our breathing slowed back down. I turned to him. "Is it always like this, for you?"

Jasper rolled to face me. "What do you mean?"

I took a deep breath. "Sex. Is it always this... explosive for you?"

His eyes lit up. "You saying I'm the best you've ever had?"

I rolled my eyes and shoved his shoulder. "Obviously. But not what I meant."

His laugh was fast becoming my favourite sound. "I

know what you meant. Is it a wolf thing?"

I nodded. But he shook his head slowly. "No. It's not a wolf thing, and it's not normally like this. It's never been this intense for me."

Oh. Jasper watched me absorb the information, reaching out to gently stroke my hair. "Wait. Does that mean I'm the best you've ever had?"

He smiled wide, eyes crinkling at the sides. "You could say that." He leaned over and kissed me.

I relaxed. "Why do you think it's like this between us? I only just met you, and it's like you're a drug I can't get out of my system."

He sighed heavily -- a sound I wasn't expecting. "I have a theory. But you aren't going to like it, so don't freak out."

A theory? Don't freak out? Not, *Wow Ava, you're really hot and that does it for me.* My guard immediately went up. Just once I wanted to hang out with Jasper and not have a bomb dropped in my lap. "Okay. No promises, but I'll try and keep calm."

He framed my face in his hands and watched me carefully. "I'm pretty sure you're my mate."

Caligo (Darkling 2)
Torri Heat

Ava's stepped out of her own reality and into another world -- a world where werewolves exist. She's slowly coming to terms with Jasper and their mate bond, but now she has bigger problems. Whatever's hunting the werewolves in her small town is still on the loose. Worse yet, her parents seem to have a vendetta against Jasper.

With Jasper's help, Ava's embracing her Venator heritage. Good thing she has a hot werewolf to teach her everything she needs to know about fighting. But will she be strong enough for what comes next?

Chapter 1

This was fine. I was fine. I could handle werewolves. I could handle Venators. I could handle anything thrown at me. Right? Maybe not. "I'm sorry. What did you say?" I immediately recalled my mom's snarky tone as she questioned me about mates.

Jasper sucked in a breath. "Well, werewolf mates are basically soulmates. But it's a bit different because..."

I held my hand up, cutting him off before he could go any further. "Jasper, I'm a bit more concerned with the fact that you think we're mates. And the fact you are only telling me now." I sat up, covering myself with his blanket and stared at him. *Mates? Us?* He must be kidding.

Jasper laughed, but his voice sounded like it was shaking and I could tell he was nervous. "Hey, if you can think of a better way to tell someone you've just met they're your soulmate, I'm all ears."

His logic seemed understandable, but his reasoning didn't stop my blood from rushing into my ears, and my pulse from racing. I knew my life had changed from the minute Jasper told me werewolves were real, but I hadn't expected this. I clutched the blanket in one hand, and waved my other arm in agitation. "It doesn't make sense. None of this makes any sense!"

Jasper put a soothing hand on my arm, but I shook him off. He looked hurt at my rejection, but I was too riled up to stop. "Hey, baby, relax. What doesn't make sense?"

I ran my fingers through the rat's nest of my hair in frustration. "All of it! Any of it!" I gestured towards his naked body, every inked muscle on full display, and then towards my covered self. "Look at you, and look at me! *We* don't make sense. We're nothing more than a fling, and I'm not even sure how that happened, to be completely honest."

His gaze turned hard, and he roughly grabbed me by my shoulders. "Don't. Don't start that. Mates give us exactly what we need in a partner. What you lack, they give, and vice versa. I know you didn't grow up with this shit, but I'm telling you whatever brought us together was done perfectly." He tipped my face, forcing me to look up at him. "Besides, I'd still think you're the most beautiful woman in any room, mates be damned."

I couldn't deny the inescapable pull he had on me. The way I felt desperate to be near him. "Is this why I felt like I knew you, even before we met?" Everything was starting to make sense in a way I wasn't sure I wanted it to.

Jasper sighed. "Most likely. I tried to downplay the feeling before you could think too much about what all this meant. I didn't think you would ever go for me at the time." My breathing hitched, and I felt my pulse slow. Despite all my concerns and my overwhelming need for independence I couldn't write off what Jasper was saying. He gently stroked my cheek, and I leaned into his touch.

He nodded, his gaze softening. "You feel it too, don't you? The bond. It has a relaxing effect when we're together, touching."

I couldn't disagree with him. But that didn't mean I wanted to agree either. "I have questions."

"I imagine you do." Jasper's face relaxed. God, he was so handsome it was distracting. His chiselled cheekbones and full lips were mere millimetres from me.

"I need complete honesty, if this is going to work. When did you first think I was your mate?"

"Well, that's a tough question." He grimaced, but I glared at him until he continued. "I saw a photo of you a few years ago, one of the times I met with your parents. I had a feeling, but I managed to convince myself that you can't find your mate through a photograph. I forgot about it until that day I walked into the coffee shop and there you were. All the time we have spent together since then has reinforced my feelings. I wanted to be sure, and then I couldn't figure out a way to tell you."

I blinked, my mind reeling. "That's why my mom told me to ask you about mates."

Jasper looked surprised. "She did?"

I closed my eyes, nodding. "Uh huh. Putting two and

two together now, I can only imagine she was hoping I would freak out and leave once I knew the truth." My mom being so cruel was a tough reality to face. So many of these lies that Jasper was having to come clean about stemmed from my parents, not him. I opened my eyes, meeting his gaze. "Why are my parents so against us being together?"

He jumped out of bed, back turned to me as he started throwing his clothes back on. "People who know about wolves can be prejudiced towards us. Some think that a human and werewolf match goes against nature." His voice was tight, and I could tell this wasn't his favourite topic.

"Are my parents like that?" I asked.

Jasper stiffened, midway through pulling his shirt on. "Do you actually want to know the answer to that?"

Did I? Could his response be any worse than them lying to me my whole life, or them not believing in me? "Yes. I do."

"Your parents are the ones who convinced me to not seek you out the moment I saw your photo. They asked me to stay away. For everything your parents have done for us, the idea of a human and werewolf match is still unacceptable." He spoke without emotion, and I realized he was worried I might share my parents' prejudices.

I slipped off the bed, wrapping my arms around him. "I don't think like them, Jasper. You being a werewolf is only a part of who you are. It's not the whole of it."

Jasper turned in my arms, gaze offering a small glimmer of hope. "Do you mean that?"

"Absolutely. Even if my parents were in my good books right now, I don't think I could ever think anything about us was unnatural. This whole mate thing does explain a lot of weird shit. But…"

His eyebrows shot so high they nearly reached the dark waves of his hairline. "But?"

"I want to do this my way."

"What do you mean?" Jasper asked.

"I mean, I don't want to act like we are automatic 'mates,' together forever, end of, period. I want to treat this like a normal relationship. I don't want to know more about the whole mate thing until I ask. I want to date at a normal pace. I want you to meet my friends." I'd have to talk to Mollie first, calm her down. But once we were over that hurdle, hopefully she'd be ecstatic. I had only brought one other guy to meet her before, and that hadn't lasted too long.

He squeezed my hands. "Okay. We do this your way."

I expected more of a fight, more indignation. "Really? You don't mind taking things slow, comparatively speaking?"

"I'm not going to lie, Green, every cell in my damn body wants to claim you as my own. I want you to be mine. I want to fuck you until you see there's no other way except for us to be together." His gaze was dark with honesty, and every word sent a shiver down my spine. "But I won't force it on you. If taking things slow means you aren't going to go running out the door on me because of this freaky wolf shit, then I can work with that." He offered me a small smile, and my stomach tightened. This was real. This handsome man thought I was destined to be his partner. *Fuck.*

"One more thing." I smiled back, hoping it was charming. I traced my fingers down the tribal tattoos on one arm, feeling the muscles tense under my light touch.

Jasper rolled his eyes, his grin widening. "Of course."

"What happened to you today?"

He tensed his jaw and averted his gaze. "I didn't think you were going to let me get away with that one easily."

"So then you might as well tell me." I was desperate to know what hurt him. I felt protective, even though it was quite obvious that there was little I would be able to protect him from. Right now, at least. I would make sure that was different next time.

He sighed, sitting back down on the bed and pulling me into his lap. "I tracked whatever is hunting around here to a bit of the forest about fifteen minutes outside of town. His scent led me to a cave, and I trailed him in expecting a fight. What I wasn't expecting was the cave to have some sort of protection around it."

He lost me. "Protection?"

Jasper nodded, focused on his story. "I couldn't see anything in the cave. I couldn't see what was attacking me, or how to attack back. It was far from a fair fight. I should've been better prepared."

"Don't you have night vision?" I felt stupid saying it out loud, but Jasper just took it in stride. *Right. Werewolf.*

"Well, that's just it." He sounded as confused as I was. "It was like the cave was designed to take away any advantage I'd have as a wolf."

"Are you sure you're okay?" I traced my hands lightly around the bruises and cuts on his face.

When he looked at me his expression was resolved, gaze hard. "I'm fine. I heal fast, and next time I'll be ready." He slid me onto the bed and stood, offering me his hand. "I should take you home. It's probably not safe for you to stay here tonight."

I hadn't yet bothered getting dressed, so I gave him a small smile. "What does safe mean, anyways?" I tugged on his hand, falling back with Jasper on top of me. He propped himself up on his elbows, brushing a stray lock of hair away from my face.

"Hell if I know anymore, baby."

I bit his bottom lip. "I think I'd rather stay."

Jasper swirled his fingertips down the soft skin of my neck, pressing his lips against mine as he spoke. "Oh yeah? What did you have in mind then?"

Ripples of pleasure ran across my body as his words reverberated against me. I kissed him deeply in response, and he helped me pull his shirt back over his head. I admired his muscled torso for a moment before Jasper turned his dark gaze onto me. "I think I'm okay with this new plan." He dipped his head to my breast, sucking and biting my nipple as I arched into his body. I whimpered as he moved his hand lower, searching for the wet heat between my legs. Jasper released my nipple as he looked into my eyes, watching me as he dipped a finger into me, and then another.

I moaned, running my hand down his side until I could reach the edge of his pants. I undid the button on his pants, pushing them down over his hips. I needed to feel him, all of him. The only thing still making any sense in my brain was how good it felt when Jasper touched me, and I needed more of him.

Jasper groaned, and the sound was loud in the small room. "Fuck, you're so wet." He curled his fingers, and I cried out.

"Jasper, I need you inside me."

He rolled off me and kicked his pants off the rest of the way, grabbing a condom from the drawer next to him, before unrolling it down his cock. I clenched my thighs together against the ache there, watching him as he turned back to me with his coal-black gaze.

"This is going to be hard and fast, baby. I don't want you having second thoughts about how your *mate* can make you feel."

He kneeled on the bed, pulling me around so I was on my hands and knees in front of him. With one swift move, he thrust himself into me. I gasped as he filled me, making me feel whole once again. Jasper gripped my hips tightly, pulling me back onto his cock as he drove in deeper. His desperate growls mixed with my needy cries as he began to move his hips quicker behind me, his rhythm driving me towards the edge of pleasure.

He kept one bruising hand on my hip, as he drifted the other one underneath me. He feathered his touch over my clit, before putting more pressure there. "Come," he commanded, and his voice was strained and urgent.

I screamed out his name, not caring who would hear in the hotel, as I shattered around him. A moment later, he cried out my name as I felt him cave to his own release.

Jasper collapsed next to me. "One day. One day you'll accept what I've known all along. Because no one else will ever make you feel as good as I do," he whispered, peppering my shoulder with light kisses.

He tossed the used condom into the garbage can before

turning around in the bed and holding me tightly to his chest. I felt him kiss the back of my head, and I immediately knew he was wrong about it not being safe for me to be here. I had never felt so warm and safe in my life.

He was right about one thing, though. There were no doubts in my mind about how good he could make me feel.

* * *

Jasper had to go out of town for a few days for another job. I threw myself into work, trying to avoid the fact that I missed him. It felt like there was an invisible tether pulling me back to him, and the best way to ignore it was to push myself even harder at the gym. I felt myself getting stronger. More capable. I just needed Jasper to come home so I could learn the details of what my new life required of me. I didn't think running on treadmills and lifting weights would be helpful in the Venator world.

Friday night came, and I had just settled into bed when my doorbell rang. *What the hell?* I thought. It was almost midnight so I turned over in bed, and ignored the ringing. Whoever was there could come back in the morning.

"Ava! Open up!" Jasper's voice echoed down my hallway.

Jasper? I jumped out of bed wearing my oversized T-shirt and headed to the door, unlocking it to Jasper's smiling face.

"Jasper!" I kissed him. "I thought you weren't back until tomorrow! What are you doing here?" Grabbing his hand, I pulled him into the apartment.

"Change of plans," he said, casting a hungry gaze towards my bare legs under my makeshift nightshirt.

"Oh?" I felt my body flush under the heat of his gaze as I waited for him to explain. It was a cool night, but he was dressed in only jeans and a T-shirt, his delicious tattoos on full display. He wasn't even taking his shoes off, and I wondered what his plans were now.

He reached towards my coat rack and tossed me a sweater. "I thought we should start your training tonight. I really hate to say this, but you should get dressed."

I caught the sweater and took a step back. He must be kidding. I had been waiting for him to train me, but at midnight? I could think of other things I would rather be doing. The main one being him. "What, now? It's late, Jasper. I thought we would train in the day. You know, when it's light out?"

Jasper ignored me and pushed past me towards my bedroom. "Come on, lazy butt. You got better things to do on a Friday night? You need to learn how to protect yourself from this thing, in case I'm not around."

It was clear he wasn't going to take no for an answer. I dragged my feet behind him into the room and pulled on the jeans he threw at me. "Where are we going to go?"

Jasper paused and considered this. "It's pretty dark tonight. I think the edges of your yard would be fine. I haven't noticed any activity in that area of the woods."

I pulled my shoes on and he grabbed my hand, leading me out the front door. I locked my door and slid my keys into my back pocket like I was sleepwalking. Jasper pulled me close and gave me a gentle kiss on the forehead. "Perk up, Green. I promise this will be good for you."

I groaned. "Just tell me I get to have some semblance of sleep afterwards."

He grinned darkly, dragging his fingertip down my neck and across my collarbone. "I was thinking of other activities we could do afterwards. But if you want to sleep, that's fine."

Oh. He didn't really leave any room for interpretation there, but the bribe definitely woke me up. I was instantly wide awake and practically sprinted from the parking lot to the field.

Jasper jogged easily to keep up with my newfound energy. "If I had known sex worked so well as a reward system for you, I would have tried seducing you much sooner." He laughed, and I joined in. I didn't even care that the laugh was at my expense. It was infectious.

Until his laugh caught in his throat, and he stopped running. I kept going, thinking he was playing a joke on me by slowing down. "What's your problem now? Hurry up!"

"Ava." I didn't recognize Jasper's commanding tone, and his severity froze me in place. When I turned around to look at his face, I realized this was no joke.

"What's wrong?"

Jasper wasn't moving and the silence was making me nervous. His gaze was fixed onto the forest, every muscle was tensed. When he didn't respond, I darted closer to him. He reached out with one strong arm and pulled me behind his body.

I was frozen with fear, and we both stood like that for what felt like years. The wind rustled through the trees, and the night air was cool around us. I was about to suggest he was simply being paranoid when Jasper dropped into a protective stance, growling. He hadn't shifted, but he was all wolf. I strained my eyes to follow his gaze and faintly saw a pair of eyes. They were the same ones I had seen before from my window. The same eyes I had convinced myself I had imagined. My scream caught in my throat when Jasper spoke in the same low tone as before. "Stay back, Ava. And for God's sakes, when I tell you to run, you run."

* * *

I closed my eyes and hoped when I opened them again this would all be a bad dream. But when I finally talked myself into looking again, the eyes had moved even closer towards the fringe of the woods. Towards us.

"Jasper. *Jasper!*" I whispered harshly to him, unable to keep a slight note of panic out of my voice. I willed the nerves to go away. We had bigger problems to deal with.

I felt his chest rise and fall in a measured breath as we watched the woods. "I know, Ava, I see him. I'm going to count to three, and then you run. You get inside. For once, don't argue. Do you hear me?" Jasper's voice was slow, making sure I picked up on each word.

I nodded, forgetting he couldn't see me. "Yes."

He squeezed my hand tightly before releasing it. "One... two..."

Panic was tightening my throat, and I tried to shake the

feeling off. It was maybe twenty-five yards to the door at most. I was a runner. I could do this. I had to do this.

"Three."

At the same moment I took off across the field, Jasper leapt into the air, instantly phasing into his wolf. His shift was seamless, poetry in motion. He landed gracefully on all fours and charged, growling aggressively. The danger we were facing was real, and I wasn't ready to take this thing on quite yet. I didn't necessarily need to stay inside, but I needed to get inside to be any good to Jasper. Adrenaline was spidering through my veins, and my lungs felt like they were screaming for air. I ran as fast as I could, the twenty-five yards seeming much longer now I was actually sprinting. Fifteen yards left, then ten. I needed to unlock the door and get inside. *Easy*. I glanced over my shoulder, but I couldn't make out Jasper or whatever else was out there with him. There was only the rustling of the bushes and the crunching of the gravel under my feet.

I launched myself at the door, fumbling for my keys. *Shit*. Where the hell were my keys? I checked my back pockets coming up short. I couldn't remember losing them, and I wanted to scream. I wanted to cry. But that wasn't going to help me. *Fuck!* I needed to get in the door. I must have dropped my keys in the field somewhere. I whirled around, hoping Jasper's bike was closer than I thought, and choked on my breath. Standing closer to me than Jasper's bike, or Jasper for that matter, was another wolf. I immediately recognized the eyes and knew this must have been what we saw in the woods. He was big, with mangy dark brown fur, and he looked like he was out for blood. And I had no way to get inside. I had maybe five seconds to figure out what to do, and none of my options were looking viable. To my right was the locked door, and I could possibly break the glass if I threw enough weight into it. To my left was an old pickup truck parked in the closest spot. Jasper was nowhere in sight. The wolf took a step closer, growling.

This was one of the moments in your life where one

decision alters its trajectory completely. I took a deep breath, and hoped like hell I had made the right call. I sprinted for the pickup truck, praying to all the gods I could think of. *Shit. Shit. Shit.* I could feel the ground trembling under the weight of the wolf barrelling after me so I gave my idea all I had, and threw myself to slide under the bed of the truck. It wasn't graceful, but it worked. The whole truck swayed with the impact of the wolf throwing his body against the rear fender, but thankfully the truck didn't flip. Rust and dirt rained down from the undercarriage on top of me, but I was alive. For now. While I was barely able to slide under the truck the wolf was too big to fit. I was going to be scraped and bruised tomorrow, but at least my maneuver gave me a couple minutes to figure out my next step. I knew it wouldn't take long before the wolf heaved the truck over. I could hear his paws crunching on the gravel, looking for the best angle, and I made myself as small as possible.

Okay. Think. You got yourself this far, you can get yourself out. I was weighing up my options -- run for Jasper's bike, or try to make it into town on foot -- when I heard an awful crunching sound, followed by a cry of pain from the unknown wolf. Another angry growl, but this one I recognized -- Jasper had found us. I crossed my fingers Jasper was the one dealing out the bone-crunching blows, and not the other way around. Finally, the wolf whose voice I didn't recognize let out a blood curdling shriek that sounded almost human. But even when I heard the bushes rustling in the distance I didn't move from my spot. A hand reached underneath the truck to grab my arm, and I instinctively shifted my body away.

I heard knees sink into the gravel, and Jasper peered under the truck. "Baby, it's okay. He's gone."

I let him pull me out from my hiding place, gently gathering me into his arms. "Is he dead?" I asked.

He shook his head. "No, he ran off. But I hurt him pretty good, and I don't think he'll be able to do much damage for a while."

"It was a wolf. Is that what you've been tracking?" I

couldn't put the pieces of this evening together.

Jasper looked as confused as me. "Yeah, I think so. But things don't add up. How can a wolf do the kind of things we've been seeing? Why would they want to hurt their own kind?" He shook his head and sternly looked down at me. "I thought I told you to get inside."

I averted my gaze sheepishly. "I couldn't find my keys. Not that I was planning on staying inside."

Jasper laughed and pulled my keys from a tattered pocket. "I know. I found these when I went back for my clothes. I've gotta say, Green, those were some instincts you had out there. You might have some Venator in you after all."

I shoved him, trying to stand up but finding myself unsteady on my feet. Jasper held me close until I caught my balance. "It's the adrenaline," he murmured. "It'll go away soon."

I sagged into his arms, letting him take my weight. I had been so focused on staying alive the danger *he* had been in was only hitting me now, and I desperately pressed my mouth to his. Jasper responded by crushing his lips against mine, and I knew he had to feel the same way. I started pulling at the shreds of the clothes he had put back on, desperate to feel his skin against mine. "I need you."

Jasper nodded, his wolf still close to the surface in his caramel eyes. He scooped me up under my thighs, wrapping my legs around his waist. "Not here. It's not safe." I tangled my fingers in his thick hair, urging him closer as I licked and nipped at his neck. A low groan escaped him as he carried me to the building, balancing me as he unlocked the door. "Ava. Fuck. Let me get you into your apartment."

The fear I had felt before was gone, replaced with craving for him so strong I couldn't think straight. "You said he wasn't coming back. My neighbours are retirees. No one is coming into the stairwell." I tugged on the waistband of his ruined jeans, feeling for the hard ridge of his erection.

Jasper's gaze got darker. "Don't test my willpower."

"I like it better when you don't have control anyways."

I was pushing him, and I knew it. But it had the desired effect. A growl tore from Jasper's throat as he pushed me against the wall, letting it carry my weight. He kissed me hard, letting one of his hands reach under my shirt to grasp my breast. I gasped as he released me from the kiss, turning his attentions to my neck.

"Is this what you wanted? Me to fuck you right here?" Jasper asked, grinding his hard cock against me.

I tore my shirt over my head in response, desperate to feel his mouth everywhere.

"I'll take that as a yes." He lowered his head, taking a nipple between his teeth. I gasped and rocked my hips against him as he sucked and teased. "Fuck, Ava. The things you do to me," Jasper ground out as he unbuttoned my jeans, slipping his hand between the thin silk of my underwear to palm me. I tightened my fingers in his hair, kissing him with an urgency I felt deep in my bones. Jasper slid a finger into the damp heat between my legs, rubbing my clit with the palm of his hand. We both groaned as he slipped a finger into me, and then another.

"Shit, don't stop," I begged.

"I don't plan to. I want to see you come now, on my hand. And then again, when I'm buried deep inside you." I moaned loudly as he picked up speed with his hand. The friction felt so good, shooting pleasure to every part of my body. But I needed a release.

He curled his fingers inside my pussy, and I bucked my hips against him wildly. "Come now, Ava." And I gladly did, crying out and clenching around his fingers. "Good girl." Jasper took his fingers out of my pants, never breaking eye contact as he sucked my juices off them. *Fuck.* Who would've thought that would be so hot?

My body felt content, but my mind wasn't satisfied yet. I shimmied the rest of the way out of my jeans, and pushed Jasper's down his hips afterwards, his massive erection springing free. This was really what I wanted, what I needed. To feel us as one.

He growled darkly as I stroked his cock, and pushed

my hands away to grab a condom from his pocket, unrolling it down his thick length. He fitted himself between my legs. "You're so wet and ready for me." Jasper's eyes were black as the night sky as he pushed himself into me, filling me perfectly.

He cursed under his breath as he started to pump hard, lost to the sensation. One orgasm in, I felt every movement, every sensation, everywhere. My body felt like it was on fire, and the only cure was Jasper. Every thrust brought me closer to the edge of ecstasy, and every kiss kept me grounded to Jasper and his body. The pleasure was building, and building, to a point I couldn't control. I felt myself surrendering to another orgasm, Jasper's pitch-black gaze staring into my soul as I shattered around him.

I felt Jasper give into his release inside me, resting his forehead on mine gently as he stopped shaking. "Fuck, Ava. What did I ever do before you?"

"I was going to ask you the same question." I smiled softly. Even with the evening we had, I felt at peace knowing we were together. Except... "We should clean up. But you don't exactly have any clothes left to walk back up to the apartment in." I looked at the scraps of fabric at our feet. I'd have to tidy that up later. Jasper chuckled against my neck, and I pushed away from him. "What's so funny about streaking?"

He pointed behind me, and I turned to read my apartment number on the door beside us. "Why didn't you just tell me we were at my apartment the whole time?" I cried.

Jasper shrugged, smiling. "You seemed pretty set on me taking you right then and there, and who am I to argue with a pretty girl?"

I punched him in the arm, but I smiled too. "You still could've told me. Let's go inside."

I cleaned up while Jasper made himself at home, and I walked out of my bathroom to find him sprawled on my bed. "I was so scared, Jasper. Maybe my parents were right, and I'm not cut out for this."

Jasper hugged me tightly. "Not even a small part of me believes that's true. Your instincts were spot on, and they saved your life. As for being scared, anyone who wasn't afraid in that situation would've been an idiot."

I fidgeted in his embrace, nerves getting the best of me. *How stupid*, I thought. *Can outrun a damn wolf, but can't talk to a man.* My fear won the battle. "Will you stay with me tonight?"

Jasper smiled gently. "I'm not planning on going anywhere, baby. Not even a teeny cat can scare me away tonight. I'll sleep better knowing you're safe."

"Watch who you say that around. Betty will take offence if she hears you!"

I yawned widely, and Jasper kissed the top of my head. "Come on. Go to sleep. I'm here if anything happens."

Jasper spooned against my back, pulling me tight to his chest. I couldn't help but notice we fit together perfectly. Being around Jasper made me feel at ease, even after the night we had. His breathing slowed and evened out, and I found myself drifting off easily. Maybe this mate thing wasn't so bad after all.

Chapter 2

"Good. Now hit me again."

I dropped my hands to my knees to catch my breath, wiping the sweat off my forehead. "Seriously? Can I have a five-minute break?"

Jasper shook his head. "Nope. Supernatural beings don't stop, Green, and there's no breaks in the real world. What happened to the girl who told me she wanted to be stronger?"

We were in the old park on the outskirts of town, and Jasper was teaching me to spar. It was a week or so after the encounter outside my apartment, and things had been going a lot smoother. Jasper and I alternated where we spent our nights, our explicit reason being we were safer together, the unspoken explanation being we didn't like sleeping apart after we first shared a bed. I found myself having an increasingly more difficult time fighting the mate bond and trying to take things at a normal pace.

We had been practicing for several hours. In between lessons, I took the time to admire his impressive form, the easy way his track pants draped perfectly on his hips. Jasper was jogging in place, shirtless and sweat free, looking like he had stepped out of a catalogue. I, on the other hand, looked like I had run a marathon. In a garbage bag. With weights. I had thought I was in shape, but that was before I trained with Jasper. Despite my exhaustion, most of the skills he was teaching me came quite naturally, as if they were second nature. I had never been more certain my parents were wrong in doubting my abilities as a Venator.

I groaned and stood up straight again, reaching for all the strength I had. I forced myself into a defensive stance. "Tell me again why I can't train with weapons. I don't think I'm going to be taking anything down with my bare hands."

Jasper laughed. "I've told you before. If you can't fight with your fists, then you won't be able to control a weapon effectively."

"Where'd you learn all this stuff, anyways?" I asked,

trying not to roll my eyes.

"Here and there." He stretched his arms out. "It's encouraged in the pack to diversify your strengths. Stop stalling. Again." He slapped his hand against his sharp jawline, waiting for my move.

My knuckles were bruised from punching, and every muscle ached, but I felt stronger every day. I threw another quick punch to his jaw before ducking back to my defensive stance. Punching him hurt me like hell, but Jasper didn't seem any worse for the wear. How did normal humans fight like this on a daily basis?

He nodded briskly. "Again."

After what felt like years of training we headed back to my car. "You did good today, baby. I'm definitely seeing improvement, and your base instincts are good. Maybe we can start with knives by the weekend." Jasper reached for my hand, kissing my swollen knuckles. His touch sent tingles down my spine, and as tired as I was, I was eager to get back to the motel. I did a small happy dance with my free arm to acknowledge my excitement of my training progress and Jasper laughed. He looked towards the near-empty parking lot and jerked his chin up. "Wonder what crime the sheriff has to investigate in this park? Someone littering? A kid riding their scooter on the wrong side of the sidewalk?"

I followed his gaze and saw Sheriff Kelly in his cruiser, talking to someone on the phone. "Huh. I wonder what kind of call they got."

We passed Sheriff Kelly's car, and he nodded a greeting to us as he hung up the phone. "Ms. Green. Out for a run?"

I paused to respond, noting the sheriff's dark sunglasses even though the day was overcast. "Yeah, just out for a jog."

He nodded his acknowledgement, revealing a healing bruise along his neck. "Rough time on patrol, Sheriff?" I gestured toward his neck.

He looked away, pulling his collar up higher. "The usual. Wasn't paying attention to where I was going."

Weird. This whole situation felt off. But Jasper was waiting next to my car, so I said goodbye and walked away. As I made my way over to my car, I glanced back over my shoulder to see the Sheriff pick up his phone once again.

"Everything okay?" Jasper held his hand out for the keys, and I tossed them to him as I slid into the passenger seat.

"Yeah, fine. Sheriff Kelly has always been a bit of an odd duck." I shook off the strange feeling I was having and turned in my seat to face Jasper. "Your place or mine?"

He grinned, and I felt the usual tightening in my belly at his smile. He leaned across the armrest, gently squeezing my upper thigh. "How about something a little different?"

* * *

Jasper drove us both back to my place so I could change out of my grungy workout attire. Yet again, I found myself in my closet struggling to find something to wear.

"How am I supposed to know what to wear if you aren't telling me where we're going?" I called out to Jasper, who was currently sitting in my living room attempting to coax a very unsure Betty out of hiding.

"What you had on looked great!" he called back, and I rolled my eyes. *Men.* I rarely left my house except to work in the cafe and I wasn't about to do so with old yoga pants on. I grabbed a sweater off my shelf, pulling it over my head, and nabbed my trusty old denim mini skirt off its hanger. I started towards my dresser to get a pair of tights, but stopped myself. If I was going to become a more confident Ava, then I had to do more things that made me uncomfortable. Instead, I dug through my closet until I came across an over-the-knee pair of boots Mollie had gifted me for my last birthday. I checked myself out in the bathroom mirror, satisfied with my outfit.

Walking out into the living room, I twirled for Jasper. He had managed to talk the cat out from under the couch, but Betty was still maintaining a safe distance. His jaw dropped when he saw my outfit, and he pulled me down onto his lap, kissing my neck. "Damn, baby. I know I said we were going out, but are you sure you don't want to stay here instead?"

Tempting. Especially when he let his kisses drop lower down my neck and I could feel his arousal growing underneath me. But I wanted to see what he had planned, so I pulled him to his feet. "You're not getting out of this that easily."

We walked down the stairs hand in hand, and I let Jasper get in the driver's seat. I didn't mind relinquishing control every now and then. Especially when he ran a caressing finger down my bare thigh. "I don't want to complain about the skin you're showing, but won't you be cold?"

A trail of goose bumps appeared and I shivered, from his touch rather than the cold. "Isn't that what you're here for? To keep me warm?" I cocked one eyebrow teasingly at him.

Jasper let his finger graze higher, sliding under the hem of my skirt. "Don't tempt me. We're already late."

Late? "How are we late for an event I didn't even know about until an hour ago?"

Jasper simply shook his head and started the ignition. "You'll see." Passing the drive in companionable small talk, he drove us through the next town over, and then took a turn down a dirt road. A lot of the roads in this area were unmarked, meaning I didn't recognize the exact one we were currently on. I didn't bother asking any questions, because Jasper was unlikely to answer them. He seemed pretty proud of his surprise trip. A few turns later, and Jasper pulled into the busy parking lot of an old bar.

"A bar?" If he had wanted to go to a bar, we could've gone to the one in town. I was baffled as to what was so special about this dive.

He smiled widely at my confusion, a perfect dimple on display in his cheek. "Not just any bar. Ivan's Bar." Jasper reached across the armrest to grip my hand, dipping his forehead to rest on mine. "This is a special bar to me, Ava. It's where the wolves in this area hang out. You said you wanted me to meet your friends. If it's okay with you, I'd like you to meet mine."

My heart was beating so loudly in my chest I was sure it was going to pop out at any moment. For some reason I had the idea in my head Jasper would have been embarrassed of me, as a human. But he wanted to introduce me to his world. "Of course, I'll meet your friends! But what if they don't like me?" I wrinkled my nose. "I don't exactly make a good first impression"

He kissed me sweetly, and I felt the swell of emotion behind it. "I like you. Therefore, my friends have to like you. Besides, my girl is training to be the most badass Venator of all time."

I rolled my eyes. "I don't know about that." I paused. "Your girl?"

He opened his door. "You rather I introduce you as Green?"

I opened my door, meeting him on his side of the car. Yanking my hair into a bun, I stuttered out, "No. But I didn't realize we were labelling this."

Jasper reached for my hand and kissed my knuckles. "Ava. I know you don't want to rush things, but you know my feelings. I don't want to pretend I feel anything less for you."

I liked being "his girl." I took a deep breath. "Okay. Let's go meet your friends."

Jasper shrugged his shoulders into his leather jacket, and I fought back my instinct to drool. Grinning at me like he knew exactly what I was thinking, he steered us inside. The bar was dimly lit, and smelled like someone had been paid to dump pitchers of beer onto the weathered floor. Booths surrounded the edges of the room, and several burly looking guys played pool at a table in the middle. I definitely stood out here. But Jasper eased into his surroundings, and I realized this must be one of the few places he felt comfortable being entirely himself. He dropped his head close to my ear to be heard over the old-style jukebox blasting Metallica. "Don't let your guard down here, Green. You're safe with my friends and me, but not too many humans come here. The ones that do definitely aren't beautiful women." He pressed a kiss into my hair and led me to a back booth, where three young men were sitting.

If I were anywhere else, they could've been members of the football team. All of them were obscenely tall and disgustingly in shape. But I knew better. When Jasper slid into the booth next to a younger guy with shaggy blond hair, I swallowed my fear and offered a timid smile to the table.

The guy with the close-cropped dark hair sitting across from me grinned widely. "Is this pretty little thing the girl you've been after?"

Jasper rolled his eyes, laying a protective arm around my shoulders. "Guys, this is Ava. Ava, this is Adrian, Duke, and Beau." He pointed at the blond, the quieter, dark haired man in the middle, and the one who teased him, respectively.

I wiggled my fingers in a semblance of a wave. "Hey. It's nice to meet all of you." I hoped they would like me. I hoped I wouldn't do anything to embarrass myself.

Adrian smiled kindly at me, while Duke watched me, as if trying to figure out how I fit into their world. Beau leaned across the table, extending his hand. "We're excited to meet you too. When you get bored with Mr. Detective here you come find me, okay?" He winked charmingly, and I had to laugh at his lack of shame. I already liked him.

Jasper, on the other hand, stiffened and glared at Beau over my shoulder. "Behave."

I rested my hand on Jasper's knee, stilling him with my touch. "Stop. He was only kidding." I felt his body relax behind me, and he began idly toying with a piece of hair that had fallen out of my bun.

Duke whistled quietly at our interaction. "She really is your mate, isn't she, man?"

Jasper changed the subject abruptly. "What trouble have you guys been getting into the last few weeks? I've been too busy to make it out here."

The guys launched into tales of everything that had

been going on in the pack while Jasper had been away. I half listened to their gossiping about who had gotten into a fight with whom and who had changed packs while I watched Jasper interact with his friends. He was a personable guy in general, but around these men he lit up the room. His laugh was infectious, and he regaled them with stories of small-town life in Merrillan. He was something to watch, and he was here with *me*. Eventually the conversation turned towards me, and the guys asked me countless questions about my family, my job, and anything else they could think of. They were a welcoming bunch, and I felt nearly as comfortable around them as I did around Jasper. I had them all captivated as I told them the story of our first date.

"Wait, you had no idea werewolves were real? And my man Jasper sprang this on you at *dinner*? I can't believe he didn't even wait until dessert." Adrian threw his head back and laughed.

Jasper graciously let us have a laugh at his expense, watching me with his friends. "If you guys had a better plan, I'm all for it."

Beau wiped tears away from his eyes as he joined in the ribbing. "Remind me to never take dating advice from you!"

The quietest one of the group was definitely Duke, but his silence wasn't out of shyness. I had the sense he was taking the whole thing in, processing it. At this point he leaned forward. "I have to say though, it's pretty cool you didn't even flinch when he phased in front of you. That can be some messed up shit if you're not prepared, and sometimes even if you are."

The current pitcher of beer was running low, so I offered to grab us another round from the bar. "Don't worry babe, I can grab it," Jasper offered. I frowned, offended he thought I couldn't take care of myself and he backed off, smiling. "All right, all right!"

I found the bar on the same level as the rest of the room -- aged, sticky, and oddly comfortable. As I waited for the bartender to come take my order my thoughts drifted to how easily I fit into Jasper's life. It felt so natural. I hoped he would fit into mine as easily. The bartender returned with my pitcher, and I turned with my beer and immediately walked into a wall. Except as I fell onto my butt and looked up, I saw it wasn't a wall. It was a giant man. "Oof, I'm sorry," I said. Thankfully the beer had just sloshed over the edge of the pitcher, so no real harm was done. "I'm such a klutz. I really can't even blame the beer..." I was rambling.

The mountain of a man looked down from his towering height, and when he slurred his words, I knew he was trashed. "Ain't no problem sugar, let me give you a hand there." He offered his hand to me, and I gratefully took it, pulling myself up to stand again.

I brushed myself off. "Thanks," I said, intending to ask the bartender for a rag to clean up my mess. Not that it mattered. I was pretty sure the bar hadn't been cleaned in years.

The drunken giant held an arm the size of a tree trunk out in front of me, trapping me between his body and his table. "Now why are you running off so soon, sugar? I didn't even catch your name." He used his other arm to grab my waist, pulling me into him.

I squirmed and tried to wiggle out of his grasp. "I should get back. My boyfriend is waiting."

He laughed, and it wasn't a pleasant sound. "Fine piece of ass like you? Doesn't seem like a very good boyfriend if he's letting you wander around a werewolf bar by yourself."

I shoved at him to no avail. The man was built like a brick house. "I need to get back to my friends."

"How about you give me one little kiss, and then we'll see if you still remember your friends' names." He leaned in, and the stench of beer wafted over me thickly.

"No," I said, pushing his face away. "Get away from me."

His hand brushed the bare skin of my leg, and anger immediately flooded my veins at his touch. I wanted to snap his fingers in half.

"I think I'm fine where I am, sweet thing."

From the corner of my eye, I caught a blur of movement

that smashed into his body, and his drunken form easily toppled over. "What the hell?" he cried, trying to stand up.

Jasper stood with his tattooed hand at the man's throat. I hadn't even seen Jasper leave the table, but my attention had been at the asshole harassing me. His strength was inhuman as he lifted the drunk off the floor and slammed him into the table. I heard the wood groan and creak underneath him, but Jasper was deadly calm as he spoke. "She said *no*. If you lay one finger on her again, I'll snap your neck. Do we understand each other?"

Hands grabbed me from behind. Instinctively I went into self-defense mode, stomping my foot down on their foot and throwing my head back with all of my strength to bash their jaw. "Whoa! Whoa, Ava. I'm trying to get you out of the line of fire." It was Beau, trying to pull me back to safety. Glaring, I let him take me a safe distance away, twisting against his hold as I watched the situation unfold.

The man's face was turning purple, but he couldn't move under Jasper's tight grip. "Do. You. Understand. Me?" Jasper repeated, and slammed his fist into the larger man's nose. The man's head grazed down in a facade of a nod. Jasper let him go. "Get the hell out of my bar."

The man bolted off, and I shook off Beau's arms to hurry back over to Jasper. I touched his back with my fingers. "Thank you."

"Give me a minute, Ava." His voice was low and emotionless, and I knew he was trying to get his wolf under control. He took a deep, shuddering breath. "Are you all right?" he asked.

I didn't remove my hand. "I'm fine. He caught me off guard. I didn't exactly think I was in danger in the middle of a bar, so I didn't try anything."

Jasper laughed darkly. "You're always in danger. We need to start training harder. This weekend. I want you prepared for anything."

Beau walked over to us, rubbing his chin. "That's a hell of a girl you got there, Jasper. I wouldn't be surprised if I actually have a bruise tomorrow."

I smiled sheepishly. "I'm sorry, Beau. My guard was up."

He grinned back at me. "Don't you ever be sorry for that, baby girl. I like a girl with some spunk." Beau winked, leaving Jasper and myself alone. Jasper finally turned to face me, his face a controlled mask. He grabbed my wrist and pulled me toward the fire escape at the other end of the bar.

"Where are we going?" I asked.

"I need some air," he responded, pushing the door open. We stood in a small driveway behind the bar. A few dumpsters lined the brick walls, and the wind whistled through the trees in the forest opposite us.

"Jasper, are you all right?" I gripped his hands, forcing him to look at me. I leaned against the brick wall, Jasper towering over me.

"You shouldn't have to ask me that. I'm fine. But if anything had happened to you it would have been my fault." He averted his gaze. "I should have trained you in reading the situation better. I should have made sure you were better prepared. I should have stopped him the moment he touched you, but I didn't hear him. I was grabbing my phone from the car. I'm so sorry. I'm sorry you're in this world where your instinct is to head bash my best friend instead of saying hello."

I shook my head. "I'm fine. Really. About all of it." I didn't want him to worry about me, to have doubts about my abilities. I would get better.

He smiled grimly. "That's not what I'm most sorry for though."

I furrowed my eyebrows. "What then?"

He smashed his lips into mine, and I tasted beer. He slipped his tongue between my lips, and I felt his desire, his protectiveness, and his need. I gasped into his mouth and returned his commanding kiss. Jasper pulled away, looking at me with a thousand emotions in his steady gaze. "I'm sorry because I know how you feel. And I'm sorry because all I could think about when I was standing over him was he touched you, and you aren't his to touch. You're mine."

These last words were said with a force I couldn't argue with.

He tangled his fingers in my hair, whispering, "I don't want to scare you off, having you thinking I'm being possessive, because that's not what this is." Jasper dropped his lips to my neck, and then along my collarbone as he spoke. He slid his hands under my skirt, inching up my thighs. "If you're mine, then it's only right I'm yours in return."

I had no words, so I leaned in to kiss him again. I could feel wet heat between my legs, and a tremor of excitement ripple down my spine. When I looked at him, his gaze was black with lust and I knew he was still barely controlling his wolf instincts. He inched my skirt higher over my thighs, his thumb softly grazing over my clit. I stilled his hands. "Really? Here? Someone might see."

"Weren't you the same girl who had me fuck her in the apartment stairwell? No one is going to see. If you want me to stop, I will. Or you can let me show you."

I released his hands, and moved to the buttons on his jeans. "Show me what?"

He kissed me deeply. "Show you how we belong to each other." Jasper undid the button to my skirt, pushing the fabric down my hips, and I released his erection from his pants. "Let me show you how you complete me." He hooked a finger into the side of my underwear, sliding through the wetness already there. He groaned, and nudged his thick length against me. "Say yes, baby."

I needed him inside me, almost more than I was beginning to realize I needed him in my life. The only logical answer was, "Yes."

He plunged into me in one swift stroke, commanding me entirely. With every full stroke he brought me closer and closer to release. I moaned loudly, as he began to rub quick circles around my clit. He put a finger on my lips. "You're gonna have to be quiet for me, baby, there's a whole bar of wolves on the other side of that door." I nodded, biting my lip to keep from crying out. I lost myself as Jasper sighed against my neck.

"Come with me." Jasper's voice shook me out of my reverie, and I looked at him to find his intense gaze on me. "Keep your eyes on me. I want to watch you."

I kept my eyes open and on him as Jasper continued to thrust into me. When I felt myself shatter around him, he didn't lose eye contact as he came inside me. After, he rested his head against mine. "Do you see now? We belong to each other, simple as that."

I considered his statement as we cleaned ourselves up and straightened our clothes. I wasn't sure if fate was as simple as he was making it out to be, but I was certain of a few things. One, Jasper was an irrevocable fixture in my life, and two, I wasn't sure how much longer I could deny the pull of the mate bond.

Chapter 3

We said our goodbyes to Jasper's friends, and started the drive back to my apartment. Both of us were lost in our own thoughts. Jasper held my hand tightly, and when we hit the main road I finally spoke up. "Your friends..."

At the same time Jasper started to speak. "I don't know what..."

We smiled at each other, and he tipped his head towards me. "Go ahead."

I shrugged. "I was going to say your friends seem like really great guys." I looked out the window. "You're lucky to have them."

"I've known them since we were teenagers. They're my brothers. I wouldn't know my life any other way. I was going to say I don't know what you were worried about. They loved you."

I sighed. "Are you sure? Duke didn't seem too thrilled about me."

Jasper squeezed my hand. "Duke is cautious. But believe me, you won him over."

I watched his handsome profile as he drove, wondering what he meant. At my silence, he turned to me with a question in his caramel eyes, so I asked, "What is he cautious about?"

Jasper pulled to a stop at a red light, and furrowed his brow. "Remember what I told you about your parents not liking humans being with wolves?"

I nodded, and he continued. "The same biases happen the other way. There aren't too many human and wolf mates, and sometimes wolves can be hesitant about the bond. They question if a human can truly understand our ways, respect our culture."

"Are human and wolf mates really rare?" I asked.

Jasper hummed in agreement. "Yeah, they are." He brought my knuckles to his lips and gently scraped them with his teeth. "Means you're extra special."

I laughed. "Now you're starting to sound like Beau."

He winked suggestively at me. I was about to tease him back when my phone rang. I shook myself away from Jasper's hand and grabbed my phone from the bottom of my bag, surprised when I saw my dad's number flashing across the screen. I hadn't spoken to my parents since my confrontation with my mom, but not for lack of trying on her part. I ignored all of the phone calls and texts I received from her, but this wasn't exactly unusual for me. But now, this was my dad calling.

I groaned, not wanting to deal with him right now, but knowing this was only delaying the inevitable. Jasper looked concerned. "Everything okay?"

"Yeah. It's my dad." My phone continued to ring as I debated answering it. At least with Jasper in the car I would have emotional support. But on the other hand, I would be forcing him to sit through what I expected to be a very uncomfortable situation. I closed my eyes, ignored the ringing, and counted to five. Then I pressed the answer key.

"Hello, Ava." My dad's calm voice rang out over the line, and I knew Jasper could've heard every word even if he wasn't a wolf.

"Hi, Dad." We had always had a better relationship than my mother and I, but I still always felt like I was failing him in some way. Now I understood why and it was the elephant in the room.

He sighed heavily. "Now, what has your mother so upset?"

"You mean, besides the fact you've lied to me my entire life?" I snapped bitterly. I hadn't realized how angry I was still at them.

"Don't be overdramatic. Your mother and I made the decision based on what is best for you. Now this whole situation has gotten her quite agitated, and I expect you to call her and apologize immediately."

My temper flared. "Shouldn't she apologize to me? My whole life has been a lie, not to mention how little you two must think of me to not fill me in on the family secret."

"This has gone far enough. You will apologize. And I

don't think I need to reiterate you will stay away from that Knight boy."

I stole a quick glance at Jasper. He was still staring straight ahead, but his knuckles gripping the steering wheel were white. "You can't order me around anymore, Dad. I'm not a child. You have no say in the matter."

My father's voice cut through me as if he was in the car with us. "I can and I will. No daughter of mine will be seen with a mutt."

Jasper pulled the car over to the side of the deserted road and closed his eyes, breathing heavily. I knew he was livid, but I wasn't sure at which part. I turned my attention back to the phone, putting as much venom into my voice as I could. "What the hell, Dad? I thought you were supposed to help the packs? How can you say this shit about them behind their backs?"

"It's one thing to aid the packs. That's something in my blood. My father did it, and his father before him. It's another to watch my only daughter run off and mate with one of their kind." I could practically taste my father's disdain, and Jasper stormed out of the car, slamming the door behind him.

"You're with him right now, aren't you?" I'd never heard my father's voice sound so cold.

"I am. Your concern is misplaced, in both myself and in Jasper. You could show me a little bit of faith for once in my life," I responded.

My father laughed. "Believe me, Ava, you have no idea what you've gotten yourself into. I'm telling you this once more for your own good. If you expect to remain my daughter, you will forget you know anything about the Venators, and you will not see Jasper Knight again."

For the first time in my life, I hung up on my father. I couldn't believe the disgust and anger that was seeping out of a man I had thought to be calm and level headed. Dark had settled around us while we were driving, and it took my eyes a moment to adjust. I spied Jasper at the edge of the woods close to where he had pulled over. His beat-up jacket was carelessly tossed on the ground, and the fabric of his black shirt strained over his back muscles as he repeatedly slammed his fists into a thick tree trunk. I got out of the car, hugging my arms around my body against the chill in the air as I walked over to where he was.

"You know I don't think like they do." I wanted to alert him to my presence.

"Ava." He stopped his attack on the tree, resting his head on his forearms. "It's not that."

I stood in front of him. "Then what has made you so upset you're hell-bent on knocking this tree down with your bare fists?"

Jasper raised his head up an inch, looking at me darkly. "I can't ask you to give up your family for me. So where are we going to go from here?"

I put a hand on his forearm, careful to avoid his scratched-up knuckles. "The family I grew up respecting taught me not to judge people by their differences. They taught me to be honest, and to stand on my own two feet when things got tough. So far, the only person in my family holding up their end of the bargain is me."

Jasper shook his head, his wild locks blowing in the wind. "No. You'll regret losing your parents eventually, and then you'll resent me. I'd never want that."

I gripped his arm with more force. "No. Jasper, they never respected me. I was a burden on them, nothing more. If they want me to ever be part of their lives, they'll have to respect the decisions I make. And one of those decisions I'm going to make is you."

I felt like he was staring into my soul. "Are you sure, Ava? That's a big decision to make. And you wanted to take this slow."

"I can't fight this," I whispered. I knew what I was admitting to, in less words than I'm sure he would have liked to hear. "Now take me home."

He enveloped me in his arms, crushing me to his chest. We stood in the dark for a moment, me breathing in his woodsy smell. Eventually he released me, and we made our way back to the car.

I lay awake all night in Jasper's arms, thinking. My mind was cycling, and I couldn't shut it off. I wasn't sure how everything would work with my parents. If they couldn't accept Jasper, I wasn't sure I wanted them in my life. What Jasper had said was true. I had wanted to take this slow, to know I was making my own choices in life, not leaving them up to some unknown fate. Unfortunately, my parents had forced my hand. My gut was telling me to trust the person who had been honest with me, and that was the man sleeping next to me. My heart told me to trust him. There was still some real danger in Merrillan, and I wasn't about to let Jasper take that on by himself. I must have made a noise of frustration, because Jasper stirred. He slid his hand down my hip. "Hey," he mumbled, his voice husky with sleep. "What's wrong?"

I didn't want to burden him with my worries, not when he was already feeling guilty about my tempestuous relationship with my parents. I turned to face him. "Nothing. Just thinking about our dinner with Mollie tomorrow. Go back to sleep." I kissed his forehead, and he gave me a small smile without opening his eyes. He settled back into my bed, the sheets slipping to reveal his sculpted abs. His tan skin shone pure in the moonlight filtering through my thin curtains, contrasting with the dark ink spidering across his body. This view in my bed alone was worth a bit of trouble. I wasn't lying to him. I had vocalized my anxiety about dinner with Mollie to him earlier. Mollie had been busy transitioning to a new role at work, and I hadn't seen her as much as I normally did, though we still kept in touch over text and the occasional call. When I had first proposed a dinner, Mollie had been wary.

"I don't know, Ava. He seems like bad news," she had told me over the phone. "You won't be able to change him."

But really, what was there to change? Jasper treated me with respect, and almost a reverence. I had convinced her to give him another shot, but her excitement had yet to build. Mollie was instinctively very protective of me, and I didn't want her to interrogate Jasper, or worse -- threaten him. I pictured tiny Mollie cornering Jasper's large frame in her kitchen, her threat ten times scarier than anything Jasper could manage. The amusing image finally broke through my intrusive thoughts, allowing me to fall asleep safe in Jasper's arms. Now that I knew what contentment was like, I couldn't imagine sleeping anywhere else.

* * *

We pulled into Mollie's apartment parking lot on Jasper's bike promptly at 5:30 the next day. Jasper was wearing a clean shirt and jeans, but with his beat-up old combat boots still on. My personal opinion was he looked hot in them, but Mollie might have other opinions. I was trying to pretend I wasn't nervous for Jasper's sake, but I was really hopeful everyone would get along tonight.

Jasper looked like he wanted to say something, so I elbowed him as I took my helmet off. "What's up? I promise, you have nothing to worry about. You'll probably like Mollie more than you like me."

"That's not what I was thinking," he said, laughing. He ran his fingers through his hair thoughtfully. "Does she know? What I am, I mean. I wouldn't blame you for telling her. I should know what I'm getting into."

"Mollie doesn't know. I didn't think any of this was my place to say. And Mollie won't even watch the trailer for a scary movie. I didn't want to be the one to break it to her all that stuff is real." I took a deep breath. "If it's okay with you, I was hoping we could keep the whole wolf thing on the downlow for right now."

Jasper immediately relaxed. "More than okay. If I'm already going to have to win her over, I didn't want to add another problem to the mix." He slipped his hand into the back pocket of my jeans as we walked towards Mollie's ground level apartment. "By the way, have I told you I love these jeans on you?"

"Once or twice." I blushed. Jasper was back to his normal self. Now I was the nervous wreck.

As we reached Mollie's door and I knocked, he leaned

closer towards me. "I'll love them even more off of you later tonight," he breathed.

Fuck. That's all I would be able to think about throughout dinner now. And from his satisfied smirk, he knew exactly what he was doing. Luckily for him, Ben answered the door before I could retaliate.

"Ava!" Ben greeted me warmly, giving me a hug when he saw me. But I could feel his judgement as he ran his gaze over Jasper, the worn leather jacket, and the tattoos peeking over the neckline of his shirt. He offered his hand. "You must be Jasper. We're so happy you guys could make it." Jasper took his hand, shaking it firmly, and I could see Ben trying not to wince with the force of his grip. Sometimes Jasper underestimated his own strength.

"Thank you for having us over," Jasper told him, smiling. I let out the breath I was holding. Hopefully we'd all get through this night in one piece. Ben opened the door wide, and gestured for us to follow him into their cozy living room. I started to walk behind him, but Jasper pulled me back by my wrist. "Relax, baby," he whispered, winking at me. "I promise I won't shift in the middle of dinner." He dragged his nail down the back of my neck, exposed by my high bun, and I squirmed under his touch.

"Ava, are you guys coming in or what?" Mollie called from the direction of the kitchen, and I tugged Jasper forward. He trailed behind me into their living room, taking an easy seat next to me on their small couch.

"Can I get you two a drink?" Ben asked from the doorway. "I think Mollie opened a bottle of wine."

"Wine is good with me, Ben, thanks." They were the perfect hosts every time I came over. And in return, I usually offered them take out and dusty drinks. He turned to Jasper.

"Wine would be great, thanks. But a small one. I've got the bike tonight and I've got to make sure this one stays upright." He glared at me pointedly, and I knew he was remembering the last time I rode his bike after a few drinks. I glared back, but not before I noticed Ben's impressed face as he headed to get our wine.

"Well, look at that." I rested my hand on his thigh, enjoying the tensing of his muscles beneath my hand. "You're already off to a great start with Ben! Who knew you were all about sobriety in case your girlfriend gets loaded?"

Jasper gave me a sharp look. "Girlfriend, huh?"

Shit. Had I said that out loud? I wasn't sure whether I wanted to admit what I had said or play it cool.

Jasper flipped me so I was straddling his lap, forcing me to meet his gaze. "Jasper!" I protested in a loud whisper. "Ben will be back any second!" I glanced over my shoulder to make sure he wasn't there.

"Then you have a second to answer my question." He feathered his fingertips down my spine over my thin shirt, pressing a kiss against my collarbone. "Do you consider yourself my girlfriend?"

I couldn't think with his hands against me and his lips kissing my neck so gently I might have been imagining it. I moaned softly, and he nipped my skin. "Shush," he scolded. "You don't want Ben to hear, do you? Now, I think you have a question to answer." His hands dipped to my front, skimming the waistband of my jeans, and I stopped breathing. Fuck. He wouldn't. Would he?

Jasper's caramel eyes were mischievous and I knew he definitely would if I didn't answer his question. He had the upper hand, and he was well aware of it. "Yes," I whispered.

His eyes were bright, but guarded. "Yes, what?"

I met his gaze, and put a hand on either side of his face. "Yes. I consider myself your girlfriend."

He crushed his lips against mine in a forceful kiss, his arms wrapping around me in a bear hug. I felt every muscle in his body straining, and could feel himself holding back his full strength. I had made him happy, and that made me happy. I kissed him back with enthusiasm until he pulled away. Jasper responded with a goofy smile, brushing his thumb against my lips. "God, baby, I never thought it would take you this long to submit to my charm."

"Sorry, are we interrupting something here?" Mollie's voice echoed over my shoulder, and I hurried to get off of

Jasper's lap and make myself presentable in the seat next to him. My face grew hot, and I was sure my entire body was a deep shade of red.

Jasper, all the power to him, merely stood and smiled at Mollie, casually holding a hand to her as if they hadn't walked in on us fooling around on their couch. "I'm Jasper. It's nice to officially meet you, Mollie."

Mollie gave him a tight smile, taking in his overall appearance. "You too." I knew what she was thinking. Jasper, for all intents and purposes, looked dangerous. Until you got to know him, like I had. Mollie only knew the bad stuff about Jasper, and it hadn't exactly left her eager to meet him. She set down a glass of wine to give me a hug.

I hugged her back. "I feel like I haven't seen you in ages!" I told her, taking the wine.

Mollie rolled her eyes, glancing over to where Jasper stood making small talk with Ben. "Yeah, well you've obviously been busy."

I glared at her over the rim of my glass. "You promised you would give him a chance, Mollie."

She sighed. "I know, I know. I will. For you. But I don't like it. He's already hurt you, and I don't know if I can get past that. And look what he's turned you into! Going at it on my couch." Mollie pulled a face, taking a long drink of her wine.

"Mol, I told you that whole thing was a misunderstanding." I could already feel my blood pressure rising. "And it's your own fault. You told me I needed to find a nice guy. And if anything, he's made me more confident in myself. Stronger."

She looked at me hard, as if searching for some sign of weakness. Finally, she nodded, and I heaved a sigh of relief - - I had won the first battle. Mollie called everyone to the dinner table, and I wandered into the dining room while Ben and Mollie grabbed the food from the kitchen.

Jasper trailed me closely, and whispered, "I think Ben likes me."

I tipped my face towards him, pulling my usual chair at

the table out. "Yeah?"

He nodded. "I guess he's a big hiker, so I was filling him in on my favourite local trails."

I raised my eyebrow at him, knowing exactly what he meant by hiking experiences. "Did you tell him most of these experiences took place in wolf form?"

Jasper shook his head, laughter in his gaze. "Not exactly." He stretched his arms above his head, rubbing the back of his neck. "Speaking of, I haven't gone on a run in a few days. Feel like doing some late-night training after this? We could take sparring up a notch."

Was he asking me if I wanted to spar with him in wolf form? I didn't think I was strong enough yet. He laughed at my shocked expression. "You're stronger than you think you are, Green. Believe me."

I did. I grasped his hand, just as Mollie and Ben returned with delicious smelling dishes. As soon as we all settled down with some of Mollie's specialty, roast chicken, she turned her sharp gaze onto Jasper. "Jasper, what do you do for a living again?"

Ben rested his hand on Mollie's forearm, and I knew he was trying to keep her from being too overprotective. Jasper cut into his chicken, unbothered by Mollie's intrusive tone. "I'm a private investigator, freelance."

She cut into her food. "Sounds dangerous."

He put down his fork and knife, and stared at her quietly. "What exactly are you implying?"

I focused on breathing in and out slowly, hoping this would blow over. In and out. In and out. Mollie met his gaze. "I'm wondering if such a dangerous job would allow you to fully commit to a relationship with Ava."

Jasper laughed, breaking the tension in the room. "Maybe you should ask Ava, instead."

Mollie looked surprised, and glanced at me. "Ava? What does he mean?"

I looked down at my plate, not wanting to get into the whole situation. "Well, you see…"

Jasper reached for my hand, saving me from the

uncomfortable situation. "Ava only admitted she was my girlfriend today after weeks of me trying to get her to say otherwise." He grinned, still enthused by my earlier admission.

Mollie's jaw dropped. This wasn't the Ava she had grown up with. That Ava would have needed the label of a real relationship for validation. "Is that true?"

"Well..." I started, "Yeah."

"Weeks of grovelling it took me." Jasper moved his hand down to my thigh before he continued. "Showing her how good we could be together. A slip of the tongue was her downfall. Otherwise, I could've been waiting years to find out if I had a girlfriend or not!"

That was all it took. Mollie beamed at Jasper. "You really are good for her!" She leapt out of her seat and ran around the table, snaring us both in a big hug. "Ava! I'm so proud of you. And Jasper! I'm sorry I've been tough, but I had to make sure you weren't going to hurt her again."

Jasper turned to me, questioning, and I mouthed "*I'll explain later*" over Mollie's head.

"I'm glad Ava has a friend like you, Mollie," Jasper told her, trying to detach himself. "She deserves it."

She grinned, and raced back to her seat. The rest of dinner went smoothly, now I knew my best friend approved of Jasper. We talked about hiking, and travelling, and food, and by the time we were heading out the door, Jasper and Ben were making plans to meet up at the local sports bar later in the week. Apparently, they shared the same favourite football team. Mollie rolled her eyes at me, and pulled me in for another hug. "I'm happy for you, girl."

I smiled at her, overwhelmed with emotion -- happy she approved, grateful for Jasper -- and embraced her back. "Thanks."

I gave Ben a quick hug, and then turned to Jasper, who had shrugged back into his coat and was offering me mine. We walked back to the bike. "Where to now?" he asked.

I tilted my face to the starry sky, content. "I thought you said you wanted to go for a run."

He nodded, tipping his face skyward as well. "I do. But we got interrupted before you could tell me if you were okay with that kind of training."

Jasper swung on the bike easily. My dexterity was getting better by the day, and I grabbed my helmet and jumped on behind Jasper. My blood was pumping from the dinner and Jasper, and I needed to blow off steam one way or another. I pulled him back to me and kissed him hard. "I'm ready for anything."

Chapter 4

My heart felt too big for my chest. The streets were quiet and dark as we stopped at the motel for Jasper to change his shirt and grab his gear bag. Not having any other clothes, I grabbed one of his faded sweatshirts to throw on top of my jeans. Jasper watched me with a funny look on his face the whole time.

"What?" I asked.

He smiled faintly. "Nothing."

I raised my brow. "Seriously?"

Jasper held me at arm's length, brushing an unruly lock of hair away from my face. "You're so damn beautiful. And you should keep the sweatshirt. It looks good on you." He kissed my forehead and let me go.

I cuffed the too-long sleeves, blushing at his sweet words. "Come on, it's time for me to kick your ass."

We took the bike out to the old park, which I now thought of as "our park", seeing as we seemed to be the only ones ever in it. Jasper dug through his gear bag. "Before I shift, there's something I want to try," he told me, half his face obscured by the oversized bag.

"Oh yeah?" I took my helmet off, admiring his butt in those tight-fitting jeans. I hoped whatever he wanted to try involved removing clothing.

"Check these out." Jasper turned and presented me with two short wooden blades.

I took them carefully, turning them over in my hands. "What are they?"

Jasper took one of the swords in his hands. "Bokken. They're a traditional martial arts practice sword. Also known as what you will be training with tonight."

Nerves shot through my body. "I know I said I wanted to learn weapons, but are you sure I'm ready?"

He carefully handed the blade back to me. "You're ready. You have to remember all of this runs in your blood. Weapons should come quite easily to you once you know the basics."

"The basics? I don't just point and stab?"

"Not in the slightest, Green. These are designed for close combat. You'll want to slash your opponents, not stab them. Don't want to lose your blade, especially not in the middle of a fight."

"Okay, slashing, not stabbing. Got it. Where do I aim?" The swords were a nice weight in my hands, and I felt almost graceful as I slashing the air.

"Here." Jasper grinned and pointed to this throat, teeth gleaming in the dark. "Although I would prefer if you didn't actually hit my throat tonight. They might not be sharp, but you could still do some damage. But in all seriousness, most of your targets are going to be bigger than you. You're going to want to aim for the easiest spots that do the most damage." He pointed to several spots on his body. "Throat. Armpits. Stomach."

I nodded, taking the details in. "What about the back?"

Jasper shook his head. "Too many bones. Stay away from it. You probably won't have much time to aim." He dug in his bag again, coming up with two Bokken of his own. Jasper swung them around in the air expertly a few times, looking like he was born fighting with them. "Okay, you ready?" My stomach tightened, but I could do this. I knew I could. These blades felt like an extension of my arms already.

We started out slow. "Stay close to your opponent." Jasper was speaking so easily he could've been at a party, not in the middle of sparring. "Your size will be your advantage. If you stay close, they won't have the range to do as much damage." I nodded, not enough breath left in me to respond. Soon, the talking stopped, and the pace picked up by an unspoken agreement. I found my blades easy to use, but I felt clumsy and slow compared to Jasper. It didn't take long before Jasper had one of his swords at my neck. We were both breathing heavily, caught up in the moment. "Get out of your head, Green. Don't focus on my strength, think about your speed," he told me, pushing me a few steps away to start again.

I closed my eyes and took a deep breath. He was right. I wasn't going to beat him with strength alone. My instincts were good, and I had to focus on that. I *could* do this. Turning off the logical part of my brain, I went on my instincts alone and dropped into a defensive stance.

Jasper mirrored my movements. "Now we're talking."

I focused on matching his blows with speed instead of strength. Jasper's smile dropped, and the only sound in the dark night was the cracking of wooden blades as they met each other. I found myself beginning to outpace Jasper's moves, and I could see him concentrating as he tried to stay on top of things. There was nothing in my current world but me, these blades, and Jasper.

"Okay, okay! I give!" Jasper laughed, the deep sound reverberating in my belly, waking me from my stupor. I looked down and saw my blade at his stomach, his entire side unprotected. Pride echoed through me at the fact I had managed to best him, and I could see admiration reflected in his face as well. I walked over to the gear bag to put the Bokken away, and Jasper handed me another set of swords from his bag. Their sharp edges gleamed brightly in the moonlight, their curved blades looking menacing compared to the Bokken.

"What are these?" I asked, balancing the weight of them in my hands and getting used to the different way they felt slashing through the air.

"Makhairas. A Greek slashing sword. And they're yours."

I couldn't believe myself, but I was getting emotional over a damn set of swords. "Thank you." My voice sounded thick. My gratitude wasn't for the makhairas, it was the fact that he believed in me enough to trust me. I felt like I was truly on my way to becoming a Venator.

Jasper met me with two sets of sheaths. "Here. I'll show you how to store them on your body." He strapped the sheaths on underneath my shirt, and then carefully showed me how to store the swords. "I thought you would like these. They're smaller, which means you can hide them when you need to."

I practiced pulling them out, down along my hips. "I can't get over how natural it feels to have a weapon on my body," I marvelled.

Jasper watched me, his gaze serious. "I told you, you could do it. Venator blood runs in your veins." He reached his long arms overhead, his focus shifting. "Are you ready to try these against me in wolf form? I'm going to take a quick lap, and then we can jump back into it."

Was I ready for this? I wasn't sure. But I nodded, and he backed away. While Jasper stripped off his shirt and folded it carefully, I took a seat in a comfy patch of grass to watch the show. He grinned when he saw me. "Didn't you know it's rude to stare?" he taunted as he started unbuttoning his jeans.

Pop! Went the top button, and I couldn't take my gaze off him as I responded. "Didn't you know it's wrong you look this good when I'm supposed to be thinking about how best to beat you up?"

Pop! Jasper unsnapped the second button, pushing the denim over his hips. He raised an eyebrow at me. "I didn't say I was going to make this easy for you."

Something about what he said kick-started the nerves in me. He was so physically perfect, and he wanted me to mar his body with a sharp weapon. I covered my eyes, only peeking the tiniest bit to admire his long muscular form. "But this isn't playing fair! And you won't have a weapon while you're a wolf! What if I hurt you?" I buried my face deeper into my hands.

Jasper knelt in front of me, pulling my hands away from my face. "Do your worst, Green. I know how you fight. I won't let you get in too bad of a blow. You need to learn, and I'll heal quickly. You had lots of practice with the Bokken."

I tipped my head up to him. "You sound so sure! I don't want to make a mistake."

Jasper walked away again. "You won't," he called over his shoulder. I heard the cracking of bones, and the twist of his back told me he had started to shift again. It should've repelled me, watching his body contort. But the shift captivated me, and I could see the beauty in his changing form. The change only took a couple seconds, and then Jasper's wolf stood in front of me. He sprinted off and I admired his lean shape as he ran around the field, dipping in and out of sight. When Jasper returned to stand before me, head cocked to the side, I knew he was waiting for me to let him know I was ready. I focused on my breathing, repeating to myself I had speed and maneuverability to my advantage. And swords. Couldn't forget the swords.

Some semblance of a plan in place, I crouched. My feet dug into the soft earth to gain some solid footing. Jasper did the same. I said a quick prayer to whoever was listening that neither of us would end up too badly hurt, and waited for him to make the first move. He leapt towards me. He would probably expect me to stand my ground, but I didn't want to go on the offensive right away. I ran, sprinting underneath his airborne form so we ended up in each other's spots. I smirked at Jasper's confused reaction -- he had probably expected to take me down on his first attempt. He was wrong. He attacked again. I dodged. I moved towards him, and he maneuvered out of my reach. This dance went on for some time, only a few minor scrapes on both of us. He was right -- we knew how the other fought.

I was out of breath, and a continual growl reverberated deep in Jasper's chest. I was going to run out of energy before he did, and I wanted to win. I needed to do something unexpected to end up on top. It was like a light bulb went off in my head -- I literally needed to end up on top. I hoped all of the push-ups would pay off. The next time Jasper charged me, I ran at him head on. We had been dodging each other, which meant he wasn't expecting me to come at him. His surprise slowed him down a fraction, which gave me the advantage I needed to drop one of my swords and grab the fur on his shoulders and swing myself onto his back. I was barely clinging on as he thrashed, trying to shake me off. The move wasn't graceful, but I was on.

Jasper growled loudly, a warning. But I knew what I was doing and ignored him, pulling myself upright around his shoulders. Now I had to figure out how to maneuver myself on a moving animal. A moment later, and my blade sat at his neck as he stood frozen in place underneath me. I whooped and slid off his back, Jasper glaring at me, a disgusted noise coming from his throat.

I ruffled the fur on his head, kissing him right on the nose. "Bet you weren't expecting that!" I felt high on adrenaline, blood pumping furiously through my body. Jasper shifted and I tossed him his jeans. I was exhilarated, smiling from ear to ear.

Grabbing me, Jasper kissed me. "I'm pissed you got the better of me, but damn if that wasn't hot."

I kissed him back, needing a release. My skin felt ten sizes too small. Jasper gripped me closer, and the heat of his body pressed against mine was too much. "I want you," I told him between kisses.

I wrapped my hands around his broad shoulders, and he laughed, tracing my spine with his hands. "Well, Ava Green. Not only did you best me twice tonight, but now I find out fighting turns you on? Have I died and gone to heaven?"

"Shut up and kiss me." I pulled his face down to meet me, trying to undo my own jeans while we kissed. I couldn't get my clothes off fast enough. Jasper brought his hands around, taking over for me, sliding my jeans off.

"I know what you need. Let me take care of you," Jasper told me, running his fingers through my hair, under my shirt. Touching me everywhere. It wasn't enough, and he knew it. He laid me down on the grass, resting on his elbow beside me. Reaching back, he rummaged in his discarded jeans to find a condom, sliding it down his cock. He didn't take any time before he pulled my underwear off and thrust into me. I was running so high on my own power him entering me alone nearly made me come. I moaned into his mouth as he lifted me up and down on his cock. I tried to change our pace but Jasper stopped me. "Relax. Let me take control."

Jasper continued his rhythmic thrusts, holding tight to my hips. It didn't take long. I needed him for my release, and I felt his need for me, too. We had grown up in two completely different worlds, but we operated on the same wants, the same needs. He understood how I felt without me having to explain. The sensations built until I couldn't hold back anymore, and I cried out as I felt him come to his own release.

We laid in the grass afterwards, content. "Did you ever think we'd end up like this, the first time we watched the sky in this park?" I asked him.

Jasper stood up, passing me my jeans. "Naked with swords?"

"Ha ha, very funny." I pulled on my jeans, resisting the urge to roll my eyes.

He kissed my wrist, releasing me to toss his shirt over his shoulders. "I had hoped. Obviously. But I don't control you."

I pulled my sweatshirt on, carefully storing my swords on my back. "I hoped, too. But I didn't want to admit it to myself." Our path back to the bike was illuminated by stars and park lights alike. A gentle breeze picked up the stray hairs off my neck and cooled me down. A scrap of fabric blew in front of us, interrupting our idyllic walk. I stopped walking towards the bike and instead headed towards a bush at the edge of the forest that seemed to be accumulating most of the scraps.

"Where are you going?" Jasper asked. "It's a little late for a walk."

"There's a ton of garbage blowing around, and I'm wondering if raccoons dragged some junk out here or something. We should tidy the mess up before it wrecks our training ground though," I told him, picking up scraps along my way to the edge of the forest.

I heard him following in step behind me. "Great at sex and an environmentalist. I must be the luckiest guy around."

I ignored his comment and reached down to pick up

the scraps out of the bush. "What the hell? It's fabric! Why would there be fabric out here?" I had started to accumulate quite the collection of material and wasn't sure what to do with it all.

Jasper's voice carried over to me. "Huh. Maybe another pack wolf uses this area to shift too. It might be scraps of a shirt. Probably a young one who doesn't know how to clean up his trace yet. Funny I can't smell anything though."

That hadn't occurred to me. I still wasn't used to the fact there were not one, but multiple werewolves in my life. "Makes sense. I'm gonna grab the big pieces here. You can crack the whip on your wolf buddies later." I grabbed a large scrap wrapped around a branch, but the fabric was stuck around the back of the bush. As I reached around the bush, I touched a bit of something which was definitely not cloth. It was cool to the touch. And clammy. And oddly soft. I felt sick to my stomach. I think I knew what I was touching before I wanted to acknowledge it. Before I pulled away the branch, revealing the mauled body of a young man. I slapped my hand to my mouth to stifle a scream, and fell back onto the hard dirt. His face was torn and bloody, and a deep cut ran the length of his slender neck. He was young, barely out of his teens.

Jasper was close and jogged the last few steps to see what had scared me. "Baby, don't tell me you startled a sleeping racco... shit!" The joking tone of his voice cut off as he realized what my discovery actually was.

"Jasper. He's..." I couldn't even bring myself to say the word. *Dead.* I had never seen a dead body before. He tugged me away from the bushes, and didn't stop until we were in front of the bike.

"I knew him. Cody. He was new to the pack, from California." Jasper shoved my helmet into my hands. "From the looks of his injuries, another wolf took him down. And he hasn't been dead long. Why the fuck couldn't I smell him?"

I tried to strap on my helmet with shaking hands but kept missing the latch. Jasper leaned over and did the clasp for me. "Don't we need to call someone, or do something? We can't leave him there."

Jasper shook his head. "I'll call the pack leaders when we get in. They'll want to take care of the body themselves. But with how fresh the kill was, my priority is getting you home and safe. You're a natural, and you're quick, but I'm not about to throw you into something dangerous when it's not necessary. I'll bet you anything whoever did this is still out in those woods as we speak."

He tapped his fingers on the handlebars and barely waited for me to get on the bike before he was turning over the engine, racing through the empty streets towards my apartment. I couldn't help from glancing over my shoulder towards the woods, seeing eyes in every dark hollow. My heart thudded in my chest, and I was sure the sound of that alone would keep me awake until we took this killer down.

* * *

Jasper stopped travelling for work. I tried to talk him out of it, but he wouldn't hear any of it. "I know you can take care of yourself. It's only while you're still training. I'm the one who told you everything. It's my fault you're a target."

"Jasper, you know I would never think any of this is your fault. You're not going to be able to protect me forever," I protested.

"I know," he said, his face hard. "But I feel better knowing when I can, I have your back."

If this small thing was going to help him sleep at night, then I wouldn't push the matter further. Our training sessions adapted, too. Instead of going to our park we drove outside of town, to the pack lands. We trained every day without fail, until I was exhausted and could barely move. Jasper pushed me hard and I pushed myself harder. I couldn't fail, not now. I grew muscles in places I didn't know muscles could exist.

My father's Boy Scout lessons finally came in handy, and I passed Jasper's lessons on wilderness survival with ease. The guys usually offered to join us, and I readily agreed. I didn't want to get complacent, defending against Jasper. They all had different styles, and the change definitely kept me on my toes. Duke was by far my toughest opponent -- he was quiet, but quick. I had to work hard to best him. Adrian was unpredictable, confident in his youth. But my favourite to spar against was Beau, because he always made me laugh and kept things light.

"Goddamn, baby girl, you got a sister? You're ten times tougher than any wolf chick. Wouldn't mind if she was my mate." Beau waggled his eyebrows at me as we grabbed some water. I had had my blades at his stomach for the fourth time in as many rounds.

"Watch yourself, Beau." Jasper warned, but he was smiling.

I grinned at Beau. "Just me. I doubt you would've been able to handle two of us anyways."

"The real question is, could you have handled me?" Beau winked, making me laugh.

It felt good to feel in control, able to be carefree like this. These moments were few and far between. Cody's death had made it into the news, and the pack leaders barred Jasper from actively hunting the other wolf. Defensive measures were another matter, but they didn't want to put the pack into the spotlight any more than necessary. The killer seemed to be laying low, too. The lack of control left Jasper feeling frustrated, and he grew more protective of me. But his protective nature didn't translate into coddling.

"Okay, break's over. Let's go again." Jasper clapped his hands, walking over to us. "This time, Beau, I want you to shift, and don't go easy on her. Don't tell her your plan ahead of time. Let Ava think on her feet." He turned to acknowledge me with no warmth in his voice. "Green, you need to stop leaving your left side vulnerable. It's going to get you killed."

Jasper was a good teacher, and he trained from a place of concern, but sometimes he could be blunt. I sucked in a breath through my teeth. Beau whistled. "Shit, Jasp, I know you're not a guy who minces words. But Ava isn't one of the guys, she's your girlfriend."

Jasper whirled around, with an apology written across his face. "I'm sorry. I didn't mean to say that."

I shrugged him off. "It's fine, Jasper. I'm not dumb, I know what I'm getting into isn't safe. But it's different hearing how dangerous this really is out loud."

He watched me with concern, but nodded once he saw I was being honest. I unsheathed my swords and glanced up at Beau. "You ready?"

Beau had already undressed and was getting ready to shift. He smiled. "Born ready, Ava."

The sky was purple with dusk by the time Jasper let us wrap up our session. The air smelled like snow was on its way.

"You guys wanna come back to Adrian's place?" Beau asked as we packed up our stuff. "I think we're gonna hang out there tonight."

I wrinkled my nose and Jasper stifled a laugh. I had been to Adrian's house a few times. I loved the kid, but his place was like a college dorm. His dining room table was a pool table. Like, an actual pool table.

"Thanks, man, but I think we're going to head back into town," Jasper answered for both of us.

Beau pulled Jasper in for one of their intricate bro hugs. "Suit yourself. More beer for me. Catch you later, Ava!" He waggled his fingers at me and took off into the budding twilight.

Jasper pulled me close as we walked to the parking lot, kissing the top of my head. "You did really good today, baby."

I leaned into his touch, finding comfort in his body. "Thanks. I happen to have a pretty good teacher."

He sighed heavily. "Even if he reminds you about stuff you don't want to think about?"

I stopped and pulled away from him. "I knew what I was getting into when I asked you to train me. This situation happens to be accelerating the timeline, but danger would have happened at one point or another." I ran my hands over the delicate skull tattoos on his hands. "*Memento Mori*," I murmured under my breath.

He stared deeply into my eyes, shaking his head. "You really were born for this."

I was beginning to think that myself, but it still made me feel good to hear it from him. I leaned over to kiss him, but was interrupted by my cell ringing. Mouthing an apology to Jasper, I lifted the phone to my ear. I had been doing better at keeping my cell charged, but hadn't been so good at staying in contact. I was reminded of this when I heard Mollie's voice on the other end of my phone.

"Girl! I know you're in the honeymoon phase, and I totally get that. But please, please, please tell me you two are coming to my holiday party!" Mollie's voice was full of excitement.

Shit. Christmas. With all the commotion going on in our lives, I hadn't even had a moment to focus on the holidays fast approaching. I knew Christmas was soon, but shopping hadn't been at the top of my priority list -- and neither was Mollie's party. I slapped my hand to my forehead and tried to sound like I hadn't forgotten all about it. "Of course, we'll be there! What day did you decide again?"

"Friday. You know, Christmas Eve," she answered dryly. "I'm on break and I don't have a lot of time, but don't forget!" Her voice was sweet, but I heard the implied threat behind it.

"I won't, Mollie. I promise."

"Good. Okay, gotta go, love you!"

The line went dead before I could respond, and I pocketed my phone again, shaking my head at my best friend.

Jasper picked up my hand again. "What was all that about?"

"Mollie's holiday party. You know, for Christmas. Which is this weekend, and I'm completely unprepared."

Jasper peeked at me out of the corner of his eye. "Uh huh. So why does a holiday party make you look like you're about to cry, but the thought of possibly dying in your new career doesn't?"

I gulped in breaths, trying to calm myself. "I haven't spoken to my parents since I hung up on my dad. I'm really hoping they aren't planning on coming here and pretending we're some big happy family right now. But also, if they don't come, do I sit at home eating Doritos on Christmas Day?"

I could picture the day now -- sitting on my couch with Betty, both of us stained with orange dust. "No. We spend Christmas together. If you want more excitement, then we could always invite the boys over. Or if you want less, then you could come meet my mom," he said casually, as if he hadn't just dropped one of the biggest bombshells.

His mom? I tried to remain calm. "Oh. Um. Okay. What does your mom know about me? I thought she didn't live around here." *Does she know I'm human? Does she know I'm a Venator? Does she know who my parents are?* Unspoken questions raced through my mind. Doritos with Betty were looking better by the second.

Jasper smiled reassuringly. "She doesn't, she lives in Chicago. And she knows enough. But we don't have to think about meeting my mom right now. Mainly because I'm starving. Get your fine ass in the car so I can make us some dinner."

Chapter 5

Thankfully, Jasper was a great cook. Which was great because the one time I had tried to make him a casserole ended with the smoke detector going off and us ordering pizza. But even his perfect spaghetti couldn't pull me out of my funk. I pouted through dinner. And the washing up. I still hadn't gotten over the holiday thing by the time we sat down on the couch together. Jasper was right. I was facing imminent danger, and I was more concerned about who I would be eating Christmas dinner with. Luckily, I had bought a few presents last month, but my mind had been firmly on training the last few weeks.

I tried to focus on my work as Jasper researched our unknown wolf friend. But there had been too much going on today, and the words were becoming blurry on my screen in front of me. I slammed the lid of my computer down, rubbing my eyes. Jasper absentmindedly rubbed his hand along my calves where they rested in his lap. "Everything okay?"

"I can't think about work right now," I complained.

Jasper set down the tablet he had been researching on. "So, don't." He swung my legs off of his lap and walked into my kitchen. I buried my face in a throw pillow. How did I manage all of this insane shit in my life on a day to day basis, and yet I was going to let a stupid holiday unravel me? I needed to pull myself together. I was supposed to be a Venator, for Christ's sake.

"Here. Drink." I peeked out from behind my pillow mask. Jasper stood beside me holding two double shot glasses of whiskey, one considerably fuller than the other. At least I hoped it was whiskey.

He passed me the fuller one, and waited for me to take a long sip. "Better?" he asked, and I nodded.

"Thank you," I told him as he sat down beside me on the couch again, pulling me into his lap. He looked as worried as I felt, and I wondered if he had found new information. "Any good research tonight?"

"No, nothing." Jasper took a swig of his own drink and closed his eyes. "None of this is adding up. I want to understand what we're actually up against, so I can train you appropriately. And with the limits the pack put on me, I'm stuck with the fucking Internet."

Huh. I considered this. "Can't you go out and not tell the pack?"

He shook his head. "Doesn't work like that, Ava. What the Alpha says is law. I can't disobey him."

The alcohol had hit my bloodstream, and I felt my fingertips tingling. The combination of Jasper's chest underneath me and the whiskey finally had me feeling relaxed. He took a deep breath in, and when I felt his shoulders droop, I knew he was starting to relax, too. I sipped my drink, thinking. "Hey, Jasper."

"Mmmm?" He was toying with my hair, not paying attention.

"Were your parents mates?"

He stopped playing with my hair. "No."

"Oh. I was wondering why you never talk about your dad." I regretted asking, but I wanted to understand. I wanted to know all of him.

"It was a fling that ended up with me, and they tried to make the relationship work. But eventually my mom got frustrated she couldn't get what she truly wanted from my dad. Love." He took another sip of his drink. I had so many questions, but I didn't want to interrupt. "She left. Moved to Chicago. My father met his real mate soon after, on a scouting trip to California. He lives there with his new family now." His voice sounded level, but there was an old bitterness underneath it.

I bolted upright. "Your father left you alone? Oh, Jasper, I'm sorry. I didn't mean to pry."

He stroked my hair. "It's okay. I was a teenager at the time. I moved in with Duke's family, and Beau's too for a while."

I hurt for a young Jasper I didn't know. "I can't believe he left you."

Jasper's voice was soft. "I used to be a lot angrier. I used it as an excuse for going off the rails. But especially now, with you, I understand my father's decisions a lot better. The mate bond, it's hard to fight."

"Can you tell me more about it? The mate thing, I mean." Something about the evening made it okay for me to ask the things I was scared of.

He was instantly guarded, which was fair of him, as I had shot the mate thing down pretty hard when he first brought the topic up. "What do you want to know?"

I sorted through all of the questions swirling around my head, choosing one. "Well, like how does the bond work?"

"Okay. But no getting freaked out." Jasper took a sip of his drink and settled in. "It's kind of like love at first sight. But different. Because it's meant to be."

"What do you mean?"

"I mean it's difficult to fight once you've met your mate." He turned me to face him. "One has what the other doesn't, and vice versa. They're two halves of a whole. Once you've experienced feeling complete, how could you go back?"

"Oh," I said, watching the mixed emotions behind his eyes. "And you think that's what we are?"

Jasper nodded solemnly. "Besides the obvious, it's the only explanation I have for the other stuff going on."

"What other stuff?" I frowned, trying to follow his logic.

"Well, you already know how we comfort each other by being close. And normally mates have a telepathic bond, but it's a little different for us because you're human." He hadn't stopped looking into my eyes, and I couldn't look away.

"How does the mate bond work for us?" I whispered. The whole conversation felt like it deserved reverence. Respect.

"The sparks when I touch you." He ran his finger down my arm. "I can usually sense where you are. I'm beginning to feel your emotions."

I didn't respond. The whiskey was helping me remain calm, but to be honest, everything he was saying made perfect sense.

His eyes shone in the warm light, happy with my acceptance. "Usually, the bond gets stronger with marking. But I don't think we'd ever do that. I'd be too afraid of hurting you."

"The marking?" I asked.

Jasper hesitated. "It's when the wolves bite each other. Marking them. Claiming them as theirs. Here." He trailed a finger across the delicate skin of my neck. I shivered as he followed his finger with his mouth, kissing me. I leaned into his touch, eager for more. But he jumped up, leaving only the couch under me. Jasper already had his phone in his hand, but I hadn't even heard it ring. He ran his fingers through his hair. "Shit. I have to take this."

He stepped into my bedroom, and I could barely make out the low murmur of Jasper's voice. I set my drink down on the table and laid back on the couch. Was I okay with being someone's mate, with having no say in my own destiny? I couldn't deny everything he had said rang true. I couldn't deny *him*, for that matter.

Jasper stepped back out into the living room still holding his phone, a look of shock on his face. "You need to get dressed. Beau's been attacked."

* * *

I stood numbly in my room, processing everything that had happened. It was only a few hours ago we had seen Beau, and he was healthy. Happy. Joking.

"He's alive," Jasper had told me a few moments earlier. "Stable. But he's in critical condition. We need to get out to the pack lands now. The leaders want to see us."

"Us?" I questioned. I wasn't sure what I had to do with the situation.

"You were one of the last people to see him. But it's more than that. You're a Venator now. They are going to want your insight as well."

I pulled a sweater out, pausing with it over my head. It

could have been me laying in that hospital bed. It could have been Jasper. Beau had been attacked on pack lands, where we'd thought they'd be safe, but we thought wrong.

A sharp knock on my doorframe shook me out of my thoughts. "Ava, we need to leave, now." Jasper's voice sounded calm, but I knew that was for my benefit alone. I could sense the panic not far beneath. I shook off my negativity and finished putting my sweater on. Jasper didn't need me worrying about the *what ifs* right now, he needed me to be there for him. I walked out of my bedroom and straight into Jasper.

"Shit! I'm sorry." Jasper caught me in his arms before I went sprawling.

He smiled. "I got you."

And he did, he always had my back. So now, I was going to have his. I smiled back at him, staring deep into his beautiful eyes, trying to convey all the things I felt for him without having to say the words stuck in my throat. I righted myself, and moved past him towards the door. "Come on, I'll drive."

The snow I'd expected earlier in the day had started to fall, shining in the dark under the glow of the streetlights. I stuck my tongue out, trying to catch one of the delicate flakes. A perfect moment, dissolving before you could even taste it.

"What are you doing?" Jasper asked me, amused. He hadn't stopped walking towards my car.

I jogged to catch up to him. "It's a beautiful night. Come on, try it. It'll take your mind off things for a minute. The pack can wait, and Beau is in good hands." I held my head back again, spinning in circles, letting the cold drop onto my tongue.

"It is beautiful, isn't it?" His voice sounded funny, and I snapped my head forward to look at him. He was watching me, an uncertain smile on his face.

I took his hand and squeezed. The look he was giving me made me feel uncomfortable. "Just try it. Then we'll go."

He tipped his head back, letting his tongue catch

several flakes. Then Jasper bent his head to me, his lips and tongue still cold from the snow as he kissed me. I sank into the kiss, grateful for his touch. All too soon he pulled away, his lips still brushing against my own. "I do feel a hell of a lot better. Now the problem is I'd much rather go back inside and lose myself with you." He sighed heavily. "But the pack awaits."

We stopped at the hospital to see Beau. His injuries had been too severe to heal without medical attention, so they had taken him to the nearby emergency room. It was a shock to see him in the bed, tubes sticking out everywhere, his usually tanned skin a pasty white. His arms had countless stitches in them, his head and neck bandaged in a soft gauze. I didn't want to think about what the rest of his body must look like beneath the hospital sheet. I held myself together as Jasper dropped into the chair next to his bed, holding his best friend's hand. He spoke to him in a low voice I couldn't make out. I tried to imagine Beau as I had seen him only hours ago -- laughing, full of life. This immobile body wasn't him. There must have been some mistake.

Jasper stood abruptly. "I'm going to find a nurse who can give me more information. Can you sit with him for a minute?"

I nodded, taking Jasper's place in the bedside chair. I squeezed his hand as we swapped, and he gave me a grateful smile. I sat there for a few minutes, watching Beau. Eventually, I reached out to take Beau's hand in my own, trying to will his eyes to open.

"I'm so sorry, Beau. You were only out there because of me. This is all my fault. I'm going to fix this. I promise." The words fell out of my mouth before I could stop them.

"He wouldn't blame you." I whipped my head around to see Jasper's dark frame leaning against the door of Beau's room, arms crossed.

"How long have you been standing there?" I asked him.

"Long enough. Thank you for sitting with him." He walked towards me, placing a gentle hand on my shoulder.

"I mean it though. He wouldn't blame you. I know I don't. He would probably make some joke about how he was only there to see me get my ass kicked by my girl. Regardless, it's not your fault."

I leaned into his body. "Did you find a nurse?"

"Yeah. Apparently, they found him just in time, and they were able to get him into surgery immediately. They have him pretty heavily sedated for the time being, but she said he's stable now."

I kept watching his face. "He'll be okay." I felt certain, if only because it seemed impossible to think anything otherwise.

Jasper agreed with me. "He will. I gave the nurse my contact info. She'll call me if anything comes up."

"Is that allowed? I mean, you're not actually related. Would they be allowed to call you?" I questioned.

He smiled. "The nurse is part of the pack. She gets it. How else do you think we could sneak him into the hospital?"

"Hey." We both turned at the new voice to see Duke joining us in the room.

Jasper filled him in on Beau's condition, and I stood up to let him have the chair. Duke took my hand as I moved towards Jasper. "Thank you. Beau would appreciate you coming more than you know."

I tipped my head down, so he couldn't see how touched I was. "It was nothing."

"It wasn't nothing. You're one of us. A part of the pack." Duke embraced me, and I was stunned. I was part of something. Appreciated, more so than I'd ever felt with my own family.

He sat down next to Beau as we left and made the short drive to the pack hall. The reception desk was empty, but Jasper led me down the hall. "They're expecting us."

He pulled me towards a set of ornate double doors, opening them without knocking. I immediately felt out of place compared to the three large, intimidating men sitting at the table. They had to be the pack leaders. Jasper sat down at a chair across from them, and I sat next to him. He tipped his head politely.

"Jasper. Ava. Thank you for joining us on such short notice." The man in the middle acknowledged us, and from the way everyone seemed to turn innately towards him I assumed he had to be the Alpha. The Alpha's voice sounded as smooth as silk, and had a calming air to it.

My suspicions were confirmed when Jasper greeted him. "Alpha Dean. It was no problem at all. You know I'd do anything for the pack." The other two men weren't introduced to me.

"Thank you, Jasper. I know you're committed. But I need to know if you, Ava, are as committed." The Alpha turned his stern gaze on me, but I refused to cower away.

"I'm sorry, Alpha, I'm not sure what I can really do for the pack. I'm still training." I kept my voice as strong as I could. Jasper took my hand and squeezed.

"I understand you're Jasper's mate." My gaze darted to Jasper at this point, but he didn't meet my glance. The Alpha picked up on my quick look and continued. "Regardless if you have accepted this fact or not, your bond makes you a part of this pack now. I'm also aware you have been training under Jasper. If you're willing, we'd like to call on you for your aid."

My hands shook. I was expecting him to ask me for my insight, maybe an opinion or two. But this? Was I ready to hunt a monster who had injured others, even killed? My parents certainly didn't think I was. But the Alpha had made me feel like I was a member of this pack. Jasper's grip tightened on my hand. Jasper believed in me. His friends believed in me. Beau believed in me, so much so he was lying in a hospital bed as we spoke. I owed it to him. I owed it to myself.

I met the Alpha's stare. "I'll do whatever you need me to do to protect the pack."

Alpha Dean smiled at me. "Good. Jasper, we are once again giving you free rein to track and use whatever force necessary to take this wolf down. I don't know why he's here, or why he's hurting his own kind but the violence needs to stop. You will have any resources you need. Same goes for you, Ava."

Jasper nodded tightly. "Yes, Alpha."

"I don't think I need to tell you how important it is that this is handled quickly and quietly."

"No." Jasper's voice was low and serious. Something was bothering him, but there wasn't any point in worrying about it until we were on our own.

"You're both dismissed. Stay safe, stay alive." The Alpha and the two other men who had remained quiet left the room.

Jasper waited until they had left to stand, offering me his hand to help me to my feet. "I wasn't expecting him to ask you for help as a full Venator. You don't have to do this, you know, if you don't feel ready."

"I know." I hoped I sounded brave even though nerves were shooting through me. "I said yes because I want to. But, tell me something."

"Anything."

"What did you say to Beau, in the hospital?" I asked.

"I told him we were going to take this asshole down."

I stood on my toes to give him a quick peck on the cheek. "Then let's make him proud."

Chapter 6

"Come on." We grabbed some gear from the pack hall, and Jasper nudged me out the door, pulling me out into the cool night. "We need to check the perimeter. If they got through the security there must be evidence somewhere."

We walked through the gently falling snow, our feet leaving light prints in what had already accumulated on the ground. The weather this year had been strange, and I didn't think the snow would stick around until the morning. It left me wondering if we'd have a white Christmas this year. *Christmas. Shit.* I couldn't think about that right now. We had bigger problems than who was going to cook a turkey.

I shook myself out of my thoughts, only to notice Jasper lost in his own head. I elbowed him gently. "What's up? You look like you have a lot on your mind."

"It's nothing. I don't want to bother you with my worries when we have a job to do. You need to stay focused." He tried to smile, but it didn't meet his eyes.

"Really? You need to be clear headed too. Talk to me. If it's Beau, you know he'll be okay. The nurse already said he was stable, but you know she will call you if there's any issues."

"It's not that Ava, it's..." Jasper's voice trailed off, carried away in the wind. He turned to me, a thousand emotions alight in his face. "I'm scared."

I stopped dead in my tracks. "You're scared," I repeated dumbly.

He nodded, and his voice got quiet. "I'm scared I'm going to lose you. This isn't a game. It's not training anymore, it's life or death, and I'm the one who got you involved." Taking my hands, Jasper continued. "If you get hurt, I'll have only myself to blame. I don't want to live without you, and I don't think I could if I knew your pain was my fault."

"Jasper, I... I don't know what to say. We should probably --"

Jasper cut me off, pressing his lips against mine. His

touch, his proximity -- it made all of my worries go away. All that mattered in the world was Jasper kissing me, and it was all I focused on. He grabbed either side of my face, barely breaking our kiss. "Don't say anything, baby, let me talk." He kissed me again, slipping his tongue between my lips. "I'm going to tell you something, and out of all the things I've told you, I wouldn't be surprised if this is the one that makes you want to run. Promise me you won't."

"Jasper, I don't know if now is such a great time for another bombshell. Let's set up the perimeter and go home." I tried to wiggle out of his grasp, but his tight grip left me immobile.

He continued to stare at me. "No. This is important." His voice was gentle, but firm.

"What could be more important than our safety?" I was getting frustrated now, and threw my hands out to the side. Jasper could be so stubborn sometimes. "Fine. Fine," I huffed. "If it means you'll let us do our job, I promise I won't run away."

He ran his thumb along my lip, and breathed out heavily. "Ava, I --"

"Hey, Jasp, wait up!" Jasper was cut off by a deep voice calling out to him.

"Shit," Jasper cursed under his breath. "We'll come back to this, so don't think you're off the hook yet." He tugged his gaze away from me, squinting into the dark where a tall figure was jogging towards us. His body relaxed. "It's okay. It's Adrian."

Adrian joined us, not a bit out of breath from his jog. "Hey. I passed Alpha in the parking lot on my way to see Beau, and he mentioned you guys were beefing up security. Thought you might need a hand."

Jasper ran a hand through his hair, obviously agitated at our interrupted conversation. "Yeah, man, thanks." He offered a weak smile to his best friend and immediately settled into business mode. "The pack found Beau a little east of the field." He motioned to the left of us. "We should probably set up the motion sensors for a kilometre or so on either other side. It's not perfect, but it'll be better than nothing. We can regroup at the exact spot the pack found him later to see if there's any tracks or evidence we can follow."

The three of us worked in silence, inching our way from one edge of the forest to the other. The only sounds were the occasional snap of a stick underfoot, or the eerie call of a lone owl. Looking around at the deep woods, I knew Jasper was right. The perimeter wasn't a perfect solution, but hopefully it would at least give us a buffer, or some idea as to what we were working against. We eventually worked our way back around to the small clearing where Beau was found. I rested my head on Jasper's shoulder, sending some good vibes out into the universe Beau would recover. Adrian must have been thinking along the same lines, because he shook his head. "I can't believe it, man."

Jasper wrapped his arm around me, rubbing my shoulder gently. "I know. That's why we have to take this guy down soon, so no one else has to feel like this. We need to search the area, see if anything got left behind. I'm doubtful, though, because whoever this guy is, he knows what he's doing. We'll split up, but don't go far enough away you can't hear each other." Adrian nodded, heading towards the far side of the clearing. Jasper turned me towards him. "Ava, are you armed?"

I reached behind me, the feel of my blades reassuring. "Yeah. I'm good."

He kissed my lips briefly before releasing me. "Good. Stay close. We still have to talk after this."

I groaned. At this point I'd rather be found by this wolf than hear whatever he wanted to drop on me now. I turned away, headed for some bushes outside of the clearing. I examined the area in detail, looking for any sign of the attacker. The ground wasn't cold enough for the snow to stick overnight, which meant the dirt was soft enough for footprints to stick. The heavy, large sneaker prints were obviously Beau's, unless our unknown wolf had shown up fresh from the gym. I brushed my hands through the bushes, coming up short. I searched the area for several more minutes, becoming increasingly more frustrated as I found nothing. We couldn't hunt this thing with no leads.

"I think I found something!" Adrian's voice carried over to where I was looking, and I left my own futile search to join him. He was standing over a wet patch of dirt, and beckoned me over. "Come see." Jasper was already crouched next to the spot, examining something intently.

I crouched next to him. "What did he find?"

"Look." Jasper pointed to a smeared bit of dirt. "It's a print. Fresh. It looks like someone turned away in a hurry. But this is the interesting bit." He carefully lifted his foot to sit next to the print, his own shoe engulfing the size of the dirt print by nearly double. "It's a woman's print."

I checked out what he was saying, and everything lined up with my own tracking knowledge. "Huh. So, either a woman was out here and saw the attack happen or…"

Jasper finished my sentence for me. "Or, we're looking for two attackers, not one."

Finding nothing else, we walked Adrian back to his house before leaving pack lands, finding safety in numbers. The enhanced perimeter alarm was set up, linked to Jasper's phone if anything should set it off. By the time we made it back to my apartment, his phone had already gone off for a deer, raccoon, and several birds.

"At least we know the alarm works," I told him, slipping off my shoes. "But it might make for some sleepless nights when the noise wakes us up every twenty minutes."

Jasper sat on my bed, leaning against the headboard. "I'm not sure I would have slept much anyways until we catch this guy. Guys, I mean." He closed his eyes. "I'm so angry at myself because I never considered the idea of two people working together. But they've been covering their tracks well, and I've only ever seen signs of one wolf."

"Hey, don't beat yourself up. I never thought about there being more than one, either. Will you be okay for a minute if I take a shower? I need to warm up. My clothes got soaked through." I plucked at my damp sweater.

He eyed me from the bed hungrily, all earlier signs of frustration forgotten. "Want some company?"

I rolled my eyes, chucking him a towel from the bathroom door. "Come on, then."

Turning the shower on as hot as I could handle, I undressed and stepped into the steam. I tried to psych myself up before Jasper joined me and could see my nerves. *I can do this. Being a Venator is in my blood. I'm tougher than I think I am.* Truth be told, I was terrified. But for the first time in my life, I felt like I was doing something *right*. I heard Jasper step into the bathroom, and I took a deep breath to calm myself. He didn't need to see my nerves on top of everything else. Everything would be fine.

He pulled aside the curtain, and I couldn't help but admire his thickly muscled frame. It still astounded me this godlike man was in my house, let alone in my shower.

Jasper blinked at the copious amounts of steam filling my small bathroom. "Shit, baby, I don't think you have the water hot enough," Jasper said sarcastically, running his hands over my shoulders.

His touch burned more than any water did, and I struggled to speak coherently enough to joke back. "Aren't you supposed to be super warm blooded? Don't be a baby."

Jasper bit my shoulder gently, and I stopped joking altogether. He trailed one of his hands lower, curving the other towards my chest. I arched back into his body. But before he touched anything further, he took his hands away. He gave me a teasing smile when I turned around to glare at him.

"After," he said to me, reaching for my shampoo.

"After what?"

He was quiet as he squeezed the shampoo onto his palms. His hands went to my head, massaging the shampoo into my scalp. No one had washed my hair like this since I was a young child, and it felt oddly intimate for such an everyday task. His fingers felt so good, I soon relaxed into his touch. He kept washing my hair as he started to speak. "Ava, I… I never thought I would meet someone like you. I didn't see a relationship in the cards for me. I was always on the road. My parents weren't mates. My mom isn't a wolf. A thousand reasons. A million excuses. Then when I found you, I thought I had lost you before I could have you. You parents drilled into me you would never go for someone like me." His voice was honey, sweet and smooth as he spoke to me.

"Uh huh." I was only half paying attention to his words, hypnotized by the repetitive motion of his hands.

"But I couldn't help myself. I couldn't stop myself from getting closer to you -- from trying to find ways to fall into your path. I knew I shouldn't, I knew I would end up alone and hurt at the end of it. But I had to. All these things I couldn't talk myself out of doing. And now, with so much going on, I can't stop myself. Do you remember how I told you I was scared?" He took his time rinsing the shampoo from my hair, waiting for my response.

"Yes," I murmured. I couldn't think of any excuse to get out of this conversation now, so I had to embrace whatever secret Jasper needed to get off his chest. And hope it wasn't an actual body hidden in the closet.

He pulled me to him, my back nestled into his front. I could feel his heart beating, a steady drum keeping me anchored to this moment. "Well, I am. I'm scared. I'm scared something will happen and I'll have never told you I love you."

I didn't know what to say. This guy, this man, loved *me?* I felt overwhelmed with emotion, and my tears began to mix with the water from the shower. I was grateful he couldn't see my face. He kissed me softly on the back of my neck. "You don't have to say the words back. I know you like time to process things. But I couldn't go through all of this without being honest."

My throat still felt paralysed, and I wasn't sure what words would come out even if I could speak.

Jasper filled my silence by continuing to kiss me. "Are you okay? I'm sorry, maybe it was too much."

Jasper was worried he was going to scare me off, with

love of all things. I couldn't let him feel like he had done something wrong, with such a beautiful moment. Turning in his arms to face him, I stared at his perfect face. I tried to convey all the emotion I felt but could not speak to him, saying the only words I felt capable of. "Kiss me."

Relief flooded his gaze as he saw the acceptance he was looking for in me. Jasper pulled me impossibly closer to him, bringing his lips to meet mine. He scooped me up as he brought us both back to my bed, our bodies still soaking wet.

Barely moving apart, he whispered into my mouth. "I love you." For the first time in weeks, I felt certain everything was going to work itself out.

* * *

I woke up to a weight crushing my chest. A large, snoring, *naked* weight.

"Jasper. Jasper! I can't breathe!" I tried to shove him off of me, but he weighed almost twice as much as I did, which felt like four times as much when he was asleep. My pushing was going nowhere. I took my elbow and jammed it into the side of Jasper's ribs, prompting him to jolt off of me.

"Huh? What? Baby? Is everything okay?" His voice was thick with sleep. But he didn't open his eyes, and instead threw one heavy arm over my chest instead. He probably intended to immediately fall back to sleep.

I threw his arm off of me. "You're heavy. And hot."

"Mmm…" Jasper curled his lips up in a smile, and his husky voice made my stomach turn backflips. "You're not too shabby yourself."

He crept his hand up and over my chest again, but I pushed him off, laughing. "That's not what I meant. Now get up! It's Christmas Eve and we have stuff to do. Wolves to catch. Presents to buy. You know, normal Christmas things." I jumped out of bed, opening the heavy curtains. Jasper groaned and buried himself under my pillow. If my time with Jasper had taught me anything, it was that he was *not* a morning person. He tried to be, he really did. But he failed miserably most of the time.

I walked back over to the bed to drag him out, but Jasper snaked his hand out and grabbed my wrist before I could. "How about I make a deal with you?" His voice was muffled by the pillow. "You come back to bed, and I'll let you do unspeakable things to me."

I glanced down at him. "How exactly is that a win for me?" But heat crept through me as I eyed his bare chest, and I knew exactly how it would be a win. Unfortunately, we actually had stuff to do. I snatched the pillow off of his face, tossing it on the bed beside him.

"Come on!" he protested, squeezing his eyes tighter.

"Really, Jasper? You're lucky I..." I trailed off, surprised with myself for what I was about to say. The rest of the sentence echoed in my head. *You're lucky I love you.*

Jasper opened one eye, focused only on me. "I'm lucky you what?" he asked suspiciously.

I couldn't. Could I? I was too practical, and it was too soon. Jasper had told me he loved me numerous times since that night in the shower, but I had yet to say it back. *It wasn't the right time,* the romantic in me told myself. *Maybe I'm fooling myself,* the logical part of my brain said. I struggled to finish my reply as Jasper looked on. "You're lucky I think you're cute," I finished lamely, trying to smile to cover up my awkwardness. There was no denying my feelings towards Jasper were strong, but was it love? I couldn't be sure. Not now, not with everything else going on.

Jasper closed his eyes again. "Mhmm. Cute. Great. You know, Green, you're a pro at killing my self-esteem."

I chucked a pillow at his head. "I try. Now get your ass out of bed."

* * *

It took me ages to drag Jasper out of bed, coaxing and bribing. But eventually we made it out of the door. First on the agenda was a quick stop to the pack lands so we could set up a few more hidden sensors in hopes of tricking our wolf friend. There had been few new leads on our opponent and his partner. No attacks either, which left us feeling simultaneously frustrated and optimistic. Any tracks we had found seemed to disappear as soon as we thought we were getting somewhere. Our motion sensors were all still in place, but we hadn't caught any sign of him on the cameras. This could mean only one thing -- we were dealing with a pro. We'd have to see if the new sensors worked. I hoped they would. For all of our sakes.

Unfortunately, our next stop was the small mall. Which wasn't the place you wanted to be on Christmas Eve. "Remind me why we're here again? We could be training," Jasper complained.

"Because," I scolded, "all of my clothes are ruined from your crazy ideas about coaching, and I need something presentable to wear tonight."

Jasper shrugged. "Sounds like my coaching is effective, not crazy." He held up a soft white shirt. "What about this?"

I felt the soft material. "That's actually really nice." The top was beautiful. And guaranteed to have a nice big red wine stain on it by the end of the night.

He grinned at me. "Great. So, can we go?"

"The mall is not your comfort zone, is it? But no, I have to find a present for Mollie. I've been a terrible friend lately."

We'd rushed through the crowds, trying to find a suitable gift. Which meant we had run late. Which is how I came to be standing in front of my best friend with quite possibly the worst-wrapped Christmas gift on the planet.

"Earth to Ava. Ava!" I came back to reality as Mollie called my name. As usual, her party was done up to the nines, with twinkle lights, a beautiful tree, and countless appetizers I couldn't pronounce the names of if I tried.

"Sorry, Mollie, I was distracted for a minute." Ignoring everything else racing through my brain, I smiled at her. "You have my full attention."

"Mhmm..." Mollie followed my gaze towards where it rested on Jasper, who was talking to one of her cousins across the room. Jasper looked hot as anything in a new button down, his muscles tight against the deep green material. "My mind would be elsewhere too if he was my distraction."

Jasper either felt us staring or sensed I was admiring him because he turned in our direction, gaze on me alone. He smiled at me and I grinned back, giving him a small wave. I faced Mollie again to see her smiling at me. "Okay, maybe I was a little distracted by Jasper," I conceded.

"It's okay, Ava. I'm happy as long as you're happy."

I nodded, watching Jasper return to telling Mollie's cousin a story that had him laughing. Every so often he would meet my gaze, letting me know he was there. "Yeah. I'm happy."

"Good. That's all that matters. Have you told him you love him yet?" Mollie asked me baldly.

"Mollie!" I shoved her lightly. "No!"

"Why not?" she prodded. "It's obvious you do. I can tell just by looking at the two of you."

"You cannot! Besides, it's complicated," I explained, as Jasper peeked over at me again. Seeing my agitated face, he tipped his head to one side as if to ask me if I was okay. I nodded my head slightly at him, then focused my attention back on Mollie.

"Complicated as in you don't love him, which would be a lie, or complicated as in he has a secret family in Chicago and you're the side piece?" I couldn't tell if she was joking or serious.

"You're terrible!" I couldn't help but laugh. "But to answer your question, no, I'm not the side piece."

"Then what's the problem?" Mollie made life sound so easy. I wished everything could be easy.

"It's..." I didn't know how to explain everything to her. And I didn't want to get into the whole situation at Christmas no less. "It's tricky. There's other stuff going on."

"Other stuff like your parents not approving?" When I looked up, shocked, Mollie grabbed some kind of fancy hors d'oeuvre and rolled her eyes. "Ava Green. I'm your best friend. You haven't mentioned your parents in ages, so it's only logical to think there's some tension."

I sighed. She knew me too well. "Yeah. Things aren't great with them right now."

"Girl. When have things ever been great with your parents? Even in high school, you'd come home with an A, and it'd be a week of nagging because your grade wasn't an A+." Mollie was blunt, but what she said was true. Things had never been great with my parents. I had always been trying to make amends for things I never really understood how I had done wrong.

I was also grateful Mollie had picked up on tension with my parents instead of digging for more information, and I jumped on the opportunity. "You think? It's not totally crazy I'm going against my parents' wishes by being with some guy?"

She shook her head, pointing her now clean spoon in Jasper's direction. "Not when 'some guy' has had that look on his face since I started interrogating you. He really cares about you, Ava."

I followed the direction of her spoon to Jasper's concerned gaze. "He told me he loved me a couple days ago." I couldn't believe I was admitting this to Mollie. But she was my best friend and I felt bad about all the secrets I had been keeping from her. I had to be honest about something.

And by her reaction, I knew I had fed her the right tidbit. "What!" she practically screeched, causing Ben to duck his head around the kitchen doorway. Mollie shooed him off with a motion of her hand and turned back to me at a much lower decibel. "Girl. You didn't call me? Also, he said he loved you and you didn't say it back? What is so complicated?"

Mollie's questions were coming a mile a minute, and I tried to answer all of them the best I could. "I didn't call you because it was late, and then you worked a double the next day. And no, I didn't say anything back. I already explained that to you. And as for the complicated bit… there's nothing I can do. But we're headed out to Chicago tonight to spend Christmas with his mom, if that's any consolation." I tried to head off any further questions with more gossip for her.

She tapped her spoon against her bottom lip, thinking.

"Hmm. Interesting."

"What is so interesting about it?" I hoped she wasn't suspicious.

"Nothing." But she must have been excited to talk because I gave her one look and her whole explanation spilled out. "Okay, it's just he told you he loved you, and you didn't respond. He didn't leave, *and* he's taking you to meet his mom. That takes someone who is confident in the relationship. He's in it for the long haul."

"Uh huh." I tried to downplay my reaction, but I was secretly thrilled to have Mollie's definite approval.

Mollie smiled slyly. "I hope whatever you got her is better wrapped than my gift."

I cringed, thinking about the newspaper I had wrapped Mollie's last-minute gift in. I would have to make it up to her for her birthday. "Sorry. Again."

"Don't worry, Ava. I'm just glad you came." She rested her hand on my forearm. "Wow, girl, your arm is solid! What's your secret?"

I laughed, sounding strained even to myself. "Uh, boxing."

Mollie raised her brow. "You'll have to take me with you next time."

I could feel a migraine coming on. "Um, sure, definitely."

Thankfully she dropped the topic, and smiled at me gently. "You seem worked up lately. Don't let all this bullshit with your parents get you down. It's not worth it."

If only she knew the whole story. I wished the issue with my parents was my only problem. But I couldn't burden her with more, so I smiled weakly and gave her a hug. "Love you, girl."

Mollie squeezed me back, whispering, "I know. And he does too."

I untangled myself to find Jasper headed towards me. "You ready to go?" he asked as he touched my shoulder.

"You good if we take off?" I asked my best friend. "We have a bit of a drive." I was ready to get on the road, but I was grateful for the chance to feel normal tonight. I'd needed it. We both had.

She pushed us both towards the door, shoving our coats into our hands. "Go. Bye. Drive safe. Text me tomorrow!"

We headed out the door, smiling at each other. I couldn't ask for a better friend, really. Or a better night. For all of my fears about Christmas, the day was turning out to be perfect. The only thing left was to make it through meeting his mom without putting my foot in my mouth. Jasper reached for my hand, bringing my hand to his lips. "You look beautiful tonight."

"You always say that." I attempted to deflect, but blood still rushed to my face with the compliment. "Thank you for coming tonight. I really appreciate it."

"I would do anything for you. Always." I knew he meant what he was saying. "Now, are you ready to go to Chicago?"

I hesitated to answer when I felt rather than heard his phone ring. He reached in his pocket and silenced it. I opened my mouth to reply, but his phone rang again. Jasper mouthed an apology and brought the phone to his ear.

"It's Christmas Eve, Adrian. Whatever girl you're trying to get rid of can wait until tomorrow. Or if you really want to be a gentleman, the next day." He listened quietly for a minute while I tried to figure out what Adrian was saying. But Jasper's face was an impassive mask, giving nothing away.

He hung up the phone and continued walking towards the car. His sudden silence made me nervous and I rambled in an attempt to fill the space. "What did Adrian need? Does he not know we are driving to Chicago tonight?" A light snow had started to fall and I hoped the roads wouldn't be slippery.

"We're not going to Chicago," Jasper replied tightly. "The new sensors were tripped five minutes ago. Our unknown wolf is officially on pack lands."

Chapter 7

Jasper was so preoccupied he didn't even ask me if I wanted to drive like he normally did, he just jumped in the driver's seat of my car. He barely waited for my door to shut before he took off, racing through the streets. He muttered something to himself about how the drive would've been quicker on the bike, before turning his attention to me. "Ava. Do you have your makhairas?"

I twisted to pat the compact bag under my seat. "Yes, they're here."

"Good." His voice was still strained, and I knew he was trying to stay calm. "Here's the plan. We will meet up with Adrian at the pack hall. He and I will do a quick run to make sure our friend is still around and then we can all regroup from there."

I nodded mutely before realizing he wouldn't be able to see me in the dark car. "Okay. Are you sure you don't want me to come out and do the loop with you guys as an extra set of eyes? I can back you up."

Jasper growled low in his throat. "No. No. It'll be quicker with the two of us in wolf form."

I hesitated, not wanting to make things worse. "Jasper, I don't want to add fuel to the fire, but shouldn't we, like, call your mom?"

"I'll call her later. Don't worry. She'll understand. It's not the first time I've had to cancel because of work, and unfortunately it probably won't be the last." He made a dismissive motion with his hand, and I knew he didn't want to discuss the matter further.

We arrived at the pack lands in record time, even with the slick roads. Adrian was waiting for us outside the main doors of the pack house as we pulled up. I wasn't even sure if Jasper put the car into park before he jumped out.

"You ready?" Adrian greeted Jasper, his attitude subdued compared to normal.

Jasper gripped my shoulders. "Wait inside. Please. Until we do a quick lap to make sure this isn't a trap."

I held my hands up, conceding. "Okay, okay."

He breathed out heavily. "Thank you. We'll be back in five minutes tops. Keep your blades close." Jasper kissed the top of my head and tore his clothes off. I sighed as I watched him carelessly rip his beautiful new shirt over his head and toss it to me. I folded it as he shifted, his pale grey wolf taking off through the warm lights of the parking lot. Adrian followed suit, and they split up, each heading to the woods in opposite directions. I went inside the unlocked doors and closed them firmly behind me, staring into the dark woods. I hoped they would be quick. Being alone and tracking was one thing. But being alone, waiting for people to return was nerve racking.

I watched the clock tick for one minute, and then two. The time passing felt like years. I needed something to do to keep myself occupied. Otherwise, I was sure five minutes would be long enough to drive me certifiably insane. I headed down the corridor to where I knew the equipment room was. My blades were securely strapped under my shirt, but I figured it wouldn't hurt to be overly prepared. Surely a bunch of werewolves would have an extra knife or two I could shove into my boot. I lost myself in the supplies and finally stopped paying attention to the ticking clock. They would be fine. It would be a quick run, something they did all the time. Besides, their noses were way better than mine. I was so caught up in the disorganized storage room I didn't feel someone come in behind me until a hand grabbed my shoulder firmly. My breath caught in my throat, and I tried to focus on my breathing so I wouldn't scream. I prepared myself to get out of any situation, counting to five.

Before I could reach five, Jasper breathed into my ear, sounding irritated. "Didn't you hear me calling you?"

Instantly relaxed, I twisted to face him. "Oh, it's you." He had found a pair of athletic shorts that draped low on his hips, and his eyes were the dark colour I had come to anticipate after his runs.

"Who else would it be?" He still sounded annoyed, but he looked calm. "I thought you would be waiting by the door. I was worried when you weren't there."

I held up a small knife triumphantly. "I was looking for extra gear. As a precaution, you know."

Jasper made a strangled noise deep in his throat. "You don't have to do this, you know. You can still go home."

I huffed. "Jasper. You trained me. I know what I'm doing, and I can handle myself."

"I know. You're ready, and you're capable. It's only..." he hesitated. "If you get hurt, it'll be my fault because I didn't train you properly."

Jasper's gaze was clouded with worry and I squeezed his hand tightly. "You trained me perfectly. I can do this."

He closed his eyes tightly and nodded. "I know. I can't let my own fears hold you back."

I stood on my tiptoes to kiss him, trying to reassure him the best way I knew how. I would be okay. I was scared out of my mind, but at this point I couldn't imagine doing anything else. He kissed me back greedily, letting his tongue part my lips. I pushed him away, laughing. "I'm not sure we have time for this. Don't we have a wolf to hunt?"

Jasper held my face in place with his large hands. "The wolf is still close. Adrian is on his trail. He knows the signals." He kissed me again deeply. "Please, Ava, I need you." He trailed his hand down my spine to toy with the bottom of my shirt as he kissed under my jaw, and I shivered against his touch. He had me, and he knew it. Jasper scratched his nail along the plane of my stomach, licking my neck. "Come on. It'll be good for both of us."

Jasper pressed his mouth back on mine, and I sighed into the kiss. He dropped both hands to the button of my jeans, undoing it and sliding the denim over my hips. "Do you trust me?"

Of course, I did. But I had no idea what trust had to do with our current situation. He snatched an old blanket off of one shelf, laying it down on the floor, and me on top of it. He knelt over me, hooking his fingers into either side of my underwear.

"Yes. But if we don't have time to fuck around, we

really don't have time to have an intimate conversation," I told him, focusing instead on the taunting way he was brushing his fingers over me.

"I want you to tell me something."

Jasper took his fingers away and I protested lightly, until I saw him taking his own shorts off, releasing his cock. He settled back between my legs, pressing against me but not making any move to enter me. I tried to move against him, but he held me firm in his strong grasp. "Tell me you love me, Ava."

Shocked, I pushed myself up on my elbows. "Excuse me?"

His tone was level, but his dark gaze was pleading. "Tell me you love me. I know you do. And I think you know it, too."

I did love him, so I wasn't sure what was stopping me. I laid back down, and he reached his hand under my sweater, playing with my breasts. "Jasper, I…" I couldn't focus on what he was asking me when he was teasing me, so I stopped trying to speak. He took his hands away and I tried to bring them back.

"Ava." He was waiting. Anxious.

I had been fighting it, but I had known I loved him since the first moment I had met him, since I had first laid eyes on him. My denial of this fact had forced him to beg. "I love you."

He thrust deep into me as I said the words, causing us both to cry out. Jasper moved his hips, and I matched his rhythm.

"Say it again," he said, his voice husky with desire.

I tried to speak and failed as pleasure started overwhelming every sense I had. Jasper slowed his motions, going torturously slow so I could feel every movement he made. "Say. It. Again," he demanded through clenched teeth.

I knew the slow pace was killing him, as well. He was the one who originally offered release. But I was still unable to form the words. I closed my eyes, giving in to the rhythm.

I was so close. And then Jasper stopped all together. When I opened my eyes, he was staring at me, eyes filled with emotion. "Say it again, baby," he requested softly.

"I love you." He closed his eyes in pleasure and resumed his desperate pace. I could feel the heat building, but before I could cry out Jasper shuddered inside me. His subtle release was enough to send me over the edge alongside him. I clung to him, all that mattered in the world at the moment.

"I really do love you, you know," I told him again, resting my head against his. I tried to catch my breath -- I was going to need it.

He smiled, satisfied. "And I love you. Forever. Always."

I knew he meant it. I could feel the mate bond coursing through both of us, and I thought back to our earlier conversations. Only one thing was missing. I doubted he was going to go for it though.

"Jasper."

"Yeah?" His gaze was still unfocused.

"I want you to mark me." I made my voice as confident as possible.

Shock was clear on his face. "Are you serious?"

"Yes." I was resolute. There was nothing to stand in my way now -- no fear, no denial.

Jasper considered my request, then nodded. "We can talk about it later. After all of this is done. It's a bigger undertaking than you're thinking."

I started to protest when a piercing howl shattered through the hall, breaking us apart. The moment was over, and we both moved into high gear.

I stood up, pulling my jeans back up. "What the hell was that?"

Jasper was grim. "That was Adrian."

I strapped my blades in place before jogging to catch up with Jasper's fast pace. He turned towards me. "You okay if I shift? It'll be faster."

"Go. I'll catch up." He didn't even bother to remove his

shorts, shredding them as bones cracked and fur emerged from skin. I ran behind him as fast as I could, feeling grateful for all of my early morning runs as I sprinted. I found him inside the tree line where he was examining a crushed bush. His gaze met mine. He was still Jasper, but in a different face. He pointed with his snout and I followed, snatching a blade in each hand. He led me deep into the forest, where the tree roots began to overlap each other. The evergreen foliage was so thick overhead in places it made the space nearly pitch black where we ran. I hadn't seen Jasper in several minutes, but I could hear him lightly crushing through the snow as he ran ahead of me. I had stopped for a moment, to get my bearings when I heard a sharp yelp from up ahead.

"Jasper! Jasper!" I called out his name in a harsh whisper, torn between wanting to make sure he was okay and not wanting anyone to know my location. But the woods were silent. I couldn't hear the crunching of his footsteps anymore. I made my way towards the area where I thought I had heard the yelp, and broke through into a small clearing where the trees weren't as thick overhead. The opening flooded the area with moonlight, harsh on my eyes after all of the dim light.

"Jasper!" I called, a bit louder this time.

And this time, I heard him. "Ava!"

He must have shifted back, I thought. I headed towards the sound of his voice, calling out to him again and again.

"Ava!" he shouted. "Ava! Get the hell out of here!"

* * *

"Ava, go!" Jasper's voice called out again, more desperate this time.

I immediately turned on my heel. The plan wasn't to run away, but to mark my trail back. If Jasper was otherwise occupied, then I was going to have to rely on my skills to get us home safely. Using my teeth to rip off strips of my shirt, I tied the fabric around a branch at the edge of the clearing. Even in the dim light the white stood out. Then I took off in the direction his voice had come from.

I found nothing. Jasper was nowhere to be found. Every so often I would stop and tie a strip of my shirt to a tree to make sure I wouldn't get lost. I tried to track Jasper's trail, but there wasn't much of one to go by. I would find bits of prints here and there, but I had no way of knowing if they were Jasper's. I hoped they were his. I wasn't sure if I wanted to meet the other wolf by myself. I remembered our previous encounter in front of my apartment and shuddered to think about a repeat. Except I was stronger this time. Better prepared. It wouldn't be like last time. I wouldn't let it.

I found a steady trail of prints in the crisp snow, slightly different from the last. Not finding any other choice, I started following them through the brush. At least the prints were a solid lead for once. The snow was starting to come down heavier, settling into the evergreen branches and making my coat damp. I wish I had the foresight to change into a better coat, but this wasn't exactly how I saw my night going. I kept listening for Jasper, or for anything else that might be in the woods, but it was silent. But that didn't mean no one was there. The wolf we were hunting had managed this long not being caught, I wouldn't be surprised to find out he had been watching me all along. Moonlight was breaking through the branches ahead where the tracks were leading me, and I stumbled towards the light. Except it was out of the dark, and once again into my original small clearing. The tracks must have led me around in a circle, and I had been too preoccupied listening for other wolves to pay attention. An amateur mistake. Frustrated, I closed my eyes, counting and breathing, hoping some idea would come to me.

A rustling in the bushes startled me from my thoughts. I opened my eyes and ducked into a defensive stance to see a black wolf at the opposite end of the clearing. *Adrian.*

"Adrian? Is that you?" I could pick out Jasper's wolf no problem, but differentiating the other wolves in the dark took more practice than I had.

He tipped his snout down in acknowledgement and

trotted behind the deep brush. Adrian emerged in his human body a moment later and rushed over to me. "Ava, thank God. I heard Jasper calling out for you and I thought the worst."

"We were worried about you! We heard your howl and thought you must have gotten into trouble with the other wolf," I told him, relief flooding my veins. Thank God I wouldn't have to explain to Jasper another one of his friends was in the hospital. Or worse. "I don't want to make things awkward, but you didn't happen to bring any clothes with you, did you?"

Adrian stood in the blowing snow naked as the day he was born, and didn't seem to be a bit concerned about it. I tried to keep my eyes above the waist level. He rolled his eyes. "It's nothing you haven't seen before. And wolves run hot, so I'm fine. I wasn't exactly expecting to shift back in the woods."

"Okay." I just had to ignore the nudity. No big deal. "Did you find the other wolf?"

Adrian settled his lips into a tight line. "Oh, I found him, all right. He led me on a wild goose chase for quite a way before I lost him." He looked around. "Where's Jasp? Is he still shifted? I lost track of him awhile back."

I felt my extremities grow numb, and it wasn't from the cold. "I was hoping you would have crossed paths with him. We got separated around here. I've been trying to track him down but I guess I followed your prints instead."

Adrian narrowed his eyes. "Okay. Don't panic. Jasper can take care of himself. Why don't you head back before this storm gets any worse and I'll track him down?"

I shook my head. "No. I'm not running. I'm going to help you find Jasper and take this asshole down."

His face was pure annoyance. "Jasp is gonna have my head for this, taking his mate out in a bloody snowstorm," he muttered to himself. "All right, let's go. I'll stay like this for now, but I'll shift if we run into trouble. Try to not get hurt."

"I think you'll find I'm quite capable," I told him,

irritated. I gripped my blades tighter and shoved past him into the brush. Sometimes I felt like Adrian was the little brother I never had. Or wanted. I huffed and headed deeper into the forest.

"Ava! I'm sorry!" Adrian jogged after me, apologizing. "I didn't mean it that way. Jasper is going to be pissed at me if something happens to you. So please stay safe."

"I won't let anything happen. Relax. Now let's focus. We have to find Jasper." I imagined the worst. Jasper's broken body lying on the ground. Jasper's bright red blood pooling against the new white snow. Jasper's throat, slit.

The snow was thick, and time was a vague concept. We trekked through the forest for what felt like hours, but what was probably nowhere close to that amount of time. We were silent except for me occasionally checking to make sure Adrian didn't have hypothermia (he didn't) or him occasionally pausing because he thought he heard something (a squirrel). The storm continued to pick up in intensity, making it difficult to see in some areas.

We paused for a break under a dense cover of evergreens, waiting for the snow to let up. "Can you smell him?" I asked anxiously. I spun my blades around in my hands in a lazy form of the trick Jasper had taught me, trying not to seem anxious.

He sniffed the air. "No, nothing."

I groaned. This felt like a futile mission, us tracking Jasper who was tracking the other wolf who was tracking us. I hoped we'd all make it to see the morning. But I wasn't about to give up. Not now.

"What if you shifted? Do you think you could smell a bit more then?" There had to be something I was missing, something to help us out.

Adrian tilted his head from side to side, weighing the options. "Possibly. But with the snow coming like it is, it's a toss-up and I'd rather not shift unless I have to. If something happens to you, it's easier for me to help if I have thumbs."

He spoke like he was more concerned I was going to trip and break my ankle than us coming in contact with the other wolf, which scared me. What if we couldn't find either of them?

I pushed the topic, hoping I was wrong. "Adrian, you'd be more help to me against this other wolf if you were in wolf form, too."

He stared at me for a moment. "I don't think we're going to find the other wolf."

"But the other wolf has Jasper, and we have to find Jasper," I protested. Adrian was confirming my worst fears. I was well prepared for a fight, but that meant nothing if we couldn't find the enemy.

Adrian winced and shook his head. "I don't know what happened to Jasper. He could've run into the other wolf, or it could also be something else. But the odds of us finding the other guy this late at night aren't great -- we've had a hard-enough time with weeks of planning."

"No. You're wrong," I stubbornly disagreed. The only option here was he was wrong.

"Look, the snow is getting worse. We need to have faith Jasper can take care of himself. If he was smart, he probably found some cave to hole up in for the night and can't hear us calling. Let me shift, and I'll take you home on my back. We can start fresh first thing tomorrow."

"No." I was angry, and the look on Adrian's face said he knew it. "I'm not leaving without him. You can go home if you need, but I'm staying out here as long as it takes to find him."

"As long as it takes to find who?" A woman spoke from behind me, and I whirled around to see her hand brushing aside the tree giving us cover. Two familiar figures stood amongst the trees. I couldn't let myself give in to the shock, couldn't let myself think too much on what her presence meant. Why they were in this forest, on Christmas Eve, in the snow. I had a job to do, and my focus had to be on my job. Otherwise all of Jasper's training was for nothing. I held my blades out in front of me expertly, protectively dropping in front of Adrian.

"Stay back," I warned. They had no idea what I was

prepared to do -- for Adrian, for the pack. For Jasper.

"Ava, do you know these people?" Adrian snarled, looking impressively menacing for someone who wasn't wearing a stitch of clothing in a massive snowstorm. He edged closer, and I knew he was ready to shift at the first given moment. One of them was going to end up hurt if this went any further, and I didn't know which one I was more afraid of being in danger. I held one blade gently against his arm to stop him.

"Adrian." I kept my voice as calm as possible. "Meet my parents."

Chapter 8

Adrian looked shocked. "These... these are your parents?"

"Yes," I informed him tightly, before addressing my parents. "Mom. Dad. Nice of you to let me know you were coming home for Christmas." I had never seen them looking like this before, both dressed in identical black outfits with short knives strapped to their hips. They looked deadly, and they definitely didn't look like my parents. Dangerous looked so natural on them, and I wondered how I never realized something was amiss before Jasper filled me in.

My parents gave each other an exasperated look. "Don't be dramatic, Ava, it doesn't suit you," my mother told me. "And put those ridiculous swords down before you hurt yourself."

I was angry. Angrier than I had been over finding my parents out here in the first place. They still questioned my capabilities when they had no right to do so. "Don't give me orders. Tell me what the hell you're doing out here in my woods."

My mother coughed out a laugh. "*Your* woods, are they, now? Did you magically become a werewolf while we were away?"

"No, Mom, I became a Venator. So let me ask you again. Why are you here?"

"Don't be dense. You already know why we're here," she said bitterly.

"You've been helping the other wolf." I felt numb. My relationship with my parents the last few months had been like the worst roller coaster ride of my life.

"Congratulations, you've figured us out. You must be a true Venator," my mother said sarcastically, clapping.

"But Jasper said there was a kind of magic, when he was in the cave. How did you --"

My mother cut me off. "I told you there were things he couldn't hope to understand. Obviously, I was right. Let me give you another chance to go home and forget this whole mess. You're in way over your head."

"I wouldn't underestimate her, if I were you," Adrian interjected, and I looked over at him in surprise. Up until this moment, he had managed to stay quiet and I had almost forgotten he was there. "Ava has been working hard. She can best nearly everyone, and I wouldn't be overly surprised if she could take you both down one handed."

My heart swelled with pride that Adrian thought so highly of me, but ice flooded my veins when I realized the truth of what he said. Jasper had trained me for every eventuality, every possibility. But I wasn't sure if I was prepared for taking my own parents down as enemies.

"Shut it, mutt," my mom snapped back at Adrian. "You don't know who you're talking to. Ava needs to learn her place, and this isn't it. She needs to get home before she embarrasses herself."

Adrian growled, and I rested my hand on him again. "It's okay," I told him. "And you," I said, turning on my mother, "will not speak to my friends that way. They have treated me with more respect than you ever did. Now while I have your attention, what did you do with my mate?"

My father joined in. "Don't tell me you actually buy into that bull. I told you he's no good for you. I meant it."

I gritted my teeth together. "Thanks for the fatherly advice, Dad. Now, where is he?"

He simply gestured towards the thick tree line. "Maybe our friend can answer your question. What do you think?"

The shaggy brown wolf limped into view. Before I could stop him, Adrian phased, leaping in front of me ready to attack. The brown wolf bared his teeth in return, but he looked pretty beat up. I hoped Jasper had inflicted some of those wounds. "Please. Be civilized," my dad scolded before turning his attention on the brown wolf. "Kelley, I believe Ava has a question for you. Did you deal with Jasper like we had originally discussed?"

I froze at my father's blunt words, but then hope threaded through me as the wolf shook his big head. Jasper had to be out here somewhere close. We had to find him. But something in what my father had said was ringing a bell. "Kelley…" I repeated, "as in, Sheriff Kelley?"

My dad looked at me like I was missing an obvious point. "Do you know another Kelley?"

"No," I replied coldly. "But I'm trying to piece together how my parents, who are charged with protecting the pack, have come to be attacking them instead."

"Why would I want to protect such a disgrace to mankind?" My father's voice matched my coldness. "My father was one of the best Venators around, and his father before him. So on and so forth. The kind of men you read about in… alternative histories."

My mom interrupted him. "Jim, stop. We don't owe her anything. We knew a long time ago she'd never understand. She's too soft."

"Monica, if she thinks she can handle it, let her hear the truth. Besides, picking up some toy weapons doesn't make you a Venator. There are things she still hasn't experienced." He turned his attention back to me. "As I was saying. We were the best in history. That's what I was trained for -- greatness. But as the pack grew in size and strength, the rest of the monsters dwindled in comparison. Here I was, meant to go down in history, while I was stuck babysitting a pack of half-breeds." He curled his lip.

I was dumbfounded. Did my father expect me to believe they were killing innocent wolves for glory? His reasoning was disgusting. "Your plan was to kill the entire pack off, one at a time?"

He shrugged his shoulders, unbothered. "If it came to it. Our original intention was to create enough attention surrounding the pack they would go into hiding at the very least."

"And how does Kelley fit into all of this?" I spit out.

"Kelley was a happy surprise. Imagine our amusement when we found out Merrillan's chief of police was an unwilling wolf! He had hidden his true identity, making him perfect for our needs. Don't get me wrong, he's fought his nature for so long there are flaws. He heals rather slowly.

But he serves our purpose. Doesn't have to think too much, which suits him." My father smiled. He was actually proud of himself, of this plan.

I wasn't sure how he really expected this conversation to go. "You disgust me. You both do."

"You don't agree, which is why we never told you. Your stomach is too weak for such things. They're beneath us, Ava. With them gone we can go on to do the work we were destined for. Well, your mother and I can. You will go on living your normal, uneventful life." He reached down and grabbed a knife off his leg sheath, flipping the blade in the air. "It's simple biology, Ava, survival of the fittest."

The wolves were growing anxious and I knew the time for action was drawing near. I had tried to avoid violence, but it didn't seem like peace was going to happen. This all had to be a bad dream. These weren't my parents. This wasn't happening now. And where the hell was Jasper? I wiped away a lone rebellious tear. To hell if I was going to cry in front of these people, biology be damned. Adrian and I were going to have to take care of this without Jasper. The snow was warping my sense of the landscape, but I tried to take stock. Adrian's warm body was still beside me. I subtly reached back, expecting to feel the large bush at my back. Instead, I whacked my hand into something warm and solid. But that didn't make sense. Unless...

"You looking for me?" Jasper's deep voice whispered in my ear.

Thank God. I looked at him out of the corner of my eye, thankful to see his muscular frame mostly in one piece. But celebrations would have to wait. My parents were watching.

"When I give the signal, go low. Remember, baby, speed, not strength. I'll phase and go high. Between the two of us we can take Kelley down. Are you prepared to demobilize one of your parents?" Jasper whispered.

"Hell, yeah." This had gone on for long enough. When I nodded, he spoke in a louder voice for everyone to hear, edging around the small group we had gathered. "I thought I should be in human form to see if we could talk this out, you know, as family."

My father laughed. "As if we'd ever consider a disgrace like you a part of our family. Our own daughter will have to be wiped from the family tree at this point, fraternizing with your sort."

"Yeah, I figured once I heard what you had to say to Ava." He continued to slink around my parents, distracting and dividing them. He was preying on their weakness -- their pride. If my parents hadn't been surprised to find me out here, if they hadn't been so angry I stood up to them, if a thousand decisions hadn't lined up into place, this would have never worked.

Adrian tilted his head towards me, blinking slowly, and I realized he was giving me acknowledgement that he understood Jasper's plan. Kelley, too, had figured out our plan and was growling angrily in the background.

"Hush," my father commanded Kelley. "Your part in this is almost over. Stay out of the conversation until we ask for your input." Kelley whined and slunk further back. My father was right about one thing -- Kelley didn't think too much. "Ava will learn her place if she knows what's best for her. Otherwise, she will fall with you."

Jasper had circled around their small group, until he was in front of my parents. "Oh, I'm pretty sure Ava already knows her place." He jerked his chin down sharply. Without waiting to see if Jasper shifted, I dove towards Kelley. I heard the sounds I had come to associate with the wolves' phasing and I knew I had made the right call. Our movement caught Kelley off guard, but his reflexes were still quick. He dodged our initial attack, panting across from us.

"This is ridiculous," my mother sputtered. "Ava, stop this at once." Quick as lightning she had her swords drawn.

I glanced at Jasper, then back. He understood. Three on three. We just needed to keep our cool. I left Jasper to deal with Kelley, facing off against my mother -- the woman who had brought me into this world, and had raised me. And now here we were, swords drawn.

My mother glared at me. "You probably want to

rethink taking me on, little girl."

"It's been a while since I was a little girl, Mom." We circled each other in the snow, and I could hear Kelley's cries of pain behind us. But I had to focus on the fight in front of me. "You could stop this at any time. Just turn yourself in."

She cocked her head to the side, and her hands tightened on the hilts of her blades. "Too late for that."

She lunged forward, and I immediately went into defensive mode. Every blow she powered towards me I deflected easily. The clang of the blades rang out in the still of the night, and I focused on meeting every one of her attacks. Focusing so well, that when she slashed up instead of down, I wasn't prepared and the tip of her blade caught my forearm. I cried out in pain, taking a step back. The bright blood dripped off of my arm into the snow beneath my feet, but thankfully it felt like a shallow cut. My mother also seemed surprised that she had actually drawn blood, but then her cruel mask was down again, as she shifted back into her fighting stance.

This was only going to end one way. I had to stop being on the defense and get aggressive. It was going to be me or her, and I needed to get her unarmed. This time, I met her as she lunged, watching how she moved. Like me, she had a tendency to leave her left side exposed. I needed to exploit that.

When she came at me again with her left arm, I blocked her, immediately slashing her wrist with my free blade. I felt nothing as she screamed and dropped her blade, blood gushing from the deep gash. I kicked her fallen sword away as she came back with her remaining weapon. "You think you can kill me, Ava? I'm your mother. I know you better than anyone."

I laughed as our blades met again, looking into the eyes that were so like my own, and yet so different. "Think again." I spun the blade around in my hand, pinning her as I used the hilt of my other sword to bash the back of her wrist. Her eyes flickered in pain, and she dropped her remaining weapon. "You don't know me at all. You never have." I kicked it away, spinning around in the snow with a wild cry I didn't know I had inside me, looking over my shoulder as I drove my blade towards her neck.

And then I stopped. The tip of my blade pierced her pale skin, a bubble of blood pooling from the pressure. *Could I do this? Could I kill my mother?*

Did I even consider her my mother anymore?

My mother's eyes flashed with something cruel, and she leaned into my blade the tiniest amount. "Do it. You want this life so bad? Take it. *Earn* it."

I wanted to. I could feel blood rushing to my head, and every muscle in my arm crying for release. But I hesitated. And she felt me question my judgement, taking advantage of the moment.

My mother smirked at me. "I told you. You're too weak for this life." She pushed off my blade and sprinted into the woods. *Shit.*

I caught Adrian's eye, who growled and took off after her. He would find her. I turned to check on Jasper, who had Kelley knocked out on the snow, his body shifting back into the human form I had grown up around. Sneaking up behind Jasper was my father, blades drawn.

I moved quicker than he could. He might have been better trained, but I had age and stamina on my side. Before he realized what was happening, I had my blade against my father's stomach. "Don't try it," I snarled. Jasper's wolf looked up, surprised. He had been too focused on taking Kelley down to notice my father creeping up behind him.

"You wouldn't, Ava. I raised you!" he protested.

I shook my head, putting a little more pressure on the blade. Not enough to draw blood, only enough so he knew I was serious. "You raised me to be a lesser version of myself. But I know differently now. I can go down in history the right way. Getting you out of the picture seems like a good place to start."

I kept my blade where it was, and sheathed my other sword along my back. I used my free hand to remove his weapons, double checking he wasn't hiding any.

"Ava, I'm sorry I doubted you. You've been well trained. I can teach you things no wolf ever could, things my father taught me."

"You had a thousand chances to make that choice. You made the wrong one." I brought my sword to the small of his back. "Now walk."

* * *

By the time we walked out of the woods with Kelley and my father the sun was beginning to break against the clouds, and the snow was starting to taper off. It looked like we had gotten our white Christmas after all. We took Sheriff Kelley into the pack hospital where he could be cared for until he was well enough to be taken into custody. If he made it there. A huge group of angry wolves had met us at the doors, crying out for revenge for their fallen family members.

The pack nurse patched up my forearm for me, thankfully with no stitches needed. The next stop was taking my father to the jail in the next town over. He protested and denied any wrongdoing the entire way. Jasper knew the officers there who would keep the real reason my father was being charged hidden.

"I can't imagine what you went through last night. Are you okay? How's your arm?" Jasper asked as we walked out of the jail. It was surreal, taking my own father in. But I didn't feel bad for him. I only felt bad for all the people he had hurt.

I pressed my lips together. "I'm fine. A small cut. And it had to be done, Jasper. There was no other way around it. Let's get the rest of this morning over with." I was afraid if I let any emotion out, I wouldn't be able to stop.

The Alpha had requested our presence, so we returned to the pack house. The receptionist ushered us into a private office. Alpha Dean stood looking out the window, back to us. I must have been exhausted because I had to keep myself from laughing when I realized this is exactly what everyone must think of when they picture a werewolf alpha. Jasper grabbed my hand, squeezing my fingers tightly and looking at me sternly. He must have sensed my amusement. I gave him a brief smile before taking a seat in front of the Alpha's desk. It had been quite the night and I figured I was entitled to a bit of temporary insanity.

Alpha Dean spun around to address us. "Jasper. Thank you. You have done the pack quite a service, and we will forever be in your debt."

Jasper raised his eyebrows minutely and I could tell he was surprised with the Alpha's high praise. "You're welcome. Anyone would have done what we did."

Alpha shook his head. "But they didn't. You did. I take it this was all handled discreetly?"

"Yes, Alpha. Kelley is in custody at the pack hospital, and we handed Jim over to Luke and the boys," Jasper reassured.

"Good. I also have spoken with Adrian, who made it home safely. Monica managed to evade him. We will find her though, make no mistake." This came as a shock to me -- my mother was missing? Hopefully wherever she had managed to lose Adrian was far away from here. The Alpha turned his attention to me. "Ava, I can't begin to thank you for your dedication to the pack. You took down your own family for us."

I shook my head, hoping he wouldn't think I was being impertinent. "No. I protected my family." I squeezed Jasper's hand.

The Alpha gave me a small smile. "Still. This does leave us with a problem. Your parents were our pack Venators. With your mother missing and your father in custody, we're shorthanded. Ava, we'd like to offer you the position of our pack Venator. Probationally, of course, until your training is complete. But I'd say you proved yourself and then some last night."

I didn't know what to say. I didn't want to get emotional at a time like this, but I was so honoured I couldn't focus on anything else. "Oh... thank you. Yes. Thank you. Thank you."

"Thank *you*, Ava. Now, both of you get out of here and

get some rest. I can't have either of you falling asleep on the job." The Alpha sat down at his desk, opening a thick file sat there. We were dismissed.

Out in the hallway, I collapsed into Jasper's arms. The emotions and exhaustion of the last night were finally hitting me, and I couldn't believe it was all over. "I'm glad you're okay. I was so worried."

Jasper held me tightly. "I know. I'm sorry. They must have been trying to divide us, because Kelley led me on a false trail out into the middle of nowhere. But it's okay. We're okay."

I squished my face against his solid chest. "Yeah. We are."

"You kicked ass last night, baby," he said to me, pride heavy in his voice.

"I know. I had a good teacher." The weight of what I had agreed to hit me. "Shit, Jasper, I'm responsible for a whole pack now. What am I supposed to do?"

He laughed, and I was grateful for the sounds of normalcy again. "You work your ass off."

Jasper and I held each other in the pack hall corridor for a minute, letting our emotions recover. Then Jasper pushed himself away, holding me at arm's length. "Did I hear you call me your mate?" Jasper asked me, a sly smile on his face.

I groaned, covering my face with my hands. "How long exactly were you listening for before you made yourself known?"

"Long enough," he said happily.

"I'm never going to live that down, am I?" I grumbled.

"Nope!" He squeezed me tightly, flexing the dark tattoos on his arm. "I'm glad you're finally beginning to realize I'm always right."

"And I'm glad I'm too tired to be more offended right now." I yawned. "I'm exhausted. I need my bed. Can we go home?"

Jasper took my hand. "Definitely."

"So, we saved the pack. What's next?" I asked Jasper, happy to feel his hand in mine again.

"Well... we will have to track down your mother at some point."

I nodded in agreement. I wasn't looking forward to hunting her down, but I knew it had to be done. I should have killed her when I had the chance, but I hadn't wanted to be like her -- callous and unforgiving.

I wouldn't make that mistake again.

"But that can wait a few days at least," Jasper offered. "I have to head back to Chicago first. Tie up a few loose ends."

Oh. I felt my face fall. I knew he had work and a place and everything in Chicago, but I guess I hadn't considered the reality of him going home at some point. I tried to look happy for him. For us.

"I thought maybe you'd like to come with me, stay in Chicago for a bit? See how you like city life. Your work is pretty mobile anyways. Well, except for the pack now. But you don't need to be here all the time."

I felt my body sag in relief. He wasn't expecting us to be apart. "Yes. Yes, I'll come."

"*Yes*? That's it? I'm disappointed. I was expecting more of a fight. I could already hear the words '*too soon*' coming out of your mouth." Jasper's tone was teasing, but he looked thrilled.

I shook my head. "I don't really want to be apart. If that's okay with you."

We walked outside into the fresh snow, the cool air nipping at our faces, and he gathered me into his arms again. "More than okay. I didn't want to push you, but I was hoping you'd say something like that." He tipped my face up to meet his, kissing me firmly. "Now let's get home. I have a few things in mind requiring the use of your bed."

I tried to keep a straight face, pulling him towards the car. "I hope you mean sleeping."

He raised one dark eyebrow up at me. "Are you seriously telling me you saw me half naked all night, and now you want to get me into your bed... to sleep?"

I laughed out loud this time, and Jasper joined in. I couldn't deny anymore the surety of the fact we were made for each other. Today, I was happy, strong and confident. Tomorrow, I'd worry about finding my mother.

Nighted (Darkling 3)
Torri Heat

Jasper and Ava have made it through every hurdle thrown their way -- together. Their relationship is stronger -- and hotter -- than ever. But now something new and deadly is after Ava. The pair also can't forget the minor detail that her mother is still missing.

The supernatural world is dangerous, and full of things that go bump in the night. Will they be able to find the monster before the monster finds her?

Chapter 1

If I thought back really far, I could almost remember my mother telling me a story. About creatures who lived in the woods, and monsters that went bump in the night. Bedtime stories created to scare children. Except I was no longer a child, and I knew better now than to think those stories were made up.

None of this mattered anymore. My mother and I had no relationship left, and this was definitely not the time for a casual discussion on children's stories. I had bigger things to worry about. The forest I was currently sprinting through full tilt was far from imaginary, although the scene could've been from a dream. The dense foliage was thick with new growth, lush like a fairy tale. Bright flowers bloomed in the small gaps of sunlight. The only thing missing was the bird song, preferably from a friendly bluebird. Instead, all I heard as I ran was the sound of my own heartbeat.

I wanted to stop and catch my breath, but I couldn't. He'd find me, and that was a whole world of trouble I didn't even want to contemplate. So I kept running, my heartbeat keeping time with my silent footsteps.

There were perks to being a Venator, and then there were skills I had worked my ass off to learn. The quiet way I could move through the forest was one of those skills I was most proud of, and my talent was paying off tenfold at the moment. My original plan had been to do a wide circle in the woods, coming out at the far end, which hadn't been working out for me so far. Venator or not, my stamina wasn't unlimited. What I needed was a distraction, or some way to let me loop back on myself. I eyed the aging trees as I ran deeper. The thick vines desperately making their way skyward were too new to provide any real support, but they might give me some traction if I could find a tree small enough to find good holds. Just ahead of me I found my target. A tree younger than the rest with some low limbs, but not fully covered in the twining green ropes. Perfect.

I jumped, reaching for the first low limb and pulling

myself into the tree. I continued to climb until I was high enough in the leaves that I was unable to be seen but could still hear everything going on below me. Unfortunately, this vantage point also left my vision partially obstructed. I would have to rely on a combination of my senses and hope for the best. I pulled myself as small as I could, straining my ears to hear the sounds beneath my hiding place. I needed to wait until he passed by me, and then I could make my way back out of the woods. Easy. I had outmaneuvered wolves loads of times. My breath and my heart kept an odd melody in my head, and I forced myself to slow down. I needed to listen.

I heard the heavy breathing first. I must have pulled up at the perfect time, because he wasn't far behind me. I could hear sniffing down the trail I had followed. I pulled my feet even closer to my body, willing my heart to be silent. I had come this far. I could make it a little while longer. I kept count of the seconds, tapping my finger on my tight black shirt. *One. Two. Three.* There was the swish of a tail in the bushes beneath me. I could see the edges of the damp fur but couldn't make out the whole body. Holding my breath, I waited to see if he would find my hiding spot or would move on. *Four. Five. Six.* The fur slowly disappeared, and the sniffing faded out further along the trail. I would give him a couple more minutes, just to make sure, and then I would jump down and move. *Seven. Eight. Nine.* My hiding spot had been a success. There was no more sign of him. Now I only needed to get back in one piece. I took a deep breath and jumped down.

Ten.

I took a quick look around me, feeling satisfied I hadn't been found out. I turned on my heel to head back the way I had come, before he noticed I was no longer ahead of him. But before I could move, something snaked out from the left of me and grabbed my wrist. My heart stopped. *Shit.*

"What gave me away?" My voice sounded a lot braver than I felt. Bravery was a constant work in progress, especially when the supernatural world wasn't one you were expecting to find yourself living in.

Jasper smirked. "Your scent was all over those vines, Green. You should know better than to climb on the greenery without masking your scent first."

Double shit. How had I forgotten that? I had been pleased with myself too, and my pride had knocked me down hard.

"Damnit! I thought I had you this time."

He laughed, casually running his fingers through his messy hair. His hair had gotten longer in the last month or so. I wasn't complaining. The length suited him. The soft sweatpants he stashed around the woods we used for training draped low on his hips, putting his toned and inked body on display. I loved looking at him. Jasper Knight. My boyfriend? I still couldn't believe he was real after all this time.

Jasper swung a perfectly tanned arm over my shoulder, teasing me lightly. Somehow, he managed to come out of winter looking like he spent every day on the beach. "Listen, Green. Give up now. I will forever out track you."

We often came out to the woods to practice tracking. I was technically no longer in training, but we both enjoyed the runs, and were both a little competitive.

I shook my head stubbornly. "No way. You have a weakness I will discover and exploit." Okay -- we were very competitive.

He tucked my head tight against his shoulder, trying a different tactic. "Baby, you're a phenomenal Venator. No one is doubting that. But I trained you, and I will always out track you."

I relaxed against his body, still annoyed at myself. My agitation only grew as Jasper brought his lips close to my ear. "Even if you did make a rookie mistake."

I stood corrected. I loved looking at him, but I definitely didn't like him at the present moment. I pushed away from his body. "You're a jerk."

He was laughing at me. With me? No, definitely at me. "You're cute when you're angry."

Whatever. I'd show him cute. I started jogging down the path back to town. He might still have the advantage in tracking, but I was faster than he was. On his human feet at least. "Last one back to the apartment gets dish duty," I called over my shoulder to him. "And no cheating!" I didn't bet dinner duty, because that was a joke. We both knew who would be cooking, and it wasn't me.

Jasper groaned loudly, starting to jog behind me. "Come on, you know I don't stand a chance on two legs."

Duh. "You should've thought about that before you made fun of me. See you at home!" I picked up the pace, letting my mind focus on nothing more than my feet in front of me, and my blood rushing within me.

My run put me in a much better mood. For how fit Jasper was, he really did not enjoy running as a human. I stopped in front of the main doors, catching my breath. As expected, I had gotten back to my apartment miles ahead of Jasper.

After Christmas, we had spent some time in Chicago. Then we came back to Merrillan for a while to make sure I didn't shirk my duties with the pack. And then, we went back to Chicago. After playing this game for some time, we had decided the efficient thing to do was to keep both apartments. Double apartments allowed us a place to stay when Jasper had to work and when we came back to visit Mollie and the pack. An added bonus was not having to stay in Adrian's "guest room" which I had serious doubts about even being a legal room, let alone a bedroom.

It was different, not being in Merrillan all the time. Not always working in the café or seeing Mollie every week. But I liked the city, and Jasper and I both thought a fresh start was necessary. A life far away from everything that took place this winter.

I shuddered thinking about the events from not long ago. I didn't like to think about everything too much, but my job now meant I was required to think about what happened in the woods way too much. How my parents turned on us, and how I had to take my father into custody -- and attack my mother. But I hadn't been strong enough to end her life. Not then, at least.

Jasper finally came jogging around the corner, looking annoyed but not overly strained. The guy really did not enjoy running on two legs.

"You're a pain in the ass, Ava, you know that?" he muttered, but smiled as he stopped next to me. "What's wrong?" he asked, noticing I didn't rise to his bait as I normally would.

We unlocked the door and headed upstairs. "Nothing unusual. Thinking about my mom. She's been on my mind a lot today."

"I'm not surprised. But you have nothing to worry about. I've always got your back." Jasper's attempt at reassurance was sweet, but misplaced.

"It's not that…" I sighed, walking into the apartment. "I'm not worried about myself. I hope we find her before she causes more trouble for people. I should've taken her down when I had the chance."

Jasper pulled me into his arms again, kissing my forehead. "I love you, and you made the decision you felt was right at the time. We will find her. I promise you."

I gave him a tight hug. "Thank you."

"What for?" He held me at arm's length so he could look at me.

"For being you. For having my back." I glared at him. "But *not* for besting me at tracking today. Your betrayal was unforgivable."

Jasper smiled widely, crinkling the skin around his eyes. "I'm sure I can find some way to make my mistake up to you." He trailed his finger down my neck, following with soft kisses. My traitorous body responded to him easily, and I felt his smile against my skin. But before I could suggest we take this to the bedroom, I looked over Jasper's shoulder and noticed the balcony door was ajar. Weird, because I was usually pretty paranoid about making sure everything was locked up tight when we left. Maybe Jasper had left the door open.

"Jasper?" I tried to get his attention, but he was too focused on his current task. I gently pushed him away, trying again. "Hey, Jasp?"

"Mmm?" His eyes were unfocused, but at least I somewhat had his attention now.

"Did you forget to close the balcony door?" One of us must have forgotten. It was the only logical explanation.

Jasper was instantly alert. "What? It's open?" He went over to check out the sliding door, easily slipping into investigator mode. "You sure you didn't forget?"

"Pretty sure." The lock had been acting up for weeks. Maybe the wind knocked it open. No reason to panic, right?

He sighed, face close to the latch. "I remember locking the handle before we left. I was hoping you had opened the door again. But it looks like the lock has been broken."

The idea had already been at the forefront of my mind, and I readily caught up to his line of thinking. "Someone broke in."

* * *

It had been a quiet few months, with not a whole lot of action. I assumed we had been lucky, but apparently not. Obviously, Jasper was thinking the same thing.

"Okay. Okay." Jasper ran his fingers through his hair, making it stand up in a ridiculous manner. "This still could mean nothing. Might have been some kids playing around."

"Sure." Sarcasm dripped from my response. "Playing around on the third floor. Makes sense." I was not comfortable. At all. "Who did this? What did they want?"

Jasper crossed the floor, embracing me in his arms. "Hey. Don't panic. We'll get to the bottom of this. Let's take a look around, see if anything is missing. If it's supernatural in nature, it might be someone checking out the new Venator."

"Not helping," I muttered. I knew peace wouldn't last for long, not in this job. But I didn't think when it came, it would feel quite as violating. I had been thinking more along the lines of a fight or two.

We were interrupted by a pounding on the front door.

"Ignore it. They can come back later," Jasper told me, his voice muffled by my hair.

But the banging escalated and was followed by a loud voice. "Ava Green, I know you're in there! Open up now!" Mollie. At the worst possible time.

I sighed. "Shit. I should let her in. She'll break down the door otherwise. Can we pretend nothing happened for like five minutes?"

Jasper's smile didn't quite reach his eyes. "Of course." I knew he was as uncomfortable as I was, but we would have to fake it for the time being. I swung open the front door and there stood Mollie, looking perfect in a slim colourful dress, and not a hair out of place. She took in my appearance, gaping at my messy bun and my muddy workout attire. As long as she didn't notice my agitation, she could judge my current appearance all she wanted. Thankfully, she had other things on her mind.

"You've forgotten!" Mollie had perfected the look of accusation over the years, and she was currently using it against me.

Forgotten. I had forgotten something. But even trying as hard as I could, I couldn't grasp at the wisps of my memory. "No I haven't!" I instinctively defended myself, but then immediately caved. "What have I forgotten?"

Choosing the most unfortunate moment to come up behind me, Jasper gently placed a calloused hand on my shoulder. "Oh hey, Mol. How's everything going?" He acted like he didn't have a care in the world, while I was sure I had the words "stressed out" written across my forehead. Damn him.

Mollie turned her accusing stare on Jasper. "Your girlfriend has forgotten our plans today, and I'm certain you had something to do with her lack of memory!"

Jasper held up his hands as if to protect himself from Mollie's sharp words. He had learned Mollie could mean business, and not to mess with her when she was in this sort of mood. He looked to me as if I had the answers. But if I did, I wouldn't be in this situation in the first place.

"Mollie, don't blame Jasper. It was all me."

She glared. "You were supposed to meet me at my house half an hour ago so we could go shopping in Easton!"

Shit. Shit. Shit. How had I forgotten? Probably the whole training in the woods with my werewolf boyfriend, and then coming home to find out someone broke into my house. An excuse, but a reasonable one. Also one I couldn't tell Mollie without getting into details she didn't need to know yet. I tried to play it cool. "Oh, duh! I was teasing you." I laughed, slowly starting to slink away from the doorway to get changed. Jasper was already nowhere to be seen. Coward.

If looks could kill, then I would already be in my coffin, and halfway in the ground. "Ava Green, you're supposed to be my best friend! You shouldn't be forgetting this kind of stuff when I barely see you."

Mollie was right. There was no getting out of this one, and she was on a roll. I interrupted her before she could really pick up steam. "I'm sorry, there's no excuse. Give me five minutes to shower and get ready." I ran out of the room before she could disagree.

"Five minutes!" Mollie's angry voice echoed down my hallway. I had to make this up to her, and fast. I ran past Jasper and dove into the shower, setting a world record for the amount of time it took to scrub the dirt from our tracking session off of my body.

Mollie had been wanting to check out a new boutique in Easton for weeks, and I kept putting the shopping trip off. We were too busy. We weren't in town. I knew there had been a specific reason for us to come back to Merrillan this week, but I had assumed the appointment was my meeting with Alpha Dean scheduled for tomorrow. I really needed to start keeping a calendar to juggle between pack life and my old life.

I darted back into my bedroom, fully intending on throwing on the closest possible clothes and getting the hell back out there before Mollie came and dragged me out herself. Jasper was sprawled out on the bed, eyes closed, making the bed look much smaller than its queen size.

"Nice of you to ditch me out there. What am I supposed to do? Also, what are you doing?" I poked Jasper in the ribs before pulling a pair of jeans off the floor. We used to be fairly tidy people. Constantly living in between two places changed us. Piles of clean and dirty clothes covered the floor. Gear bags filled with Jasper's various weapons were spilling out at the foot of the bed. It was probably for the best if I got dressed quickly so Mollie didn't have to come in here, because the collection of knives would be rather difficult to explain. I'm not sure we would even be able to figure out if anything was missing in this mess.

Jasper rolled on his side and looked at me. "I'm thinking. As for what you should do, you should go out with your best friend. I'll check out the place to make sure it's secure. Starting with the bedroom until after you two leave. Mollie is scary."

I laughed, grabbing what looked to be a clean sweater from the top of the dresser. "Mollie is also 100 pounds soaking wet. Are you sure you can handle the apartment on your own? Shit." The sweater I had thrown on had a dark red smear across the front of the material and I couldn't tell if the stain was blood or pasta sauce. I tore off the sweater, digging for something else suitable. "We're going to have to do something about this."

"About what?" Jasper was sitting up, pulling his laptop closer. His screen reflected a news web page for Chicago unsolved cases. He was probably already on the hunt for any new supernaturals in the area.

I paused for a moment, to admire him. He was perfect, and sometimes I was still astounded he was in my house, let alone in my bed. His delicate tattoos covered much of his flawless skin, but they only added to his beauty. I would know. I had traced them enough times. He caught my eye, smiling like he knew what I was thinking. He didn't, but he could probably sense my feelings well enough. Another one of those wolf things I still wasn't used to. I shook myself back to my senses. "About this room! We're living out of suitcases like we're in a hotel. I never feel like we're in either of our places long enough to actually feel like we're living there. And now this break-in. Shit." I hadn't said that out loud before, but as I spoke I realized the truth of my words. I felt like we were always on the move. And now my temporary home didn't even feel safe.

Jasper levelled me with a serious look. "Unfortunately, that's the way of our lives right now. But there might be a solution for the time being."

I snagged a long sleeved shirt out of a pile and threw it on after deeming its cleanliness satisfactory. "What's your solution?"

"We could… get a place midway between the pack and Chicago. Something that's ours."

"Ours," I repeated. Nerves were rushing through my body, but I was sure the feeling was still residual adrenaline from knowing someone had been in my house uninvited.

Jasper pushed his computer off his lap, coming to take my face in his hands. "Too many people know where you live, baby. It's dangerous for you. Besides, we're already living together. We might as well put some roots down together."

The moment was broken by Mollie yelling down the hallway. "Thirty seconds, Ava Green, and then I'm pulling you out by your hair!"

He pressed a light kiss to my lips, leaving me wanting more, as always. "Go. I promise to make sure everything is secure here. I won't bother telling you to stay safe, because you can handle yourself. But think about it, okay?"

I nodded. "Okay."

"I love you, Ava." A note in his voice made me pause, but when I turned to look at him, I only saw unadulterated love reflected in his eyes.

"I love you." I gave him another quick kiss and dashed out the door to where Mollie stood, tapping her feet.

"Can we go now?" Her voice was impatient, before she stopped and looked at me intently. "Ava, are you okay? What's wrong?" Her mood instantly swung from anger into one of concern. I really couldn't have asked for a better friend, and I needed to do better to be the same kind of friend for her.

Giving my oldest friend a hug, I tried to push all of the negative images from today out of my mind. "I'm good, Mollie. The travelling back and forth is exhausting. Let's go and see this new shop."

Mollie grinned. "Okay. You can make your forgetfulness up to me by trying some stuff on too."

I groaned. "Is it too late to accept your anger and stay home instead?"

She linked her arm into mine, leading me out the door. "We're gonna have a blast." Mollie chattered the whole way out to her car, and I thankfully welcomed the noise. I wanted to embrace her excitement, but all I could focus on was the clock in the car ticking down the minutes until I could get back home and find whatever had been in my house before they found me again.

Chapter 2

I found myself standing in front of a full-length mirror and squashed into a tight purple dress. Fidgeting and trying to pull the dress up over my exposed cleavage, I turned to face Mollie. "You're really sure this looks okay?"

"Girl! You look great!" She spun a finger motioning for me to turn. I needed to be a good friend. A best friend. I could go shopping, try on clothes. Act like a normal girl, not one who had an entire pack of werewolves to protect. But still. "Are you sure this doesn't come in black?" I whined.

Mollie grimaced. "Yes, I'm sure. Besides, it's almost summer. Who wants to wear black in the summer?"

I did. But I didn't say that. Instead I focused on being a good friend. "I guess the dress doesn't look too bad." I frowned, looking in the mirror. My reflection was almost a shock to my system. I was used to seeing myself in mud-stained workout clothes.

"You look hot. I can't believe your body right now either. What the hell are you doing?" Mollie sounded impressed over my newfound muscles, but I was immediately embarrassed.

"The usual. Running. I've also been trying out boxing, remember?" *Boxing. Sure. Stick with it.*

"At a club in Chicago? I don't think we have anything around here."

I wasn't sure if Chicago had any either. "Something like that." I didn't want to outright lie to Mollie, but I also didn't know how much longer I could avoid the truth.

Thankfully, she was already on to the next thing. She clapped her hands together. "My turn!" We both ducked into our changerooms, and I put my casual clothes back on. I sank in relief to be out of the dress. But I would buy the dress and wear the damn thing out with her. For Mollie. I waited outside for Mollie to come out in her first outfit. Mollie had great taste, which was completely different from my own. Despite my day, I was excited to see what she had picked.

"Ta-dah!" Mollie came out in a dress, striking a pose. The white lace dress, fitted through her delicate waist and hips, had off-the-shoulder straps emphasizing her collarbones.

I clapped my hand over my mouth. "Oh, Mol. It's beautiful." Mollie was always gorgeous. She was effortless in a way I could never manage to achieve.

"It's perfect, right? Do you think Ben will love it? Our anniversary is coming up, and he's taking me away for the weekend." Ah. The real reason we were shopping was coming out. Ever the perfect planner, Mollie was already preparing for what was likely to come. A proposal was imminent.

"Ben will be at a loss for words. Honest." My words were the truth.

Mollie continued to talk as she admired herself in the mirror. "I still need to find shoes. None of mine will match. And a necklace. What do you think about a pearl necklace?" I nodded, barely able to keep up with her speed. "Just think, Ava. I might come back from this trip engaged. And soon enough it'll be your turn!"

I choked on my breath. "I'm sorry, what?"

"Don't be dense, Ava," Mollie said, in a matter-of-fact tone. "You and Jasper are obviously soulmates."

Soulmates. I tossed the word around on my tongue. If Mollie only knew the half of it.

I shook my head. "Maybe. But I don't think marriage is in the cards for us." I tried to picture it. Me in a white dress, and Jasper in a tux. Our friends and family gathered around outside. But who would walk me down the aisle? Did I wear my blades under my dress? None of this seemed plausible.

She met my gaze in the mirror and shrugged. "Never say never."

On the drive back to Merrillan, thoughts of the break-in at home were replaced by images of the ideal family life. The one I had pictured for myself since I was twelve. The perfect wedding. The house. The man. Truth be told, that dream wasn't what I wanted for myself anymore. I wanted to make a name for myself. I wanted to be an equal, to be strong, and to go on adventures. And I wanted to do all those things with Jasper by my side. I didn't think I needed the title "wife" to get what I wanted out of life. Besides, one dream out of three coming to fruition wasn't bad. Jasper was ten times the man I had ever anticipated in my life and had made me realize I could be bigger than myself. He came with danger, and an uncertainty in life, but they were odds I'd choose again and again.

It was pitch black by the time Mollie pulled into my parking lot. Spring was coming, but daylight had yet to catch up. She killed the engine and turned to me. "Okay, you won't forget next time we make plans?"

"No chance in hell I'll forget." Literally. "Name a time and I'll be there."

She pulled me into a tight hug. "I miss you, girl. Tell me you and Jasper aren't going to be doing this back-and-forth thing forever."

I shook my head. "Definitely not. It's too much for both of us."

Mollie grinned. "Good. Speaking of, what is your insane boyfriend doing?" She pointed to the field facing the parking lot. I followed her finger to see Jasper, illuminated only by the streetlights, kneeling in the grass with his nose nearly in the dirt.

I was at a loss. "Um. Well." I had no idea what I was supposed to tell her, because I had no idea what the hell he was doing either. So, I shrugged my shoulders and went with confusion. "I'm pretty sure your guess is as good as mine, Mol."

Always a good sport, she just shrugged and laughed. "Hey, who am I to judge? Takes all kinds to make the world go 'round right?"

I joined in her laughter, unbuckling my seatbelt. "I should go check on him. Drive safe."

I made my way over to Jasper through the damp grass, about to call out to him so I didn't surprise him. But he beat me to it. "Watch where you step, Ava."

Huh. I was fairly certain the front lawn of my apartment was not a dangerous place, but I had been proven wrong several times before. I heeded his warning, stepping carefully. "What's up?" I wasn't really sure what I was supposed to be careful of.

"Come look." He waved me closer, not picking his head up. "What do you see?"

I knelt gently down beside him. "You know you look like a nut out here right? I wouldn't be surprised if the neighbours put in a complaint about my crazy boyfriend."

"Mate," he corrected. "Now tell me what you see."

He was pointing to what looked like a pile of dirt. But I knew he wouldn't be out here captivated by a pile of dirt. I mimicked his position, bringing my face close to the ground. The pile he was pointing at smelled dusty, almost like... "Ash?"

Jasper nodded, a grimace marring his perfect features.

"What would ash be doing out here? It's not the season for bonfires, and we don't even have a pit for the building." Not that any of that mattered. I was beginning to realize most things in my life made no sense anymore, and for good reason. I had learned to go along with the weirdness and hope for the best.

"Exactly. What the hell is ash doing out here? I found a dusting of this outside your door too. I originally thought we might have tracked it in from the woods. But then the trail led out this way, and not the way we came home earlier."

I sighed. "So definitely supernatural then, I'm guessing. I can't see teenage boys leaving trails of ash behind on their breaking-and-entering adventures."

Jasper stood up, dusting off his still-muddy track pants. Only he could make a look like this work. He reached out a hand to help me up off the ground. "Unfortunately, only a few beings leave trails like this, and we don't want to get mixed up with any of them."

I snaked a hand under the back of his shirt, finding comfort in the easy contact with his skin. "Unfortunately, it's my job."

Jasper snatched my wrist out from under his shirt, instead twining my hands behind his neck so I faced him. "I know." His voice was solemn. "And I never want to take that away from you -- your strength, your power. It's a beautiful thing to see."

I trailed my nails down the back of his neck, loving the way I could feel each of his muscles contract under my touch. "But?"

"But..." He sighed heavily, touching his forehead to mine. "It doesn't mean I don't feel protective over you. We're mates, Ava. I have a responsibility to keep you safe. Inherently, your job is going to put you in danger." Jasper ran his strong hands down my spine, sending electricity through my entire body.

"I have a responsibility to keep you safe too," I whispered. "It's not all on you. We're in this together." I pulled his face down to meet mine, pressing my lips firmly against his.

He groaned, deepening the kiss and crushing my body to his chest. His tongue darted in between my lips, teasing me. I slid my hands up his neck, tangling my fingers into his messy hair. I gently tugged, knowing from experience the sensation always drove him wild.

Sure enough, when he pulled back his eyes were black, riding the edge of his wolf. I eagerly anticipated what was to come. But instead he fixed his gaze onto me, slowing his breath.

"I love you, Ava. But it's more than that. We're two halves of a whole. If something happened to you... I wouldn't survive it either."

"Oh, Jasp." I didn't know how to reassure him, or how to tell him I felt the same way. "I can't tell you everything is going to be okay, because no one can keep a promise like that. But I'll do the best I can, and I know you will too."

He nodded, still serious. "There is one thing. Something we could try."

"To keep us safer?"

Jasper hesitated. "Yeah. We could try the marking."

I let out a breath. "Oh."

He mistook my exhale as displeasure and began to ramble. "I would have never brought the idea up, except you offered at Christmas. But if you changed your mind it's okay. I know the marking is a big decision, and I wouldn't ever want to hurt you."

I lightly pressed a finger to his lips. "Stop. I want to. How does the marking help us stay safe though?"

Jasper's face immediately relaxed. "The bond I was telling you about before. It's amplified. I don't know how the link would look for you, but for me I'd be able to know exactly where you are. More so than just sensing you. I would *know*. And if you're in trouble, then I could help."

I stood on my tiptoes to kiss his full lips. "I love you. I want nothing more than to make you mine forever."

He closed his eyes, turning his face to the moonlight. "I can't believe this is really happening. I guess we should decide on a day when we want to do this."

I started to giggle, causing Jasper to turn to me, his expression one of utter confusion. "What's funny about all this?"

I caught my breath. "Nothing. Nothing at all. Just reminds me of what Mollie said to me earlier. She told me I'd be next to get married and I was pretty insistent a wedding wasn't going to happen. But this whole marking thing sure feels like a ceremony."

Jasper grinned, pulling me back against his toned body again. "Green, you telling me you wouldn't ever want to marry me?" His teeth tugged gently on my earlobe. "Because if I need to be more persuasive, then just say the word."

"Hmm..." I leaned into his body. "I'm not sure I'm entirely sold yet. What else do you have to offer?"

Jasper's hands circled around my thighs, lifting me up and wrapping my legs around his body. He carried me inside the front doors. "I thought you'd never ask."

* * *

Surely it was morning by now. I had been lying awake staring at my ceiling for so long the time had to be early morning. I rolled over to blindly snag my phone off the bedside table, hoping my clock would say a reasonable enough time I could at least go for a run. Unfortunately, the blurry numbers read 12:04 AM. Shit.

I sighed heavily, turning back over to lay my head against Jasper's chest. He sleepily raised his arm to circle my body, falling back asleep easily. Within moments his breath evened out, and he was deep asleep once again. As long as we were in the same bed, Jasper could sleep through anything and come out rested the next morning. If only we all could be so lucky.

I must have fallen asleep eventually, because the next thing I knew I woke up to screams. The piercing sounds filled my ears, ringing through my body. The screams of pain.

"Ava. Ava!" I could feel Jasper shaking me, and it was then I realized the person screaming was me. I took a deep breath, slowly opening my eyes to Jasper's face, the moonlight illuminating the concern written all over his perfect features. "Ava. Baby. Are you okay?"

I nodded, focusing on my breathing. The dream wasn't real. But anxiety was already flooding my veins and numbing my fingertips.

He kept one tattooed hand on my pounding heart, stretching over me to flip on the small light next to the bed. "Why didn't you tell me your nightmares were back?"

The taste of something evil still lingered in my mouth, like a forgotten apple left to rot. "I didn't know. But this one was… different."

"Different how?" Jasper's voice was husky from waking up, but his tone was serious. The nightmares he was referring to started after Christmas Eve. Dark figures hiding in trees, Jasper's broken body on the ground, and a feeling of utter despair. These dreams felt so real they usually ended with me screaming myself awake and they made him uneasy. Something he blamed himself for, but something he had no explanation for. Nothing more than the residual of a life left behind, or of a path not taken. The ghost of the dream still lingered around me, tendrils snaking up the back of my neck.

"The monster was me," I whispered. Jasper blinked, waiting for me to continue. "I was the dark thing hiding in the trees. And you came toward me, like you were going to kiss me. Your face was serene, Jasper, peaceful. And… and then…"

Unwilling tears sprang from my eyes, and Jasper gently wiped them away. "It's okay, baby. You don't have to tell me the rest."

But I could see in his eyes he wanted, or needed, to know. Whether I liked the idea or not, I was a part of a world now where my dreams meant something more than what I had seen on Netflix the night before. So I shook my head. "It's okay. It'll feel better once it's out." I counted to five in my head and started again, this time without emotion. "You came toward me. Trusting me. And I opened my mouth to speak to you, and all of this black smog came out of my mouth. The smoke was thick, and I couldn't breathe. It covered everything, and I couldn't see. And then when everything cleared, you were…" I paused, unable to say the word. Jasper nodded, understanding what I meant. His face was unreadable. "But it was my fault, Jasp. The monster was me. I was evil… I hurt you!" My voice steadily grew more agitated, and Jasper pulled me to him, stroking my hair.

"Shh… shh. Baby. It's okay. All of that was just a dream. I'm okay. I'm here." His voice was reassuring, but we both knew he didn't entirely believe what he was saying either. "We'll figure out why you're having these dreams. Together. Someone has to know what all this means."

The unspoken answer hung heavily in the space between us. My parents would know. But asking my family wasn't an option. My mother was missing, a trial awaiting her return, and I wasn't about to go have a cuddly talk with my prison-bound father.

Jasper kissed my forehead. "Are you sure you're okay?"

"I'm okay. I'm glad it all wasn't real. I don't know what I would do if…"

Jasper pulled me up so I was looking at him. "Hush. Look, I'm okay. I'm here. Nothing is going to hurt me. And I'm never going to let anything hurt you." I nodded, trying to believe him, and leaned in to kiss his bottom lip softly. Greedily, I deepened the kiss, wanting to feel more.

He caught my lip between his teeth, gently tugging. The motion sent a shiver down my spine. Jasper noticed and raised an eyebrow. Despite everything that had happened, I wanted him. I needed to feel him here, with me. Alive.

Jasper knew and tucked his mouth against my ear. "You need me, don't you?" he whispered darkly, trailing a finger up my thigh. "You need to feel my body against yours. My heart beating in time with your own. You need to feel whole."

Every word he spoke sent a shock to my core. Both because of what he was saying, and the fact he knew what I needed more than I knew myself. He slid his hand underneath the oversized tee I wore as a nightshirt, seamlessly hooking a finger into my underwear and tugging them down. Jasper's body was perfectly fitted to my own, filling all my physical spaces the same as he did my emotional ones. He pulled my shirt over my head, dipping his head lower to caress my breast between his full lips. I put my hand on his shoulder tugging him up and he looked up at me with confusion. I normally let him take command, but tonight I needed to feel like I was in control.

I pushed him onto his back, watching the confusion in his eyes shift to satisfaction. I straddled him, tossing my messy hair out of my eyes.

Jasper's eyes were black, his gaze running over my skin with a passion that could have set me afire. "You're the most beautiful creature I've ever seen. And you're mine." He dragged the back of his hand down my neck, down my waist, coming to rest on my hips.

I smiled softly at him, emotions I couldn't explain threatening to spill out. "And you're mine, Jasp." I traced the delicate lines of the roses on his chest. Jasper closed his eyes and held still as I did so. I trailed down across the muscles of his stomach, and across the sharp contours of his hip bones. I could feel his arousal growing beneath me, and I was surprised he hadn't stopped me yet.

As if I had conjured it, his eyes flew open. "Baby. You're naked, and perfect, and on top of me. I can't be responsible for my actions from this point on."

I laughed, running my hand down the soft skin of his cock. Jasper groaned beneath me.

I repositioned myself, letting the tip of his dick inside me slightly. His eyes were hooded, watching me intently. I met his gaze as I slowly lowered myself back onto him.

Feeling complete and whole once again, my moans mixed with his.

"Shit, baby. You're perfect." He clenched my thighs with his hands, willing me to move against his hips.

But I was in control. I raised up, lowering myself down again slowly.

"I love you, Jasper." I let my body take over.

His gaze was foggy as he met mine. "I love you. Forever."

I moved faster, allowing him to pump in and out of me in time. I needed this, to feel complete. Was the lust always going to be like this for us? A constant need, a craving so deep it couldn't ever be satiated? My desire for him always kept me wanting more. Another touch, another kiss. Or like now, for him to drive impossibly deeper into me.

Our pace was frenzied, and I could feel him losing control. I picked up the tempo, feeling Jasper shake and quiver within me. My orgasm came on furiously, and I cried out, watching him shatter into me.

I sank onto his chest, our bodies still joined. "God, I love you, Ava. You are my every want, my every need," Jasper whispered into my hair.

I sighed into his neck, letting our bond envelop me in a

comfortable bubble. My energy was completely different than how I had felt when I first woke up. I just needed to figure out how to stay in this moment instead of getting inside my own head.

I propped myself up on my elbows. "There's no way I'm sleeping anymore. I'm going to jump in the shower. Maybe I can still try to have a productive day."

Jasper murmured his acknowledgment, barely awake. I left him sleeping with one last look at his perfect form.

I turned the shower up as hot as the tap would go, letting the heat fill the shower as I undressed. I stood in front of the mirror, staring at myself. I wish I knew what was happening to me, what was going to happen. I thought I knew who I was becoming, but this dream had left me uneasy about the future. What if I had made a mistake? Steam started to fill the bathroom, fogging up the mirror. I started to bring my hand to wipe it and stopped. The fog on the mirror looked like something was written on the mirror. Maybe Jasper had written me a note when he showered earlier. I smiled at the thought, letting the letters slowly emerge with the growing fog.

But my stomach sank as the phrase grew more readable on the cloudy glass. This wasn't a love note. It was written clear as day in unknown handwriting.

The debt must be paid.

Chapter 3

For the second time that day my scream woke Jasper up. He came running into my small bathroom. "Ava, what is it? What's wrong?"

I pointed a finger toward the fogged-up mirror, the message still legible on the glass. Following my gaze, his mouth settled into a tight line as he read the words scrawled there. Not saying a word, Jasper left the room, coming back a moment later with his phone. He snapped a few photos of the mirror, then took his hand and wiped the mirror clean. Instead of five haunting words, I instead looked back at my blurry reflection, my face paler than ever. I had stupidly assumed I was safe in my home. How could I have been so wrong? And what the hell kind of debt did I owe? Fuck this shit.

Jasper met my stare in the mirror, his caramel eyes overflowing with concern. "We'll fix this. We have a whole pack behind us."

Turning the shower off, I wrapped a towel around myself and shook my head. "I'm not bringing the pack into this. The wolves were endangered because of my family once before. I'm not doing that to them again." My voice was firm. I meant what I said. My job was to help protect the pack, not bring more trouble their way. Jasper would either know I meant business and back off, or he would continue to push the issue.

Choosing the latter, Jasper narrowed his eyes. "I think the pack could help. We don't know what we're dealing with yet, but whatever is hunting you, it's too much for one person to take on themselves."

"Two."

"What?" His voice was tight. I knew I needed to stand my ground on this, but I also understood his temper ran thin when it came to my safety. Normally I didn't test his limits.

"Two," I repeated stubbornly. "You said it's too much for one person to take on, but there's two of us. You, and me."

Jasper gritted his teeth. "Ava. For once take your safety seriously. This isn't us hunting a dangerous creature. This is something deadly actively stalking you. I'm telling you the pack would be more than willing to help protect you."

"And I'm telling you I'm not letting them put themselves in harm's way again for me. We will figure out another way. The end." My words echoed off the tile walls of the bathroom with a finality. I knew I was playing with fire, but I didn't care.

Jasper's eyes flashed dangerously at me, and not the kind of danger I usually liked to see in them. He flung his arms in the air. "Fine. Have it your way, Ava. Play the hero." He pointed a shaking finger at the mirror, still defogging. "Let's hope for both our sakes you find whatever left this message for you, before they find you."

He stalked out of the bathroom and my heart sank. His words struck a chord in me. Of course it wasn't only my life I was gambling on here. Jasper's was on the line too. But I knew I was making the right call. Whatever this thing was had a personal problem with me, and it seemed only fair I dealt with them the same way.

I turned on the shower again, stepping into the steam. My neck was tight, and my muscles were far too stretched. My blood pressure felt like it was through the roof. I hated fighting with Jasper, but we were both so bloody stubborn that arguments were inevitable. Sometimes I wondered if the moon goddess or whoever was in charge of pairing up mates knew what she was doing when she matched us. But of course she did. Jasper pushed me to be better, and to train harder. But he also brought me a sense of clarity when I was too focused on making up for lost time. In return, I made sure Jasper knew when he was being stubborn and overprotective. I wasn't a damsel in distress anymore. We had both made certain of that.

The water ran cold by the time I got out of the shower. I avoided looking in the mirror as I grabbed my towel. Maybe a new apartment wasn't the worst idea in the world. If Jasper and I were even still talking, that is. Who knew what would be waiting for me out there?

I made my way back into the bedroom to find Jasper with his back turned, looking out the open window. Great. He was pouting.

I sighed and started finding clothes to wear. A glance over my shoulder told me Jasper was still pissed. I didn't understand why he couldn't let me have this one. My reasoning was entirely logical.

"Are we not going to talk about this then?" I sat on the bed, and Jasper didn't turn around from where he stood.

"What is there to talk about, Ava? You've made your opinion pretty clear." A quiet fury laced his words.

"Why can't you see where I'm coming from?" Jasper could be incredibly frustrating, and my own anger was escalating with his. I flew off the bed, stalking over to yell at his back. "You don't have to agree with me. But at the end of the day, it's my life. I will protect those people. Why don't you understand that?"

He whirled around, and his gaze was ablaze with anger. "Because I don't understand why you wouldn't take advantage of anything and everything to stay safe. To stay alive."

"This isn't their problem to be brought into, Jasper. It's mine. I'm supposed to keep them safe, and that's what I'm going to do." My voice left no room for argument. I grabbed his hand, tracing my finger across his worn knuckles. "Memento Mori," I whispered.

He snatched my hands in his own. "I never wanted this for you, Ava. I wanted to protect you from this life. But I was selfish, and I couldn't help coming back to you again and again. You shouldn't have to feel unsafe in your own home. To constantly wonder what's coming for you next."

My heart cracked. "Are you saying you… regret being with me?" I hated the wavering in my voice. I knew what he was saying wasn't a matter of wanting to be with me now, but maybe he wished he had made different choices. Easier choices.

Jasper's gaze snapped to mine, softening the slightest

bit. "No. Never. Not once. I guess I hoped there would be some magical way for us to be together without all the bullshit. All the fear, and the danger."

I shrugged my shoulders, trying to exude a confidence that wasn't there. "We don't even know what's doing this. Maybe it's not dangerous at all."

Jasper barked out a laugh. "I have some good guesses. None of them are friends you'd invite over for dinner."

I freed a hand, forcing his gaze to meet mine. "So, tell me what you think did this. Let's figure this out. Together."

He nodded -- a truce struck for the time being. Jasper immediately started pacing the room. "The easiest guess would be a witch. Obviously."

"Obviously," I repeated, sarcasm dripping. Tension still flooded the room between us, and his tone irked me.

Jasper stopped pacing, glaring at me. "Don't start with me, Green."

Not wanting to pick another fight, I gestured for him to continue. "And the less easy options?"

He pinched the bridge of his nose. "I don't even want to say the name. It's not right."

Taking my chances with his eyes closed, I rolled my eyes. Really. A werewolf scared of something's name. "Spit it out, Jasper. I have only your experience to rely on here."

Jasper cringed. "An... evil spirit."

I had to stop myself from bursting out laughing. But I didn't think he'd take too kindly to my humour, all things considered. "Like, an evil ghost? A demon?"

"I know you think you're immune to all of this shit, but don't say any more than you have to. I'm serious. Their names have the power to release them and summon them, and it's better to just play it safe and not say anything." He looked and sounded serious, and I had nothing to say.

A demon. Haunting me? Seemed pretty implausible. Hell, a witch sounded more realistic. Jasper shifted and checked his phone. "Shit. We're going to be late. I need to get dressed."

I nodded silently, not knowing where we stood. On the

same team, definitely. I was mad he couldn't see my side of things, but we needed to be one hundred percent on the same page to get anything done.

Jasper seemed to notice my uncertainty and bent to kiss my forehead softly. "My love for you is never in question. Doesn't mean I'm not angry. Grab your blades. I'll be ready in five."

I snagged my short swords from the backpack I had dumped them in the night before. Easily strapping them around my body, I knew I had the short drive to the pack lands to figure out how to make Jasper see things my way. I didn't know what to tell him. He would tell the Alpha regardless, and I couldn't stop him. But I could phrase my feelings in a manner that sounded like we had it under control. *Could you have a demon under control?* I groaned, rubbing my palms against my eyes.

Jasper cleared his throat behind me, and I composed myself. He had changed out of his sweats into a slim pair of jeans, a dark shirt emphasizing the thin lines telling his story across his body. "You ready?"

"Always. Let's go." I opened the door as he shrugged into the leather jacket I loved. I wanted to embrace him, to kiss him, but the tension was still heavy. We had things to figure out first.

Jasper led the way out to his bike, passing me the spare helmet. I straddled the bike behind him, knowing we were pressed for time. I needed to say something. Anything. Or for him to say something. But we were both silent.

Jasper sped along the still-quiet roads, the wind whipping through my hair. I had hated the bike when I first saw it. The speed terrified me. And then I began to see the thrill, and feel the adrenaline rushing through my body. The feeling was definitely an acquired taste, but one I had grown to love.

We pulled up outside the pack hall, and I ran a hand through my hair to try and make myself look presentable. After the absolute hell yesterday had been, I was pretty sure presentability was a lost cause.

Jasper caught my hand gently, getting my attention. He sighed heavily. "Look. I'm not going to pretend I'm not pissed, because I am. I think not using the pack is foolish and means taking unnecessary risks." I opened my mouth to butt in, but he held his hand up. "Let me finish, Ava. Despite all of my misgivings, you're right. It is your life. And if this is how you want to do it, then I'll do my best to respect your wishes. Respect, baby, not agree with them." He twisted his mouth into a crooked smile when I grinned.

I never said I wasn't a little bit competitive. "Thank you. I couldn't live with myself if anyone else got hurt because of me. Beau only stopped physical therapy a few weeks ago!" I felt like the weight on my shoulders was finally lifted.

Jasper grimaced, but thankfully didn't disagree with me. "Regardless, we need to have a united front for the Alpha. Speaking of, we should get a move on. Don't want to keep him waiting." He took my hand, leading me past the receptionist who merely waved us through. We were a pretty common occurrence around here.

Alpha Dean was waiting for us in his office. As was his manner, he didn't offer us any greetings or preliminary talk before diving into the reason he had asked to see us.

"I have a job for you." As usual, I was impressed with his smooth voice, and the amount of power the casualness hid. In fact, I was so distracted by his voice, that I didn't pick up on what he had said until a moment later.

"Um, a job for who? Jasper or myself?" Jasper squeezed my hand. Thank God we were talking again.

"Both of you, actually. Ava, I'll need you to stay on pack lands this weekend. Most of our younger scouts are headed out for a training weekend, and I would feel more comfortable knowing we had an extra set of eyes and hands on deck. If you don't mind." The Alpha's gaze was direct, and expectant. But I still looked toward Jasper, making sure he was cool with this change of plans.

"Of course, Alpha. Jasp, are you okay to stay here this weekend too?" But before Jasper could answer the Alpha cut him off.

"Actually, I have different plans for you, Jasper. I need you to go to Chicago this weekend and check a few things out. There's an Eastern pack moving to the opposite side of Chicago, and with you living there half the time I figured you would be the best mediator to send to make sure the transition goes smoothly. Borders, rules, you know the drill." His cool gaze focused on Jasper as I turned to him with wide eyes. *What*? We hadn't spent a night apart in months. And now, with everything going on, we were supposed to spend a weekend away from each other. This whole situation wasn't sitting right with me. Surely the Alpha knew how hard this weekend would be for us. He probably didn't care though, as long as business was taken care of.

"Oh. Sure thing, Alpha." It always astounded me how nervous Jasper seemed to get around the Alpha. The boy definitely had an authority issue. "But, does that need to be done this weekend? Meeting a new pack might go a bit easier if Ava came with me."

Alpha Dean raised his eyebrows subtly. "This weekend works fine for me, Jasper. Ava will be fine without you for a few days."

Jasper nodded. I knew he couldn't refuse the Alpha's quiet command.

The Alpha turned back to his paperwork, and our conversation was over. "Great. So, it's settled then. Ava, we will see you Friday. Jasper, you can leave me a full report when you get back on Monday."

Jasper met my eyes, and neither of us were happy. This was going to be a hell of a long weekend.

* * *

Friday found us both in my small bedroom, packing our respective backpacks. I sighed loudly, shoving another pair of workout pants into my bag. "Why did the Alpha decide you needed to meet this pack the same weekend they needed me on pack lands? I'm not comfortable with you being this far away."

Jasper smirked. "I thought you were sure you could handle this on your own, baby?"

Huffing, I balled up a shirt and stuffed the crumpled fabric in my bag. Good thing weekends with the pack didn't call for formality. I couldn't remember the last time we had done laundry. We'd been at my apartment for a week now, but between pack meetings and training, clothes just tended to pile up. "I believe what I said was the two of us could handle whatever this was, together. Not me on my own."

Jasper froze with his hand on a pair of black jeans. "Have you... seen anything else?"

"No, nothing." I shook my head. "But what if I do?"

"You call me." He acted like this was the obvious answer.

I glared at him out of the corner of my eyes. "Great. When some evil demon is cornering me in Adrian's bathroom, I'll ask him politely to wait a couple hours until my boyfriend can get there."

"Mate," he corrected me automatically, then glared back at me. "Don't say that out loud if you don't have to, even if it's not the name. It's an unnecessary risk. Anyway, whoever is playing games with you isn't going to attack you. They're going to drag the torture out. So yes, if you see something, you'll call me. I'll come as quick as I can."

"How are you going to get around the Alpha's orders?" I was curious. As far as I was aware, he couldn't disobey a direct order.

"Leave that to me to figure out. And I'd rather you stayed with Duke this weekend. If you wouldn't mind."

"I don't mind." Duke's guest bed was a thousand times better than a mattress tossed on the floor. "But will Lucy be okay with me staying?" Lucy was Duke's mate. She was a very sweet, gentle girl. But I didn't want to bring danger and drama into her placid life if having me over wasn't necessary. We usually avoided staying with them due to the general nature of both of our jobs. I knew why he was asking now. Duke's place was a bit more secure than Adrian's bachelor pad.

Jasper returned his attention to his bag, zipping the pack. "I've already asked them both. Lucy would love to have you. And before you ask, yes, I've told them the situation." I hadn't even opened my mouth to speak. But of course I had been planning to ask him.

He crossed the room to hug me, and I sank with relief into his strong arms. No one warned me it was this exhausting being strong all the time. "It's going to be okay, baby. It's only a weekend."

I rested my head against his warm chest -- my happy place. "I know. You'll be safe too won't you?"

Jasper tugged on my messy braid, turning my face up to meet his. "I'm always safe. Relatively speaking," he added, before I could make a face at him. "Besides, we have more important things to consider."

"Such as?" I wondered where he was going with this. I was pretty sure nothing took priority over the hell this weekend was going to be.

"We have a marking to discuss," he murmured, trailing his finger along my neck. I shivered against his touch, my heart contracting nervously. Jasper laid his hand on my heart and smiled. "Are you scared, or is that excitement?"

"A little of both." I wanted to give myself to him fully, and have Jasper be mine forever. But participating in a ceremony traditionally reserved for werewolves was still intimidating. At the end of the day, I was human. "Will the marking hurt?"

Jasper eyed me with caution. "I'm not going to lie to you. The bite is going to hurt. It's why I was hesitant in the first place. But I think the potential benefits outweigh my hesitations now. That's all you're worried about? If it's going to hurt?"

I shrugged my shoulders. "I mean, yeah. Should I be worried about something else? Side effects? Am I going to start howling at the moon?"

He laughed. "No, Ava. Nothing like that. I thought you might be a bit more concerned about the commitment side of things. You know, having second thoughts about being trapped with a dude who spends a lot of time running around as a wolf."

"It also means you spend a lot of time wearing minimal clothing, which I am definitely okay with." I dragged my finger down his chest to emphasize my point.

Jasper grinned. "I'll take it. I love you, Ava Green."

I stood on my tiptoes to kiss his soft lips. "I love you. One more thing though."

He lightly kissed me again. "Anything."

I hesitated. I wasn't sure how to say what I wanted to ask. Finally, I decided on spitting my thoughts out all at once. "Do I mark you in return?"

He looked at me seriously with his beautiful eyes. Eyes I constantly found myself lost in. Eyes I'd get to look at for the rest of my life. However long that ended up being. "Only if you want. It's kind of a grey area, with human/wolf mates. So, it's entirely up to you."

I bit my lip, considering, and then I nodded. "I think… I'd like to. If that's okay with you."

Jasper's face lit up. "Of course. More than okay."

"I don't want to be yours." His eyes narrowed at me as I continued. "I want to be each other's. Equals. And the only way that works is if I mark you too."

His expression softened immediately. "I understand completely."

How could I have ever thought Jasper, with his cocky attitude and dark clothing, would be cold and cruel? Those memories seemed like a different life.

Jasper cradled my face between his large hands. "So, how's Monday night then -- after I meet with the Alpha?"

Too soon. Too far away. I was half ready to tell him to mark me before he left tonight and half expecting myself to run out the door. "Perfect."

He kissed me deeply, moving his firm lips against my own. I knew the time apart was only a weekend, but my heart was acting like the time was going to be an eternity. I didn't want to let him go.

But too quickly he held me at arm's length. "I should

go. I don't want to, but I should. And you should too. Duke and Lucy are expecting you for dinner."

Jasper picked up his backpack off the bed. "Call me when you get there, okay? And make sure you double check all of the locks on the apartment before you leave."

"Got it."

He pulled me close for one last embrace. "I'll see you Sunday. And I mean it. If anything weird happens, you call me."

I smirked. "You mean, if I don't take care of them myself first."

Jasper pointed his finger at me, trying to look menacing as he walked out the door but his expression only made me laugh. "Be good, Green."

His laugh echoed down the stairwell with his footsteps, and I moved to the window to watch his bike roar out of the parking lot. I sighed, looking at the microwave clock. Only forty-seven hours and thirty-four minutes to go. I triple checked all of the windows and doors and swung my bag over my shoulder as I headed out.

The drive to the pack lands was quiet. There was no Jasper next to me cracking jokes or using every conceivable moment as a coaching opportunity. But there was no point in moping -- it was only a weekend. I was being ridiculous. I turned on the radio, flipping through the stations until a band Jasper couldn't stand came on. There were some perks to a solo drive. Smiling, I sang along with the radio, my mood brightening with every mile I drove. I could deal with a weekend apart. God knows, I had dealt with worse shit than a bit of loneliness. Besides, I could handle myself if anything happened. Everything would be fine.

I pulled up outside of Duke's cosy house and shot Jasper a quick text to let him know I had made it to the pack safely -- no funny business involved. I grabbed my bag off the back seat and walked up to the front door. Everything about Duke's house screamed Lucy's delicate touch, from the artfully arranged wreath on the front door to the perfectly landscaped flower beds encasing the wide windows. Before I could figure out where to knock without damaging the large wreath, the door swung open under my fist.

"Ava. Hi!" Lucy's voice was warm and excited. I liked Lucy. She was kind and had a great sense of humour. But her excitement didn't stop her from peeking behind me before she closed the screen. "You didn't see anything weird on your way here, did you?"

She pulled me into a quick hug and I laughed. "No, nothing weird. A normal everyday drive. You're as bad as Jasper!"

Lucy's smile lit up her delicate features. "I know. Don't tell Duke. I told him I wasn't the slightest bit nervous about any of this."

"Don't tell Duke what?" Duke walked out into the living room, slinging an arm around Lucy's slim shoulders. She bit her cheek, looking at me conspiratorially.

"Don't tell Duke how crazy Jasper is being about this whole break-in thing," I replied smoothly, eliciting a grateful glance from Lucy.

Duke was naturally reserved and cautious. But around Lucy his personality was a lot more easy-going, and he was quicker to laugh. I wondered if the differences in my personality were as apparent around Jasper. His laugh now was full of life. "Yeah, I don't doubt Jasp is being a little paranoid. I probably would be the same. Thankfully, Lucy has no interest in twirling knives or actively hunting down creatures in the night."

He playfully squeezed Lucy, who wrinkled her nose in return. "I'll stick with gardening, thanks. No danger involved. Speaking of, how is Jasper handling this weekend?"

She lifted Duke's arm easily off her body, motioning me to follow her into the kitchen. I took a seat at one of their barstools, and she slid me over a glass of red wine, taking a sip of her own glass as she waited for my answer.

I shrugged. "As okay as I am, I guess. It's not ideal. Thanks for letting me stay here by the way. I know it's not how you were probably hoping to spend your weekend."

"Ava, you're always welcome here. Seriously. I don't know why you guys continue to pay for two places when you can just stay here." She put her glass down and turned to stir a bubbling pot on the stove, muttering to herself the whole time. I smiled. Something all the wolves had in common was their stubbornness. Even those of them who didn't appreciate everything that came along with being a wolf, like Lucy. Jasper had explained to me that even for those who grew up in the environment, sometimes people struggled with their wolf half. Lucy was one of them. She played her part in the pack. She participated when called upon and shifted when necessary. But she avoided doing any more than the minimum, and Duke respected her wishes.

My phone started ringing in my pocket, and I held the speaker up to my ear without checking the caller I.D.

"Hey, baby." Jasper's smooth voice washed over me, and I instantly felt better. Not as great as when we were together physically, but a hell of a lot better than I had five minutes ago. And then I remembered everything else going on.

"Hey! Everything okay?" I asked.

"Of course everything is okay. I wanted to hear your voice." I immediately relaxed. But he sounded like I felt. Tired, lonely, and on edge.

I curled my knees up into my chest, balancing my toes on the edge of the leather barstool. "Is it stupid that I miss you already?"

Jasper chuckled. "Not in the slightest. I'm not looking forward to my lonely bed tonight either. Only thing getting me through this weekend is knowing I have Monday to look forward to."

Monday. Maybe I should add our marking to my list of things to stress over this weekend. I sighed. "This sucks."

"I know, baby. But I'll tell you what, if you get super lonely you can give me a call and tell me all the naughty things you want to do to me when I get home." Despite myself I laughed. I could picture him lying on the new bed I had forced him to buy and knew exactly what I wanted to do to him. "I should probably go. I have an early morning. Call me if anything happens. I love you, Ava."

"I love you too," I mumbled, and shoved the phone in my pocket. Stupid Chicago. Stupid Alpha.

I looked back up to see Lucy smiling sadly at me. She was a mate too, and she understood how I was feeling. How the time apart felt like I was being ripped in two, even for such a temporary time. I sighed and buried my head into my knees and let the smell of Lucy's pasta sauce fill my senses.

Only forty-five hours and fifteen minutes to go.

Chapter 4

I woke up in the dead of night, rolling over and expecting to find Jasper's warm body next to me. But I had forgotten where I was, and the other half of the soft bed was cold and empty. Duke and Lucy were nothing but the perfect hosts, and the spare room I slept in was small, but warmly furnished. The two of them distracted me with stories throughout Lucy's delicious dinner, and I found laughs coming easily with them. I felt at home.

But now, alone and in the dark, I missed Jasper. The hollow ache spread out from my stomach, encompassing my limbs and I knew there was no chance of me getting back to sleep. I groaned and snatched my phone off the dresser. He had said he had an early morning, but surely he could run on a little less sleep. I rubbed my blurry eyes and sent him a quick text, asking if he was awake. His response pinged back almost immediately. *This bed is too big.*

A trace of a smile spread across my lips. I knew he would be awake too. My eyes slowly adjusted to the dimness of the room, dappled in faint moonlight. Another message popped up. *Everything okay?*

No. Yes. Technically. I didn't know how to put my feelings into words. Surely the tingles of rebellion in my body were me being overdramatic. You couldn't miss someone this badly when you had seen them only a few hours prior. This feeling couldn't be healthy. I typed back an easy message. *I miss you.* Simple, but summed my feelings up. Concise, but barely scraping the true depth of my emotions.

Believe me, Ava. I miss you too. I knew Jasper did. I could feel him in every ounce of my blood. Sitting up in bed, I leaned against the headboard, settling into his words.

Why does the separation hurt like this? It's only a couple days. I feel like a drama queen. My fingers flew across the screen, sending the message before I could doubt myself.

My phone began to vibrate, waking me up even more than I had been a second ago. "Hello?" I whispered, not wanting to wake Lucy or Duke up. They were wolves, so this was a futile attempt, but I felt better all the same.

"Baby." Jasper's voice was warm on the other end, and I relaxed into hearing him. "I forgot you wouldn't know."

"Know what?" I continued to whisper, tiptoeing down the quiet hallway and silently sliding open the glass door. The moonlight was strong. We were close to a full moon, and the sky was free of clouds. In the bluish light, Lucy's garden looked like something out of an artist's mind. I took a seat at the painted picnic table, waiting for his response.

"About the distance." His voice was raspy with the night, and I could picture him lying under the duvet -- eyes closed, dark hair a mess. "Being apart is hard for mates, more so if there's actual distance. Especially if the pair haven't been marked. It's the soul's way of making sure the heart gets what it wants."

"Oh." I was quiet, considering his words. In a lot of ways, the mate thing was something I continually had to adjust to. I loved Jasper -- body and soul. But the idea separation would make me feel like a black hole was tearing me in a million directions was a lot to digest.

"What's on your mind, Green?" Jasper's voice was rich with amusement, knowing the gears in my head were working overtime.

"I guess, I…" I sighed, turning my face toward the cool moonlight. "I constantly worry maybe I'm not strong enough for this."

Jasper's laugh was quick, startling my eyes open. "Not a chance. I'm certain you were born for this. You're the strongest woman I know." My blood rushed with the compliment, but I still hoped for some sign among the night sky to tell me I was destined for this. That my body could and would handle anything thrown at it.

We were far from the bright lights of the city, and a thousand stars twinkled in the clear night. I chose the brightest one, and squeezed my eyes shut to make an ironic wish.

It was only when Jasper's soft voice caught me off

guard, I realized I had spoken aloud. "Oh, baby. How long have you been wishing on false stars? You were always the only one strong enough to control your destiny."

His loving tone made the words spiral in my belly, and I curled my toes in the damp grass underneath my feet, letting my body feel everything. He was right. I was strong enough. I stood up, turning to go back inside. But I wasn't ready to hang up.

"Will you stay on the phone with me until I fall asleep?" I asked, returning to my whisper.

"Of course. Anything." I made my way back to the spare room as silently as I could. My bed was ice-cold as I crawled into it, enough to send a shiver shuddering through my body. As I turned my body to get comfortable again, a shadow caught my attention. I whipped my head around, staring at the foot of my bed.

My heartbeat was loud, hammering in my ears. "Ava? Ava? You okay?" Jasper's voice sounded like it was miles away.

I shook my head, clearing my eyes of the tricks being playing on me. The room was empty, and nothing was at the foot of my bed. "I'm fine. I thought I saw something, but my eyes are tired."

I let his voice lull me to sleep, telling me stories about everything we would do when we were together again. Before I knew it, I was asleep.

* * *

The warm morning sun woke me up the next day, promising a beautiful day. Thirty-four hours and twenty minutes to go. Usually, weekends on the pack lands were pretty uneventful. We had left the additional cameras up from the winter, and I would usually check those, or hang out with the guys. I was there as a "just in case." A backup for a backup. After the massive breakfast Lucy cooked up, Duke followed me out to the woods. A companionable silence accompanied us. The grass was becoming green with all the rain we had gotten lately, and new buds were popping up on all the small trees. A new season. I breathed in the warm morning air, a light breeze ruffling my hair.

"So…" Duke sounded nervous, and that made me anxious. It wasn't like him. He was quiet, confident. Always level-headed, and always watching. I kept walking, waiting to hear what would come next. "We found Monica's scent the other day. Nearly had her too."

Monica. My mother. My mother who was supposed to be missing. Who I was supposed to have killed, if I hadn't been too weak. I stopped dead in my tracks. "I'm sorry, what?"

Duke's gaze was direct as he nodded. "Caught her smell while I was doing patrol ten miles out or so. She's smart though and knows what she's doing. Led us all over the damn place before we realized she had us crossing paths with each other."

I started walking quicker, as if I could outrun this whole problem, meaning Duke had to rush in long-legged strides to keep up with me. I shook my head fiercely. "What would she be doing this close to the pack lands? She knows being here is a death sentence. Maybe you had her scent confused with someone else." The thought actually running through my mind was… would I be strong enough to do what needed to be done this time? I needed to see her brought to justice for what she had done, and what she had wanted to keep doing. Killing all of the werewolves, and for what? Because she felt like she was destined for more?

Duke curled his hand around my upper arm, pulling me back. "It was definitely Monica. You forget I grew up knowing her, learning her scent. She was here."

My shoulders sagged with the knowledge. If she was close, I would have to come face-to-face with her again. I needed to prepare myself for seeing her. I closed my eyes, steadying my resolve. Justice needed to be done. Any feelings I had toward my mother were residual. Mere emotions I thought I should have for a maternal figure. The feelings weren't real.

"Are you okay?" Duke asked. Everyone kept asking me if I was okay, and if everything was okay. I was sick of it. I was fine. So I shook off Duke's hand, and started trekking toward the woods again.

"I'm fine, Duke. We'll find her and we'll do what needs to be done. Like we do every other day." He opened his mouth, looking like he wanted to say something. But he closed it, thinking better of whatever was on his mind. His footsteps fell into line behind mine as we did what needed to be done. Just like every other day. And one day this job would include taking down my mother.

Thankfully the rest of my day went by easily. Some of the sensors were in rough shape, which meant I didn't even have time to check my phone to count down the hours until Jasper came back. Duke also stayed quiet on the topic of my mother for the rest of the day. Thank God. We walked back through the field. Dusk was beginning to break through the trees. A light breeze tickled the back of my neck, bare from where I had pulled my hair up earlier in the day.

"I can't wait for the days to start getting longer again. Less darkness is always a plus in my books," I said, trying to make light conversation in an effort to apologize for my snappiness before.

"Soon enough." Duke gave me an amused look. "Although I'm surprised you didn't say you were looking forward to Jasper getting home."

"I figured it was a given. Only one more night."

He nodded. "I remember the first time Lucy and I were apart for a weekend. It was after we had acknowledged our mate bond, but before our marking. I felt like I was watching a lion eat my heart in front of me." It was the most poetic I had ever heard Duke speak. "You'll get through it. We all survive it. It's worth it, in the end."

It was worth it. I reached out to squeeze Duke's arm. "Thank you."

He looked bashful, like he had said too much. "Don't mention it. Now let's get back before Lucy sends out the cavalry."

We arrived back at their cottage to find another incredible dinner. Lucy must have been in the kitchen for hours. I let the aromas and warmth of the dining room settle around me like an old friend. This weekend really hadn't been as bad as I had anticipated. One more evening, and Jasper would be back in my bed. We joked and laughed throughout dinner, enjoying each other's company. I headed out to the front porch after dinner, letting my feet dangle from the old porch swing hung there.

Lucy poked her head out the screen door. "Everything okay out here? Do you need anything?"

I smiled at her. "No, believe me, you've fed me enough for weeks. I'm going to call Jasp and then turn in for the night."

She returned the grin. "Okay. We're going to head to bed. But maybe you can tell Duke's mom how much food I make next time you see her? For some reason she seems to think I'm starving her baby boy." Duke's indignant response came hollering out the door, and we both laughed. "Night, Ava. Double check the locks before you come in."

"Will do." She turned to go back into the house, and I dialled Jasper's number. The phone barely rang before he picked up on the other end.

"Ava." I smiled at the relief in his voice, echoing my own body. "How did the day go?"

The porch swing creaked gently beneath me as I briefly filled him in on the work Duke and I had done, leaving out any mention of my mother. That was a conversation better held in person.

"Good." His brisk manner was typical whenever we discussed anything to do with the pack. All business. Jasper's voice dropped an octave. "Now tell me how much you missed me."

The ripples of his voice were like electricity to my body. But I wasn't going to cave to him easily. "Oh, are you gone? I hadn't noticed."

I could practically hear his smirk as he responded. "So, then you wouldn't mind if I had to extend my trip a few days?"

"Don't joke." My response was quick, and it elicited a

soft chuckle from him.

"Maybe it would be easier for you to show me how much you miss me." Jasper's voice was raspy and quiet, leaving my ears straining and my heart wanting more.

"I guess you'll have to wait until tomorrow to see then." I trailed my foot through a small dirt pile on the porch. My voice was light but if I was being honest, tomorrow felt like years away.

"Or you could show me now." My head shot up so fast I nearly gave myself whiplash. Jasper stood at the base of the steps, looking beautiful as always. Leather jacket smudged and hair messy from the ride, and a sexy smile on his full lips. The only difference was the dark circles under his eyes. Obviously, he hadn't gotten a great night's sleep either.

"Jasper!" I leapt off the swing, running the few steps to throw myself into his waiting arms. His large body squeezed me tight, and I never wanted him to let go. "How are you here?"

"I drove," Jasper said drily, and I narrowed my eyes at him. "Alpha said I had to be in Chicago for negotiations. He was less explicit about where I had to spend my nights. I decided to take a chance, and luckily for both of us, my guess was right."

He gently tugged my hair back, bringing my lips to his, crushing me to him. "Thank God," he murmured. "I couldn't have made it another night." Jasper tugged my hand desperately, dragging me off the porch beside him. "Come on, let's take a drive. I believe there was some mention of you showing me how much you missed me."

"Jasp, I'm not even dressed!" I protested, motioning toward my loose tee and cotton shorts. His eyes darkened as he followed my hand's gestures, his gaze slipping down my legs as smooth as a touch.

"You're perfect." Jasper's words were flirtatious, but I always heard the underlying danger lacing his words when his eyes looked like this. "Now, come on. I love Duke, but I don't need him seeing what we're about to do." All my inhibitions went out the door with his honest statement, and

I let him pull me down the dusty path into the moonlit night. *Perfect.*

Jasper's movements were quick and desperate as I struggled to keep up with his pace. He stopped abruptly after the curve in the path, swinging around to face me head-on. He tangled his fingers in my hair, and his gaze drank me in. "God, baby, you have no idea how much I missed you." Both Jasper's actions and his words were tinged with restraint, like he was barely holding himself back.

Part of me wanted to laugh, to reassure him I had only seen him a night ago. But the bigger part of me knew exactly how he felt, because my body rang in tune with his own. I wrapped my arms tight around his neck, breathing in his woodsy smell. I greedily pressed my lips against his skin, eliciting a growl deep in his throat. "Don't tease me, Ava. I'm already at my breaking point, and I'll take you here if you don't stop." Jasper raked his warm hand down my back, fingertips dragging on my skin. His lips captured my own, hungrily pressed against mine.

I felt drunk in his presence and intoxicated with his obvious desire for me. I needed more, wanting to feel whole again. Standing on my tiptoes I put my lips to his ear. "So, stop talking and start doing."

He groaned, closing his eyes. "Fuck, baby. We're not going to make it to the bike, are we?"

"Not a chance." This time I pulled him behind me, through the brush beside the path until we were in the forest. The moon was so full I could see Jasper perfectly, his face glowing with the blue light. I stripped off my shirt, standing in front of him in my thin shorts, picturing his pupils dilating. But he still stood there, eyes full of longing. What was his problem? Definitely wasn't like we hadn't ever done this outside before. I took his warm hands, placing them over my breasts.

He sucked in a breath through his teeth. "There was somewhere I wanted to take you, first," he ground out.

Somewhere was going to have to wait. I shook my head.

"After. You're the one who proposed doing this now."

Jasper's dark chuckle sent shockwaves to my core. "Okay, fine. I'll stop complaining." Eyes flashing dangerously, he stepped toward me until my back was against a tree, the coarse bark scraping into my skin. "I'd ask you if you were okay, but you won't be noticing anything but me in a minute." He squeezed my breast, any pretence of gentleness now gone. Jasper dipped his head, replacing his hand with his mouth.

Gasping, I tipped my head back to rest against the tree. He was right. I didn't notice the scratchy bark. And I wanted more. I grabbed at his shirt, pulling the fabric over his head. Jasper helped me, desperately trying to get closer to me too. He tore my shorts down my legs, and I undid his belt buckle, pushing his jeans over his hips. I wrapped my arms around his neck as Jasper picked me up around my thighs, tightening my legs around his body. His hard cock pressed firmly against my wet pussy, but he made no move to enter me. I tried arching my hips into his body, but he wouldn't come any closer. His mouth sucked at the delicate skin under my ear. With my back against the tree again, and Jasper's mouth on my body I rode the fine line between pleasure and pain.

It wasn't enough. I needed all of him.

"Mark me," I begged.

Jasper was momentarily shaken from his reverie. "What? Now?" His voice was hoarse, and his gaze was unsure.

I nodded. "Now. I don't want anything else to be between us."

His eyes grew resolute, words tender. "Anything for you. Forever."

Jasper brought his mouth to my neck again, teeth pushing against the firm skin. I closed my eyes, my heart beating erratically in my chest. He was worth the pain.

The exact moment his sharp teeth broke the skin, his cock plunged deep inside of me. Pain tore through my neck as my body adjusted to the joy of having Jasper inside of me again. Colours flashed behind my eyelids. "Oh, Jasper!"

As quick as the pain was there, it was gone, Jasper delicately kissing the spot he had opened. "You did so good. You did perfect. You're perfect." Feeling me watching him, he glanced at me, our eyes meeting with a new intensity. "Perfect," he whispered.

My blood tingled with a rush of something new. It was like I could feel the emotion flooding Jasper's veins, in addition to my own. Jasper reared back and thrust into me. I clutched his strong biceps, kissing his chest as he moved within me. My body swelled with pleasure, but I couldn't give in. Not yet. I met his gaze, a question in my glance.

He moved deeper within me, turning his head to the side so I had access to his neck. "Do it. There was never any question I belonged to you." Jasper's movements didn't slow as I positioned my mouth on his smooth skin, making it hard for me to concentrate. I heard a smile in his voice. "Bite hard, baby."

I did. My teeth pierced his skin and immediately the taste of rust overwhelmed my senses. Jasper's growl echoed off the trees surrounding us, and he threw his arms around me, bringing me to the ground as gently as he could. I knew the focus took all of his control.

He rested on his forearms on top of me, bright teeth flashing in the dark. "Keep your eyes open. I want you to see me fall in love with you all over again." I locked my gaze onto his, feeling him drive into me again and again. I didn't close my eyes when I felt myself peak, or when I orgasmed around him. I kept them open the whole time, watching the unharnessed love reflected in Jasper's stare as he fell apart inside of me.

He rested his head in the crook of my neck after, our heartbeats returning to normal. Gently I touched the spot where Jasper had marked me.

"Does the bite hurt?" Jasper's soft voice surprised me. I had thought he had fallen asleep, because his eyes were closed next to me.

"Not really." I lightly trailed my finger over the mark

on his own body. My human teeth had barely damaged his perfect skin, but the bite was there. "I guess I expected I would feel different."

He opened one eye, propping himself on an elbow and squinting at me. "You thought I'd mark you and you'd instantly start hearing my thoughts?"

"Well… yeah," I admitted. I was clueless to how this whole thing worked. I thought I felt different. More connected. But I wanted some physical reminder of our permanency.

He leaned up on one forearm, and his muscles tensed under his tattooed skin. "Doesn't work like that. It'll take some time. Your body has to adjust to the feeling, like anything else. And honestly, I'm not sure if we will ever be able to share thoughts." He ran his finger across my mark, sending shivers through my body. Jasper smiled. "Looks pretty badass though, baby." He gently rolled off me, pulling his clothes back on. "As much as I would like to show you exactly how hot I find it, I really did want to take you somewhere."

Following his lead, I got up and put my shorts and shirt back on. "Does this trip involve the general public or am I dressed appropriately?"

Jasper pulled me to him, kissing my forehead. "It'll just be the two of us. Do you want to let Lucy know you won't be coming home?"

Shit. Lucy. I grabbed my phone from Jasper's pocket and filled her in on Jasper's surprise visit. A message came back almost immediately, telling me she already knew. Of course she did. *Wolves.* I shoved my phone back in Jasper's pocket. "All good. Let's go."

He led the way to the lot where his bike was parked, passing me my helmet. He kicked the bike into action, the motor roaring to life underneath us. I was regretting my decision to not change into pants, until Jasper squeezed my thigh, fingers digging into my leg. Maybe my wardrobe wasn't so bad after all. Was it just me, or did my spine tingle even more with his touch? To my surprise, he didn't turn toward Merrillan when he left the lands. Instead, he turned the opposite way, toward Chicago.

The drive didn't take long, and soon enough he pulled into a parking lot beside a small, rural apartment building. He parked, waiting for me to get off the bike. "Jasp, what is this place?" I asked, as he got off the bike behind me. If this was a work investigation I was really underprepared.

Jasper turned to face me, a broad grin on his handsome face.

"This," he said, pulling a small silver key out of his pocket, "will hopefully be our new apartment."

My jaw dropped open. I hadn't even seen the place. What if I hated it? "We only started talking about getting a place a few days ago!" I was in shock.

Props to him, Jasper was completely calm. "Yes. And a friend in Chicago was subletting this place. Perfect location, and zero paperwork in your name."

I rolled my eyes. This was exactly like Jasper to spring this on me. But I couldn't help the excitement flooding my veins. A home which would be ours. He kissed me gently, my mark tingling with the touch. "At least come look inside, Ava. If you don't like it, I'll talk to my buddy and we'll go back to your place. Okay?"

"Okay," I agreed. But unable to contain my excitement any longer, I smiled. "You didn't tell me this was what you wanted to show me!"

Jasper dragged me toward the small complex. "You didn't give me much of a chance before you jumped my bones and demanded I maul you."

A little dramatic, but yeah, points for accuracy.

The apartments were low, all on one level. Jasper stopped in front of the end one, juggling the key. As he opened the door I gasped, the theme for the evening seeming to be perfection. The space was small, but cosy. A bedroom, a bigger bathroom than my current one. An open kitchen. And best of all, a view of the woods.

I threw my arms around Jasper, hugging him. My heart felt like it was going to burst with the number of emotions I had for this man, the bite on my neck tingling pleasantly. "I love it. I love you."

Jasper laughed, the sound filling his lungs. "I think either the marking or the sex has gone to your head. Hopefully it was the sex, and not the injury causing your delusion."

I punched him on the arm. "Jerk."

He leaned into me, resting his chin on my head. "Mmm. I am pretty great, now you mention it." He twined a strand of hair around his finger, letting the lock run through like water. "Did the pack have a bonfire tonight?"

"No?" I was confused. What did a bonfire have to do with anything?

"Your hair. You smell like smoke. I thought maybe..." Jasper trailed off, and a pit grew in my stomach.

"Like the ash we found outside the apartment," I whispered. We locked eyes. "But I was only with you tonight, in the woods. We would've noticed something. And before I was having dinner with..."

We finished the sentence at the same time. "Lucy and Duke."

Chapter 5

Jasper flew down the empty streets, the drive back taking less than half the time of the original drive. I squeezed his waist tightly as we sped through the dark night, begging whatever god was out there we had made a mistake. We had read the clues wrong, and we would get back to Duke's house and Lucy would be fine. Duke could handle himself, but Lucy… I had pulled out my phone to call Lucy at the apartment, but it was dead. Same with Jasper's -- dead. Jasper peeled into the parking lot, and I was off the bike before he even fully stopped. I couldn't be certain what was moving faster, my brain or my feet. All I knew was my sweet, gentle friend was in danger and everything was most likely my fault.

"Ava! Ava! Wait!" Jasper's desperate yells followed me through the trees as I ran. "We don't know what we're getting into!" I almost paused, knowing he was right. I was unarmed, undressed, and literally running into a potentially dangerous situation.

Danger had also never stopped me before. I knew he wanted me to stop, make a plan. Think things through. But we didn't have time for planning. I didn't stop running and instead waved him ahead. "Go! Shift! I'll meet you there."

I heard his exasperated sigh from behind me, followed by the cracking sounds that told me he was shifting. Tree branches beside me rustled and shook as Jasper took off through the forest. Good. For once he could listen to me.

Duke and Lucy's cottage was at the opposite end of the lands from the parking lot. Because why wouldn't their house be so far? On a good day the distance was a ten-minute walk, meaning Jasper could do the run in a minute. As long as nothing intercepted him. Shit, I hoped Lucy would be okay. I imagined the worst, shaking the thoughts from my head as I ran. After what felt like years I could see the warm glow from the rustic porch light and urged my feet to move faster.

As their small cottage came into view, I almost tripped

on my own feet over what I saw. On the porch stood a very naked Jasper, a very angry Duke, and a frightened looking Lucy. Thank God. I exhaled loudly, trying to catch my breath.

"Lucy! You're okay!" I called over to her, catching the attention of all three.

Duke's voice was cold, catching me off guard. "Of course she's okay, no thanks to your jackass mate dragging her out of bed in the middle of the night." He wasn't angry. He was *pissed*.

Jasper shrugged his shoulders, glaring at Duke. "We had to be sure."

I ignored their arguing and climbed the steps. I embraced Lucy who stood woodenly with her arms at her sides. "I was so worried. Are you sure you're okay?"

She didn't try to return the hug, and I stepped back. Maybe Duke and Lucy were both pissed. "I'm fine, Ava. Ready to go back to sleep if this interrogation is over." She met my gaze blankly before glancing nervously at Duke.

"Yes, we're done." Duke glared back at Jasper. "Do you not think I know my own mate well enough to know if something's wrong?"

Jasper huffed. "It's our job to make sure she's safe."

"No, it's your job to keep the pack safe. It's my job to keep Lucy safe. You do your job, and I'll do mine." Duke's voice was filled with finality, and Jasper looked absolutely livid. Duke turned to me, and his voice was slightly softer. "Do you need a place to stay tonight, or are you okay?"

I opened my mouth to speak, but Jasper butted in before I could say anything. "She'll be fine. My job, right?"

I was still checking out Lucy. She wouldn't meet my stare and kept shivering in the warm night like she was cold. Something was definitely off. But we wouldn't be able to figure the problem out tonight without one or both of the guys ending up in the emergency room.

I put a gentle hand on Jasper's hot shoulder, feeling the tense muscles relax under my touch. "It's okay. I'll come back and pick up my stuff sometime tomorrow." I grabbed

Jasper's hand, tugging him down the stairs.

Duke and Lucy didn't say goodnight, but silently stepped into their house, the quiet click of the door the only sound in the dark.

Jasper didn't speak as we walked back to the bike, hand in hand. I knew he was upset about his fight with Duke, so I broke the silence first. "Please tell me you took your clothes off before you shifted. I don't even want to think how uncomfortable it's going to be for you to ride your bike in the buff." I tried to crack a joke, hoping to lighten the mood.

I was rewarded with a small smile. "As much as I think you'd enjoy seeing the nudity, baby, I was conscientious enough to take my clothes off before shifting."

"I'm sorry you fought with Duke," I murmured, meeting his dark gaze.

He shook his head. "It's not your fault. Duke can get high and mighty sometimes. He's always been like that. He'll get over it."

I nodded, hoping he was right. Duke and Jasper had been friends for so long, I'd hate to think of anything coming in between them, and I'd especially hate for *anything* to be me. "Did Lucy actually seem… okay to you?"

"No." His answer was quick, silencing any doubts I had in my own head. "But Duke was being possessive from the word 'go.' I couldn't get more than two words out of her. What did you think?"

"Something was definitely off. I don't know though. Lucy's such a skittish person it's difficult to see the difference between her normal level of anxiety, and something being seriously wrong." I wasn't sure what to think. I didn't want something to be wrong, but I also didn't want to make any rash decisions based on an assumption. "Why didn't Duke notice something wasn't right with his own mate?" I already knew I'd be able to feel if something was off with Jasper, and the mark had barely begun to sink in. He was everything.

Jasper shrugged. "Duke is a very protective person, especially when it comes to Lucy. His need to protect her from me is probably outweighing him seeing anything being wrong."

I nodded, processing. It was a lot to take in. What I really needed was sleep. We had made our way back to the parking lot and paused beside Jasper's strewn clothes so he could get dressed again. The night felt like months had gone by. Had it really only been a few hours ago we had marked each other? I subconsciously ran a finger across my neck, feeling the tingling sensation once again. The mark felt like those raised bumps had always been there, hidden under the surface, waiting for the right time to break free. "Where are we staying tonight anyway?"

Jasper tugged his shirt over his head, unsuccessfully hiding a smile. "I have a plan, but you're not going to like it."

I raised an eyebrow at him. "As long as it's not on the bike and I actually get to sleep, I'll love it."

"Remember you said that. Because we're going to Adrian's house."

He had to be kidding me.

I groaned dramatically and Jasper pulled me close to him. "Cheer up. It's for less than a night. Soon enough we'll be in our own place. That is, if you're still okay with the plan." His voice was cheerful, but I could hear the concern underneath. But he had no need to be worried.

"Definitely. Absolutely." He laughed gruffly at my quick response, the sound reverberating against my body. I peeked up at Jasper through my lashes. "You realize you're stuck with me now, right?" Rising up on my tiptoes, I kissed the slight mark I had made on his neck, feeling his body shudder under my touch.

"I'm not sure 'stuck' is the word I'd use, baby." His golden stare warmly locked onto mine. "Now come on. We have a blow-up mattress calling our name."

I wasn't surprised when we knocked on Adrian's door and he immediately answered, looking dishevelled but wide-awake. The time was late, but Adrian looked like he hadn't yet gone to sleep. If the pool table in the living room didn't scream frat boy, his erratic sleeping habits definitely sealed the deal. Emphasizing this point, Jasper poked his head around Adrian's lean frame to peer inside his small rental. "We're not interrupting anything, are we?"

Adrian ran a hand through his sandy-blond hair, laughing unabashedly. "Nah. You missed her." Narrowing my eyes, I pushed past him, collapsing on his worn couch. He was well aware of my disapproval toward his ever-revolving door of girls. Adrian threw his hands up in the air, feigning defence. "Don't look at me like that! She knew the score when she came home with me!"

He was digging his grave deeper. I remained quiet, pursing my lips. Adrian wisely took notice and changed tactics. "What's up with you guys anyway? I thought my air mattress was beneath you."

I caught Jasper's eye and shrugged in response to the question I saw reflected there. Secrets didn't keep for long in the pack, so he might as well spill everything now. At least that way he could get a handle on how the story came out. Neither of us needed more bad press in the pack. Jasper nodded, took a seat on the couch arm next to me and ran down the events of the evening. The explanation didn't take long, but by the time he finished, Adrian was slack-jawed.

"So, wait. Let me see if I have this straight." He pointed his finger at me, and then at Jasper. "You, a human, marked him, a wolf?"

The warmth of a blush spread across my face, along with a bit of pride. "Adrian!" I scolded, glaring at him again. I mean, I didn't expect Jasper to throw the marking into his rundown either, but was that seriously what he had taken away from everything going on? Men.

"I'm kidding! Kidding!" Adrian grinned at me. "Besides, we can circle back around to your marks later." I rolled my eyes as Jasper rested a reassuring hand on my shoulder.

Jasper turned his attention back to Adrian, expression serious. "Something is up, Adrian. We have responsibilities elsewhere and can't be here all the time to keep an eye on things. Beau won't be back from his camping trip for a while yet. We need you to be our ears and our eyes when we aren't here."

Always eager to please, Adrian nodded. "Whatever you need. You know that." Jasper did. As did I. Trust ran deep in the pack. The feeling of this instantly made me feel at home and was something missing in my own family. We never had honesty, so how could we have true loyalty? That was an impossibility. But I had found a family here, with these young werewolves. And I never wanted to lose the feeling. The powerful loyalty was also what made watching Duke and Jasper argue difficult. The rift slowly opening tonight would take time to heal.

"Baby. Ava. Are you listening?" Jasper's voice sounded like it was miles away. I was exhausted and lost in my own thoughts. I stared blankly at him, wondering what had been said.

Thankfully, he knew what I was thinking and repeated what he had said previously. "Adrian's had exposure to demons before. He'll be an asset. Okay?"

Adrian quietly beamed from Jasper's praise, before solemnly turning to me. "My aunt. In another pack. My mom made us all learn the signs and defences to be on the safe side. If that's actually what we're dealing with here, the situation isn't pretty." Yet again, I felt like I was in over my head. But I would figure the problem out. I smiled gratefully at him, before yawning uncontrollably.

I felt like I had been awake for weeks and I wasn't sure I could keep my eyes open another second. "Man, Ava, you look beat. We can talk about this stuff tomorrow."

I nodded. "I think the whole night caught up with me. I'm going to head to bed if that's okay."

Adrian gestured down the hall. "Bed's all made up." I glanced sharply at him, shocked. He shook his head. "Listen. I've been friends with Jasper for a long time, and I've learned it's always better to be prepared."

Instinctively I opened my mouth to ask what he meant, but thought better of it. I didn't need to know. At least not tonight. Jasper joined me in the hallway. "Thanks, man, I appreciate it."

Adrian's voice carried out down the short hallway. "Don't worry! You can tell me all about the marking ceremony I wasn't invited to tomorrow!"

"Yeah. Sure," Jasper muttered, following me into the tiny bedroom. "Really wishing I had left out that detail now."

"I heard you!" Adrian's voice was muffled but cheerful. Jerk.

I fell into the bed, fully clothed. I didn't care the bed was an air mattress. At this moment the mattress was the most comfortable bed I had ever slept in. With my eyes closed, the spare room could've been a five-star hotel in Tahiti. "Everyone would've found out eventually. People usually notice new marks right away, unless you cover them up."

I felt the weight of the mattress shift as he settled into the bed next to me, the warmth of his large body spreading through my own. "I know. Just would've been nice if we had been the one to tell people instead of Adrian running his big mouth." I heard Jasper sigh and felt him press a soft kiss to my temple. I thought he had fallen asleep, and I was close enough to sleep myself I wondered if I was dreaming already. But I heard his soft voice as he whispered into my skin. "Tonight was more than I could've ever hoped for."

* * *

Sunlight filtered in through the window in Adrian's small spare room, waking me up before I felt ready. I struggled to open my eyes, finding Jasper already wide-awake, caramel eyes watching me.

"Morning," I mumbled, trying not to be self-conscious. I probably had drool all over my face, and I could feel the imprint of the coarse pillow still on my cheek. But as usual, Jasper's eyes reflected none of this.

"Good morning," he whispered, brushing an unruly lock of hair out of my face. "I have to go. My first meeting is at ten and I've already waited too long. I didn't want to wake you up though. You seemed peaceful, for once."

I knew the urgency had to be the pull of the Alpha's order calling him back. Jasper wouldn't be up this early of his own volition. "I'll see you tonight?"

He nodded. "I'll see you at your apartment." He started to say something, then stopped himself, hesitating. His muscles tensed under his shirt in the usual manner when he was holding something back.

I poked his chest. "Spit it out, Jasp. Don't tell me you're regretting last night already." My tone was light, but it didn't stop a spark of worry from running through me.

Jasper closed his eyes, words spilling out. "There's a party on the new pack's land this week. I have to go. Alpha wants you to come with me, representing our pack."

"But...?" I waited for him to continue, mentally preparing myself for the end of his sentence. A party couldn't be enough to stress him out.

"This pack. They're old fashioned. Most aren't the biggest fans of human and wolf mates." His face was apologetic, and I knew it wasn't a conversation he wanted to be having.

I groaned in frustration. "Oh, you have to be fucking kidding me. As if we didn't deal with this enough from my parents, now we have to be professional about it?"

Jasper lightly kissed my forehead. "I know. Believe me - - I know. I want nothing more than to shout about our marking from the rooftops and tell everyone we're mates. Marked. But it's probably safest we keep the bond under wraps. Because you still read as human for most wolves, and we can cover up the marks it should be fairly simple. We can talk about the party more later."

"Under wraps, my ass," I muttered. I was not okay with this. What did he expect me to do, buy out the concealer aisle at the drugstore?

Jasper smiled, knowing exactly what was going through my mind. "I'll see you tonight baby. Be careful today." The door clicked softly behind him as I flopped back into bed. As soon as he was out of sight, I was desperate for him to return. To make me feel whole once again.

Ugh. I was awake anyway. I might as well make the most of it. I had one last day to hang out on the pack lands. Originally, I had planned to spend the day with Lucy. I didn't think girl time was still in the game plan. But there was always work to do. I dragged myself out of bed and headed into Adrian's small kitchen. Hoping for the best but prepared for the worst, I scavenged in the fridge to try and pull some breakfast together.

I closed the fridge and jumped -- Adrian stood leaning against the counter, arms crossed. "Jesus, Adrian, you'll kill me one of these days." Fucking wolves and their fucking stealthy walks.

He ignored me. "Duke dropped your stuff off early this morning. Like, really early." He gestured to my bag next to the front door, my blades set carefully on top. "You know, you're the first human I've met who marked a wolf."

I huffed. Men. One track mind. "First time for everything, Adrian."

"It's a pretty big deal. Did Jasper explain everything about the marking?"

"You mean about the mind reading, and basically owning each other's souls? Yeah, I got that much." I couldn't help traces of sarcasm from threading through my voice. The mark was not subtle as it pressed through every cell of my body, demanding Jasper's presence.

"It's more than possession. It's two bodies functioning as one." Adrian sighed, putting his hands on my shoulders. "You know I love you like my own sister, Ava. But you have to take the marking seriously. Which means you need to take your safety seriously. You two are linked now. I don't think Jasper could take the pain if something happened to you."

I met his gaze. I knew what he was saying was true. I had felt the connection in my own body for weeks now, and more so since last night. I doubted I could handle if anything happened to him either. It was why Adrian needed to know he was safe with me around. "I know. My intention is to keep both of us out of harm's way. We're going to take this demon down before they can touch either of us."

Adrian made a face at my casual use of demon, before smiling. "I don't think either of you understand what it means to not be in danger."

It was a joke, but his words sank like a brick in my stomach. He was right. I needed to take care of this demon before I put Jasper into any more danger. I gave Adrian a brief hug, dumping all the food in my arms on the table as I tugged my shoes on. I pulled my bag on my shoulder and grabbed a blade in either hand.

"Aren't you hungry?" Adrian called out to me as I ran out the door.

"I'll eat later. Thanks, Adrian!" He had made some good points, and I knew where I needed to go today. I had to look up demons at the pack library.

Chapter 6

Six hours later I rubbed my blurry eyes, all of the words on the page spinning in front of me. The decision not to eat before I left had been a mistake. Now I was frustrated and hangry. Not a great combination. The pack library was devoid of any information about demons, except for the repeating warnings to avoid them at all costs. Looked like even big bad werewolves had some scary enemies. *Fuck.* I really wanted to be able to take care of this on my own, to be able to keep everyone out of danger. Especially Jasper. I needed to protect him at all costs. But if the books couldn't help me this was going to be useless. As if I summoned him, the bite on my neck started to tingle. A voice called my name, and I turned toward the door. But no one stood at the door. I turned back to my book.

Again, the voice called me, and it sent a chill down my back. Jasper's voice. Desperate, and in danger. "Ava, help!" The only image in my mind was that from my dream -- Jasper bleeding out onto the ground in front of me.

I reached behind me to make sure my blades were securely strapped to my back, and slammed the useless textbook shut in front of me. Jasper wasn't supposed to be back for a few hours, so the fact he was already on pack lands was a warning signal I couldn't ignore. The small town square was devoid of people, so when he yelled my name again I could hear it clear as anything. It was coming from the tree line, near the sensors we always checked. Maybe something was wrong with one of them. I ran out past the main buildings, and paused for only a moment, wondering if I should let Duke know. Usually, I took him or Jasper with me for situations that might be dangerous, but there wasn't time to argue with Duke right now. I could feel that down to my core. So I turned away from the lane leading to Duke's house and picked up speed, running across the field as fast as I could. I hit a rock just beyond the tree line, but caught myself before I could stumble and fall.

"Fuck," I muttered, gaining speed once again. "Jasper?

Jasp, where are you?" I paused, waiting to hear where his response came from. A light sweat coated the back of my neck as I yanked my hair up into a tight bun. "Jasp, this isn't funny anymore." If he was playing some kind of sick joke on me, then he was going to get dish duty for a month.

"Ava! Hurry!"

From the left of me. I sprinted through newly budding saplings and the still dense evergreens, the sun bright above me. Until I ran through a cluster of trees and stumbled into utter darkness.

Shit. I couldn't see my hands in front of me. Somehow I had wound up in one of the small caves dotting the forest. I tried to retrace my steps back, waiting for my eyes to adjust to the thick blackness surrounding me. *What the hell did I get myself into?* Jasper was not going to be happy. I touched my blades, making sure they were still there. "Jasp? Jasp, can you hear me? I think I'm in a cave. I can't see a thing."

I was trying to steady my heartrate, and not let fear get the best of me. It was just one of the caves. Tons of boulders had shifted over the years, making these small caverns that were dark as anything. The fact Jasper still wasn't responding though... that made me nervous. I took a deep breath and counted to ten. This was nothing. "Jasper!"

I felt the presence near me before I heard them. "Jasp! Jasp!" The voice was a weak, mocking imitation of my own calls for Jasper.

I would *not* let the fear control me. I whipped my swords out and down spinning around in the darkness as if that could help me. "Who the hell are you?"

"So weak. Weak little Ava Green. Yes, I've heard about you. And the rumours must be true, because you fell into my trap so easily." The voice laughed, but it might have been a cough -- a dry, croaking sound.

"Don't fucking mess with me," I gritted out, sounding a hell of a lot tougher than I felt. I gripped the hilts of my blades tightly, ready to strike and get out of this darkness.

And then something was around my neck, choking me. I gasped, trying to suck in any air I could. "Stupid girl. Did you really think you were going to get me before I got you? I need you compliant, and for you that means unconscious."

Fuck. That. Shit. I needed to keep my head, and I couldn't do that if I was desperate for air. I relaxed my body, thinking back to all the trainings Jasper and I had done. Not running away from my fear, but using it as leverage. The thing behind me felt human. At least, human enough to have an arm. I cranked my head to the side and the air pocket in the crook of this arm gave my throat just enough space to expand. I sucked in a couple quick breaths as quietly as I could, oxygen pulsing through my blood once again. Now I could breathe, I could focus on taking this thing out. I still had my blades. Thank God for that.

"Yes, my master will be so pleased." If I never heard this voice again, I would die a happy girl. I twisted my hips to the side, feeling nothing behind me. Good.

"Your master is going to have to wait." I threw my weight back, and the thing screeched as I caught it off balance. It stumbled far enough away from me that I took a blind aim, slashing toward where I guessed its thigh would be. I hit my target, hearing another ear-piercing cry as I turned and ran. Hopefully it was the right direction, but I had no idea. I couldn't see anything behind me or see anything ahead of me, but I put one foot in front of the other. Finally, I stumbled into blinding sunlight once again. I wanted to cry. I wanted to scream. I wanted to run right back into the darkness and make sure that thing was never coming out again. I ran as fast as I could through the woods, bushes and branches scratching my arms and face as I moved.

"Ava? Ava!" I could hear Jasper's desperate cries again echoing through the forest, and I was ready to turn and run the other way. But then I saw his dark shaggy head peek out from behind a tree, and my heart stuttered.

"Jasper!" I had never been so grateful to see his face and leapt into his arms. He squeezed me back tightly, and I could feel his fast heartrate levelling out. "How did you know where I was?"

"The bond... the bond told me where you were the second I stepped onto pack lands. I could feel your fear." He put me down gently, running his hands over my face. "Are you okay? What the hell happened?"

"I'm fine. I'll have a few bruises in the morning, but I'm okay. I think it was the demon." I paused, taking in his scowl. "Do you remember when you told me you tracked Sheriff Kelly into a cave, and you couldn't see?"

Jasper nodded, and his mouth was set in a hard line.

"It was like that. I couldn't see, but I should've been able to. It was unnerving."

He placed a light kiss on my forehead. "What happened next?"

"It lured me out using your voice. It knew my name..." I trailed off, gathering my thoughts. "It tried to choke me, but I got it pretty good." I glanced down at my sword, covered in a light sheen of blood.

"So it had a human body?"

I shrugged, finally coming down from the events of the past few minutes. "It must have."

Jasper pulled me to his side tightly but released me when I winced. "Sorry, baby. Bruises. I forgot."

I squeezed his hand. "I'll heal. Is it safe to leave with this thing on the loose?"

He sighed. "I hate to say it, but whatever this thing is seems to be after you. I'll tell Adrian to give us a shout if anything unusual happens, but I think we're going to have a harder time than him."

I nodded, willing the fear in my body to be replaced with the knowledge that I was going to take this asshole down. "I just need to grab my stuff from the library and then we can go. I want to get far away from this forest right now."

We made our way back to the library, Jasper quizzing me on every second of my interaction with the demon while we walked. If I hadn't been so grateful to see his handsome face, I would've been a lot more annoyed with his nonstop questions.

"Jasper, it was dark. I'm telling you as much as I can remember." And honestly, I'd rather remember less. I wanted to go back to my research and figure out how to take this thing down without Jasper winding up as collateral damage.

We walked inside the library and I started tidying up my stacks of books, making sure to keep aside the ones that seemed to have anything at all. Jasper started stacking books as well, haphazardly, and the papers I had been taking notes on began to fly everywhere.

"Fuck," he muttered, and started grabbing the ones falling to the ground. But he laughed as he recognized my handwriting. "Back in school then?" His laugh trailed off as he realized what was written on the paper. I knew what the page said. It was only one word.

Orcus.

"Ava... what is this? Do you think this is what's hunting you? I thought I told you to avoid names. They have power. More than either of us will ever understand." Jasper's voice was quiet, and I knew he was unimpressed.

"I needed to know more. I was hoping I could find something to fix everything. Before the problem got worse. I thought maybe if I knew the name of it, I could figure out how to get rid of it." I couldn't look him in the eyes, couldn't acknowledge how terrified I now was for my friends. My family. My bruises ached -- a reminder that this thing was very real, and very dangerous.

Jasper crumpled the paper in a tight fist, before pulling me into his arms. "We're going to figure this out, Ava. Together." His voice was tender and reassuring, but I could feel the panic racing through his veins as easily as if the feeling were in my own body. He was scared. The mate bond was going to betray us both.

* * *

I woke up in the night, but I wasn't cold. The air was humid, and beads of sweat were forming on my skin. I tried to push the blankets off, but the covers weren't on top of me anymore. I needed to open a window. I needed air. Opening my eyes, I looked around, and then did a double take. I wasn't even in bed. I was outside, on the stretch of highway between Merrillan and Easton where there was nothing except for farmer's fields. A heavy thunderstorm was brewing in the distance, the culprit of the thick humidity. It was turning the still-dim sky a bruised shade of purple. I had to be dreaming. But the scene felt so real, I could practically taste the approaching rain, and could almost feel the lightning in my bones. This wasn't my normal nightmare. The storm rolled ever closer, darkening the bright fields. Somewhere close, someone screamed.

"Ava, why are you screaming?" Jasper's quiet voice tickled my ear.

I whirled around. Jasper was never alive in my dreams. Why was he there?

His face was alight with wonder as he tucked a loose piece of hair behind my ear. "How did you do this, Ava?"

"I… I don't understand," I whispered.

"Show me how you summoned the storm. Show me how, and I'll show you how it feels to be truly awestruck." Jasper bent his head, kissing me as the storm broke over us, kissing me until I was alone once again. The storm raged as I screamed.

I woke up screaming.

"Ava! Ava! It's okay. You're okay." Jasper's perfect face was above me, gaze concerned in our dark bedroom. His fear was quick in my own veins, a reflection of the marking tying us together.

I took several deep breaths as I took stock and patted the sheets around me. I was awake. This was real. But I needed to be sure. Needed to know my mate was physically next to me, safe.

"It was different. You were there, talking to me, and…" I trailed off, shaking my head. It didn't matter. "Kiss me," I begged. I need something to centre me in this world. Not a dream.

He obliged, crushing my lips against his until I wasn't thinking of anything except for the feeling of his skin on mine. Jasper slipped his hands down my body, urging my thighs wider. He stroked the soft skin between my legs, and I could feel myself growing wetter with each gentle pass of his fingers.

"Let me help," he whispered, curving his body over mine. I parted my legs without thinking, and he groaned as he discovered for himself how wet I was. I arched my back as he dipped his finger inside of me, the pleasure snaking up from the tips of my toes. Jasper slipped another finger into my pussy, and there was no doubt in my mind this was real. I gasped as he curled his fingers up, rubbing my swollen clit with the heel of his hand.

His movements were intoxicating, and *he* was a drug I couldn't get enough of. I could feel the pressure building deep within me, needing a release. Jasper's fingers stroked the perfect spot as he pressed down with his hand and I cried out as I rode out my orgasm. I smiled at Jasper, my mate, knowing there wasn't anything more I needed from this life than him.

* * *

I checked my neck in the mirror again. And again. I barely recognized myself anymore. The dark, fitted clothes. The muscles I had worked hard for. The face of someone betrayed one too many times, by those who she assumed loved her. I tugged my shirt down, hoping the fabric was long enough to hide the sheaths I wore on my back. I patted the thick concealer, hoping the makeup wasn't too noticeable. It felt wrong to cover up something so precious. Thankfully my bruises from the other day had healed, so that was one positive. The memories still lingered though, and I knew I was running out of time to solve this problem. I was directing my focus on looking up one -- *Orcus*.

"Baby. Stop touching the makeup. You look perfect." Jasper tugged me away from the tall mirror, spinning me in his arms to meet his warm caramel gaze. "Now, remember what I told you?"

I sighed. "Don't go anywhere alone with anyone. Always be on my guard. Always be ready for a fight," I parroted, raising an eyebrow at him expectantly.

"Perfect." He tipped my chin up with his finger, kissing me so deeply I could feel my bones crying out for more of him. I had thought I couldn't get enough prior to the marking, but I had been sorely proven wrong. "That'll have to last us both until later."

We were getting ready to go to the new pack's party in Chicago. I had fought tooth and nail to not have to hide our mating, but Jasper had stood his ground. The man was immovable when he wanted to be, and I had to pick my battles. To the costume store I went, to get the thickest possible concealer for both of us. The thick paste would have to do. And even though this was a getting to know you party, Jasper insisted I arrive armed. Both of us would be.

"This pack isn't like ours, baby," he had said. "They don't have a Venator. They aren't fans of human mixing. But Alpha wanted to be clear on where we stood. Your presence is necessary."

Necessary, but the image they were presenting of me was a lie. I wasn't innocent. I wasn't harmless. I had the blood of a thousand Venators running through my veins, and the possessive mark of a deadly werewolf on my neck. This pack may not believe in Venators, but they had another thing coming for them if they expected a passive human to toy with.

Jasper drove us to the outskirts of Chicago, where the houses were still spaced far apart and set back from the road. He led us down a narrow road, to where a small home was nestled in the tree line, cheerfully lit in the full dark. I don't know what I had been expecting, but I definitely wasn't expecting a normal looking house party. Music blasted out of the bright windows, with people milling about in the yard. I could see still more guests inside.

I subtly touched my blades again, for reassurance. A party full of werewolves. Easy. Jasper reached across the seat and squeezed my hand. "It'll be fine, baby. You can kick all of their asses if you need to."

I groaned. "Not the motivation I was looking for.

Mingling isn't really my thing."

Jasper chuckled. "You'll do great." He brought my hand to his mouth, kissing my knuckles softly. "Don't let anyone else sweep you off your feet."

I snatched my hand away and rolled my eyes as I got out of the car. "As if. Besides, hiding our marks was *your* idea."

Jasper grabbed my wrist back, pulling me into the dark shadows on the other side of the car. He pinned me between his firm body and the car, trapping me between his arms. I watched his muscles tighten and ripple beneath his fitted shirt as he struggled to control his emotions. "Don't think for a minute this isn't hard for me," he breathed. "Acting like I didn't have you screaming my name from underneath me this morning. Pretending like I won't be fucking the hell out of you again later tonight."

I could feel desire flooding his body, coursing through the mate bond which only amplified my own cravings. *Shit.* How was I going to focus now?

Jasper smirked, and I knew he was fully aware what he was doing. "Let's go, Green. Our new friends await." He ran one last longing look over my body as I tried to catch my breath.

We walked into the party together, but far enough apart we seemed like colleagues. Nothing more. He introduced me to several burly men, all of their names and faces blurring together. They gave me polite nods, but didn't seem to care who or what I was. After all, to them I was nothing more than a lowly human. Some people sniffed openly at me as I brushed past, knowing I smelled… different. Other. And without Jasper holding my hand, I was either a threat or a meal. Jasper tugged me over to where a few women stood, drinking sweating cans of beer.

"Ava. This is Sage. She's the Beta for this pack." Jasper introduced me to the tallest woman as her friends looked over me curiously. A female Beta? I had thought the pack was old-fashioned. Sage was stunning, with bright blue eyes and masses of golden hair spilling down her exposed back.

She certainly didn't look like a deadly Beta.

"Don't hurt yourself trying to figure it out." Sage's voice was cool and laced with disdain. "You humans and your emotions are so... easy."

Easy. Irritation pricked under my skin, and I was ready to snap back until I felt Jasper place a tense hand on my shoulder. For the pack. I was here for the pack. "Ava is our new Venator."

I gave Sage an icy smile and offered my hand. "Pleasure."

She looked down her nose at my offered hand before turning to Jasper. "Jasp, you ran out before we could finish our dinner the other night."

Jasp? Why was she familiar with my mate? And why were they having dinner? I could feel anger bubbling in my stomach. He needed to have a damn good explanation for this. Jasper shot me a warning gaze out of the corner of his eye, but I ignored him, waiting to hear his response.

"I had other matters requiring my immediate attention." His voice sent sparks through my carefully hidden mark. *Oh.* Still didn't explain why they were having dinner.

Sage tossed her casually curled hair, arousing the attentions of several wolves in the surrounding area. She was obviously used to getting what she wanted. "We'll have to find another time for us to get together then. I had *so* much fun." She glanced at me as if to dare me to interrupt the conversation.

"Yes. We will." Jasper took my elbow, steering me toward a leaning table stacked with beer. "I have to be on Sage's good side. She's the Alpha's sister," he murmured under his breath, covering up the sounds of his whispers by opening a can of beer. "Can you handle making the rounds on your own now?"

I glared at him as openly as I dared. "Yes. But we can talk about your convenient memory lapse regarding your dinner with Sage later."

He handed me the beer and grinned. "I had other

things on my mind. Come find me in a bit."

I scowled at his receding back as he turned and walked into the crowd, immediately striking up a conversation with another man who had called him over. And then I was on my own, at a party. How hard could mingling be?

As I leaned against the wall near the beer table, I'm sure I scared away everyone within a ten-foot radius. Some of the teenaged wolves smiled and giggled as they walked by in groups, but I was left alone for the most part. I nursed my beer, wanting to keep a level head as I kept an eye on Jasper's tall frame as he worked his way around the room. I was always awkward in group settings. Alpha Dean had really made a mistake sending me into a party to build relationships. The anger I could feel radiating off me toward Sage probably wasn't helping things either. She was currently laughing loudly with her hand on another man's chest. Fucking Sage. Telling me I was human. Telling me I was *easy*.

"You're the Venator right?"

I startled from my angry inner monologue to find one of the werewolves standing in front of me, smiling warmly.

"The one and only." I raised my beer in a sarcastic toast, giving him a half smile. "But you can call me Ava."

He clinked his own beer can in response, humour alight in his eyes. "I'm Mick. I've never met a Venator before."

I shrugged my shoulders. "Not much to it. At the end of the day, it's a job." Small talk was not my forte. But I had to do my best for the pack. Mingle. Make people like me.

"Come on. I can see those pipes hiding under your shirt. You must work out nonstop. I bet you could even take me down." I raised my gaze to look directly at Mick. Was he flirting with me? A quick glance over his shoulder to Sage's evil glare told me he was. Time to have some fun.

I smiled sweetly at Mick, tossing my hair over my shoulder the way Sage had done. "I'm sure I could take you down in more ways than one."

Mick's smile grew larger, taking on the hungry quality I had learned to notice in Jasper's amusement. He *was* hitting on me. I hoped Jasper was watching. *Would serve him right if another wolf hit on me after the way Sage was eyeing him.*

Ava. I heard someone call my name, clear as anything. I spun around before turning back to Mick and gave him an apologetic look. "I'm sorry, did you say something?"

He cocked his head. "No?"

I brushed the strange feeling off, and ran my fingers through my hair, enjoying knowing Mick was watching me. I would've put money on the fact Jasper was keeping tabs on Mick. I took a sip of my beer and nearly spit it out as the voice echoed through my head again. *Behave, Ava.* I knew whose voice that was -- Jasper's. But when I tried to meet his gaze, he was trapped in conversation with one of the elders. Couldn't be him. Could it?

The mate bond. He said the bond usually allowed for telepathy, but he didn't think such a thing would work for us. Obviously, he had thought wrong.

Did you hear what I said? Holy shit. Fuck. Fucking hell. What was I going to do now? Could he hear *everything* I was thinking?

If Jasper could hear my questions he ignored them, the slight smirk on his lips the only indication I had telling me he understood what was going on. His voice purred in my head, equal parts warning and seducing. *Don't play this game with me, Green. You'll lose.*

Asshole. We'd see about that.

Chapter 7

I gave Mick my full attention. "Sorry, I thought someone was calling me. Obviously, I've had too much beer." I giggled, hating every second of the sound, and placed my hand on Mick's bicep. "What were we talking about?"

Point proven, Ava. Now stop. I looked up at Jasper's voice in my head to see him still talking with the elder, but his shoulders were tense, and he was clenching his jaw.

Mick was all too happy to encourage my advances. His gaze flickered over my tight clothes before returning to my face. "I believe, Venator, you were going to tell me all the ways you could take me down."

I smiled, toying with my prey. "Maybe that's something better demonstrated?"

Mick raised his eyebrows and opened his mouth to respond when a weight hit my side. Jasper. He wrenched my arm and proceeded to drag me away from Mick.

"What the hell is wrong with you, man?" Mick asked, confusion and anger written all over his face.

The room fell quiet, and people were staring. Sage was gaping at what was happening. I tried to figure out how to talk to him, shooting thoughts at him mentally before he said or did anything he regretted. *Jasp. Jasp!*

He was either ignoring me or I wasn't doing the mate bond thing right, and he continued to pull me toward the door. "What's wrong with me is that Ava is my mate. Which means you all better back the *fuck* up." *Shit.*

Mick was silent, and I mouthed an apology, unable to tear myself away from Jasper's tight grip. Another werewolf whistled as we strode by. "Dude, if she's your 'mate' we have some problems because I definitely had a dream about your human whore in my bed last night." His buddies all laughed and high fived at his witty joke. Jasper didn't think the joke was as funny.

A frenzied growl tore from his throat as he finally let go of my wrist, stalking over to where the now frightened teen stood.

"Jasper!" I yelled at him, trying to get his attention. Anything to stop a fight from breaking out.

Jasper shuddered, trying to gain control over himself. His voice was quiet and dangerous. "That 'human whore' is my mate. And you will not disrespect her again."

The teen was shaking in front of Jasper, but he still didn't quit. "Wha... what are you going to do about it? She's just a human."

The smile Jasper gave him was deadly. "It's not what I'd do about it. It's what Ava would do about it." He dragged his palm down across the carefully arranged makeup on his neck, exposing his fully healed mark to all the wolves in the room. "Ava's not 'just' a human. She's a Venator. She has earned and deserves your respect. And if my words alone don't convince you to respect her, maybe my mark will."

The room was quiet, and the only noises I could hear were Jasper's laboured breathing and my own heart beating rapidly. Jasper was staring all the wolves down, daring any of them to challenge him. Even Sage looked shocked. I gathered my remaining courage and smeared off my own makeup before I made my way to Jasper, taking his hand tightly. Relief flooded my body through the bond. "I assume this won't be a problem for anyone." I didn't ask. I didn't make requests anymore. This was an expectation.

When there was no response, Jasper shot one last disgusted look to the now cowering teen before turning on his heel and leading us out to the porch. There were a few people mingling on the porch still, but I gave them a deadly glare and they wandered back inside.

"How the hell are you in my head?" I snapped at him as soon as we were alone.

"The mate bond. We're connected now."

I narrowed my eyes in frustration. "I know we're connected. But I thought you said the whole telepathy thing wouldn't happen for us."

Jasper was quiet for a moment. "I guess you're more

capable than either of us gave you credit for."

"How does the link work? Can you hear everything I'm thinking?" Everything could be a disaster. I loved Jasper, but I wasn't sure I wanted him in my head every second of every day.

"You have to project the thought to me. Think about me, what you want to say to me. Which is why I could hear you in the party, flirting with *Mick*. You wanted me to hear." His voice dropped ominously with Mick's name, and I glared at him before focusing on projecting my thoughts.

I focused on Jasper's handsome face and thought about what I wanted him to hear. *Can you hear this? When I say you were a jerk to the pack we were supposed to be making friends with?*

He heard, because he shrugged and answered calmly, unbothered. "I got angry."

I tried to project again, finding the effort easier now I knew what I was doing. *You can't lose your shit at people because you don't like them.*

"They weren't respecting you." He said this like the statement was common sense, like everyone threatened people because they were disrespected.

"Is respect what you were mad about? Or were you angrier they didn't know I *belong* to you?" My voice was dripping with sarcasm.

Jasper locked his gaze on to mine, stalking closer to me until I could feel the heat radiating from his body. "And what if I was?" His voice was as quiet and dangerous as it had been with the teenager inside the cottage, and his eyes were dark with need.

"Again. You were the one who wanted to cover up our marks." I tried to sound bored, but my traitorous heart was beating furiously, and I licked my lips in anticipation at his proximity. I knew what happened when his eyes got dark.

"Drop the act, Green." He ran a slow, longing gaze over my body.

"What act?"

"The angry act. I can sense you now, you know. Your

wants. Your needs. Your... desires. You want to be mine, and you want everyone to know you are too." He gripped my waist so tightly I knew I would have marks. But common sense always went out the window with Jasper. He dipped his head closer, sending shivers down my spine as his warm breath tickled my neck. "Strip."

"Jasp, we're outside a party," I breathed as he kissed his way across my collarbone. Every touch sent electricity through my body. I wouldn't have been surprised if we had an audience watching through the window as if we were a spectacle at a carnival.

Jasper growled quietly, but he knew as well as I did the Alpha would hear about the events of tonight. Jasper threatening a teenager was bad enough. Jasper screwing his human mate on the back porch would not be the relationship he was hoping for. He tugged me off the porch toward the dimly lit patio. The space was private, away from the prying eyes of the partiers. They'd probably still be able to hear, but I wasn't sure if I cared anymore. He pushed me onto a lone lounge chair, standing over me, breathing heavily. He watched me intently as I raised myself up on my elbows to watch him.

Strip. Jasper's command echoed through my mind.

I could feel a blush warming my cheeks as I met his intense stare. I didn't move, but neither did he.

If you want to see the power you hold over me -- strip.

I glanced over my shoulder to confirm no one was watching us before I undid the harness holding my blades, letting it drop to the ground. I tugged my shirt over my head with shaking fingers. *Are you going to join me?* I asked him.

He shook his head. *I think I'll watch.* Every word echoed through my head in a resounding demand. I unbuttoned my jeans, sliding them over my hips as he looked on hungrily. As I laid back in my simple black underwear, his control slipped, and I watched him curl his hands into tight fists.

What now? The projection of my thoughts was coming naturally. As if this was how we always fooled around, reading each other's minds.

Jasper cocked his head to side. *Touch yourself.*

I met his steady gaze, challenging me like he dared those teenagers at the party. Inviting me to take control. I raised an eyebrow at him. *Fine. Try and control your jealousy.* I trailed my hand lower, dipping underneath the waistband of my underwear to the wet heat there. A moan escaped my lips as I rubbed my fingertips on my clit, imagining my touch was my mate between my legs.

I felt Jasper's desperate groan in my body before I heard the noise. I kept going, and his powerful stare focused only on me. His intensity was always a turn on. I moaned loudly, and Jasper's voice cut across my mind. *Try and control your volume, Green. I'm not planning on sharing you tonight.* His voice was steady, even as I watched his hands tremble with need.

I grinned at him. *Come over here and control my volume for me. Unless you think I'll need help?*

His control, stretched as taut as a rubber band, snapped, and he growled as he knelt and forced my legs wider. Jasper locked his gaze on mine, the sight of him wild and needing between my legs seared into my memory. *Like I said, baby, I'm not planning on sharing you. Ever.* He pulled my underwear off, tossing them carelessly to the side. I gasped as he kissed his way down my thighs, his warm breath sending a shiver across my spine.

"Fuck!" I cried as his soft mouth sank onto my pussy. He glanced up at me, never stopping his licking and his kissing, everything sending sparks throughout my body.

I have never tasted anything as good as you, baby. Fuck.

I couldn't focus on projecting anything back. Not with him worshipping me between my legs. I felt his finger stroking the wetness there and gasped as he immediately slid two fingers inside of me. The rhythmic pumping of his fingers and the gentle caress of his mouth on my pussy was a sensory overload. I moaned again, letting my body give in to the sensations.

You're going to come like this. And then you're going to come with me inside of you. You're going to keep coming until you admit you like being mine. He curled his fingers, knowing exactly how I needed it. *Come now, Ava.*

And I did, shattering around his fingers and his mouth. Crying out through the pleasure and the overarching need that never went away with him. Jasper pulled himself up between my legs, licking the taste of me off his lips. He looked like he was about to say something over the mate bond, but instead he spoke aloud. "Fuck, Ava. You are the most beautiful thing I've ever seen. I will hurt anyone who tries to disrespect you. And I will kill anyone who tries to take you away from me."

I leaned forward and kissed him as I fumbled with the button on his jeans. *I love you too. Now make me yours.*

He groaned as I released his thick length from his pants. Jasper propped himself up with his elbows on either side of me and I felt the broad tip of his erection pushing against me. He leaned down to rest his forehead on mine. "I swear to you. I will never make you hide our mate bond again."

In response, I tipped my hips up, letting him sink inside of me. Jasper hissed through his teeth as he pushed himself deeper, until there was no space between us. No room for doubts, or fear, or silly arguments to distract. *I love you.* His mental voice was quiet, but passionate. Then he began to move. At first we moved as one, his lips kissing my mark. Declaring me as his, and Jasper as mine. But I felt the ecstasy rising in my veins, the pleasure pounding through my body. I cried out softly, and I felt him lose his edge. "Hold on," he whispered, and flipped us so I was on top of him, my legs straddling his taut stomach.

I couldn't control the moans as he sank deeper into me. I shifted back and forth on his cock, so damn close. *Ride me.*

He didn't have to tell me twice. He thrust deeper and I rocked my hips, needing more, needing to be closer. Jasper's breath was soon laboured, his eyes unfocused. I held the power with my body, and such a feeling was a head rush. I could feel my orgasm building, and I needed a release. I needed to be *his.*

Let go, Jasper ordered. I let my body give itself over to the fullness of having him inside, of letting go of control as much as I had the control.

I love you too. I shook and trembled around him. He picked up my hips, thrusting through the aftershocks of pleasure as he lost control and released himself inside of me. Mine. His. I'd call myself whatever he wanted me to. Titles didn't matter -- we were one.

He gently stroked my bare back as we lay together. My heart beat in time with his own, and I couldn't imagine a time when there hadn't been an us. I felt like we were a world away from the party, from the stares. Until I heard the side door slam shut, and heavy footsteps walking toward us.

"Jasper. Someone's coming." He cursed quietly and sat up next to me on the lounge chair, zipping his jeans up. I yanked my own pants back on and combed my hair with my fingers as the footsteps got closer and a tall man walked off the back porch toward us.

I hurriedly pulled my shirt back over my head, and tucked my blades underneath the chair, but Jasper was unaffected by the precarious position we had almost been caught in. "If you have a problem with my mate or our relationship you can take your issue up with your Alpha." His voice was tense, and I knew he was ready to defend if it was needed.

The young man walking into the patio light held his hands up. He had short brown hair, and friendly eyes shining brightly in the light. "Nothing bad. My name's Merrick. I came looking for Ava."

A growl rumbled deep in Jasper's chest, and I placed my hand gently across his heart to still him. He sighed and ran his fingers through his hair. "What do you need with my mate?" Again with the *mate* thing. Jasper hadn't been kidding around -- he wasn't taking any more chances.

"Um. It's kind of personal." Merrick's gaze darted around nervously.

He's scared of you. Don't be a dick, I mentally shot over to Jasper.

Jasper rolled his eyes in response to my mental message. "Whatever you want to say to Ava, you can say in front of me."

Merrick looked to me, widening his eyes. I nodded, gesturing for him to continue.

"Okay, then. There's no easy way to say this. Ava, I'm your brother."

My mind started spiralling and I burst out laughing. "I don't have a brother. And no offense, Merrick, but my dad is definitely not a wolf."

Merrick looked away from me, and then back. "No. My dad's a wolf. But Monica is my mom. They were a college fling. My dad told me Monica never wanted you to find out. But I knew I needed to say something when I saw you here tonight."

I shook my head. "This is insane. My mom hates wolves."

Merrick sighed softly, a sound filled with hundreds of emotions I understood all too well. "Yeah, I know. My dad probably has something to do with the distance. When she realized what I was, she dumped me off on his doorstop real quick and my dad spent most of my life resenting her for it. I haven't seen her in years."

Jasper had been quiet throughout the entire exchange, and now he tipped his head toward Merrick. "His eyes."

I turned my head to look at Jasper, narrowing my own eyes in confusion. "What about them?"

"He has your eyes. Monica's eyes," Jasper murmured.

I looked back at Merrick, trying to see what Jasper saw there. "You're... you're right, Jasp. You're telling the truth, aren't you?" I asked Merrick.

Merrick nodded. "Like I said, I haven't seen Monica in years, but I knew you had to be her daughter. Of all the Venators to visit..." He shook away some unspoken thought. "How is she doing? Not that I should care. But I can't help myself."

Jasper and I exchanged glances. I spoke first. "She's... missing."

Merrick creased his forehead in a frown. "Missing? How?"

As gently as we could, Jasper and I explained the events of the last few months to Merrick, including my failed fight and our current fruitless search for Monica. His expression shifted from one of shock, to disbelief, to anger.

"I really shouldn't be surprised," Merrick said. "But I'm shocked."

I nodded. "We all were. But now we're trying to make things right."

"Anything you need. I'm there."

The three of us sat on the patio, facing the deep woods to the side of the house. While the party raged on inside, this side of the porch was quiet with the exception of our quiet talking and the occasional lonely call of an owl. My eyes had adjusted while we sat and talked, slowly learning about each other's lives. A half-brother. A half *wolf* brother. It was a lot to take in, but maybe there was a relationship here that could grow where my own family's hadn't.

A flash of light in the corner of my eye caught my attention, and I turned to watch a pale, slender figure darting through the trees. Familiar. Too familiar. "Lucy," I breathed.

"Ava, we're miles away from town. Lucy wouldn't be here." Jasper squinted at me, trying to figure out if I was playing a trick or trying to get out of an uncomfortable conversation.

I shook my head. "No. I saw Lucy. I'm sure of it." With an apologetic smile at a very confused Merrick, I unsheathed my blades and took off running after her through the dense trees.

Damnit, Ava! You can't take off like that! Jasper's growl echoed through my mind.

I ignored him, jogging to catch up with Lucy's slim frame. If she had followed us out here, then she was definitely in danger.

"Lucy! What are you doing here?"

She stopped and spun around, and her expression

made me freeze. Her gaze was cold and vacant. Whatever was happening, Lucy wasn't aware of it.

"Your friend is… indisposed." She had Lucy's face, and Lucy's body, but definitely not Lucy's voice. No. But, I knew this voice. *Fuck.* This was the voice from the other day. The voice that trapped me in the darkness. I tightened my fingers on the handles of my blades to keep the numbness tingling there from spreading through my body. How was I going to explain this to Duke?

"You're the thing that trapped me. Who are you?" I asked. "What do you want from Lucy?" Lucy better not be hurt or there would be hell to pay. How I would hurt a demon, I didn't know but I would make damn sure I figured it out.

"It's not what we want from Lucy. It's what we require from you. Your friend was the… easiest target." *Goddamnit.* Sweet Lucy, so innocent.

"Let Lucy go. What do you want from me?" I repeated.

"Your mother owes us a great debt."

"My mother? I haven't seen my mother in months. You're tracking the wrong person if you're hoping to find her. I tried to kill her last time I saw her." I had my knives firmly in my hands. There was no space for fear in my body or mind.

The demon's voice was bored. "All the same, she owes us payment. And if she can't be found, then your blood will do in her place. We were hoping to bring you in as leverage, but obviously that doesn't seem like it's going to work."

"Fuck that shit. Your problem is with my mother. You can find her and deal with her." I was not about to clean up any more of my mom's messes, especially not with my *blood*. But wait. *We?* "Do you work for… Orcus?"

Quicker than I could track her movements, Lucy was in my face. Her breath smelled like blood and ash, and it took everything in me not to flinch away. "Do not say that name. And you Venators do not ask questions of me," she hissed. "He will have my payment one way or another. Bring your mother here, or we'll collect from you."

"My mother is on the run. How do you expect me to find her and then convince her to come with me to her death?"

Lucy shrugged, holding a tendril of my hair between her fingers. The sight was unnerving. My naïve friend looking menacing, all the while I knew she wasn't in control of her actions. She whispered in my ear, and every word was a nail scratching a chalkboard. "Not my problem. You have a week, Venator." I blinked, and Lucy was gone into the black of the night.

Ava! For fuck's sakes, where are you? Jasper's angry voice echoed through my mind. I could feel his fear, taste his desperation as he tore through the forest looking for me.

Shit. A week. What the hell was I going to do? One thing was certain, I had to find Monica and fast. I hoped Merrick was up to the challenge, because I was going to use him as bait.

Cimmerian (Darkling 4)
Torri Heat

A demon has possessed Ava's best friend in the pack. Jasper and Ava are fighting an unthinkable deadline to complete an impossible task. It's Monica's life against Ava's in this race against the clock.

But new secrets, new allies, and new mates within the pack turn even the most practical plans into the most dangerous. Werewolves, witches, and weddings make for a deadly combination...

Chapter 1

Thump. Thump. Thump.

The thumping had been the soundtrack to my life since we had returned to the pack lands, and I was about to snap. I wasn't sure if I was going to smack Jasper upside the head, or go certifiably insane, but one of the two situations was guaranteed to happen. I was staring at my computer, willing my brain to work, but all I could focus on was the fact I had seven days, and that God awful thumping.

Thump. Thump. Thump.

I slammed my laptop shut, swinging my feet over the edge of Adrian's worn couch, and made my way to the back door. On the back patio, where Adrian had set up a makeshift punching bag, was my boyfriend, Jasper Knight. Who just happened to be working the bag like it had done him wrong in a previous life. We dealt with our nerves and agitation in different ways. I threw myself into work. Jasper threw punches.

I leaned against the frame of the screen door, watching him for a minute, all muscle and tanned skin. If only this were a different time, a different life. "Something bothering you?" I asked.

Thump. "No," Jasper grunted. He gave the bag a solid right hook that sent it swinging, then reached across, pulling it back into place.

I sighed, crossing my arms. "Jasp. We have to talk about this." *This* meaning the demon currently cohabiting Lucy's body, while expecting me to bring my mother to them.

He gave me a quick glance out of the corner of his eye, before hitting the bag with a deadly uppercut. "Nothing to talk about."

Jasper hadn't come to bed last night after we got home from the party. The party where I had run away deep into the forest, after Lucy who wasn't really Lucy. Where a demon demanded my mother or myself pay the debt in seven days. We had decided it was safer to be on pack lands while we sorted all of this out and had arrived at Adrian's doorstep. Adrian hadn't seemed surprised to see us at his door again and had sleepily gestured toward the already prepped air mattress. I had tossed and turned on the half-deflated mattress, cold without Jasper's warm skin next to mine. The upside to not sleeping? No dreams to haunt me. Small miracles.

I ran a hand through my hair, glaring at my stubborn boyfriend. "Fine." I turned to head back into the house, the screen door slamming shut behind me. He'd come in when he was ready, and I wasn't about to fuel his pouting any more than necessary.

"Wait." Jasper's voice called out behind me, and I stopped and looked back. He steadied the bag with a wrapped hand, using the other to wipe the sweat off his forehead. He looked up at me with hooded eyes. "Ava. I... I can't lose you." His voice broke, and I nearly broke with it. We had been through so much, more than any two people should. Surely this wouldn't be enough to bring us down. Fuck that. I wouldn't *let* it.

"Jasp, I..." I what? I was sorry? Because I wasn't. I wouldn't go look for my mother? Because I would. Anything I was planning to say would've been a lie. I met his dark stare, his caramel eyes pleading with me. I shook my head. *No.* I wouldn't cave. "Jasper. I have to do this."

His expression hardened. "I don't know what kind of hero complex you've developed, but you don't have to."

Rich coming from him... Jasper happened to be the king of hero complexes. I raised a brow, making sure to keep a lock on my thoughts the best I could. Last thing I needed right now was Jasper hearing everything I was thinking about him, including some choice curse words. "And how do you suggest we deal with the situation at hand? Pretend it's not happening? Maybe we could offer Beau up as another sacrifice?"

Jasper groaned, opening his mouth to speak, but at that exact moment, Beau rounded the corner. His skin was tanned, a light smattering of freckles covering his bronzed face. He looked healthy, so at odds with the man I had seen in the hospital. He gave me a roguish grin, his teeth white and bright. "What kind of sacrifice are you offering me up as now, baby girl? Are there going to be other girls involved?"

Jasper and I both whipped around, glaring at Beau who merely smirked, raising his hands in defense. "Whoa. Don't let me interrupt this couple's spat."

"I didn't know you were back." Jasper ran a hand through his thick, dark hair, giving me a stern look. I knew the look. It meant this conversation wasn't over.

Beau shoved his hands into his pockets. "Just got back like five minutes ago. Was about to drag my ass to bed, but I heard you working the bag and figured I should stop by first."

"I'll let you two get caught up," I said, refusing to meet Jasper's glare. His stare bored hotly into my face. "We weren't talking about anything important."

I turned and stormed toward the guest room, Beau murmuring apologies to Jasper behind me. He didn't have anything to apologize for. Jasper was being impossible, immovable, and he needed to understand I *had* to find Monica.

"*Ava*." Jasper was tapping down our bond, trying to get my attention. I didn't want to hear it though. He could stay out there and play with Beau like the children they were. I grabbed the small bag we had brought with us to the party the night before and started to shove my clothes in it. There wasn't much to pack. There never was. We had become experts at packing lightly.

"*Ava*." Jasper's voice again, firmer this time. He was pissed.

I didn't have time to listen to all the reasons why I shouldn't do what I was doing. I had less than a week at this point, and Jasper was either with me or he was going to slow me down. I huffed, swinging the backpack over my shoulder, and nearly slammed into Jasper, shirtless and sweaty, glowering at me in the doorway. His body still called to me in a way I couldn't describe, even when I was annoyed with him. Was that the bond? Or was that something that had always been there? I wanted to reach my hands out, run my fingers down his glistening chest. I wanted to press my lips against his, smooth out the furrow in his brow as he stared down at me. I just couldn't tell him.

"Why didn't you respond to me?" His voice was quiet and hard, and he wrapped his hand around my wrist, keeping me in the room.

I rolled my eyes, my residual attraction to him quickly evaporating. "Sorry. I didn't realize you needed tabs on me every second of every day."

"Only when you decide to make foolish deals with creatures you shouldn't be messing with," he snapped. Tension was thick in the air, and heavy in my limbs. The connection between us had steadily been amplifying since the marking, and it made it difficult to differentiate our emotions. Especially when one or both of us were agitated -- the mental walls between us weakened.

"*Asshole.*" The thought popped into my head before I could stop it, and Jasper narrowed his eyes. The fucking mate bond.

Jasper worked his jaw for a moment, before releasing my wrist. "I'm just trying to keep you safe." He walked around me, unwrapping the black bindings from his hands. I was surprised they weren't torn to shreds with how long he had been beating the bag outside.

I stood in the doorway, waiting to hear what he would say. I knew he wasn't actually angry at me. I knew it as surely as I knew my own name, his feelings flooding my own veins. We were one soul existing in two bodies, which made moments like this even more difficult. I knew he was worried for me, but Jasper being Jasper and unable to voice his concerns like a normal person instead decided to beat the living hell out of Adrian's punching bag. He finished silently unwrapping his hands, flopping back onto the air mattress and running a hand down his face. "When do we leave?"

I edged closer toward the bed, trying not to let my relief seem too evident. "We?"

"Yes, Ava, *we*. If you're insisting on continuing to put yourself in mortal danger, then we're going together to find Monica." He peeked out at me between his fingers, glaring. "I don't know why you're so thrilled with the situation."

I sat down on the air mattress, the bed sinking under my weight and rolling me closer to Jasper. "I'm not exactly ecstatic there's a demon who wants me." Jasper cleared his throat at my mention of the demon, but I ignored him. "They already know who and where I am."

"All the same, I would still rather you didn't tempt fate."

"Anyways. I'm just relieved you're coming with me. I didn't want to do this on my own."

Jasper sighed, rolling and propping himself up on an elbow. "I said it before, and I'll say it again. Ava, you're your own person. You can protect yourself. You can make your own decisions. And I will *respect* the decisions you make. It doesn't mean I'll like them, but it also doesn't mean you'll ever do anything alone. We're a team."

I smiled, sliding down to my side to rest my forehead against his. "You're not bad for a wolf boyfriend."

Jasper smiled, looking every inch the predator. "Were*wolf*. And I'm your *mate*."

"Oh yeah?" I breathed. "Can you remind me again?"

"Gladly," he murmured against my lips, brushing his hand down my hips. I arched my body into his touch.

"Not to interrupt or anything..." Adrian's voice had us breaking apart, once again glaring at an intrusion. I didn't realize he was still home, the house had been so quiet this morning. When Adrian was home the house was typically filled with loud music, or the TV running nonstop reality TV shows. His expression was amused, and he obviously didn't give a shit about what he had just interrupted. These fucking wolves. I couldn't wait to go home, in my own space, with my mattress that didn't deflate every time I lay on it. And where werewolves didn't interrupt my every waking moment.

"How long have you been standing there?" I

demanded.

Adrian crossed his arms, giving me an easy smile. "Long enough."

I groaned, pushing away from Jasper's embrace. "You've been spending too much time with Beau."

"As I was going to say," Adrian continued, leaning his lanky frame against the door. "I'm coming with you."

Beau popped up behind Adrian, swinging an arm over his shoulder. "No you aren't. You need to stay with the pack because I'm going with them."

"Jesus Christ," I muttered. If I were lucky, this discussion wouldn't end with them shifting and attacking the shit out of each other as wolves.

Adrian looked pissed. "Are you kidding me? You just got home."

"Yeah, but I almost died." Beau raised an eyebrow at Adrian, who groaned. This had been Beau's winning argument point ever since he had gotten out of the hospital, no worse for the wear. Didn't matter there were no lasting effects. If Beau wanted to win an argument, he was going to win the damn argument.

I raised my hands up, attempting to cease the brewing altercation before blood was drawn. "Look. Adrian, someone needs to look out for Duke. He doesn't even know that Beau is back yet, so it makes more sense than if you come with us." *Duke. Shit.* I hadn't even thought about Duke with everything that had happened, but what the hell must be going on in his mind? Did he know Lucy had left?

Adrian didn't seem impressed with the situation, but Beau clapped him on the shoulder. "Excellent."

"Speaking of Duke…" I began, hesitating. Duke was still a sensitive subject, refusing to speak to Jasper. But we needed to make sure he wasn't in danger, especially with a possessed Lucy running around.

"What about him?" Jasper asked, the muscle in his cheek jumping.

Adrian cut in, usefully for once. "I checked on him this morning. He's still pissed at Jasp, but he has no idea about

Lucy. As far as he's aware, she's visiting her sister this weekend."

I slid off the deflating air mattress, clumsily getting to my feet. "It's safer for him to think that for the time being."

Jasper nodded, standing up with a grace I still envied, even after all my training. He made even the smallest of movements look elegant. "You're probably right."

Beau was practically bouncing with untamed energy -- I so wished I could bottle his enthusiasm for life. "So when do we leave?"

I tossed a look over toward Jasper, who merely tipped his head back toward me. "This is your show, baby. When do we leave?"

I knew what he was doing. Jasper never stopped training me, ever. This was another test, and like hell if I wasn't going to pass it. I tucked my thumbs into the straps of my backpack, taking a deep breath in. I could lead. I could do this. And when I saw Monica, I would do what needed to be done. I wouldn't falter like last time. First things first, we needed provisions. Monica wouldn't be staying at hotels and inns. She'd be keeping off the beaten path. "As soon as possible. Beau, is all your camping equipment still packed? We're probably going to be roughing it for a few days."

"*Good, baby.*" Jasper's voice echoed down our bond, and I smiled despite myself.

Beau nodded. "Sure is. We just might need a few more rations. For you at least. Jasp and I can fend for ourselves if need be."

I shuddered. Poor rabbits. "Okay. I'll snag some food on the way out. Adrian, you can handle Duke right?"

Adrian nodded glumly, still disappointed in missing out on what he deemed an adventure. I stepped up close to the young wolf, giving him a tight hug, and waiting for him to return the embrace. I pulled back, looking Adrian straight in his warm eyes. "We need you here, Adrian. You've had experience with demons before." There was a sharp intake of breath from all three of the men, and I rolled my eyes again. "Seriously, guys. I think we're in enough shit as is without worrying about a stupid word."

"Speak for yourself." Beau muttered.

I shook my head and turned back to Adrian. "Look. You're the only one who knows the signs and what to look out for. We need you here to protect the pack. Can you handle that? I wouldn't trust anyone else."

Adrian nodded, brightening slightly. I knew he would do whatever it took to keep his pack safe. I stepped up onto my toes, ruffling his shaggy blond hair. I felt better knowing the pack would be in his hands while we left. Jasper clasped Adrian's hand, the two of them doing their complicated bro handshake. Beau rounded up the end, grabbing Adrian into a tight bear hug and lifting him off the ground as our friend protested and complained.

The walk to the parking lot was quiet, an uneasy silence stretching between Jasper and myself. Things weren't resolved between us, but there was no way for us to talk with Beau nearby, chattering on about his camping trip, and a girl he had met on his way home. I couldn't focus on his story, my thoughts drifting toward what we were about to do. Adrian was going to stay behind and watch over the pack, so that was fine. We had rations and were on our way to grab the camping gear from Beau's truck. Now we just needed a plan. Duke had said they saw Monica near the pack lands recently. Would she still be hanging around there?

"You're thinking so hard I can hear your wheels turning from here." Jasper's words sprang into my mind unannounced. I had been so focused on the plan I had let my guard down.

I tipped my head to the side, meeting his caramel eyes. I took a moment to admire him before I responded, Beau now happily humming to the side of me. How could I ever stay mad at him? His thick dark hair was swept off his tanned forehead carelessly, not that it mattered. Jasper could make anything work. He didn't need to try like the rest of us mere mortals.

"Just trying to figure out a plan." Speaking to Jasp this

way, in my mind, still wasn't natural for me, but it was becoming easier.

Jasper narrowed his eyes. *"The plan is to try and not die."*

I opened my mouth to snap at him, but we arrived at the truck. Beau and Jasper were already unloading the camping gear from the truck and discussing if we needed anything else. Besides, what was there to say? If I were being honest the plan *was* to try and not die. And find Monica. And make her see what a shitty mother she was. I had considered using Merrick originally. Would Jasper go for it though?

Jasper had said we were together. Always. And I trusted him implicitly. But it didn't mean the tension between us wasn't palpable, ripe enough to cut through with a dull blade.

"Do you have a plan?" Jasper's voice was tight, but I knew him well enough to recognize the tightness came from a place of concern, not a place of irritation.

I nodded. "Merrick."

Both men froze, and Beau frowned. "Merrick?"

"Long story," Jasper muttered, turning toward me. "What does Merrick have to do with any of this?"

"I want to use him as bait."

Chapter 2

We made our way into the woods where Duke had told me they first scented Monica. I didn't want anyone else in the pack asking questions about why we were decked out to go camping, or start quizzing Beau on his camping trip, so I decided it was safer for us to wait in the dense forest for Merrick to arrive. I had caught him on his cell phone as he was driving out of town, and once I explained a brief summary of what was going down, he immediately agreed to meet us out here.

Another reason for meeting out in the woods instead of the parking lot? We were off pack lands. Other packs used the forest as they travelled from coast to coast, so Merrick's scent in the woods wouldn't be seen as a threat to Jasper's pack.

Jasper and Beau were sparring in the small clearing where we waited, having tossed both backpacks and shirts off to one side. They never changed, the two of them. I paced, watching them fight. I kept my mental walls up as I debated my plan, wondering if this was the right call. What if Beau got hurt -- again? What if Not-Lucy got to Duke before Adrian could intercept her? What if we didn't find Monica? That was the worst one of all. I could imagine Jasper's pain all too clearly if we didn't find her. I wasn't going to put my blood's debt on the pack. *No.* I decided. If we didn't find Monica, I would write Jasper a note, and leave in the middle of the night when he was dead asleep to meet my fate -- whatever that may be.

I watched him grapple with his larger friend, taking Beau's legs out from underneath him with a swift kick to the back of his knees. His pack needed him, his strength, his determination, and his leadership. What the pack didn't need was a liability, which at the moment was me. Beau went down with a grunt, and Jasper immediately offered his hand to help him up, both of them laughing. I smiled. Maybe everything would work out for the best, and we would find Monica, and resolve this whole mess. But it was best to be prepared, just in case.

"Ava!" A gentle voice called out behind me, and all three of us turned to look at the newcomer. I held my hand to my forehead, shielding my eyes from the sun. *Merrick.*

I smiled, waving. "You made it!"

He grinned back. "Of course I did." He turned to look at Beau and Jasper, both formidable creatures, shirtless, and frowning. "Uh, hi."

Apparently it was going to be entirely up to me to make the first move, as Jasper had shifted into caveman mode. I sighed. "Beau, this is my brother, Merrick. Merrick, this is Jasper's best friend, Beau. Who is going to *play nice.*"

Beau's eyes nearly bulged out of his head. "Since when do you have a brother, baby girl?"

Good question. Thankfully, Merrick beat me to the punch. "Seeing as I'm older, she's always had a brother. But as for when she found out, that would be last night."

"Right." Beau tugged his shirt over his head, snapping his backpack into place. "Makes complete sense."

"All right, all right." Jasper was still shirtless, and still on edge. "Can we get a move on now?"

I rolled my eyes, sharing a grin with Merrick. Is this what it would've been like to have a sibling growing up? "Let's go."

We headed down the narrow path single file. Beau went first, full of energy. Next was Jasper, still radiating irritation. I wanted to know what his problem was, but he was keeping a tight lock on his emotions. Whatever it was, he didn't want me to know. I trailed close behind, and quietly bringing up the rear was Merrick. I had filled him in on the rough idea of my plan while he had driven over, but he hadn't said much either way.

As the trail disappeared, and the woods took over, I slowed my pace so Merrick could catch up with me. "It's a lot, eh?"

Merrick perked up his head, his gaze watching the two other men trample around in the forest like they had been born to it. Which, in some ways, they were. The ultimate predators. Silent, able to sneak up on you before you'd even thought twice about that sound you had heard a mile back. Cunning, willing to do whatever it took to get the job done. Merrick was one of them too. I knew this. But something about him was softer. Gentler. A quiet soul, so at odds with the dark world around him.

I guess in a way I was just as much of a predator as they were. I had learned to become stealthy, to obscure myself in the shadows as I stalked my prey. But when push came to shove, it didn't matter. I still was too weak to do what needed to be done and remove my mother from the situation, and now that was coming back to bite me in the ass. Whatever. That had been round one, and I was more than prepared for our next encounter. I nodded to Jasper ahead of us, muscles tensing in his broad back as he shifted his hiking backpack. "The guys. They can be a lot to take in sometimes."

Merrick laughed, a gentle sound that echoed the soft bird calls around us. "Ava, I grew up in a pack far rougher than Jasper's. I can handle a few big personalities."

I grinned at him. "You only say that because you haven't spent a full day with them yet." We walked in a companionable silence. *My brother*. Shit. "You know, I always wanted a sibling."

"So you really had zero clue?" He shook his head. "My dad told me some pretty fucked up shit about Monica, but I never imagined you'd be that out of the loop."

My laugh lacked any humour or emotion. "Believe it. I didn't even know about werewolves or Venators until Jasper showed up in my life."

Merrick gave me a look of utter disbelief. "But, I thought... I thought Venators passed the title down."

Join the club. "They do. My parents -- *our* mother -- seemed to think I wasn't capable of handling such a title. So they did what any good parents would, and lied to me about it my entire life." A pang of disappointment, or regret, passed through me. What would life have been like if I had known about Venators from the start? Jasper shot me a sharp look over his shoulder, obviously wondering what was wrong. I smiled at him, hoping it was reassuring. We could talk later when we were alone. And then he could also explain his problem with Merrick to me, and why he was being such a jerk to him. He knew my reasoning for using Merrick. Knowing I was alone, my mother would never come to me. But seeing that I had found my brother... I hoped that would be shocking enough to draw Monica out of hiding.

Next to me, Merrick nodded. "Well you caught up quickly. People in my pack were talking about the Venator who took down the wolf killer."

I laughed. "Yep, that's me. The killer of wolf killers, Ava Green. Besides, I heard rumors that your pack didn't like humans."

Merrick was about to speak when Beau whipped around, miming for us to be silent. I crept up behind him, the four of us clumping together.

"What happened?" I whispered. "What is it?"

"Monica's scent." Jasper's response was so faint I had to strain to hear it. "She's been here recently."

"Well what are we waiting for? Let's go!" We were wasting time sitting here on our asses.

Jasper shook his head, his gaze boring into me as he spoke through our bond. "*Monica is tricky. This could be a trap, and we need to be careful.*"

It was kind of crazy, thinking back over how rapidly my life had changed since I met Jasper. Here we were now, discussing my mother as if she were the enemy, a villain in a cheap comic book. But in all reality, she was. She had fucked up a lot of shit during her time as pack Venator, and now we were left to clean up all of her Goddamn messes. So yeah, if Jasper were describing her as a villain, he was pretty close to the truth. I looked between Jasper and Merrick, making sure Jasp knew Merrick understood exactly what was at stake here.

"*Believe me, baby. If his dad hates Monica as much as we do, he'll know without me saying anything.*"

"*I don't hate her.*" My response was automatic, but I wasn't sure if it was entirely truthful.

Jasper merely raised a dark brow in my direction. Did I hate her? Shit.

Beau grumbled low, spearing a finger in both mine and Jasper's direction. "If you two are done with your secret little lover's chat, we can move. She went south. Probably less than a few hours ago. Why the hell does she keep coming back here? She knows she's wanted." He tugged Merrick ahead with him. "Come on, Ava's brother. You can walk with me and stand guard."

"Uh, my name is Merrick…" Merrick shot me a bewildered look but allowed Beau to drag him further up the forest, toward the almost indistinguishable fork in the trail. If you knew what you were looking for, the signs were there. If you didn't, the trail wasn't for you.

* * *

Jasper and I trailed behind them, both of us quiet, listening for the sounds that might give Monica away, on alert for signs of where she might have gone. The forest was thicker here, similar to the woods outside my apartment. Branches stretched against one another, growing out of trees as old as time itself, with roots thicker than my leg. This wasn't the greenery of new life. This section of the world was ancient, and I felt like if I listened close enough, I would be able to hear the trees whisper the secrets of time into my ear.

Jasper bumped my shoulder. "What are you thinking about, baby?" he whispered.

"Nothing important." I tipped my face up toward the canopy of branches above us, shielding out the dwindling sunlight. It seemed unlikely we would find Monica tonight, so we'd have to make camp soon. Otherwise, we'd be stuck pitching our tents in the dark, which did not sound like my idea of a fun time. I bumped him back, giving him a stern look. "Why are you being such a jerk to Merrick? He's just trying to help."

"I'm not being a jerk." God, he was stubborn

sometimes.

I stuck my tongue out at him, every inch the professional, deadly Venator. "Yeah, you are. You've been in a mood since I brought up his name this morning. So what gives?"

Jasper narrowed his eyes. "Okay, fine. Don't you find it suspicious all this stuff with Lucy and your mom comes up, and then Merrick just happens to find his way back into your life at that exact moment?"

The thought hadn't even crossed my mind. Merrick was too gentle to be wrapped up with anything evil like that. "No. I don't. I think it was a coincidence, and I think you need to be happy for my new family."

"*I'm* your family," Jasper stressed, tugging on my hand until I stopped next to him, looking up into his eyes. "I'm serious, Ava. Just keep your guard up, okay?"

"Okay, fine, whatever. Even though I'm beginning to think you're just jealous you might not get one hundred percent of my attention now."

"Mmm…" Jasper tipped his forehead to me, pressing his lips against mine in a hard kiss. "I'm not worried about attention, believe me."

I pushed away from him laughing, jogging lightly to catch up with Beau and Merrick. I couldn't help the doubt snaking into my mind about my brother though. It curled around my thoughts, making its home in what I thought I knew to be true. I had been wrong before. It was entirely possible for me to be wrong once more. But my instincts had also told me to trust Jasper and look at the beauty stemming from that decision. Merrick couldn't be evil.

Beau grinned at me as I caught up, still excited about the idea of an adventure, regardless of the danger that might lie ahead. "You doing okay? We're probably going to have to make camp soon. Monica would have no reason to expect we're trailing her right now, so she probably won't be moving at night."

I nodded. "I was just thinking that. Next clearing we hit we can make camp. How many tents did you bring anyways?"

"Two. So I figured you and Jasper would obviously share one, unless you've changed your mind on your brooding private investigator, and Merrick and I can take the other."

"Don't be putting the moves on my girl, Beau. I let you off easy last time, but I'll kick your ass if I need to." Jasper's tone was light and teasing, but there was an undercurrent of venom lacing through it.

I glanced at Beau, knowing he wanted to bite back. "Don't," I murmured under my breath. "Just drop it." Jasper was riding the edge of protectiveness and anger, and I didn't want him to lash out at any of us. It had been a hard week with his fight with Duke, and the situation at the party yesterday. On top of it all, he would be dealing with double the emotion like I was, and nowhere to put it. Beau had a tendency to poke bears, just to see if they'd bite, but this time he needed to leave it alone. Last thing I needed was Merrick seeing Jasper lose his temper.

Beau looked at me out of the side of his eye but nodded. I tipped my head and pulled my braid over my other shoulder so my mark was on display, letting Beau get a good look at what was driving Jasper crazy. Realization flashed across his eyes, even as he blinked in surprise. "And him?" he whispered.

I nodded, glancing over my shoulder to make sure Jasper was still distracted. "Yeah."

Beau whistled quietly. "Damn, baby girl. You're tougher than I gave you credit for."

"And no more of that baby girl shit, you hear me, Beau? She's my baby. Find your own," Jasper called over my shoulder as we all piled into a small clearing.

"Good fucking lord," I muttered. I couldn't take another moment of Jasper's overprotective, pissy mood. I dropped my heavy backpack on the ground with a loud thud and whirled around to Beau and Merrick. "You two start setting up the tents." I turned my head back toward Jasper, glowering darkly at me. "And, you, you're coming with me."

Beau mock saluted me, swinging one of the small tent bags over his shoulder and leading Merrick out to the flattest area. I hope Merrick knew what he was getting into, sharing a tent with Beau. Come morning, they'd either be best friends or one of them would be dead. I dragged Jasper behind me, stomping through the dense forest until I knew we were far enough away to not be overheard by sensitive wolf ears.

I turned, glaring at my boyfriend. "I know this isn't what you want to be doing. I know you don't agree with this plan. But this is what we're doing, and you're either with me *completely* or you're not. Using the excuse of a fresh mating mark is getting old."

Jasper scoffed. "Of course I'm with you, baby. Have I not already said that enough?"

"You have. But your attitude and the way you just snapped at Beau for calling me a pet name that, spoiler alert, he's called me since day one, says otherwise."

He slumped onto a large boulder. "You're right. I'm sorry. I'm a dick."

I sat next to him, leaning against his firm shoulder. "You're not a dick. You're just acting like one." I tipped my nose into his neck, inhaling the overwhelming smell that was Jasper. Being around him was intoxicating, more so since we had marked each other.

"I just… I don't know how to manage all of these emotions. It's like all of a sudden every one of my nerves is on overdrive around you, and I can barely control myself." Jasper ran a hand through his dark hair. "I want to kiss you. I want to touch you. I want to *fuck* you. All the time. And adding the fact this… this thing wants you. I don't know what to do with myself. If I had my way I'd lock you up in your apartment until all of this blew over. Not that you'd let me."

I sank into his body further, Jasper reaching out to wrap his arms around me. "I understand."

Jasper tipped my head up so I was looking up at him,

pressing a light kiss to my lips, darting his tongue into my mouth. He pulled back slightly. "I love you, Ava. But I'm not sure you could understand. You can understand feeling two things at once, and our connection. You can feel the bond, and the love we have for each other. But these urges I have... they aren't mine, or yours. They're primal -- my wolf calling out to its mate. To make sure every other man on this planet knows you're mine."

My breath caught in my throat. I knew Jasper was being more possessive as of late. But him laying it out like this... it was all falling into place. I swung my legs over Jasper's lap, wrapping my arms around his neck. "But you already know I'm yours. Hell, if you ever forget, there's a big ass reminder on my neck." I grinned up at him, but his dark gaze was solemn.

"That doesn't stop my wolf from wanting to lay claim to you." Jasper snaked his fingers under my shirt, feathering them along my skin. "It doesn't stop the *hunger*."

I trailed my hand up his nape, tangling my fingers into the curls at the back of his neck. "What are you waiting for?"

Jasper groaned, tightening his fingers into my skin. "Ava, baby. My wolf is so close to the surface right now. I'm not sure I could stay in control."

I smirked. "When have I ever asked you to stay in control?"

A low growl escaped Jasper, and he pressed his teeth into my neck, lightly scraping along his mark. I shivered, so sensitive to his touch.

"Do you like knowing you're mine?" he whispered against my skin. "Do you enjoy seeing the animal you turn me into?"

"*Yes.*" I didn't intend to answer over the bond, but Jasper pressed a smile into my neck all the same.

"*Would've made things a hell of a lot easier if you had just admitted that from day one.*" He dragged his fingers down my side, pushing into my ribs. His cock hardened against my leg, telling me just how close his wolf was. Jasper pulled me closer to him, zapping all of the air still lingering between us until it was just his breath and mine.

"I was distracted…" I murmured as Jasper stood with me in his arms. He put me down, and then took a step forward, pushing me back until my shoulders hit the bark of one of the large trees.

"Sounds like a lame excuse to me, baby." He was pushing my pants over my hips, pressing desperate kisses against my neck. His own pants joined mine in a pile at our feet, gasps escaping my lips as Jasper wound his talented fingers between my legs. He slid his fingers into the wet heat he found there, lazily stroking me as pressure built in my stomach.

"Jasp," I breathed. But he didn't increase his pace, thrusting and twisting his fingers as if he had all the time in the world. He grinned, knowing exactly what he was doing to me. Which he did, because now thanks to the bond he was feeling everything I was, just like I felt all of the desperation running through his body.

I clung to him, forcing my hips against his hand, desperate for more friction. For more of *him*. "So wet for me. So needy. I'd love to bury my face between your legs, but the only way you're coming tonight is around my cock."

"Please," I begged. I didn't care how pitiful I sounded. I never did. Because I knew Jasper was just as desperate as I was.

Jasper looked at me, his caramel eyes shifting to the dark ones of pure need. He nodded, moving his hands back to my hips and lifting me up, supporting my weight against the tree. I eagerly wrapped my legs around his waist, and the only thing driving my actions was the desire flooding my body. Jasper's emotions were taking over the bond, his wolf edging him on as he fit his heavy cock between my legs. The moments came in bits and pieces as Jasper thrust inside of me with a deep groan. The sensation of stretching, of feeling whole. A quick breath in through clenched teeth. A low moan in the back of my throat. The scratch of the rough bark against my shirt we hadn't taken off in our urgency to move as one. I tried to hold off my release, enjoying the rough way Jasper was commanding my body from the inside. Each thrust was driving me closer to release, while I was trying to figure out how to make this moment last forever.

"Baby," Jasper whispered my name as he moved within me. I clutched at his shoulders, pleasure building at the base of my spine. "If I don't get to have control, neither do you. Let go." He dipped his head into my neck once more, his teeth lightly piercing the mark he had left. Electricity sparked through the bond, and I cried out my release, Jasper's bite tipping me over the edge.

Something in Jasper's energy shifted, and he moved with a fury I hadn't seen in some time. His thrusts became more desperate, frantic in their pace. He clenched my sides with his hands, his fingernails digging into my skin. "*One more mark to show people I'm yours...*" I thought.

He roared as he found his release inside me, shaking and clinging to me even tighter. We stayed like that for a moment, as one. Our breathing steadied, and he let me go. I rested my head against his chest, listening to the steady beat of his heart against my ear. Jasper ran his fingers through my hair. "It beats for you, you know."

I smiled, happy and content. "I know." I pushed him back, straightening my shirt and finding my pants. "Come on, we should head back and find the guys."

Jasper leapt to his feet behind me, grabbing my hand. "I just hope Beau hasn't talked Merrick's ear off."

The tension between us had evaporated, and for that I was grateful. I couldn't have managed another moment with things being awkward between myself and Jasper. We found our way back to camp, arriving to find two tents set up on either side of the clearing, and a small fire blazing in the middle.

Beau immediately got to his feet, giving Jasper a knowing grin. "I thought I was gonna have to come rescue you guys."

"In your dreams, Beau," I muttered.

"You know it." If anything, his smile grew bigger.

Jasper threw himself down on the ground, scrounging through the food we had brought, but before I could do the same Beau tugged me toward him. "Anyways, it's sparring time."

I groaned. "You've got to be kidding me." When Beau was gone I didn't have to deal with his constant impromptu sparring matches. Jasper was on Beau's side, saying it was good for me to stay in practice, but really Beau was still trying to best me since the first day I had kicked his ass. Sometimes winning was exhausting. But even as I moaned and complained, I was getting into position, bringing my fists up to protect my face.

Beau smirked. "Knew you wouldn't be able to refuse."

I rolled my eyes. "Or I'm just hungry, and I know you won't let me eat until I've whipped you into shape yet again."

Merrick was whispering to Jasper at the edge of the fire, their profiles illuminated in the bright flames of my peripheral vision. "Are you seriously going to let them fight? I know she's a Venator, but he's like twice her height."

Jasper's low chuckle made me smile. "Watch. Ava can hold her own, make no mistake about it."

Beau came rushing at me, trying to catch me off balance. I stuck to my ground, knowing he favoured his right side. When he was close enough to reach out and touch me, I stepped to the side. Merrick was right. Beau was twice my size. But that also meant twice the weight to knock off balance if he wasn't paying attention. Which, he never was. I swung my knee out at the last possible moment, Beau flipping over my leg and toppling to the ground.

Unfortunately, he brought me down with him. I managed to stay on top as we fell, slipping my arm underneath his neck to keep him in a headlock. The trick with Beau was to never let him get on top. His size could easily overpower me, so I needed to be one step ahead at all times.

Beau was gasping, tapping at my arm tight around his neck, so I loosened my grip, concerned I was hurting him.

The extra space gave him the chance he needed to roll over to his side, both of us covered in dirt as we laid side by side. "God, Ava, when will you stop falling for that?"

"Probably when you start winning." His arm was still trapped underneath me as we grappled, but he would have it free soon, and it'd all be over. I had to think quickly. My arms were still free, and his chest was fully exposed. I brought my elbow up and slammed it right beneath his rib cage.

I hit the exact right spot, and Beau fell back with a gasp, all fight leaving him in one go as he struggled to catch his breath. "Maybe next time, big boy." Jasper laughed somewhere to the side of me.

Merrick's mouth dropped open as I stood, brushing off my pants. I gave him a smile, leaving Beau behind me.

Jasper shrugged. "Told you. Also, Beau, when will you give this shit up?"

"When I win." Beau's response was interjected with heavy breaths. *Served him right.* I happily sat down, accepting the slightly melted granola bar Jasper offered me.

Right now, at this singular moment, it didn't feel like we were hunting my mother down. It didn't feel like a demon was expecting my life if I didn't return with her. None of this was important. We sat around the campfire, Beau rubbing his sore ribs and Merrick regaling us with funny stories from his childhood. We laughed, joked, and ate, enjoying each other's company around the dying flames of the fire. But as the embers gave way to the night, one by one we filed into our tents, darkness surrounding us as we slept.

Chapter 3

It was like all of us woke up on another planet, so different from our lighthearted laughing the night before. Jasper took off on an early morning run before I was even able to comprehend what he was saying. He eventually came back grimacing and sweaty. Merrick was more quiet than normal, and even Beau's smile seemed like he had to force it to be there.

Tensions grew as we hiked deeper into the forest, all of us silent. The only exceptions were the lone crack of a twig, or a boot scraping against a rock. Not even the birds made a sound. It was unnerving, leaving me hyperaware of all my surroundings. Something wasn't right. Our presences were intruding on something we shouldn't be, and it made me want to turn around and immediately run the other way. But I wouldn't. There was a job that needed to be done, and I was going to make sure it got done.

Jasper brushed up behind me, making me shiver with the unexpected touch. I knew it was him and could sense him from a mile away. But I couldn't stop the sensation from rushing through my body.

"*Leave. Leave. Leave.*" The words echoed through my head, but I shook them away. I met Jasper's eyes over my shoulder, tipping my chin toward him. Just to know he was here, with me.

"*Baby. You okay?*" Even Jasper's voice through the bond was a whisper, as if he didn't want to break the silence we trekked through. We were walking on delicate eggshells, and so long as we didn't disturb the environment around us, everything was going to be okay.

I attempted a weak smile, before it faltered and I frowned. "*Something's not right.*"

"*I know. I feel it too.*" His voice was a caress, reassuring even in its acceptance we were headed somewhere dangerous.

"*What do we do?*" If anything, the trees seemed to have grown closer together in our short conversation, leaving the light limited. If it weren't for the watch on my wrist, I wouldn't be sure if it was noon or midnight. Ahead of me, I could barely make out the shadowy forms of Merrick and Beau.

"We keep walking. Turning around means giving up, and I refuse to do such a thing. Not with your life on the line." Jasper's gaze as it met mine was deadly in its certainty, leaving no room for arguments or disagreements.

"When do we stop?" I needed a line in the sand, something to tell me when to stop.

Jasper pressed his lips into a tight line. *"When we find her."*

I was quiet. I didn't know what to say. I had brought Merrick here, into what was potentially a dangerous wild goose chase, and now I didn't know what I was leading him into. Darkness for one, but what dangers waited for us in the shadows? A chill raced down my spine, at the exact moment a cold wind whipped through the trees around us, blowing up T-shirts and whipping my braid over my shoulder. We all froze, Beau and Merrick coming back toward us to form a makeshift circle, the wind howling around us.

"What the hell is this?" Merrick asked, shouting to be heard over the wind.

"I'd like to say it's just a spring storm." I could barely hear Jasper, even as he stood right next to me. "But..." He trailed off. It didn't matter. We all knew what he meant.

Something was here, with us. Something wasn't right.

"Do you think it could be her?" Beau's question was punctuated with a loud boom of thunder, a crack of lightning brightening the dark forest around us. I could see the flash of fear in Beau's eyes, as quick as the blade of lightning.

Jasper shrugged, pulling me closer to his side. The wind was still howling, the lightning coming closer together. "I don't know. What I do know is we have approximately five minutes to get these tents set up before we're all going to get soaked."

Another burst of lightning. We all nodded, our faces

stark and pale in the artificial night. There was no more talking. Jasper and I lugged our tent to one side of the trail, bracing it between two trees for a bit more cover. Beau and Merrick did the same on the opposite side of the narrow trail. Tent pitched, I chucked my backpack inside and dove in. Jasper followed behind me, and I watched as Merrick and Beau did the same before Jasper zipped the tent closed. Another round of thunder, and then the rain came.

I watched it come down through the small mesh window, flooding the barely existent dirt trail we had been walking on. I could hardly see the orange tent across the way through the rain, even though we were close enough for us to touch hands if we both reached out.

"Fuck," Jasper cursed to the side of me. I knew what he was thinking without him saying anything. None of us were very comfortable with where we were, but it was either wait out the storm, or make the long trek home with limited visibility. Even with the guys as wolves we would struggle if the whole forest was flooded out. Plus wolves didn't do much as defense from lightning strikes.

I sighed, flopping over and using my backpack as a pillow. Discontent was heavy on my bones, telling me to get far away from this part of the forest as fast as I could. "Now what?"

Jasper laid his head on my stomach, and I ran my fingers through his hair restlessly. "Now we wait. At least until the worst part of the storm is over and we can travel safely."

"To go back home, you mean."

"No. To find Monica. I thought that much was clear. I'm not letting that bitch get away with this."

I closed my eyes, listening to the rain come pouring down on the nylon of our tent. I hoped it would withstand the winds still whipping through the sides. The day hadn't been cool, but now with the moisture and the wind, a chill was seeping inside of me. I wasn't sure I would ever be rid of it. "Do you ever regret it?" I asked.

Jasper hummed lightly, the noise shaking against my

ribs. "Regret what, baby?"

"This. Me. All of this bullshit we have to put up with. Don't you wish you could ever go back in time?" I didn't know where my fears were coming from. The darkness maybe. The horrible awful chill I couldn't shake, and the sensation I had missed a giant sign saying "Turn back now."

In the blink of an eye, Jasper was sitting up, pulling me into his lap. His warm honey gaze was dark in the dim light, but I could feel him better than I could see him. He pulled my hand to his chest, placing it flat against the bone and muscle. "Do you feel that, Ava? Do you feel how it beats in time with your own?" He brushed his fingers down my cheek, pulling me in for a deep kiss. "Do you hear the way your soul calls out for mine?" he murmured against my lips, vibrations ricocheting through my entire body.

"*Yes*," I thought, pushing the word out toward Jasper, toward his soul I could see and feel as clearly as my own. "*Yes.*"

Jasper laced his fingers through my hair, crushing my lips against his once more. "*There's no going back from this, baby. From us. From you. I don't regret a single moment that brought you to me.*"

"*I know.*" I didn't want to go back either. And if it had been a mistake that brought Jasper into my life, I didn't want to know reality. I only wanted to feel Jasper's skin against my skin and hear the low timbre of his voice in my mind forever.

Jasper's groan broke the silence between us, and he pulled away to give me a crooked grin. "I love you."

And in my head, I could hear the echo of the words he spoke aloud. "*I love you.*"

The words weren't enough. I needed to feel it, to have his skin seared onto mine for all eternity. The mark wasn't enough. I wanted to spend the rest of my life with Jasper's body pressed against mine, our souls moving fluidly as one. I clawed at his damp shirt, too much fabric between us for my liking. I wanted to see every inch of Jasper's thickly muscled body, his smooth skin. Every part of his being was mine -- body and soul.

"Ava." Jasper stilled my hands with his own. "What's wrong?"

I shook my head. "Please, no talking. I need you to touch me."

In the grey light, Jasper smirked. "*I can do that, baby.*" He pushed me back slightly, so he could pull his shirt over his head, leaving his godlike chest exposed to me. I bent, kissing his neck and dragging my tongue down every muscle and piece of bone. His groan was quiet against the raging storm outside the thin walls of the tent.

He sat up, pulling my shirt over my head with no words. Jasper tipped his head toward me, taking a nipple into his mouth and sucking on it hard. *Shit.* He moved his other hand toward my free breast, tweaking and rolling the hard bud between his deft fingers. I swung my leg over his hip, pulling my pants off, desperate to expose myself to Jasper's hungry eyes. Jasper took the opportunity to tug his pants down, kicking them into a puddle of rain that had seeped into the corner of the tent.

I laughed. "Your pants are going to be soaked."

Jasper grinned, taking my face between his hands and kissing me. "No talking," he whispered. "And I don't give a shit."

I leaned closer to kiss him again, my tongue swirling against his own, drawing out soft moans from both of us. I raised my hips, positioning Jasper's cock at the entrance to my soaking, waiting pussy. I sank back, taking his thick length inch by inch. I cried out softly, and Jasper cursed under his breath, pressing his hands into my hips. I wasn't about to let him take control.

Perfectly stretched, and whole once more, I began to move, rolling my hips against Jasper. I circled to take him in deeper, his eyes locked onto mine. This was all there was -- Jasper inside me, and the feeling of absolute pleasure beginning to take hold as I ground my clit against him.

Jasper began to lift his hips to meet my urgent pace, tipping into me to press against my swollen clit each time.

"Ava," he whispered, and I could feel him start to spiral out of control underneath me, as I rode him.

"Shh. No talking. Just feel." I arched my back, driving myself quicker toward the edge of bliss. Jasper gripped my hips, slamming me down hard on his cock, and I cried out, trembling around him as I came. He shook inside of me, whispering my name like a prayer as he released alongside me.

I collapsed on top of his body. Jasper chuckled, the sound shaking my body where I lay. "Who would've thought my sweet little Ava Green wanted to take control in the bedroom?"

I rolled my eyes, pushing off him to pull my clothes back on. "Shut up. And this is a tent, not a bedroom."

He pulled me back to him, pressing a kiss against my forehead. "*I love you.*"

"*I know,*" I replied, exhaustion threatening to take over.

I pulled my clothes back on, not wanting to wake up cold, and then I curled against Jasper's chest, my favourite place to be. He swung a strong arm over my body, tugging me closer. "Sleep, Ava. I'll watch over you."

I wanted to stay awake. But the steady rhythm of Jasper's heartbeat and the rain lulled me into a false security.

I woke up with a gasp the next morning, Jasper still clutching me tightly. The rain had slowed to a steady drip against the roof, and the night just barely still dark. The grey light of dawn was fast approaching, but my eyes still needed a moment to adjust. The remnants of the dream hovered on my tongue, and I clawed at it, desperate to remember.

"*Show me how you summoned the storm, Ava.*" The same dream I had before, that night in my apartment. So similar to the storm we had been in when we made camp the evening before, appearing out of nowhere. But why the hell would I have anything to do with summoning it? That was an insane thought. "*Show me how…*"

"Utterly insane," I muttered to myself, suddenly feeling claustrophobic in our tiny tent. I shoved away from Jasper's hard body, needing a moment to breathe. I rolled away, only to find myself staring at a pair of shiny black combat boots. I should've fucking known. Or maybe we all had known. *Monica*.

* * *

My mother crouched over me in an outfit that looked no worse for the wear despite all the time she would have spent on the run. Her hair was in a tight braid similar to my own, and she grasped a gleaming blade in each of her hands.

"Say anything, and one of these carves the heart from sleeping beauty there," she hissed. My chest was tight, but not with nerves. It was tight with anger, and disgust. That she tried to put all of this on me. That she dared to threaten us. I glared at her but got to my feet. Monica tsked. "I see you don't sleep armed. Step one in not getting yourself killed as a Venator." She jerked her head in the direction of where my makhairas rested in the sheaths. *Shit.* I always slept armed. Always.

But there was one thing my mother hadn't accounted for -- the mate bond between Jasper and myself. I didn't have to speak aloud in order to get his attention. Monica kept one blade pressed tight against my skin as she opened the tent door, shoving me out into the drizzling rain.

"*Jasp…*" I called my mate as Monica led me just outside of our makeshift encampment. "*Jasp!*" I dug my feet into the mud, refusing to move another inch, and she pressed the blade in firmer. I didn't want to be out in this part of the forest, and I definitely didn't want to be out here with *her*.

"For fuck's sake, Ava. Move," my mother commanded.

"What the fuck do you want?" I asked, lacing as much venom into my voice as I could.

"To talk, without that nasty dog hanging over your shoulder."

Yeah. Sure. I didn't know what she wanted, but we had walked far enough away from the tents. I could just make out the tip of Beau's orange tent through the murky gloom. "I'm not going anywhere with you."

"We'll see about that." But she didn't dig the blade in any deeper than the slight pinch on my back, and we didn't walk any further. She sighed, sounding for a moment like the mother I remembered. "There was a time when you used to trust me, you know."

I laughed quietly. "That was, oh let's see. A few murders ago? Give or take?"

"You never used to be this cynical. I knew this life wasn't for you. That dog in your tent has corrupted you for a life you weren't ready for."

I rolled my eyes, wrapping my arms around my body to protect myself from the damp chill in the air. "Keep telling yourself that. Maybe one day it'll actually be true."

"Look, Ava." The pinch of the blade was gone, and I spun around to look my mother clearly in the face for the first time in months. She had aged, far more than she should've in the few months it had been. Her face was lined with wrinkles, her once bright eyes deep set in the hollows of her face. Where was the strong, powerful woman who took no shit? "I need your help."

I couldn't stop my mouth from dropping open. "You have to be fucking kidding me. You want *me* to help *you*, after what you did to my friends? Me? Not in a million years." She couldn't be serious. But no, this was Monica, my mother, master of deception and zero shame to make note of. Of course she would drag me out of bed at knifepoint, and expect me to go along with whatever she was going to say next. I wouldn't be surprised if she anticipated me begging her to let me be a part of whatever she had planned. But she wasn't dealing with Ava, her sweet, naïve daughter anymore. She was messing with Ava, Venator of werewolves, and I had been preparing for this moment since the last time I had seen her.

I shifted my neck further into her arm, just enough she wouldn't notice. Where the hell was Jasper?

As if on cue, Jasper burst from the tent with a roar, half shifted already. The door to our tent lay in shreds behind him, and he charged toward us with speed I knew for a fact he didn't have as a human. His fury was pumping through my veins, his anger flooding my head. I had almost slid out from her grasp entirely, but Monica whipped my back against her, pressing her blade once more to my skin -- this time to my throat.

"Back the fuck off, dog. Take another step closer and I'll bleed her dry. I don't care she's my daughter. She's a means to an end." My mother brought her mouth closer to my ear. "How did you summon him?"

I shrugged, using the movement to once again give myself a bit more room to move. Just an inch. I just needed one more inch. "You're the expert. Figure it out."

Jasper growled deeply in front of us, not breaking eye contact with me. *"Are you okay?"* he asked.

"I'm fine. I don't think she'll actually hurt me. She wants something from me." I was angry, and I was disgusted, but I wasn't afraid. Monica needed my help, which meant she needed me. Which meant for a moment, I had the upper hand.

Monica squeezed her arm against my stomach. "How are you communicating with him? You're a human, barely a Venator." She dragged the tip of her knife along my neck, brushing the loose strands of hair out of the way, until she came to my mark. "Ah. So you've decided to taint your blood. Still doesn't explain the communication. That's supposed to be for wolves only."

I squirmed against her touch, not wanting her to be near my mark. It was sacred, holy. Not for her fingers to maul and examine. "Yeah, well we can. So there's that. Can we get on with the Monica show now?"

She dropped my hair, bringing the blade back to my neck. "Oh, silly girl. Still so naïve. This was never the Monica show. No, there are much larger players at work here. I'm surprised you haven't worked that out yet."

Her fascination with my mark allowed me to finally get myself into a defensive position, and I gave Jasper a look. *"I'm unarmed so we're going to have to do this old school. You ready?"*

"Always, baby."

A rustling from the other tent had us all looking in that

direction, only to see Beau pop his head out. "What the hell is going on out here?"

"You've got to be fucking kidding me." Monica cursed under her breath. "Did you really need to bring this asshole with you?"

"Yes," I gritted out between clenched teeth. She was getting on my last nerve. What did she have against Beau? And if she actually expected me to help her, this wasn't exactly winning me over to her side.

Beau was out of the tent and ripping his shirt off before I could blink. Monica pulled her blade off my stomach, brandishing it at Beau. "Don't even think about shifting. One of you is bad enough. I don't need my daughter communicating with you in some fucked up telepathic way too."

Beau shot me a sharp glance. Somewhere along the way, we had forgotten to mention to him our bond extended to a mental link, but that explanation was going to have to wait. Behind Beau, Merrick stuck his shaggy head out of the tent. He had to know what was going down out here.

Monica laughed, a cold sound over my shoulder. "I see you two have finally met. The two greatest disappointments in my life, in one place. Lucky me."

I twisted against her tight grip, trying to look her in the eye. "As far as I was aware, you still need my help. So maybe tone down on the condescension for a minute or two."

Merrick walked toward us slowly, hands up in defense. Jasper was still crouched, growling, unable to take his eyes off me. "*I'm good,*" I shot him. "*For now at least.*"

"*I want to rip her limb from limb.*" Jasper's voice should've frightened me. There was no emotion, just simple, matter of fact. For him, it wasn't a question of if, it was a matter of when.

Just not yet. "*We need her,*" I reminded him. I didn't know if Orcus needed her alive or dead, but I'd rather not make that mistake too early. Jasper growled and shook his big wolf head. He wasn't impressed.

Merrick was still maintaining eye contact over my shoulder, with Monica I'd assume. "Mom?"

"If you want to get technical, yes. Now can all of you fuck off so I can have a private discussion with my daughter?"

"Over my dead body," Beau growled.

Merrick was still walking closer, the insecurity on his face a look I hadn't yet seen. "Why'd you leave?"

Monica huffed. "Seriously? This is what you want to talk about right now?"

"I waited, you know. After the last time you left. I waited and waited for you to come back and see me, even after Dad told me it wasn't worth it. I still hoped you'd prove him wrong. Why didn't you come back?"

"You really want to know why? Okay. I'll tell you why. I got drunk one night, and you were a big old mistake. Is that the story you wanted to hear? At first I thought you might be a Venator, like me. But when I found out you took after your dad, I dumped you on his doorstep. Are you happy now?" Monica's voice was like ice, like she couldn't care less what had happened to Merrick from then on.

My heart was breaking for a young Merrick, but at the same time, he was giving me the opportunity I needed to take advantage of Monica. I raised a brow at Jasper. He'd be ready. He was always ready.

I couldn't believe I had been dumb enough not to strap my blades back on last night, but it was no matter. I could do this, armed or not. I slid sideways in her grip, and immediately shoved my hand across her face, forcing her head and her blade in different directions.

"Ava!" my mother scolded me as if she didn't just have a blade pressed to my neck. I forced her arm back further. I just needed her blade. She cried out when I had her arm overextended, glaring at me, but dropped the blade. I snatched it up and ducked out of her reach. "Are you serious right now?"

"Dead." I held her knife pointed toward her. "You need to come with me."

She scoffed. "I'll do no such thing."

I grimaced, tightening my grip on the hilt. It wasn't my blade, but it was going to have to do. For now. "As far as I can tell, I'm the one with the wolves and the weapons, and you're standing there with nothing."

"Is that really what you think, Ava? Surely you can't be that dense." A wild grin stretched across her face, and she reached her arms out wide.

Jasper was frozen, waiting for my signal. *"I'm going to keep her talking. You and Beau loop around behind."*

Out of the corner of my eye, Jasper nodded, and Beau crept over to swing his large body on Jasper's furry back.

I focused on Monica. "What do you mean?"

"Haven't you figured it out yet?" she cried, and her face twisted in a grotesque mask of pride. "I can summon the storm." A crack of lightning sliced through a tree to my side, and I forced myself not to jump.

Thunder boomed in the distance, and somewhere, an owl called. "What have you done?"

"I've made some powerful friends." The rain was starting to grow heavy once more, and I used my free hand to push an unruly lock of hair off my face.

"That's why we couldn't track you."

Monica clapped, a mocking sound that echoed the rolling thunder. "Congratulations." Behind her, I saw Jasper leap out of the bushes, Beau still on his back. Monica whipped around just before they could land, leaning back and giving Jasper a powerful kick to the chest. Jasper yelped as he and Beau flew across the forest, and I could hear the smack of a tree as they hit.

"Who the *fuck* do you think you are?" I screamed, running across the small distance toward her, ready to destroy her. How dare she lay a finger on him? But before my blade could slice through her perfect black shirt, she blinked out of sight.

"Your mother, Ava. And I have *so* much to teach you."

I whipped my head around, but I couldn't see where she was hiding. I pointed at Merrick, still frozen where he had stood moments before. "Don't let your guard down. She could be anywhere." He nodded, on the offensive at once. Now where the hell was she? Her laugh bounced off the trees, circling and taunting me.

"*I'm okay.*" Jasper's soft voice echoed through the bond. Small miracles. I whirled around, trying to pinpoint where Monica's laugh was coming from.

"You think you're so tough don't you, Ava? A big bad Venator. But when push comes to shove, will you make the decisions you need to?" Even through the howling wind I could hear her voice, as clear as day. Taunting. I turned around brandishing her knife, only to see Monica standing with another knife at Merrick's leg, blood running from where she was pushing. I could hear Jasper howling as he and Beau made their way back from wherever they had been thrown. It was just Monica, and me, and a decision between us. "I'll give you a choice, dear daughter. Me, or him?" she snarled, sounding more like the beasts than the wolves I ran with, and she squeezed Merrick's arm as hard as she could. It sounded like glass was shattering, and Merrick yelped, his eyes going wide with pain. She dropped his arm, leaving him to collapse to the ground while she backed away into the forest. "Your choice. Will you lead with your heart or your brain?"

Chapter 4

"Merrick!" I screamed. I only had a moment to decide. Would I leave the man who had come to my aid suffering in a storm? Or would I capture my elusive mother? There was no decision. I glared and sprinted to check on Merrick. And once more I watched the woman I had thought to be my mother run into the darkness, smiling. *Fuck.* I couldn't think about that. I had to focus on Merrick's arm. I had heard something snap, but when I picked it up to check, it was nothing more than a limp noodle in my hand. She had shattered every bone in his arm. *How?* Merrick needed to see a doctor before his accelerated healing set the arm completely wrong.

"*Ava!*" Jasper called to me down the bond, and I turned to see Beau and him running back into our small clearing. "*Where the fuck is she?*"

"She's gone!" I screamed. I wasn't sure what was rain and what was tears running down my face.

"*I'll go after her.*"

"No!" The wind was picking up again, the drizzling rain turning heavier by the second. "We can't stay here!" I yelled over the downpour.

"*We need to go after her,*" Jasper commanded. "*She can't get away.*"

"There's no time! If we stay out here we're going to drown. Merrick needs a doctor. We need to head home. It's over, Jasp."

Jasper growled, and I couldn't tell if it was out of anger or disappointment.

Beau knelt next to me. "Go. Get on Jasper. I'll carry Merrick."

"What about the gear?" The wind was howling, and I could barely make out what Beau was saying.

He shook his head. "I grabbed your blades as I went by the tent but as for the rest of it... you're right. It's not worth it. We need to get home."

I nodded, leaving Merrick and making my way to

Jasper. I tugged on his fur to pull myself onto his broad back. *"I know you're pissed, but please don't drop me."*

A low chuckle echoed through my mind. *"Hold tight, baby."*

I looked over my shoulder to see Beau already shifted, Merrick awkwardly arranging himself on his back. His bad arm hung limply at his side, but he clung to Beau's fur with his good arm. Beau wouldn't let him fall off. Once he was on, Beau gave us a sharp nod, and we were off.

We raced through the storm that seemed to be getting worse with every moment we lingered in the woods. The wind screamed, and the rain poured. Thunder boomed, getting closer every time, and I clung to Jasper's fur. I could've sworn I heard someone calling my name. Every so often I would look over my shoulder, making sure Merrick was still clinging to Beau's golden wolf. I could barely see them through the downpour, but I'd catch a glimpse of a big paw, or a hand, and I knew they were still behind us.

Lightning sliced through a tree right in front of us, forcing Jasper to skid to a stop and change direction. *"Too close,"* I thought. *"Too damn close."*

"Worry about staying on, and I'll worry about the lightning." Jasper's voice was calm in response to the thoughts I hadn't meant to say to him.

I was soaked through to the bone, and my hair stuck limply to my face. I tried to wipe it out of the way, but the rain just pushed it back into place. I didn't know how long we had been riding in the storm -- it could've been seconds, or hours. A moment, or a week. Time was nonexistent. There was just the wind, and the rain, and Jasper's fur under my hands.

The lightning grew further apart. The wind stopped, and the rain soon followed suit. Up ahead, I could see the edges of the tree line. Somehow, we made it through. A quick glance back told me Merrick was still clinging onto Beau. If we didn't get him to medical attention soon, the bone was going to heal funny and would need to be rebroken.

"*Merrick needs a doctor,*" I reminded Jasper, keeping my eyes fixed on the light growing brighter and brighter.

"*We'll take him to the pack house. There isn't time to call an ambulance, and we can't show up to the hospital like this.*"

The four of us burst through the trees. I don't know what I expected to find, but it wasn't the bright sunshine of a new day, and pack kids playing soccer in the field. They froze, watching us as we didn't stop racing toward the pack house. Jasper must have said something to Beau because he followed us unthinkingly.

As we neared the pack house, I leapt off Jasper's back, shaking my dripping hair out of my face. "Help!" I screamed. "We need help!"

Beau skidded to a stop beside me, and I helped a wincing Merrick off his back. His arm still hung at a weird angle, but thankfully the bleeding on his leg had slowed. Alpha Dean's secretary came racing out through the main doors, took one look at us and turned around, calling for the Alpha.

Alpha Dean stormed to the front door, where I was helping Merrick hobble up the steps. "What the hell happened?" He looked to Jasper for an answer, who I heard shift back into a human behind me.

"Monica, sir. We found her," Jasper responded.

"And she did all this?" He gestured toward our soaking clothes, and Merrick's arm. "How?"

"It's a long story," I muttered. "Can you help him? I think the bone is shattered."

Alpha Dean took one look at Merrick's arm and nodded briskly. "Follow me."

The sounds of Beau shifting behind me followed us as we walked the maze of the pack hall. Alpha Dean led us into a part of the building I had never seen before, and into a small room set up with a hospital bed. I brought Merrick over to the bed, looking around the room.

"It's for emergencies," Jasper murmured. "If we can, we go to the hospital where we took Beau. The one with our nurses. But sometimes there's just not enough time."

"I'll go get someone to fix him up, and then I expect to see the two of you in my office immediately." The Alpha's stern glare left no room for arguments. He left the room, just as Beau walked in, fully clothed and handing Jasper some clothes as well.

"Figured you wouldn't want to go into your meeting with the Alpha completely naked," he said with a grin.

Jasper shrugged and got dressed. "Wouldn't be the first time."

Merrick had his eyes closed and was breathing heavily. He would be okay, but I didn't envy the healing for him. It was going to hurt like a bitch. A small woman I had never seen before hurried into the room, smiling at us. Jasper pulled me out the door. "Mary will fix up his arm, and Beau can stay with him. Come on. We should go see the Alpha."

Beau nodded, so I gave one last look to Merrick lying limply on the bed and let Jasper steer me toward the Alpha's office. We were in trouble, that much was obvious. How much was another question.

"Let me take the blame, okay?" Jasper whispered, squeezing my hand.

I shook my head, frowning. "Absolutely not. This was my idea."

"I don't care. I can handle the heat. You don't need to worry about it."

I pressed my lips together, not bothering to fight a useless battle. I wasn't going to let him take the fall for my decisions, but I'd wait until we were in front of the Alpha when he wouldn't dare disagree with me. We walked into the open office door, hand in hand. Jasper took a seat immediately, but I remained standing.

Alpha Dean gave me a look. "Take a seat, Ava. Please."

"I'm sorry, sir. I would, but I'm still a little wet." I gestured toward my still sodden clothes.

He waved a hand. "There have been worse things on my chairs."

I sat down with a grimace. Now I wasn't sure I wanted to be sitting somewhere "worse things" had been. Jasper looked at me out of the corner of his eye, and I heard his laugh echo down our bond.

"*Asshole,*" I thought.

He didn't get a chance to respond, because Alpha Dean began to speak. "So you found Monica? Seeing as she isn't with you, what the hell happened?"

Jasper hesitated. "She eluded us again. We almost had her, but she shattered Merrick's arm."

Alpha Dean frowned. "How did she have that kind of strength?" He stopped, looking at me. "No offense, Ava. Venators are quite strong, but I wouldn't think she should be able to shatter a wolf's bone."

"There's... there's more, sir." Jasper paused, as if unsure how to explain what we had seen in the forest.

I jumped in before he could speak. "Monica appeared to summon a storm."

"She... what?" Alpha Dean furrowed his brows, trying to work out what I had just said. "Are you certain?"

"It was basically a hurricane in the forest, sir. Once we left the contaminated area, there was no sign of a storm in sight. And it got worse the more agitated she got," I added, thinking about the way the rain had poured as Monica screamed.

"Okay. Okay. Well this is a development I wasn't expecting." The Alpha steepled his fingers, leaning back in his chair. "But what were you doing that far out in the forest in the first place?"

I took a deep breath in, wanting to explain everything before Jasper could take the fall for me. "It's my fault, sir. I thought I had a good lead on Monica, and asked Jasper to come with me. We have reason to believe she's working with a demon. Orcus, I believe is its name." Jasper hissed through his teeth, and the Alpha frowned at me. I threw my hands up in self-defense. "I know, I know. Don't say the name."

"What is your evidence? And why is this the first time I'm hearing about this?" The Alpha did not sound impressed. Whoops.

"Well you see, sir --" Jasper began, but I cut him off.

"Lucy showed up at the Chicago pack party the other day. She wasn't herself. She spoke to me about debts my mother had that needed to be paid." I paused, biting my lip. I shook my hair out of my face, straightening my shoulders. I could do this. I was doing this for the right reasons. "As for why I haven't informed you yet. That's because it was my family's debt, and it was up to me to handle it. I wasn't going to drag the entire pack into my family's problems once more. I made a decision, and I will accept full blame and responsibility for that decision."

Jasper sighed, but the Alpha looked at me with something undefinable in his expression. When he spoke, it wasn't what I was expecting to hear. "Ava. I understand you didn't want to bring more trouble into the pack, but when you mated with Jasper, you became a part of this pack as well. This is your family, possibly more so than your own parents. I thought you understood that."

Appreciation was tightening my throat. Accepted. I was accepted here. "Yes, sir, I do. But I didn't want to bring more danger than necessary to my family."

He nodded. "Understood. But danger will come all the same. We might as well face it as one, instead of apart. How long did it give you?"

I played dumb. "How long?"

The Alpha raised a brow at me. "How long do you have to fulfill the debt?"

I breathed out heavily. "Less than a week now."

He nodded again, tapping his fingers on his wooden desk. "Okay. This is what we're going to do."

Jasper squeezed my hand, and we both leaned in. But before we could discuss plans, the door swung open, and there stood a fuming Duke. If looks could kill, Jasper would've been six feet under already.

"What did you do with her?" Muscles strained against Duke's arms, and his teeth were bared.

"What the hell, Duke?" Jasper jumped to his feet.

Alpha Dean's receptionist came hurrying in behind

Duke. "I'm so sorry, sir. He refused to wait."

The Alpha waved her off. "No matter." He turned to Duke. "You will stand down. You will not threaten another member of this pack." By the tone of his voice I could tell he was commanding Duke, and no matter how much Duke wanted to get at Jasper, he wouldn't be able to.

Duke's muscles remained tight, but his fists slowly uncurled. "What did you do with Lucy?"

"I didn't do anything to Lucy," Jasper growled. "Watch your mouth before you blame me again."

"She was fine!" he roared, and the pain lacing his anger was evident. "She was fine. And then you came over, and then she didn't come home from her sister's house. So what did you *do*?

"I didn't do anything," Jasper repeated, gritting his teeth. The Alpha's command was starting to affect him as well.

"Duke," I interrupted, keeping my voice calm. "Duke. We tried to tell you something was wrong with Lucy. Remember?"

"Nothing is wrong with Lucy."

"Stop it! Stop it at once!" The Alpha's command had all of us freezing, looking his way. "Now one of you, and *only* one of you is going to explain to me what is going on here."

I looked at Jasper, gave him a nod, and turned back to Alpha Dean. "While I was here on the weekend, Lucy was acting strange. Jasper and I both noticed it. Then when we were at the Chicago party we saw Lucy again, and she definitely wasn't herself." I bit my lip. "Lucy is the pack member being possessed by the demon."

The Alpha looked stunned, and Duke raged, clawing at the doorway since he couldn't get to Jasper. "This is all your fault. Both of you! Lucy didn't deserve any of this."

Tiny shards of remorse were burrowing their way into my heart, sending pain throughout my body. This was my fault. This was what I wanted to avoid, but unfortunately it had found its way toward me anyways. "Duke. I'm going to fix this," I begged. "Believe me. I'm going to fix this." Duke wouldn't meet my eye, and Jasper looked like he was being torn alive.

"Lucy…" Alpha Dean mused. "This changes things."

I swung my head back to look at him. "It does?"

He nodded, and all three of us waited for him to continue. "I've known Lucy since she was a young girl. She's struggled with being a shifter for most of her life."

I chewed on the inside of my cheek. I knew this. Lucy had always been uncomfortable with her werewolf status. But what did that have to do with demons?

"Because of her uncertainty with the supernatural way of life, it should be easier to dispel the external force. *If* we can catch her."

"Don't worry about that," I said, trying to force Duke to make eye contact with me. "I *will* find her."

"Like you found Monica?" Duke snapped. "The receptionists were already gossiping about your so-called *mission*."

"You weren't there. You don't know what it was like." But already doubt was creeping into my mind. Was it my fault Monica got away from us again? Could I have done anything differently? Was I too weak, too unprepared?

Jasper caught my eye, shaking his head.

Alpha Dean cleared his throat. "Duke, you will go home and await news from me. I don't want to hear anything to the contrary. Jasper and Ava, you will find Lucy and you will bring her home so we can expel the darkness currently inhabiting her body." While I was all for some nice language, the way these wolves avoided saying "demon" seemed to run the line of excessive. "We will deal with the debt once Lucy has been found. You are all dismissed." With that, the Alpha ushered us out the door, closing it with a sense of finality.

"Duke, I…" I began, but he shook his head and turned away.

"Don't bother, Ava. It'll just be another excuse I don't need to hear."

I sighed heavily, my shoulders sinking with the weight

of Duke's accusations. Jasper pulled me into his body. "Are you okay?" he asked.

"No. Why the hell would I be okay? Duke is right. I'm full of excuses. I'm the reason Monica got away again, and if it weren't for my family, Lucy wouldn't be in this situation in the first place." I wanted to wallow and have a bit of a pity party for myself. Having time to do such a thing was rare, but this seemed like the perfect opportunity.

Jasper squeezed my shoulders, and I relaxed into his touch, and the comfort of his thoughts reassuring my own racing ones. "Ava. None of this is your fault. You cannot take the blame for Monica's actions, especially when you've had no control over them. Every decision you've made, and every action you've taken you have done with the best interests of the pack in mind. Don't let Duke get in your head. He's just out of his mind with worry."

"I can't say I blame him," I muttered. I couldn't imagine knowing something was wrong with Jasper and being helpless to fix it or make it better. I needed to find Lucy, and at the same time figure out a way to pay Orcus's debt without compromising the safety of the pack. No big deal, right?

* * *

Jasper and I trailed our way back to the small room they had put Merrick in, and I knocked lightly on the partially open door. "How's the patient?"

Merrick was sitting up in bed, looking a thousand times better than he had when we left him. A tensor bandage was wrapped around his arm, keeping it straight, and Mary was checking a small bag of fluids draining into an IV in his hand. Merrick smiled at me. "Never been better."

Beau laughed from his chair next to the bed where he sat scrolling on his phone. "He says now. You should've heard the big bad wolf cry when Mary set his arm."

"Beau!" I scolded. "Don't forget I saw you in the hospital too, and you weren't exactly the toughest guy in the room then either."

He gave Merrick his trademark grin. "He knows I'm

kidding, baby girl. Just showing him how easy you are to wind up." Merrick smiled back, and suddenly I didn't want them to be friends anymore. That was a dangerous idea. One I could probably do without.

"How'd it go with the Alpha?" Beau asked. "How much trouble are you in?"

"Surprisingly not a lot." I sank into the chair next to Beau, tipping my head back to look at the ceiling.

"You're shitting me," was Beau's eloquent response.

I laughed. "I'm not. But we do have to find Lucy. Duke stormed in and made a whole scene. So now we have to figure out how to get Lucy here for an exorcism, which sounds like buckets of fun, as well as somehow convincing a centuries old demon they don't want me to pay my mother's life debt."

Beau hummed. "So just your average Tuesday?"

Jasper groaned, sinking to the floor in front of me and resting his head against my knees. "Basically."

I looked over at Beau. "You should go home and get some sleep. I'll watch over the patient."

He gave me a look of disbelief. "You have to be just as exhausted as I am."

"Beau," I warned. "Just go home. I've got this. Go shower -- you smell."

Jasper chuckled. "I'd do as she says. She's not in a mood to fuck with."

Beau shook his head and walked toward the door. "I'll let Adrian know we're home and grab a nap at his place. Then I'm coming back to swap off with you, and *then* we can worry about Lucy and all of your mom's pleasant friends."

"Yeah, yeah." I waved him off. "Now go!"

Beau left, and I turned my attention to Merrick. "How bad was it?"

He shrugged. "Shattered, as we expected. Mary set it so it'll heal straight though, and I should be good to go by tonight. My leg had already healed itself by the time we got here."

I nodded. "That's good. You should close your eyes and

get some sleep too."

Merrick closed his eyes, letting the medicine carry him off toward sleep. Jasper and I sat silently in the room, waiting for his breathing to level out. When I was certain my brother was asleep, I tapped Jasper's shoulder, gesturing toward the hallway.

I had so many emotions, I wasn't sure where to begin. All I knew was that this wasn't the kind of conversation one had in their mind. I closed the door behind me quietly, making sure Merrick was still softly snoring on the bed. Once I was confident he was still asleep, I slumped to the ground, cupping my head in my hands. "Oh God, Jasper. What the hell are we going to do?"

Jasper slid down the wall to sit next to me, cradling me in his embrace. "We're going to wait until Merrick can go home, and then we're going to find Lucy. We're going to scour every book in every Goddamned library until we find something that will break you from your family's obligations. I don't care what it costs. I don't care how long we have to search. I *will* protect you, Ava. I'm not letting you go."

I nodded, letting his heartbeat soothe me. At this moment, I wasn't sure if there was anything else we could do. I couldn't let Lucy get hurt for me -- out of anyone, she was the most innocent in all of this. "Merrick should come home with us."

Jasper tightened his arms around me. "Yes. And I'll call my buddy and see if we can stay in the new place a bit early. No one but he and I know about it, and I would feel better knowing you both were somewhere secure."

The new apartment. Yeah. That made sense. But my heart was racing in a way I couldn't explain or describe, and I suddenly wished it weren't this situation forcing us into our new home. This move should be exciting, and happy, and everything I had dreamed about when I pictured Jasper's and my life together. Not cloaked in secrecy and veiled in a darkness that weighed heavy on my soul. I chewed my lip. "I probably should give Mollie a heads up."

Jasper pulled away slightly so he could look me in the eyes. "Are you sure that's a wise idea? Right now the apartment is secure. I know you love Mollie, but the fewer people who know, the better."

I sighed. "I know. But you and I are also both well aware if I disappear when I'm supposed to be home, she'll sound every alarm in the Goddamn city."

"*Touché*, Green, *touché*." Jasper chuckled, and the sound was out of place in the empty hallway where we sat.

"Besides, maybe if we have a stable place then Betty can come home." My fluffy cat had been living with Mollie while we jumped between each of our apartments.

"Oh, gee, can she?" Jasper didn't bother to contain his sarcasm and I smacked him with the back of my hand.

"Be nice."

"So you tell Mollie. But bare minimum please. Don't tell her specifics and blame it on my work if you have to."

I rolled my eyes. "Mollie will love that."

Jasper pulled my chin up to look at him. "Mollie has no other option. And you'll take Beau with you into town, okay?"

"Where will you be?"

He grinned, the kind of smile that sent electricity ricocheting throughout my entire body -- bond or no bond. "I'll be setting up our new home."

"Mmm..." I kissed him lightly on the lips, unable to stop myself when he looked so damn pleased. "This is more what I expected when you asked me to move in with you."

"So I shouldn't mention I'll be going in to rig the place with booby traps and weapons?"

Despite myself, I laughed. Jasper had always had that effect on me, to lighten the mood even when the situation was dire, and the outcomes seemed bleak. He pressed a kiss to my forehead. "Go check on Merrick. I'll make a few calls. You have your makhairas?"

I patted my sides. "Always."

"And your phone?"

I grimaced. Months of training and danger, but I was

still no better at keeping the damn thing charged.

Jasper raised a dark brow in my direction, and I wasn't sure if he was trying not to laugh or was going to scold me. "Seriously?"

"In my defense, it wasn't exactly like we were planning on having cell signal out in the forest."

"Mhm…" He smirked at me. "A likely excuse."

I rolled my eyes. "Go. Go do whatever it is you're planning on doing, and I'll head into town when Beau wakes up."

Jasper stuffed his hands in his pockets and began to walk away. "I'll see you at our house later tonight."

Our house. I couldn't lie -- I liked the way that sounded. Our house. Now we just needed to figure out a way to stay alive long enough to enjoy it.

Chapter 5

In the end, it wasn't Beau who made the drive with me to meet Mollie. The lack of sleep had obviously caught up to him, and even after I went and did all but kick his door open, I could still hear the loud snoring coming from the window at Adrian's house. The *open* window -- Beau didn't fear a lot. No, in the end it was Merrick who sat in the passenger seat of my car, as dirt roads turned to gravel which became the small highway that would lead us to Merrillan. Mary had come in just after Merrick had woken up, deeming his arm satisfactorily healed, and releasing him from her care. He needed to take it easy for the rest of the day, but we both figured a drive shouldn't be overly stressful. Definitely less stressful for all of us than if Jasper were to find out I had gone into town on my own.

I slowed my speed as we rolled into the small downtown. It seemed so different since the last time I had been there, but really had anything changed? The post office still needed a new coat of paint, the peeling grey wood so at odds with the friendly clerk I knew would be inside. The hardware shop, the grocery store, and the small florist who only ever seemed to be busy on Valentine's Day and prom. Everything was the same as it had been when I'd driven here last, so why was I so at odds with my hometown?

"So this is where you grew up." Merrick looked around as we drove, rubbing his arm.

I waved my hand around in a grand gesture, giving him a wry smile. "Sure is. Doesn't get much finer than downtown Merrillan." I frowned as he continued to run his hand down his arm. "Does it still hurt?"

"What?" Merrick looked down at his arm, as if he were unaware he had been rubbing it. "No. I guess it just feels funny still."

I nodded. Somehow I knew what he meant. It wasn't the pain, or the healing that was bothering him. It was the reason the arm was hurt -- Monica. Still at large, hopefully a little bit slower and worse for the wear, but who the hell knew with her anymore. I hadn't brought up the conversation they had in the woods. If I were in his shoes, I certainly wouldn't want to talk about it. Maybe one day, when the wounds were less fresh, less raw. Maybe then we could talk about Monica. I flipped on my turning switch, pulling into a vacant space a block away from the diner.

I used Jasper's phone to make a quick call to Mollie -- all it took to arrange a last-minute meeting at our usual haunt. She didn't ask any questions, just let me know when she'd be there waiting for me. That was Mollie. If there was a chance she could get the information in person, she'd wait. It was about the only time she would be patient.

I got out of the car, Merrick trailing behind me. "Won't your friend mind me tagging along?" he asked.

I scoffed. "Mollie would never turn down an opportunity to make a new friend."

Merrick stopped for a moment, scuffing the toe of his sneaker on the sidewalk. "Ava."

I was ahead, already anxious to meet Mollie and fill her in the best I could. "What's up?" Potential explanations for my anticipated disappearance raced through my mind, and I picked through them to figure out what would be the most believable. *Jasper was sick...* No. She'd see through that right away. *I got fired.* Also a definite no.

"Something feels off. We should go back."

I rolled my eyes. Paranoid wolves were going to be the death of me. "We're going to see Mollie. And then we'll meet Jasper." I pointed toward the tarnished sides of the diner, aged aluminum that must have sparkled in its prime. "It's a public place. We're a block away from the car. I'm armed, and you're a werewolf. What's the worst that can happen?"

Merrick huffed but started walking once more. I could see the top of Mollie's blonde head through the glass, her expression focused as she pored over the menu. She did this every time we went to the diner, acting like she was going to choose something new, even though we both knew she was going to get the grilled cheese and side salad. A pang went through my chest as I realized just how much I missed my best friend, and I eagerly pulled Merrick along toward the front door.

"Mate." Merrick's harsh whisper had me tripping over my feet. I froze, looking through the smudged glass at my best friend, the girl I had grown up with.

"Excuse me?" No. No. *No.* This wasn't happening. Not to Mollie. Not to my sweet best friend who couldn't bear to watch *Casper* with me as kids. As if she had heard us, she swiveled in our direction, giving me a bright smile and a wave. Her expression shifted into something I had never seen on Mollie's delicate features before.

Merrick tipped his head toward Mollie, who was staring right back at him. "She's my mate. It's why my wolf was going crazy in the parking lot. He must have scented her."

I whipped my head around to look at him dead on, his dark gaze leaving no room for argument. "No. You have to be mistaken. Jasp told me human/wolf mates are rare." Not Mollie. I didn't want this life for her. Merrick was a good man, of that I was certain. But this life... it would destroy her. Mollie deserved the white picket fence, the house in the suburbs. The two kids, a husband who worked a reliable job and spoiled her rotten. Not danger and knives, and a new apartment because the other one might be compromised.

He raised his brows, severing his stare-off with Mollie to meet my gaze, frowning. "They are rare." His words trailed off, like I was missing something important in the whole situation.

"So what are the chances of us *both* having werewolf mates? Nearly impossible. No. You're mistaken. We'll go eat with Mollie and you'll realize you were just hungry or something." I pulled him, wanting this conversation to be over. I wanted to sit at the table with my best friend, and listen to her order the grilled cheese, and figure out some way to tell her I was leaving town for an undetermined amount of time.

"Jasper is right. Human/wolf mates are rare," Merrick

began gently, willing me to keep calm. To not draw attention toward us. "But, Ava, surely you know Mollie isn't human."

I was pretty sure my heart stopped beating for a moment. "Excuse me?"

Merrick shook his head. "Mollie. She's a witch."

I forced myself to keep my focus on Merrick, even as the sidewalk was being ripped out beneath my feet. Surely I wasn't that clueless. *Mollie, a witch*? No. Mollie wouldn't go trick-or-treating with me. She wouldn't go into the woods at night and refused to watch any horror movies. Mollie was tiny, and perfect, and blonde, and one hundred percent not a witch. *Right*?

I looked back into the window, at my beautiful best friend who I had tried so long to protect. I don't know what I was hoping to see. But her confused face met my own, and within a second blinked into something that looked like realization. Resolution. *No*.

Behind the smeared glass, Mollie mouthed my name. An apology of sorts. "Merrick. What the hell is going on?"

"You… you didn't know?"

I turned my head to give him an incredulous look. "Do you really think if I knew my best friend was a *witch* I would be reacting like this?" I wanted to go into the diner and tell Mollie everything. I wanted to run far away and let someone else deal with the fallout. I didn't know what I wanted, but I knew I didn't want to be in this situation. I sighed. "I need to meet Jasper. I… I can't do this right now."

I turned and began the short walk back to the car, looking over my shoulder when I noticed Merrick wasn't following me. "Are you coming?"

Merrick looked back and forth between me and the diner he didn't want to come to in the first place. "You're asking my wolf to leave his mate," he muttered, tossing a mournful stare into the diner.

I sobered. I knew how that felt, to be apart from your mate once you found them. I felt it even now, the urge to run back to Jasper just to be whole once more. I wouldn't make him leave Mollie, but I couldn't stay either. "I'm sorry. I have to go."

The only sound on the way back to the car was my shoes hitting the sidewalk. I couldn't get images of Mollie out of my head, as a tiny child -- determined even then. On our first day of high school, Mollie shielding me from the upperclassmen as we wandered from class to class. Mollie laughing, smiling, giving Jasper a hug. Did she know? Even when I first met him, when I tried to run? Did she know who Jasper really was? Who I was? I threw open the car door, slouching into my seat. I needed to collect myself and drive to the apartment. Ten seconds. That was all I needed. I shouldn't be leaving Merrick alone in town, but he was a werewolf, and now apparently his mate was a witch. He'd be fine.

I groaned, running my hand down my face. One day. One day without chaos and craziness, that's all I wanted. I wanted to lie in bed with Jasper and laugh at mindless TV shows. For Lucy and Duke to come over for dinner in our new apartment -- a dinner I would most likely burn. I wanted to see Mollie get married, and to not worry about what creature was going to come crawling out from the underworld next.

But I had made a decision when I chose Jasper. I chose to be aware of the things that went bump in the night, and to learn about monsters from children's bedtime stories. I wanted to be a light in the darkness, and to have strength in moments where others faltered. So right now, I needed to take a deep breath, suck up my own personal feelings, and figure out my next step without feeling sorry for myself.

A tap on the window startled me from my pep talk, and I pulled my hands away from my face. At the window was Mollie, and several feet behind her stood Merrick. I glared at him, and he shrugged his shoulders as if to say there was nothing he could do. Which, in situations involving Mollie, was probably true.

I rolled my window down but didn't make a move to get out of the car. My emotions were mixed, and I didn't want to be doing this right now.

Mollie bit her lip. "Ava."

Tears pricked my eyes. Betrayed. I was betrayed. "How could you not tell me?"

"I'm sorry, okay? I'm the worst friend alive. I understand if you never want to see me again." Mollie took a deep breath in, steadying herself. "But I can help."

I nearly choked. "Excuse me?"

She nodded, pressing her lips together. "I can help. With Orcus."

I ignored Merrick grimacing behind her. *Paranoid wolves.* "How do you know about Orcus?"

"It's a long story." Mollie looked like she was about to cry, fidgeting with her hands and tapping her feet. "Uh, I did some bad shit, Ava. Some real bad shit. But you have to believe me, I didn't want to do any of it."

I tapped my fingers on the steering wheeling, squeezing it so the leather squealed beneath my hands. Mollie was a good actress, but she wasn't *that* good. Or at least the Mollie I had thought I had known. The woman in front of me was a stranger dressed in my best friend's clothes. But I had limited time to figure out a solution, and I wasn't sure what else I could do. I weighed my options. I could use her without trusting her. I met her gaze, letting no emotion seep through the cracks in my emotional defense. "I should warn you I'm armed."

She nodded once, an acknowledgement. "I wouldn't expect anything less from a Venator."

"And I can't guarantee Jasper won't try to rip you to shreds."

Mollie stiffened her shoulders and steeled her gaze. "I can handle myself."

* * *

"I really hope I'm not going to regret this," I muttered. I unlocked the car doors. "Get in. We don't have much time."

Molly slid into the passenger seat next to me, and Merrick folded his large body into my small backseat. Subdued. That was the word that came to mind to describe Mollie as we pulled out onto the road once more. She was small, pulled into herself. I sighed, the only sound in the quiet car.

"Look, if this is going to work, which for all our sakes it better, we're going to have to talk about things." I kept my eyes focused on the road, telling myself it was for safety and not because I didn't want to meet Mollie's gaze.

Merrick was the first to speak up. "You're my mate."

My mouth dropped open. "Jesus, Merrick! Can we not start on the small scale of things?" I glared at him in my rearview mirror, but he just shrugged.

"I know," Mollie responded. "I knew as soon as you got out of Ava's car."

This time I turned to stare at her, Merrick yelping as the car swerved too far to the right. "You knew?"

"It's kind of hard not to know." She twirled a blonde curl around her finger.

"But... What about Ben?"

"Who's Ben?" Merrick growled from the backseat.

I ignored him. "What are you going to do about Ben?"

Mollie sighed sadly, looking down at her hand. I followed her gaze to see a perfect engagement ring circling her finger. She twisted it off, sliding it into her pocket. "I always knew this day might come. I just hoped it wouldn't." I watched her out of the corner of my eye as she stared out the window. "When you grow up a witch, you understand the potentials for supernatural mates. You can't fight fate, Ava."

I was beginning to realize how true that statement really was.

"Can we circle back around to who Ben is?" I glanced into my rearview mirror, stunned to see the normally placid Merrick glaring back at me with his teeth bared.

Mollie sighed again, and I rolled my eyes. "Ben is Mollie's fiancé," I replied, my voice catching when I thought of sweet Ben -- so in love with Mollie. But that had been a different Mollie. One who wasn't a witch.

"Oh." Merrick looked like he was fighting with himself to get his wolf back under control, regaining some of his gentle nature. "Um. Well. We don't have to..." His voice trailed off into the silence of the car.

"We both know that's not an option," Mollie snapped, her voice matter of fact. "You really want to spend the rest of your life as a rejected mate?"

"No."

A cold laugh came from the passenger seat, and if I hadn't known it was my best friend sitting there, I would have never guessed it was her. "That's what I thought. And it's tenfold worse for a witch. I would lose most of my power."

The three of us sat in uncomfortable silence as the suburbs of Merrillan became farmer's fields. There was nothing more to say. Broken relationships stretched between us. Merrick and my mother. Mollie and myself. And poor, sweet, Ben. Did he deserve any of this?

Did any of us, really?

The rest of the drive to the apartment was eerily quiet, none of us sure what to say to reassure the others. As I turned into the parking lot, Mollie spoke up. "Where are we?"

"My apartment. I mean, Jasper's and my apartment." I couldn't help but notice a small spark of joy when I spoke the words aloud. It was ours. A piece of the life we would build together.

Mollie hummed. "I guess I assumed you were going to bring me to the pack lands."

I shook my head. "It's not safe there right now. Come on. You said you could help, and we don't have a lot of time."

The ground floor apartment was lit up warmly, and I could see Jasper through the open window, carrying a box of clothes into another room. He must have gone back to my old place to get our things. I didn't bother knocking as I entered the door -- this was my home now, after all. "Jasp?" I called.

"Baby!" I heard the crash of something hitting the ground, and Jasper was rushing through the doorway lifting me off my feet.

I laughed nervously as he squeezed me tightly in his broad arms. "I just went to town, Jasp. You knew where I was."

He tipped his forehead to mine, meeting my gaze. "Right now, until we catch this thing, anytime you come home to me is a cause for celebration." He looked over my shoulder, nodding at Merrick, and I saw the shock hit him when he noticed Mollie standing behind him. "Baby. What is Mollie doing here?" His voice was tight and quiet, and his anxiety was seeping through my veins down the bond.

"Um. Well. You see." How did I even begin to explain what all had transpired at the diner?

"I'm a witch," Mollie piped up, softly.

Merrick shifted his body in front of her, protecting the small blonde. "And my mate."

Jasper closed his eyes, cursing under his breath. He opened them again, blinking at me. "Seriously? You've brought a witch here?"

Mollie threw her hands up defensively. "I'm here to help!"

The growl that escaped Jasper was dark and dangerous. "How can I know for sure? You've lied to both Ava and myself about who you really are. We can't trust you. Maybe you've been working with Monica this whole time."

"I have," Mollie admitted, and all three of us took a sharp breath.

"Mollie," I whispered. "How could you?" Betrayal was too slight of a word to describe the emotions pounding through my heart. This couldn't be happening.

"Ava, you don't understand." Her big blue eyes were begging me to listen to her. In them I saw a glimpse of my best friend. "It wasn't me, not really. It was my family. They've been helping her. But I knew. I knew, and that makes me just as bad as the rest of them, and I'm so sorry."

Jasper growled. "You need to leave, now, before I make you leave. And you don't want me to make you leave."

I pressed my hand against Jasper's chest, his heart

steadying with my touch. *"Let her finish,"* I begged him through the bond. I needed something to cling to, some scrap of Mollie was still there.

Jasper tipped his chin up at Mollie. "Go on."

Mollie mouthed a thank you my way, before fixing a stare back on Jasper. "I knew. But I couldn't stop them. And I couldn't tell anyone. You understand, don't you? You have that in packs, right?"

"Yes." Jasper gave her a brisk nod. "But I would never put Ava in any danger with my actions. You have by allowing her parents to get away with their bullshit. Multiple times."

The knife to my heart was back, twisting its way deeper inside. I couldn't think of all the times she had lied to my face or knew the turmoil bubbling inside of me. "You said you could help."

Mollie met my stare gratefully. "I can. I mean, I think I can. You need to get the demon and Monica both in the same place right?"

"Preferably before Saturday at midnight." I choked on the words. We only had a few days left.

She was quiet for a moment. "What did Orcus ask for if you couldn't offer up Monica?"

I peeked at Jasper underneath my lashes, whose face had become a mask of stone. "Me."

Mollie cursed under her breath. "Okay. This is what we're going to do. We're going to summon both of them here at the same time. It's going to be tricky, timing wise, because we need to make sure they both arrive at the same time. If Monica comes too early, she'll run. If the Orcus's lackey is here too early, they'll take Ava. We only have one shot."

"Are you sure you can handle this?" Jasper asked, crossing his arms in front of his body.

Mollie met his glare, and I saw a fragment of the old Mollie in her determined eyes. "Yes. Monica is tied to my family's magic. She'll have to come if summoned. But I'm going to need some things, and you and Merrick are going to have to get them for me."

Merrick growled, still in his defensive stance. "No."

Mollie took a step forward, her back to me, tipping her head up to look at her newfound mate head-on. "Look. If you want to be my mate, you're going to have to get used to this. Get used to *me*. I need you and Jasp in your little wolfy forms to run off and find some shit for me. You're going to do that, and then we can celebrate this fucked-up form of fate that brought us together."

Despite myself, I laughed out loud, and Merrick scowled. Jasper just nodded. "Whatever it takes. When do we need to leave?"

Mollie fixed her attention back on Jasper. "As soon as possible. It should be easy to get the stuff, but I'd rather not leave this to the last minute. And grab a few of your wolfy friends on the way back. Some extra muscle wouldn't hurt if things don't go to plan."

Jasper grabbed my hand, pulling me into the small kitchen. He forced me to look at him. "Do you trust her?"

I looked back at the small blonde, already ordering Merrick to be safe with equal parts affection and fierceness. "Yeah. I think I do."

He kissed me briefly. "Then I'm going to go get the things she needs. You will stay here, armed, and on alert at all times."

I patted behind my back, making sure my blades were still secure in their hiding place. Although, what I could do against a witch I wasn't sure. I had seen my mother in the forest, and if that was only a part of the power she had taken on... I shuddered to think of the entirety of it.

"Merrick," Jasper commanded, turning away from me. "You're with me. Let's go." Mollie gave Jasper a quick list of things she required for both summoning spells, and then they were gone, disappearing into the grim light of the late afternoon.

Mollie turned toward me, hands on her hips. "So, I guess it was about time you made the whole living together thing official."

I shrugged, suddenly uncomfortable around Mollie without the barrier of Merrick or Jasper. "Yeah. As of like, an hour ago."

"Jesus, Ava," Mollie muttered, shaking her head. "Who the hell would've thought we'd end up here?" She laughed, no humour evident in her voice.

My blood was pumping furiously through my veins, my heart racing. She was so calm. Why was she so calm? I sure as hell wasn't calm. "How could you lie to me? How could you lie to your best friend's face for years?"

She pressed her lips together, tears welling behind her baby blue eyes. "I wanted to tell you, Ava. Really, I did. My family, they've been witches for a long time. I physically couldn't tell you myself."

I frowned. "So how could an entire pack of wolves not know you were a witch? That seems like something they would notice pretty damn quickly."

Mollie shrugged. "We've enchanted ourselves not to smell like witches to other species. It's a spell that's gone by the wayside in recent years, but my family still remembers it. Monica insisted we use it on her as well."

The whole encounter in the forest suddenly made sense, why the guys couldn't smell her until they were aware of her presence. She had been enchanted. Was Monica using both witch magic and demon magic? *Jesus.* But one thing still wasn't adding up.

Chapter 6

"Merrick smelled you. The second we stepped out of the car."

Mollie's expression softened for a moment, and her voice grew soft. "The mate bond overpowers anything else. Even enchantments."

That made sense. Everything else in this crazy, fucked-up world in which I'd found myself confused me, but the idea the bond between soulmates would outweigh even the strongest of magic? Yeah. I got it. A piece of the ice I had so carefully layered my heart in chipped away. The mate bond between Merrick and Mollie was real, and I knew she would never do anything to hurt her mate. And part of that would include keeping me safe. I was safe with Mollie. For now.

Trust was another issue, something to be discussed later, when multiple lives weren't at stake. I wasn't sure I would ever be able to rebuild our friendship to what it used to be, but if Mollie's situation were anything like the wolves' Alpha command I could kind of understand it. But to help my mother murder innocent wolves? Hopefully she had been a naïve bystander regarding those deaths, but even so I couldn't imagine Mollie's mild-mannered parents racing out to summon demons and cast evil spells. Maybe Monica's influence was greater than I expected.

I shook my head. *All* of that could wait until we figured a way out of this. Enemy of my enemy and all that shit, right? I sighed. "So what's first?"

A small smile crossed Mollie's face. "We need an open space. A big one. Normally you can summon a demon wherever you want, but we're going to need space for both Monica and the demon. Plus the wolves will need space too."

"The backyard," I said, walking through the kitchen. I so wanted to run my hand along the countertops, explore every square inch of my new home. *Our* new home. But that was also on the Things to Do After We Destroyed a Demon list. "We're still on the edge of the pack's forest out here, so we should have enough privacy and space for you to do your witchy shit."

Mollie laughed under her breath. "Witchy shit," she muttered. "You know, I could say the same about your Venator stuff. Do you dress all in black, whipping knives at people's heads?"

I waited for Mollie to follow me out to the small patio, closing the sliding door behind her. "All black yes, although I prefer not to throw my weapons." I ran my hand down my back reassuringly. Jasper was always calling me out on touching my makhairas but it made me feel better to know they were there if I needed them. "Do you wear pointy hats and stir cauldrons?"

This time her laugh was full and true. "You've been watching too many movies. Definitely no pointy hats. They don't suit my features." Mollie pushed aside my hair, and I forced myself not to flinch away from her touch. "He marked you," she whispered, running a finger lightly down the bite on my neck.

I shook my head. "We marked each other." I spun around in a circle in the middle of our large backyard. "Will this do?" We were surrounded by trees, but the clearing was large, and the grass was recently trimmed. In the distance, the last smudges of daylight were dropping over the horizon, blush bleeding into night.

I glanced over at Mollie, who was already pacing out a large circle on the ground, her small feet leaving imprints in the damp grass. "This will be fine."

"So, uh, what happens next?"

She paused, crossing back on her path to slice through the middle of her circle. "Next Jasper and Merrick bring us back the things I need for a summoning spell."

"Jasper doesn't like being apart since..." I trailed off, embarrassed.

Mollie tipped her head to the side, not understanding what I was saying.

"Jasp. He's my mate. He doesn't like it when we have to be apart for a long period of time." The heat of a blush was spreading over my cheeks, but thankfully Mollie wouldn't be able to see it in the dim light.

"No shit, Ava. Wolves are possessive. If you're marked, he's going to have a bit of separation anxiety."

I frowned, irritated. What did she know about my relationship? "Thanks for the tip. I'll keep it in mind next time I'm working as a Venator. For the wolves. That I happen to know fairly well."

Mollie stopped, tripping over her feet. "Shit. I'm sorry. I didn't mean to sound like such a bitch. Of course you know all that."

I crossed my arms against the chill of the night, already seeping into my bones. "What are you pacing out?"

"A pentagram. I need it to be just the right size to summon two different beings. They're technically two different spells, and I'm going to have to try to perform them at the same time." I could hear her counting under her breath as she crossed back and forth.

I nodded, acting like I understood what she was saying. "How do you know it'll be the right demon you summon, and not some other random spirit?" Exactly what I needed right now -- another demon to track me around town.

"Different sacrifices summon different beings. Same thing with candles, and the incantation I'll say..." she trailed off, counting once more.

My heart caught in my throat. "Sacrifice?"

Mollie stopped once more, staring at me with a look of fear. "Yes, Ava. I'll require a blood sacrifice of someone close to the summoner, which in this case is me."

I couldn't breathe, and I stroked my back again to reassure myself that my knives hadn't disappeared in the five minutes we had been out here. "Okay. Okay. Um. So what's our plan there?"

Mollie burst out laughing. "Oh my God, you should've seen your face." When I didn't join in her laughter she bit her lip. "I'm sorry. I couldn't help it. I don't know how else to deal with this shit except humour."

My heartbeat was slowly returning to its normal rate,

and I tried to force a smile on my face. "So. No human sacrifices?"

She shook her head. "No. That used to be the way of things, but not anymore. Most of us understand that a blood sacrifice only requires a drop or two of blood to activate the summons. The only witches who still slice throats for their sacrifices are the super old school ones -- they like it messy." She shuddered, and I could only imagine Mollie grimacing in her tidy, posh clothes as she tried to not get blood on her shoes.

It's why Venators wore black.

"Lucy... she's my friend. The one the demon is possessing. She'll be okay, right?" Sweet Lucy. Duke was right, she didn't deserve any of this. I needed to know she was going to be unharmed through this whole process.

Mollie gave me a soft smile. "I'll do my best."

I smiled back. I knew what that meant, because I had to say the same thing once or twice myself as well. But I was going to make sure Lucy was safe if it was the last thing I did. Before Mollie had come into the picture as a witch, I had been ready to sacrifice myself for the safety of the pack, and I was still willing to do that for the sake of my innocent friend. Whatever it took, Lucy would be okay.

"*Where are you?*" Jasper's urgent voice carried over the bond.

I shot a glance over to Mollie. "*In the backyard. What's wrong?*"

"*Meet me in the apartment. I'll send Merrick out for Mollie.*"

I brought my attention back to Mollie. "The guys are back. I'm going to go meet Jasper in the house, and it sounds like Merrick is on his way out here." Jasper sounded worried, and I wanted to make sure everything was okay.

"Mhmm..." Mollie was preoccupied with her pentagram and didn't even look up in my direction.

I turned to walk away, and she looked up briefly. "Don't be too long. We need to get this done right away in case it doesn't work the first time."

Merrick's howl was close, so I knew he would be back

here with her in no time. Besides, Mollie could handle herself right? She was a witch after all.

I jogged back into the house, the sliding door closing behind me with a resounding clunk. "Jasp?" I called.

"In here," he replied. I followed the sound of his voice toward the bedroom -- *our* bedroom. I stopped in the doorway, frozen at the sight of Jasper naked in the middle of the room. His carved muscles were illuminated by the slice of moonlight coming in through the open window, every inch of him on display. For me.

Mate. I couldn't stop the thought, and Jasper turned unsmiling toward me. "Ava. I got back as soon as I could." He crossed the room in two quick steps, taking me into his arms and kissing me hard.

I pushed away from him, Mollie's reminder to not be gone long still lingering in my head. "You weren't gone long at all. Did you find everything Mollie wanted?"

He nodded. "Adrian is going to round up a couple of the guys and meet us here around eight."

"Thank God." I breathed out heavily. "Does the Alpha know?"

Jasper shrugged. "Probably. Not much happens that he doesn't know about. But he's letting it happen this way for whatever reason."

"He has too much faith in me." I leaned into Jasper's firm body, letting his heartbeat steady me.

"Or you don't have enough faith in yourself."

I sighed against his chest. "So what did you actually need? You sounded worried."

He placed a large hand on either side of my face, pulling me into a kiss once more. "I just wanted to make sure you were okay," he whispered. "And to do this." He kissed me again, moving his lips against mine firmly, and teasing me with his tongue.

"Jasp," I breathed out his name with a gasp, pushing my hands along his firm abs.

"Just let me feel you," he whispered, trailing his fingers down my back, pushing his nose into my neck, and tickling my mark. "Let me know you're here. That you're safe."

He trailed his fingers down my side, pulling my pants down and over my thighs. My sheathed blades were unclasped, tossed alongside my clothes. I gasped as he dipped his fingers into my underwear, stroking the damp heat he found there. "Fuck," he cursed under his breath. He slipped his fingers into my wet pussy, and I cried out softly. "Just let me see you like this, Ava. And then we can risk our lives. But right now, I want this." He circled his thumb luxuriously over my clit, and I rocked into his hand.

It felt so good. But it wasn't enough. "Jasp, I need you," I begged, not stopping riding his hand.

He nodded, his eyes already black with lust and hunger. "You don't need to ask me twice."

I complained lightly when he removed his hand, but he was pushing us back against the wall, lifting me up, and I had nothing to complain about anymore when I felt the hard tip of his cock pressing against me. I wrapped my legs around his waist, sinking onto him. He hissed out a breath through his teeth, thrusting into me as well. We both moaned as he sank into me fully.

"I love you," he whispered.

"*I love you,*" I thought back, and he grinned wildly.

He lifted my hips, sliding me up and down his cock, my back pressed to the wall. "That's so fucking hot, baby."

"The part where I'm telepathic and speak to you with my mind? I bet you say that to all the girls." I fluttered my eyelashes and stopped when a groan broke through my lips as Jasper thrust firmly into me.

"The fact that you're *mine.*" His movements were growing quicker, my breaths keeping time with his own. We both needed release, needed to move as one.

I forced my hips forward, grinding against him as he moved. "Of course I'm yours."

His hips stuttered. "Say it again baby," he murmured, grabbing my thighs and forcing me closer.

"I'm yours," I whispered, and I cried out as Jasper drove himself deeper and my body orgasmed around him.

"Fuck," Jasper cursed again, and his thrusts were no longer timed and precise. They were wild, animalistic, as he pushed himself to release, roaring out my name.

I wrapped my arms around his neck as we both came down from our high. I loved him so much. So much more than I thought was ever possible. I just had no idea how to put such a feeling into words. Jasper smiled against my neck. "*I love you too.*"

A lone howl broke through our moment. "Shit," Jasper muttered, getting to his feet and digging through his duffel bag of clothes. "That's Duke. He must have come with Adrian."

"Are you really going to bother getting dressed if you're just going to shift anyways?" I asked, pulling my own clothes and blades back on. "And what is Duke doing here?"

Jasper tugged on a loose pair of athletic shorts. "It's for Mollie's benefit. And as for Duke... he's here for revenge."

* * *

Revenge. How ominous. I knew Jasper didn't mean revenge on us, even though Duke's angry wolf glare was enough to make me think otherwise. No, Duke was here for revenge on the demon possessing his mate, and the one who had brought the demon here in the first place -- Monica.

We stood in a circle around the pentagram Mollie had outlined with salt. The list of things Jasper had been asked to grab was oddly simple. Salt. Candles. A knife. Paper. Things Jasper would've had on hand if we hadn't hurriedly moved in like we had done. We could've been having a romantic dinner, or a double date. But instead we were summoning a demon, and a woman who owed them a debt.

I looked between the wolves standing around me -- my friends. My family. We could handle this. Right? Next to me was Jasper, already shifted, the shorts he had pulled on for modesty shredded next to him. Beau was on his left, Adrian's lean wolf next to him at the next point of the star. On my right was Duke, his tension and anxiety palpable even through the distance between us. I wanted to reassure him and tell him that Lucy would be okay. But there was no time for that. So instead I listened to him breathe, growling low. Jasper's voice was in my head, telling me to be prepared for whatever came next.

In the middle of the pentagram stood Mollie and a still human Merrick, who was helping the small blonde to light a series of black candles. "So I'll finish lighting these candles, and then Merrick is going to swap places with you, Ava."

Merrick growled, sounding displeased with this fact. "Oh, stop it. You'll be like five feet away from me. And I need Ava's blood for this to work."

This time it was Jasper's turn to growl, and Mollie rolled her eyes. "Paranoid wolves are going to be the death of me," she muttered, meeting my eyes with a wry smile.

I smiled back, something loosening in my chest. "Tell me about it."

"Maybe that's not something you should say surrounded by a pack of wolves," Merrick chimed in, but Mollie just shrugged, unbothered.

Mollie handed Merrick the last candle, carefully encased in a glass jar. "This one goes there." She pointed to the tip of the star near Duke, and Merrick obligingly placed the candle gently down. All five candles now sat at the tips of a star, the small flames flicking in the moonlight. Mollie began to tick things off on her fingers, speaking under her breath. "Okay. I think we're ready. Ava, come stand near me. Merrick, shift and take her place."

Bones cracked, and skin split as Merrick quickly shifted into his light grey wolf, trotting to take my place. I caught Jasper's eyes, and he nodded at me. *"Be safe. Be strong. Don't back down."* His warning thrummed along the bond with love and concern.

"Always, Jasp." My knives were strapped tight against my back, digging into my ribs as I made my way next to Mollie. "What now?"

She was scribbling on the pieces of paper with the chalk, scrawling something I couldn't read. "Now, we summon them. There's going to be a small gap of time in between the two summonses, so we need to decide who is less of a liability."

I thought for a moment. Neither was a good situation, but I'd much rather not see Monica's face as she ran away from me again. "Demon first."

Mollie nodded, crumpling up one of the sheets of paper into a ball. "Give me your hand."

When I hesitated she grabbed my hand, flipping it upside down and efficiently slicing into it with the small blade. "You're connected to both the possessed, and the one who owes a debt," Mollie explained, pressing my now bleeding palm to the ball of paper. "Your blood will have the strongest connection."

"Lucky me," I muttered, snatching my hand away.

"Don't go far," Mollie warned. "I still need you for Monica. Okay, are we all ready? I don't know how long it will take for the demon to arrive, but with this many supernaturals in one area and Ava's blood, it shouldn't take long." Around the circle, all the wolves growled their agreement. Mollie looked at me as she flicked the small lighter she held back and forth. The only thing I could see in her eyes was determination.

I grabbed her arm, squeezing lightly. Like it or not, we were in this together now. "Let's do this."

Mollie lit the piece of paper on fire, the ball blazing brightly in her hands -- she didn't seem to be affected by the heat. She was chanting under her breath, whispering words that meant nothing to me. I hoped she knew what she was doing.

When there was nothing more than a pile of ash in her hands, she stopped. It was silent, not even an owl calling its mate. "*Jasp.*" I pulled at him through the bond.

"*I'm here.*

The silence was making me uncomfortable. Surely it hadn't been this quiet only a moment ago? I turned to Mollie. "Where are they?"

She shrugged. "It takes time. We should use the time to summon Monica. This one should be a little easier. Monica is tied to us by blood, and it's hard for her to not obey the summons."

Once again, Mollie began to scribble on a piece of paper, balling it up and reaching for my other hand. She grimaced. "Sorry. It needs to be fresh."

I nodded. It definitely wasn't the worst I was expecting. A couple of small scrapes in my hands was nothing, and once my gloves were on they wouldn't hold me back at all. She held my hand over the paper, the blood staining the once pure sheet. Is this what my soul looked like? Once pure and naïve, immune to the darkness of the world. And now here I stood, surrounded by wolves, my hands sliced open by my best friend who was a witch. Ready to take on a demon -- and my mother. How stained was my soul?

"*Stay alert.*" Jasper's reminder nudged me to pay attention. The paper was already nothing more than ashes in her palm, the silence thick between us.

"*Where the hell are they?*" I reached behind me, taking the hilts of my blades in my hands. The longer we waited, the more uncomfortable I was. What if the spells didn't work? What if only the demon showed up? I still had time before my seven days were up, but that didn't matter if an angry demon dragged me back to the underworld.

"*Patience.*" Jasper's voice was a whisper. Next to me, Mollie gritted her teeth, and I could hear the grinding clear as day in the deafening silence. One of the wolves pawed at the ground, whining anxiously. A growl rattled my spine -- Duke was ready to get this over with. I couldn't say I disagreed with him.

I didn't know how I expected the demon to appear. Maybe a cloud of smoke, or a flash of lightning? Or perhaps, fire rolling through the field we stood in, announcing their presence. But it was much more subdued than that. A crackling sound split the quiet between us wide open, and one second it was just us. The next there stood the demon still inhabiting Lucy's body. The wolves around me sent up a cry as one. A warning.

Lucy smiled at me, a sinister grin that was not Lucy's. It spoke of death and darkness, and things Lucy had no idea about. Next to me, Mollie gripped my hand. We waited to see who would speak first.

"Venator," the demon greeted me as if we were old friends. I still couldn't get past the voice coming out of Lucy's mouth -- gravelly and ancient. "You have summoned me. I take it that means you have prepared my payment."

"I have." I expected my voice to waver, but instead it was clear and strong, carrying across our small circle to where Orcus's lackey stalked. "I found Monica. She should be here any moment." *Hopefully...*

Lucy raised a brow. Not Lucy. *Demon.* "You expect me to believe that?" They strode closer, and Mollie squeezed my hand tighter. Beside me, Jasper growled. The demon stopped before me, meeting my eyes through Lucy's gentle blue ones. They reached out a soft finger, stroking my chin. "What's to stop me from claiming you as my due payment? You definitely have more life left in you than the other one."

I forced myself to meet their twisted gaze, hoping to see some scrap of Lucy still behind those eyes. "That may be, but I'm not the one who owes you a debt. You'd much rather have Monica, so you'll wait."

The demon narrowed their gaze. "You have five minutes," they hissed. "Five minutes, and then I'm taking you, and this body I'm currently inhabiting."

"I still have more days," I argued. I needed a backup plan in case Mollie was wrong and Monica didn't heed the pull of the blood bond. They couldn't end our deal early.

They waved their hands dismissively. "I'm bored of your realm. Five minutes."

Well, *shit.* I tightened my hand on the leather wrapped knives so hard I was almost certain I could crush the steel. Where the hell was Monica? *"Patience, baby,"* Jasper reassured me down our bond. *"She'll be here."*

I watched the demon with careful eyes, not wanting them out of my sight. They paced uneasily, as if being around this many wolves was making them uncomfortable. Too fucking bad. *"Remind me again why we can't just perform an exorcism?"*

If it was another time, I'm sure Jasper would've laughed. Instead his response was quiet and serious. *"Because an exorcism would be more dangerous to Lucy. We need the being to leave willingly, which they'll do once they're paid."*

The demon was still skulking around, and I was spinning in place to watch them. They came face to face with Duke, who bared his teeth and snapped furiously. "The body I'm using has a relationship with this one," they announced, and Duke growled again.

Mollie and I stared at each other for a moment. The last thing we needed was for Duke to bite Lucy's head off -- literally. I knew he would never do anything to harm his mate, but this creature currently inhabiting her body, well, that was a different story.

"Ticktock, Venator. Where is the other one?" The demon stretched Lucy's mouth in a horrifying grin, sending a wave of disgust through me.

"She'll be here," Mollie confirmed next to me.

"We'll see." Orcus's lackey sounded bored, like it didn't matter to them who they got. They were getting their blood one way or another, so I supposed it really didn't.

There was a crackle in the air. The smell of burning meat was thick around me, and I wrinkled my nose against the onslaught. Even the demon frowned, creasing Lucy's delicate features. I twisted my makhairas in my hand again, ready for whatever was going to come next. Nothing.

But then I blinked, and there in front of me stood my mother. She sneered at me, looking nearly identical to the day I saw her back in the winter. Practical black clothes, heavy black boots, and dark bags under her eyes that spoke to sleepless nights. "Ava," she greeted me. "Always a pleasure to be summoned by my loving daughter. I see you finally worked out Mollie's true nature. Certainly took you long enough."

My teeth hurt with how hard I gritted them together. "Yeah, well, it was no thanks to you. But I didn't bring you here to argue. I brought you here to meet... *a friend* who was looking for you." I stepped to one side, closer to a lowly growling Jasper.

Monica gasped when she realized what stood behind me. "No. No! I know I've done some terrible things, but I don't deserve this."

"You've done a lot more than some. It's time for you to realize that your actions have consequences." I wasn't going to let her get away. Not this time. Behind me, the demon cackled.

"The one who owes a debt. Your daughter said you'd be coming but I didn't believe her." Orcus's lackey snaked around me, stepping closer to Monica who took a step back. The wolves closed in on her, narrowing in the circle, and my mother glared at me.

"Surely you wouldn't do this to your own flesh and blood. And what about your so-called friend standing next to you? She was involved with this as well." Monica slid her hand down her leg, grabbing her blade from her thigh strap.

I sighed. I needed to compartmentalize, to put my emotions aside for the good of the pack. For the good of *myself*. "Well, like you said to me -- you're a means to an end. I need to keep my friends -- my family -- safe. And the only way I can do that is by giving Orcus you."

In front of me, the demon hissed. "Do not speak the name, Venator."

Baby, Jasper warned.

I was tired. I wasn't scared of the demon in front of me, or my mother cowering. I wasn't afraid of what would come next. I was just tired of having to watch my back again and again for my family's poor choices. I was exhausted, and I was *done*. "I apologize. I brought you Monica. Can you take her and give me my friend back now?" Was I seriously reasoning with a demon? Jesus.

The demon shrugged, lifting one of Lucy's slim shoulders. "Very well."

Monica looked at me, imploring me to save her, to do something. But there was nothing left to be done, and I shook my head. This was her fate, just as mine was next to Jasper. Something shifted in her eyes, and all hell broke loose. "No!" she cried. "I refuse!" She turned to the closest shifter, who happened to be Adrian, and charged him, knives out. Adrian didn't have any time to dodge, and her blade sliced through his shoulder. The young wolf yelped, and Monica barreled past him.

Chapter 7

"*I've got her,*" Jasper called.

"No!" I shouted. "She's mine." I narrowed my gaze and steeled myself for what would come next, sprinting after my mother.

Orcus's lackey was cackling in the circle. "I was expecting payment. I wasn't expecting such delicious entertainment. Maybe I should come to your realm more often."

"Shut the hell up," I muttered, quickly catching up to my mother's dark form. I sprinted after her, grateful for all my early morning runs and Jasper's endless training. I tucked my blades back into their sheaths, and leapt for Monica, tackling her to the ground. Her blade flew out of her hand, landing softly on the grass in front of us.

We landed with a heavy breath, and a moment later Monica was kicking me in the chest, pushing me away. "No. I will not go willingly, Ava. You don't know what this means for me."

I wrestled her arms away from my face. "You don't have to go willingly. You just have to go."

"No!" She clipped me with a short uppercut to my jaw and I went sprawling back, clutching my chin. I looked up at her, already standing, blade in hand once more. She stood between the pentagram and myself, chest heaving. "You don't know what this means for people like us."

"Venators?" I jumped to my feet, grabbing my blades from my back once more.

Monica got into a defensive stance as well. "And then some."

What? "Don't play games with me."

She shrugged. "Fine." Monica ran at me, blade directed at my stomach. I blocked her attack, steel ringing against steel in the night. The wolves had moved, blocking her escape, but they knew this was my battle. My fight. My moment. The demon skulked behind Monica as I blocked attack after attack. Somewhere ahead of us lightning flashed.

Thunder boomed. A storm was coming -- how fitting.

Monica raised her knife at me once more over her head. This was what I had been waiting for -- her tendency to not protect the soft skin under her arms as she ran. She was used to being the quickest in battle. Not anymore. I ducked underneath her outstretched arms, slicing my blade into the unprotected flesh there, and she cried out. Behind her, the demon sniffed, smelling the fresh blood.

Monica was game after game, lie after lie. I was done with it. She wasn't my family. These wolves were my family, and I would protect them at all costs. I met her eyes as she clutched her wound, and I kicked her back into the waiting arms of the demon.

They grinned, a toothy smile I had never seen on Lucy's face before and reached for Monica. She didn't even have time to scream before the demon's arms were wrapping around her, clasping her tight.

"Thank you, storm summoner," the demon whispered in a voice I was certain only I could hear.

There was a crack so sharp I was certain my eardrum was being split into two. Above me, thunder rolled and rain poured. I dropped to the ground, covering my head with my hands until the nausea passed. Had I really just done that? Had I really just sacrificed my mother to whatever lay beyond this life?

Did I even really consider her my mother? Besides, it had to be done. I had a pack counting on me here. *Jasper* was counting on me. No. I had done what I had to do, and what I should've done long ago. I had protected myself. When the world stopped spinning I peeked up from my knees. In front of me, a now human Duke was bent over Lucy who was stroking his face with a gentle hand. *Thank God.*

"Lucy?" I called.

She turned to smile at me, Duke also offering a grateful smile. "I'm okay." Duke mouthed a thank you to me before turning back to embrace Lucy. She looked pale, but alive.

Relief flooded my body, and I wanted to sink back to the ground. But there were still others I needed to check on, so I got to my feet, willing my legs to move. Mollie and Merrick were locked in a passionate kiss in the middle of the pentagram. I probably should've been more shocked at the scene of my best friend kissing someone other than her soon-to-be ex-fiancé, but I also knew the mate bond was hard to fight -- especially after a scene like we had just experienced. Ben would be a tomorrow problem.

Behind them a human Beau was checking out Adrian's slash wound. I jogged over to them, making gagging sounds as I passed Mollie. She shot me the finger, never stopping and I wanted to laugh. Just like old times. We had lots of things to talk about, and time to make up for, but that could wait. A tomorrow problem, like Ben. I pulled up in front of the shaggy wolf. "Beau, is he okay?"

Beau gave me a grin. "He'll be fine. Already close to healed. It was a clean cut. Might scar a bit, but that's just more ammunition for the ladies." I could've sworn the wolf Adrian winked at me. Good lord.

There was just one more wolf I needed to check on. "Jasper!" I called, putting my hands around my mouth. And then, once more in my head, down the bond. *Jasp*! Where the hell was he?

Before I could get worried, his grey wolf trotted out of the woods toward me, shifting in mid stride like it was the most natural thing in the world. "Ava!"

I ran to him, leaping into his arms. "Where did you go?"

"I just wanted to make sure they were actually gone." He pressed a kiss against my collarbone, and I sighed into his touch.

"And? What's the verdict?" I held my breath, hoping for the best but knowing anything could happen in this crazy world.

"They're gone." Jasper gave me a broad smile, kissing me over and over again until I was laughing. "You did it, baby."

"I'm pretty sure we did it."

He put me down on the ground, pulling on my hand

and dragging me toward the house. "I have something I want to talk to you about."

"Now?" I looked around at my friends, celebrating our win. "Shouldn't we stay with them?"

Jasper was on a mission, his one-track mind in full swing. "They'll be fine. There's no more danger. Tonight at least."

I rolled my eyes but squeezed his hand. "Fine." He led me into the house, stopping when we reached our bedroom. I only just noticed he had brought my comforter from my apartment. We would have to buy a new one. This one had a lot of good memories, but a lot of bad ones too. It was something I had picked out on my own, and I wanted something from us together. One that was ours, just like this home would be. A fresh start -- for both of us. I sat on the worn bedspread, feeling the soft fabric. It had been with me for so long. "So what's up?"

Jasper leaned over me, pressing a hand into each side of the bed -- trapping me where I sat. "I wanted to kiss you."

I laughed, but still tilted my face up to press my lips against his. "It's never just a kiss with you."

"It could be!" he protested. But already his eyes were turning dark with need, and my own desire was making my body hot.

"Lying doesn't suit you," I whispered, tugging his arms so that he lay on top of me.

"You're right. My plan all along was to get you into bed, naked, so that I could have my deviant, wolf-like way with you." He gave me a crooked smile that spoke to his hunger, already stripping me of my pants.

"That's more like it." I raised my arms above my head, letting him pull my shirt off. My sports bra snapped off in the front, leaving me bare to Jasper's eager stare.

"You're beautiful." He pressed a kiss against my collarbone, and trailed kisses down to my chest. He took one of my nipples into his mouth, sucking on it softly and drawing a gasp from my lips. "And I also think you like the idea of my wolf-like ways more than you'd admit." He was dragging his hand down between my legs, stroking my wetness there as I spread open for him, eager for his touch. I was always desperate for his touch.

"Please, Jasp," I begged.

"Please, what?" He was fisting his heavy cock, watching me with a heavy-lidded gaze. Shit, he looked good. I needed him inside me. *Now.*

"Please fuck me. I don't want your fingers or your mouth. I want *you.*"

Jasper nodded, sliding the head of his cock between my legs as I moaned and writhed, desperate for him. He pushed against my stomach, forcing me to stay still as he froze me with his stare.

He finally began to ease inside of me with a slowness and a grace I wasn't sure he had -- in bed, at least. Our bodies moved as one, urging each other to release. I scraped my nails down his arms as he thrust inside of me leisurely. When Jasper spoke, it was quiet, reverent in the midst of our lovemaking. "I did have something to talk to you about."

"Mhm." I wasn't sure this was the best time for conversation, not when Jasper was sucking at my nipple and running his fingers between us, rubbing circles on my aching clit.

"Marry me," he whispered, moving inside of me so softly I could've been imagining it.

I froze. "What did you just say?" My voice was too loud for the sanctity of the moment, but I couldn't control it. I was desperate for something to keep me centred in this moment, searing it to my skin.

"You heard me, Green." Jasper nipped at my bottom lip. "Marry me."

I dug my fingertips into his skin. "But… but we're already mates."

Jasper pulled back, pushing a loose lock of hair out of my face. "I want you to be mine in every sense of the word. Human, Venator -- I don't care about either of them. The only title that matters to me is that you're mine."

I rolled my hips against him, desperate for him to move

within me once more. "Of course I'm yours."

He smiled at me, the crooked smile I loved so Goddamn much, his honey eyes melting as they stared at me -- through me. "Is that a yes?"

I grinned back. "You seem to have me at a bit of a disadvantage, Jasp. Withholding orgasms seems to be a cruel way to get what you want."

Gently stroking his hand up my body, he pinned my wrists above my head. "Maybe you should just say yes then." Jasper pressed his nose into my neck, breathing deeply, and I shuddered from the sensation of him touching my mark.

"Do you even have a ring?" I circled my legs around his hips, digging my heels into his firm flesh to force him to move.

He paused, looking down at me with a furrowed brow. "Is that a deal breaker?"

His expression was so stricken that I leaned forward to press a soft kiss against his lips. "I would love to marry you."

Jasper's brow smoothed, and his joy radiated so far out of his body that I was sure the pack could feel it miles away. "I love you."

"I know. But you already bit my neck and marked me as yours. Was it really that much of a stretch that I would agree to marry you?" I smirked, and Jasper responded with a quick thrust of his hips.

"I can never tell with you, baby. But what I will say is that I'm grateful for whatever you're willing to give to me." He began to move inside me once more, pulling back and sheathing himself deep inside again and again.

My breath was coming heavier, gasps mixing with the pants as Jasper forced my hands deeper into the bed. The last few days disappeared, the week from hell evaporating from our minds as if it never existed. Jasper was imprinting himself on every cell of my memory, leaving no part of me untouched.

Pleasure was blooming inside me, building to

uncontrollable levels. My hands were pinned, even as I was desperate to claw at his back and make him mine on the most visceral of levels. "Come for me, Ava," Jasper growled, licking my neck.

I did as he commanded, letting go of everything besides the pleasure he was giving to me. He was close behind, roaring out his release as he shook and trembled.

"Fuck, baby." Jasper pressed his forehead against mine, kissing me softly before he rolled off me and fitted me to his side.

I was warm and content, drifting off into sleep. "Shouldn't we go make sure our friends are okay?"

Jasper just pulled me closer. "I can hear them through the bond. Duke took Lucy to the hospital. She's getting fluids, but she's fine. Beau and Adrian are crashing in the living room, and they said Mollie took Merrick back to Merrillan."

I muttered my acknowledgement, letting sleep carry me off.

Jasper interrupted the lull of my dreams. "Baby?"

"Yeah, Jasp?" He was stroking my arm with his hand, leaving goosebumps with his touch. I didn't think I would ever get enough of him.

"What did that... thing mean? When it called you storm summoner?"

I froze. I thought I had been the only one to hear that. I chewed on my lip, unsure how to explain that I wasn't sure myself and the one person that would know we just booted to the realm of the demons.

"I can hear you worrying down the bond. You might as well just tell me." He made a good point.

I sighed. "I don't know what they meant. Maybe Mollie will have a better idea about what that means. But, Jasp?"

"Yeah?"

I rolled so that we were face to face in the bright moonlight, his eyes warm honey and filled with love. "Can we worry about that tomorrow?"

Jasper laughed, a sound so filled with joy and love. "Of

course we can. Sounds like tomorrow will be a busy day. Witches, weddings…"

I groaned. *Shit.*

"I'm teasing you." He pressed a soft kiss to my lips. "Get some sleep. You're safe. We're safe."

I turned back around, snuggling into Jasper's warm body and letting him drape his arm around me. *Safe.* I was safe. My best friend was a witch, and my fiancé was a werewolf, and I was… I was something. But those were tomorrow's problems and for right now I was safe. I sighed with contentment, and let sleep carry me off into a dreamless sleep.

Tomorrow's problems could wait.

Umbra (Darkling 5)
Torri Heat

Jasper and Ava's relationship has been nothing but dramatic. From werewolf hunters to demons and everything in between, a nice, normal wedding is exactly what's needed. Their mating will not only affirm their own relationship, but help to cement the alliances between the wolf packs and the Venators.

But a rival wolf pack is dead set against Jasper and Ava's union, and everything their love stands for. Will the couple make it to their wedding day, or will deep seated prejudices keep them apart forever?

Chapter 1

A wedding. A wedding. Was this really happening? Was I really standing here, looking at a reflection of myself in the mirror, standing in a wedding dress? The dress was awful. I looked like a cupcake. Worse, I looked like a cupcake that had been squashed. I frowned, turning around and facing my best friend, Mollie. "Do we really need to go through all of this? I feel like I have a nice white dress hidden in my closet somewhere already. That'll be good enough, won't it? Jasper won't care."

Mollie sipped at her champagne, staring me down over the rim of her glass. I knew better than to mess with her when she gave me the look. It was the look that meant business. "Ava Green. I love you to death. But if you take away my one opportunity at wedding dress shop --"

I rolled my eyes, cutting her off. "Like you and Merrick aren't going to do the whole marriage thing at some point."

She ignored me, steamrolling over my argument. "This is my one chance to sip champagne and choose perfect white dresses. Do *not* take this moment away from me."

Mollie was impossible on a good day. With a wedding on the horizon, she was like a dog with a bone. I closed my eyes and took a deep breath. I could do this, right? I could be the perfect bride. Choose the white dress, throw the party. Eat cake, dance in front of a crowd of family and friends.

Except my family was a pack of wolves, and my husband-to-be was my werewolf mate. My maid of honour was a witch. My mom was in hell, and my dad was in prison. Normal. Just your everyday average life. The champagne I had drunk out of nervousness rolled in my stomach, and my fingertips began to tingle. I collapsed to my knees, the crushed cupcake of a dress poofing up around me. It was like I was in the middle of a pool filled with whipped cream, and the thought made me burst into laughter.

"Ava! Are you okay?" Mollie dropped her champagne glass to the table with a clatter, rushing to my side. "Ava, what's wrong?"

I was choking and gasping as I tried to stop laughing, burying my face in my hands. I wasn't surprised Mollie thought I was upset -- it sounded like I was sobbing.

"Talk to me! Girl, what's happening?" Mollie tugged at my hands and glared at me when my hands dropped revealing me in hysterics. "You're kidding me, right?"

"Mol, what the hell are we doing?" The snooty salesclerk eyed us with contempt, probably more concerned about the ugly dress I was crushing than the two women having a breakdown on her sales floor.

Mollie just shook her head. "What do you mean, what are we doing? We're trying to pick out a wedding dress for you, and apparently that's the funniest thing you've ever heard of."

I buried my face as another round of laughter hit me, still able to make out Mollie's sigh. Composing myself, I looked up at her again, checking to make sure the nosy salesclerk was nowhere in sight. "Mollie, I'm marrying a werewolf. A fucking werewolf. He bit me. And I'm sitting here in a white dress, pretending like I'm pure and Daddy is going to walk me down the aisle. None of that is my reality. Picking out the *perfect* white dress just seems pointless."

My best friend grabbed my hands. "Ava Green, you look at me. I know this seems silly now, especially with everything that's gone down in the last year, but you are getting married in two weeks. *Jasper* wants to marry you. He wants to do this right -- for you. Now you can walk down that aisle in whatever you want, but I think you'll regret it in ten years if I let you get married in your workout gear. This is just as important as training, Ava. This is important for you, and me, and Jasper, and the entire pack. This is a chance for everyone to feel... normal. Which is something I think we've all been missing out on lately."

I let Mollie's words sink in. She was right. I knew she was. Even when we were teenagers she knew what to say to make me see things her way. And I knew the wedding was a big deal to Jasper. Today was about more than a stupid white dress that I would just end up spilling wine down the front of anyways. Today was about fresh starts. I nodded slowly. "All right. So where do we begin?"

She got to her feet, offering me her hand with a smile. "First we get you out of this awful dress. You look like a Goddamn cupcake. Then we find you a dress that you love."

Thank God. I grinned and took her hand. "I was really worried you liked this one. I can't breathe, and I don't think Jasper would even know how to find me under all this fabric."

"Jasper's a wolf, Ava. I'm sure he'd figure something out." She had her back turned to me as she rummaged the racks, mind obviously set on something specific. The salesclerk watched her carefully, obviously not used to a tiny force like Mollie wreaking havoc in her perfectly curetted store. "This one!" Mollie whirled around triumphantly, and I inspected her selection. I shrugged, willing to try anything at this point if it meant I got to leave this store. I knew it was my own fault for leaving wedding dress shopping to the last possible moment, but it also hadn't been my top priority.

The clerk hurried me into a changeroom, taking me out of the Godawful cupcake dress, and I slipped into the lightweight dress. It fit like a glove, no alterations needed, and I felt like I could breathe. Who was I kidding trying on those cupcake dresses?

I was actually thrilled to show Mollie the dress, and as soon as I stepped out of the room, I knew she felt the same way. "Told you!" she chirped. I tuned out the conversation, Mollie telling the clerk we'd take the dress today, and other things that I knew she had handled. I was captivated by my reflection in the mirror. I wasn't Ava Green, meek and shy. I wasn't Ava Green, Venator for a local pack of werewolves. At this moment, in this white dress, I was an Ava I hadn't met yet. But if I was being honest, I was pretty excited to see who she turned out to be.

* * *

Mollie drove me back to the apartment -- Jasper's and mine. Ours. It had a nice ring to it. And the apartment wasn't bad either. In a lot of ways, it made a lot more sense than the back and forth between each of our respective apartments ever did. Plus, Betty got to move back home with us, and this was a fact I knew absolutely thrilled Jasper. Or not.

The dress hung from the plastic hook in the backseat, swinging in my peripheral vision -- a constant reminder of exactly what was happening in two weeks. Mollie chatted beside me, talking about flowers and the venue, invites and what she planned on wearing as my unofficial maid of honour. Mollie being Mollie had just assumed the title without me asking. I really didn't mind, even though I wasn't really planning on a bridal party, but the fact still made me laugh that she had just *decided*. The treeline grew thicker as we drove, edging closer to the road, and I knew I was almost home.

"So I'll bring the dress back to my place," Mollie said. "It'll be safer from Jasper's nosy eyes there."

I smiled. "You're probably right there. Although I'm not even sure your place is safe enough from a wolf."

Mollie pulled into the small parking lot next to the low-lying complex and threw the car into park. She turned to me, putting her hand on my thigh. "This is the right decision, Ava. I know you're in your own head about this, but we all need something to celebrate. That means you as well."

"I know." I sighed, rubbing my hands up and down my leggings as if that would stop the sweating of my palms. "I know."

"Go inside. Take a shower. Stop overthinking for five minutes, and you'll realize how great this is going to be." She patted my leg, effectively kicking me out of her car.

I got out of the car, shaking my head. "Love you, Mol."

"Yeah, yeah, I know." Mollie blew me a kiss as I closed the door, and all I could do was smile. I hadn't been sure if our friendship would survive the lies. The fact that she was a witch and had never told me. The fact that her parents had helped mine kill innocent wolves, and for what? *Glory*. But our friendship was stronger than I could've ever imagined, and if anything, knowing I didn't have to hide anything from Mollie anymore was a relief.

Mollie peeled out of the lot, turning in the direction of Merrick's house, and I knew exactly where she was going. She could say my upcoming nuptials was her only chance to experience a wedding of her own, but everyone who knew the two of them knew that was a lie. Mollie had Merrick wrapped around her little finger, and if Mollie wanted a wedding, she was going to have a wedding. It was only a matter of time.

I unlocked the door to the -- *our* -- apartment, and Betty immediately came running out to greet me. Having my cat with me once more really made our house feel like home. She had yet to warm up to Jasper, but we were getting somewhere, especially with Jasper's incessant treats he would bring home.

I tossed my bag on the couch, and gave Betty a quick pet, immediately taking Mollie's advice and heading for the shower. Jasper wasn't home yet. With me going dress shopping, he had taken the opportunity to head onto pack lands and see the guys. I doubted they were going suit shopping. At this moment, they were probably sparring in the field like a bunch of teenagers.

The shower immediately began to steam up the bathroom, so I opened the door a crack before I stepped into the hot water. Mollie was right -- as usual. The heat eased the tension in my shoulders, and I stopped overthinking. For a minute at least. I wasn't sure I explained my emotions clearly, the intrusive thoughts churning my stomach as we shopped for dresses and called caterers. Having the "perfect" wedding felt silly when my family was filled with supernatural creatures, yes. But little things bothered me as well. Who would walk me down the aisle? Did I cover my mark so the reverend marrying us didn't see, or was he a wolf as well?

And all of this wasn't even getting into the bigger issues. What had the demon meant when they called me "storm summoner"? The name rang in my head, day in and day out. I couldn't make sense of it. The taste of the dream still lingered on my tongue, a vision that felt more like a memory. Watching the dark clouds roll in, as Jasper stood there in awe. How could the demon know of my dreams? The only person I had ever mentioned them to was Jasper. So the only conclusion I could draw was that I was missing something, and the problem with missing something was that it usually led to danger. I didn't need any more danger than necessary with my supposed "perfect" wedding looming on the horizon. *Storm summoner...*

"Penny for your thoughts."

Startled, I jumped, catching myself on the side of the shower before I slipped and fell on my ass. One perk of Venator training? My reflexes had never been better. On the other side of the glass door stood Jasper with a smirk, arms crossed over his thick chest. "Shit, Jasp, some warning would be nice!"

He shrugged, rolling his lip between his teeth. "I was enjoying the view. Also I called your name when I got home, and you didn't answer. Obviously too deep into whatever you're thinking about."

"Just... everything." I sighed. My chest tightened. "How were the guys?"

"Good." Jasper tugged his T-shirt over his head, leaving me ogling his cut abs. It had been an unseasonably warm fall, and to be honest I was surprised he was wearing a shirt at all.

"What do you think you're doing?"

Jasper shoved his sweatpants over his hips with a crooked grin. "Conserving water. I'm sweaty as anything, and you were kind enough to start a shower for me. Figured we could solve each other's problems with one solution."

I knew they had been sparring. I had been trapped, getting the evil eye from a woman who hated working in a small-town boutique, while they had been having fun. Typical. But still I rolled my eyes and opened the glass door. "Get in."

Jasper stalked over to the shower, knowing he

would've gotten his way regardless. I was a total and complete sucker when it came to my mate. I didn't mind, because I knew the feeling went both ways. Jasper would do anything -- and I meant *anything* -- to ensure both my safety and my happiness. I had witnessed it firsthand more than once. He got in, wincing at the temperature of the water, but I shrugged. He knew how I liked my showers, and had still decided to get in. Grabbing my shampoo off the ledge, he began to wash my hair. A routine now, for both of us, since the first time we had stood in the shower, and he had shampooed my hair. The first time he had told me he loved me. And now, here we were. Mated, living together, and a wedding on the horizon. I sighed again.

"Tell me what's on your mind," he whispered.

He knew me. He knew how to relax me enough that I would spill my guts, tell him all my darkest secrets. The motion of his hands were soothing to my soul, his touch easing the tension that had lived in my body since Monica had first run away from us that night in the forest. "Is a wedding really the... safest idea?" I murmured, leaning my head into his palms.

He paused for a moment. "Is this a 'I'm rethinking marrying you' question, or a legitimate 'is it safe' question?"

I whirled around, throwing my arms around his neck. Shampoo ran down my hair and my face, but I didn't care. I hadn't thought about how the question would sound coming out of my mouth -- to my fiancé no less. "Jasp, of course I want to marry you. There is absolutely no doubt in my mind." His tense face relaxed. "I just can't get the idea out of my mind that having such a public event, involving the two of us, isn't really the smartest idea. We kind of thrive living under the radar."

Jasper raised a dark brow, shaking his wet curls out of his face. "That we do. But, Ava, I think we've lived in fear long enough. We can't be afraid for the entirety of our lives. At some point we're going to have to step out of the shadows."

I chewed on my lip. "I'm not sure I know how to do

that anymore."

He tipped his forehead to mine, resting his lips against my mouth, but when he spoke it wasn't out loud. *Let me show you.*

I'm listening.

Jasper slipped his hand down my neck, sliding it across my slick breast. My body immediately came alive under his touch, listening to his every command. I leaned forward, pressing my lips against his in a fervent kiss.

You're the light in my life, Ava. Jasper's words flooded my brain, every nerve on fire as he took control of all my senses. He slid his hand further, grabbing my thigh and wrapping it around his hip. We never broke our kiss, our tongues toying with each other as we danced a rhythm we had done so many times before. It never got old. His heavy erection pressed against me, and I couldn't help but grind myself against it. *You're my light. I won't let the shadows scare me off. Not anymore.*

Jasper took a step forward, and then another, until my back was pressed against the shower wall. He lifted me slightly off the ground, and then sank his cock into me with a groan.

I responded with a moan of my own, digging my fingertips into his hair, into the skin of his neck, into any place on his body I could find traction. I just needed to know he was there, moving inside me, moving with me. He was there, and he wasn't going anywhere.

"Fuck," Jasper cursed as he finally broke apart our kiss, pushing me harder against the slippery wall as he pistoned his hips deeper. "Fuck, Ava. Does any part of this feel wrong?"

I clung to his shoulders as he rocked into me, pleasure beginning to build in my core. My world had shrunk to the hot water, Jasper's touch, and Jasper's words. Nothing else mattered. "No," I murmured, crying out when his mouth sank down to suck on my nipple.

Does this feel wrong? Feeling this good, knowing I'm in your head? His mouth was teasing my nipple, his hand digging into the flesh of my ass. His cock was driving into me, and I was going to explode. *Let go, Ava. Let go of it all.*

I came with a cry of his name, Jasper coming moments after me with a grunt and a sigh. Fuck. It would be okay, wouldn't it?

I rested my head against Jasper's chest, letting my heartbeat sync with his. Everything would be okay. I had no idea what I was worried about. There hadn't been signs of danger in the area for weeks.

And maybe if I kept telling myself that, I would eventually believe it.

* * *

I dreamed. I dreamed of a road, lonely and desolate. Of a storm rolling in, clouds thick and bruised, rushing in overhead. Of lightning, brightening the dusky sky in the distance. Of being alone in the middle of a tempest brewing around me, and no shelter in sight.

Storm summoner…

I woke up in bed, Jasper's snoring body next to me, his arm squeezing me as he slept. The window was open, and the light patter of rain hit the sidewalk that surrounded our building. Just rain. Not a storm. And definitely not a storm I had *summoned*. I lifted Jasper's heavy arm off of me, getting out of bed as quietly as I could. Not that it mattered, because I was almost certain Jasper could sleep through anything.

I padded out to the kitchen, Betty immediately joining me and twirling around my ankles. I just needed a glass of water. A glass of water and then I could sleep, without the dream that hounded me whether I was asleep or awake. I sipped at my glass, gripping the edge of my countertop with my free hand.

Wasn't being a Venator enough? Sending my father to jail, and my mother to hell? I wanted to be normal -- or as normal as possible for someone in my situation. I wanted to be excited about my wedding. Not awake in the middle of the night, my mind turning circles around a name a demon had called me months ago. I rested my back against the countertop, clutching my water to my chest and watched the

Torri Heat   **Darkling**

rain pour outside the window.
    Storm summoner.

Chapter 2

As usual, things were absolutely chaotic when we should've been walking out the door ten minute previously. I had thought that officially moving in together would actually mean Jasper and I would arrive on time for things. I had been sorely mistaken.

"Have you seen my green sweater?" I called over the sounds of the shower, where Jasper still was, despite me telling him we needed to leave. *Men.*

"Baby, can't you just wear one of your other sweaters?"

I was on my knees in our bedroom, a pile of clothes around me, wearing only a pair of jeans and my bra. The green sweater I was looking for was currently my only clean top, and we were supposed to be at Merrick's house for dinner in fifteen minutes. Laundry wasn't my strong suit, and putting clean clothes away was even worse. Added to this was the fact that the warm fall meant mud everywhere, and our washing machine was broken, and Jasper was *still* in the shower, and…

Shit. "No, I can't because every other sweater is covered in mud from sparring with you!"

"Maybe you should stay on your feet more, and then your clothes would be less dirty."

I was going to kill him. We were a week out from our wedding, and I was going to kill my fiancé.

You know I can hear your thoughts, right? Jasper's amused voice thrummed through our bond. Shit. I had forgotten to keep up a barrier while I had been plotting his imminent death.

Get out of my head, Jasp, I threatened, still digging through the mountain of clothes that surrounded our bed.

But I was too focused on finding something halfway decent to wear, and his voice kept coming. *I definitely wouldn't go with drowning. Wolves are pretty strong swimmers.*

I got to my feet, stormed to the bathroom and twisted the shower faucet to icy cold, giving Jasper a deadly glare. The water shifted, and he jumped out of the shower immediately, cursing me the entire time. "Okay, okay, you win!"

I sat on the bathroom vanity, watching him struggling (and failing) to find a semi dry towel, and enjoying his struggle. "Didn't Beau go to school for plumbing?" Under normal circumstances, I would've gone to my landlord. But Jasper's friend who was renting us the place was out of the country on "business," and I was pretty sure that meant he couldn't be bothered fixing a washing machine.

Jasper finally gave up, grabbing a random towel off the floor and shot me a look. "I'll call him tomorrow morning."

I smiled at him and walked out of the bathroom. We were still going to be late, and Mollie was going to have my head, but at least I had come out ahead on one aspect of the day. Jasper and my lives meshed so seamlessly, it was like we had always been living together. With one small exception. The laundry. As a wolf, used to living either on his own, or with a bunch of other wolves (I was imagining Adrian specifically…) dirty clothes were just a fact of life. As long as they weren't blood stained, it was fine to wear out in public. Sometimes even then exceptions could be made. So a broken washing machine? Not a big deal to Jasper until he literally had not a single stitch of clothing left to wear.

I, on the other hand, occasionally enjoyed wearing clean clothes. Like for example, when I was going to my very clean best friend's house for dinner. *Merrick's house*, I meant. The two of them had been attached at the hip since the Orcus incident, so I was honestly surprised they hadn't made it official and moved in together already.

You could always go to dinner dressed like that… Jasper's voice thrummed through the bond again, oozing seduction.

Last warning, Jasp… My tone left no room for argument. He knew I would do a lot worse than turning the shower cold on him.

"No threats! I'm getting dressed." Jasper strode out of the bathroom, pouting. He dug through the clothes on his side of the laundry, triumphantly pulling out clothes while I still struggled to find my missing green sweater. "If you don't get ready soon, we're going to be late."

I closed my eyes, taking in a deep breath. *You're right. Drowning would be too good for you.*

Jasper only laughed, kissed my forehead and walked out the bedroom door. "I'm going to get the wine ready. You'll look great no matter what, baby."

Brownie points awarded, I amended my thoughts from death to bodily harm. Five minutes later I joined Jasper in the living room where he stood, ready to go. The green sweater was officially M.I.A. and everything else was dirty or ripped. So I was set to go to dinner at Mollie's house in my nice jeans, and a *very* oversized sweater of Jasper's I had bought him for last Christmas and he had yet to wear.

He smirked, his smile accentuating his chiseled face. God, he was gorgeous, even when I was pissed at him. "Told you that you'd look great no matter what." When my eyes narrowed in his direction, his smirk spread into a full-blown grin -- the one I desperately loved. "I'll call Beau tomorrow. I promise."

"You better," I huffed. But then I stood on my tiptoes and pressed a kiss to his lips. Fuck, I loved him, even when he drove me crazy. I loved him so much I was surprised I managed to keep both feet on the ground. Being mates, my soul called out for his -- two halves of the same coin. We were infinite, impossible to separate. When he had marked me, he said something that stuck with me.

There was never any question I belonged to you. There wasn't any question. Ever.

Jasper deepened the kiss, circling my body with his strong arms as he crushed me to his chest. "Fuck, I love you, baby."

I pushed back away from his chest. "I love you. But if we don't stop this now, we're going to be even more late than we already are. And then Mollie will drive here herself and kill both of us with her bare hands."

Jasper shuddered. He was terrified of Mollie -- even more so now he knew she was a witch. "You're right. Let's go."

The drive to Merrick's house was quick. After he had become an unofficial member of Jasper's pack, he had moved into a small rental house not far from our apartment. It also made it more convenient for him to visit Mollie, and vice versa. Merrick's pack, the one we had visited the night I saw Lucy disappear into the woods, wasn't the most accepting of interspecies mating. While Alpha Dean still insisted we maintain some form of treaty with them, Jasper and I usually stayed out of most interactions. And after the pack had discovered Merrick's mate bond with Mollie, he had basically been tossed to the curb.

Jasper's pack had become my family, one way or another, and I had never been more proud of them than the day Mollie had called me sobbing -- Merrick was on his own, nowhere to go, and no pack for support. I hadn't even said anything to the guys. Jasper and Beau had just met each other's eyes and headed out to Beau's truck. A couple of hours later, a dazed Merrick showed up on the pack lands. The guys had helped him find a new job, a new place to stay. Got him back on his feet. He was one of us, whether he liked it or not. I preferred to think he liked it.

I grabbed Jasper's hand as we walked up the steps of Merrick's warmly lit porch. Jasper squeezed my hand, and I caught him smirking out of the corner of my eye. *I really would've been just as happy with the first outfit you had on…*

"I swear you have a death wish," I muttered, knocking on the door. Even so, I couldn't stop the smile from spreading across my face, and he knew it. The low chuckle he released was one of my favourite sounds in the world -- and the most dangerous. I immediately blocked him from my mind, not needing him to know how turned on I was walking into dinner with my best friend and my brother.

"Come on," Jasper complained. "I want to know how much you need me."

I turned to him, opened my mouth with a teasing remark ready on my lips, and was immediately saved by Mollie's smiling face as she opened the door. "I don't know why I ever bother telling you guys a time. You just show up when you want to."

I grinned and gave my best friend a hug. "We're getting better."

"Mhmm." But Mollie grinned back at me as we pulled away. "Hopefully one of you will be on time for your wedding, but I'm not holding my breath." She closed the door behind us, pulling us down the hall to a dining room that had obviously been decorated by none other than her. Merrick was by no means a slob -- and definitely not compared to Adrian -- but I couldn't imagine him picking out the velvet curtains or arranging the vase of flowers.

Merrick appeared in the door, carrying a steaming tray of food. "Hey, guys. Perfect timing. Lasagna just came out of the oven."

I raised my brow at Mollie as I took a seat next to Jasper. She merely shrugged. "I'm prepared, what can I say?"

Jasper reached out and grabbed my thigh with his hand, squeezing, and I gave him a smile. Merrick sat down in the chair next to Mollie, a loving look passing between them. Life felt good today. Simple. Easy. And honestly, did it get any better than that? We ate and laughed, making small conversation with each other like we had been for a lifetime. Which in some ways, we had. In other ways, it had been a lifetime getting to this point. Would it take another lifetime before it felt normal? Natural? Dinner passed with quiet conversation and laughter, and then we all found ourselves finishing a second bottle of wine, empty dessert bowls still sat in front of us. Mollie and I were speaking about the florist we still needed to visit in the next few days when I overheard Merrick's conversation with Jasper.

"... like they think I'm not going to notice they're sneaking around here. They aren't exactly subtle. Sage is the worst of the lot."

I tipped my head toward Jasper. "Who's been sneaking around where?"

Jasper reached over and pulled me to his side. "Just the other pack. They weren't exactly thrilled when Merrick chose Mollie over them, especially when they already knew about us. Nothing to worry about, baby. Just some scare tactics."

"Uh huh. I've definitely heard that one before." Scare tactics had also wound up being my murderous parents and a demon, but what did I know?

Mollie rolled her eyes, taking a sip of her wine as she joined the conversation. "They slashed my tires before work the other day. Ruined my perfect attendance streak."

I laughed, unable to stop myself. "Mol, this isn't exactly high school. I don't think your boss was about to hand out awards at the end of the year."

"You never know!" She shot me a glare over the rim of her glass. "If I ever catch them, they're dead."

"Ladies." Jasper squeezed my side, bringing me back to the here and now. "Regardless, we should keep an eye on it. It's annoying right now, but if it escalates we'll need to let the Alpha know. He might have more sway diplomatically before we end up lashing out in retaliation." He looked at Mollie expectantly, until she rolled her eyes.

"I promise I won't do any witchy shit on the other pack," she huffed, crossing her arms. Merrick pressed his lips to keep himself from laughing before he rubbed Mollie's shoulder reassuringly.

I sighed, leaning into Jasper's embrace. "Will things ever be quiet?"

His laugh echoed through his chest, shaking me gently. "Would you really be happy if they were?"

"For a little while." I shrugged. "And then I'd probably be bored out of my mind."

"Exactly." He rubbed my back, still laughing.

Merrick met my gaze, giving me a smile. "Hopefully it stays quiet for another week at least, until the wedding."

"Well now you've jinxed it!" Mollie complained, pushing away from Merrick as she got to her feet and began to collect our dirty dishes.

"The wedding will be fine, Mol." *I hope.* "So what do we actually do about the pack? Like, I've never been Sage's biggest fan, but if it's just low-level stuff is there really anything we can do about it?"

Jasper and Merrick were both quiet for a moment, and then without another word Merrick got to his feet and helped Mollie with the dishes.

"You don't think it'll stay quiet, do you?" I murmured, pushing away from Jasper's embrace so I could look at him. His warm caramel gaze was worried, debating how much to tell me -- in other words, how much I would tell Mollie.

Finally he shook his head. "Things are escalating quickly. I don't know what their goal is, but they're not happy with the way our pack is doing things. I need you to keep an eye on both yours and Mollie's backs, until all this is sorted out."

I nodded. "And if things escalate?"

Jasper sighed, chewing on the inside of his cheek. From the kitchen, the content sounds of Mollie and Merrick drifted toward us. Easy. "Then we do what needs to be done."

Chapter 3

I woke up to the sounds of fat raindrops smacking against the window. Fall was slow to leave this year, and it was dragging out the cold, wet rains. I didn't mind, because it meant less snow for the time being, but I missed the sun. I missed the warmth of it as it shined on my face while I ran or trained with Jasper. I missed the brightness streaming in through the windows we still hadn't gotten curtains for -- finally comfortable in our own space. I missed not being in the dark, in more ways than one.

"What's on your mind, baby? I can hear the gears turning from here." Jasper, still not a morning person after all our time spent together, had his eyes closed. But he turned into me, wrapping an arm around my side and pulling me against him. I relaxed against his touch, the mate bond easing my racing thoughts.

"Just thinking about all the wedding shit Mollie wants me to do," I mumbled. A weak excuse, but a valid one all the same. With one week to go until the supposed best day of my life, Mollie had every hour of every day down to a strict schedule. Jasper would see through it, but I hoped he wouldn't push. I was worried about Mollie and Merrick, and the other pack, and all the complications that were sure to come with that. Did Jasper think things would escalate before the wedding? Should we even be having a wedding?

"Yes, we should be having a wedding. Don't go there," Jasper murmured. "Come here." He turned me so I faced him in his arms.

I tipped my chin up, pressing a light kiss to his lips. "I love you."

"I love you more than life itself, Ava Green." Jasper deepened the kiss, darting his tongue in between my lips. He pulled back, sliding his hands down my body and under my shirt, tugging the oversized tee I slept in over my head. "I love you more than the sun or the moon. I love you more than every single one of the Goddamn stars in the sky. And I want to show the whole world exactly how much I love you."

"Mmm…" I pressed my body against his naked chest, enjoying the way I could feel his heart beating. His touch aroused my body like no other, awakening things inside myself I didn't even know were there. How could I possibly ever think this was wrong? *I love you.*

And I, you. He bent his head, taking one of my nipples into his mouth. I moaned and arched into him. His tongue swirled as he sucked, and I couldn't help the noise of pleasure that escaped me.

I cursed under my breath, and Jasper smiled against my breast, knowing exactly what he was doing to me. His mouth returned to focus attention on my other nipple, and he slipped his hand down my waist, tugging the panties I had slept in over my hips. I groaned and swore, his hand expertly finding its way to the wet heat between my legs.

I fucking love the way you get wet for me, baby. So damn soaked. All of it just for me. Jasper's words echoed softly in my head, just as he sank two fingers into me.

I cried out, the sensation of mouth, fingers, and words overwhelming me. They always did, and he knew it. Jasper pumped his fingers as if he had all the time in the world, curling them in a way that made me thrust my hips into his hand.

Just like that, baby. Ride my hand. Jasper's tongue licked, and his fingers fucked me, and pleasure was building deep inside me in a way I knew I wouldn't be able to stand for long. "You're so fucking beautiful, Ava. The way your body comes alive in my hands… fuck. The way your soul comes alive with my words. I'll never get enough of you."

"Oh, Jasp," I sighed. My body was moving of its own accord, driving me closer and closer to that edge of pleasure, and I wanted nothing more than to topple over it. Jasper's erection was heavy against my thigh. As badly as I wanted him to fuck me with it, I knew he would do no such thing until he had his way with his hand first.

Come for me, Ava Green. Come for your mate.

I shuddered, riding his hand to my release as my body

shook and trembled. I moaned his name, letting my eyes close and my body come back down to Earth as his fingers guided me through my orgasm. It was never enough with Jasper. It never had been, and it never would be. I opened my eyes and pulled him up toward me with a smile.

"How can you not be sated after an orgasm like that?" Jasper smirked, but he was already lining his cock up with my entrance, teasing me.

"I'll let you know if two does the trick." I dragged my nails down his back, and his eyes darkened, a low growl escaping from deep in his chest. I knew what that growl meant. I was his. Not Jasper's, but the animal's within. It only turned me on even more, knowing that at his most primal level Jasper still couldn't resist his urges for me. I raised my hips, inviting him, and he began to slowly edge inside me.

A knock on the door startled both of us. I pushed him away and started to get out of bed. Jasper groaned, pulling me against his chest. "Ignore it," he whispered. "I want to see you come again."

I laughed, curling up against him. He dragged his fingers down my side, and my body curved into his touch. And then someone knocked on the door again. This time it was my turn to groan.

"Jasp! You told me this morning was fine! Let me in before I drown Goddamnit." Beau's voice carried easily through our small apartment to our bedroom.

"Fuck. I completely forgot he was coming to look at the washing machine today." Jasper leapt out of bed, grabbing the first pair of sweatpants he could find, and jogged out of the bedroom. I rolled over, pulling the blankets over my head, simultaneously annoyed at Beau's arrival, and excited about the prospect of clean clothes.

Clean clothes. Yeah. The interruption was definitely worth it. I followed Jasper's lead and jumped out of bed, tugging a sweatshirt over my head. Beau and Jasper were in the small laundry room off the kitchen, talking. When he saw me round the corner, Beau gave me a smile. "Hey, baby girl. Heard you had some issues with your washing machine."

Betty circled my legs, crying for food. I gave her a pat and smiled at Beau. "Thank God you're here. If I had to smell Jasp's dirty workout clothes for one more day there might not be a wedding."

Jasper flipped his middle finger at me with a wink, but Beau laughed. "I'll see what I can do, but if it's anything crazy you might need to get an actual technician out here. However, I can testify to Jasp's workout clothes. The man *reeks* after our practice sessions."

Jasper groaned, throwing his hands up in the air. "Is this pick on Jasper day? After I get a laundry machine fixed for my fiancée, and offer a job to my best friend?"

I laughed, leaving the two of them as I filled Betty's food dish and started the coffee pot. "Doesn't it make you feel better to know we love you despite your dirty clothes?"

"Not really," Jasper grumbled. "A coffee would make me feel better though."

I rolled my eyes at Betty, who looked at me with contentment as she munched her breakfast. I had already gotten three mugs off the shelf, anticipating I wouldn't be the only one who needed caffeine on this rainy, damp day. "Beau, coffee?" I called.

"Please, baby girl." His voice echoed, and a loud clatter followed his words. *Shit.* I hoped the two of them weren't making my washing machine worse. I hadn't even considered it until this very moment. My eyes widened as another clank followed, and a curse from Beau. I turned my attention back to the coffee pot, as if it was the most exciting thing I had ever seen. The washing machine would be fine. Absolutely fine. I poured coffee into each of the mugs with the utmost of care. Beau knew what he was doing.

"Guys, coffee's ready." I had to shout to be heard over the racket they were making in the laundry room.

"Coming!" Jasper called back.

They couldn't have been in the laundry room for more than ten minutes, but they walked out as if they had been working in a garage for weeks. I slid a mug across to each of them and settled myself at the dining room table before I dared ask the question. "How bad is it?"

Jasper grimaced, and Beau shrugged. "Good news and bad news."

"Okay…" I took a sip of my coffee. "What's the good news?"

"I know what the problem is." Beau slurped his coffee, not bothered at the steam rising up from his mug.

I closed my eyes, forcing myself to not make a snarky comment back to Beau's usual sass. "And the bad news?"

"I can't fix it. You're gonna have to get a technician who knows how to fix this brand." He grinned at me. "But this is a damn good cup of coffee."

Shit. This meant more days without clean clothes. I sighed, resting my chin in my hands. "Thanks for trying, Beau."

"Anything for you, baby girl." Beau drained the rest of his coffee and rinsed out his mug in the sink. Always courteous, even when he was acting like a rebellious teenager. "I'm gonna head out but let me know if you need anything else before *the big day.*" He shot me finger guns, slapped Jasper on the back, and walked toward the front door humming the funeral march.

"That's the wrong… oh, forget it." I tried to correct him, but he was already out the door. He'd figure it out soon enough. "Well. That sucks. What a waste of a day."

Jasper set his coffee mug down with a grin, coming over to wrap his arms around me. "The washing machine can wait. I can think of more than a few things we can do with our newfound time."

I smiled, leaning into his touch. His hands swept down, feathering his fingers across my breasts. "Oh yeah? And what would they be?"

"I think it's better if I show you." Jasper pulled me away from the table, sweeping me into his arms and carrying me into the bedroom.

Jasper was right -- the washing machine could wait.

Right now all I wanted to think about was my mate's hands on every inch of my body.

* * *

More rain. I didn't think the rain was ever going to stop. I laid in bed, the covers tucked around my face to ward off the damp. *At least it isn't snow*, I reassured myself. *It isn't snow.*

I needed to get out of bed. Jasper was long gone -- a meeting with Alpha Dean forced him to be up earlier than his internal clock deemed okay. Any other day, I'd take the morning slow. Eventually getting out of bed to get myself a coffee and respond to a few emails. But today Mollie was coming over to discuss yet *more* wedding plans, and if I crossed my fingers hard enough, the washing machine repairman Jasper called would be arriving as well. But they could all wait five more minutes. Five more minutes while I dozed and dreamed, imagining my wedding taking place in only a few days. My dress, perfect in a way I never thought possible. Jasper, looking sharp in a smart suit. The rest of it didn't matter. All that mattered was Jasper's eyes, locked on to mine, looking at me like I was the only thing in the universe.

Perfect.

A loud rapping at the front door interrupted my daydream, and I rolled my eyes. I knew that knock anywhere. *Mollie.* "I'm coming!" I called. I resentfully got out of bed, tossing on one of Jasper's dirty sweatshirts over the cotton shorts I had worn to bed. Trudging out of the bedroom, I gave Betty a quick pat, noting Jasper had already fed the wild beast. But I really shouldn't have worried about rushing. Before I could even reach the entryway, Mollie was opening the door, arms loaded with bags and coffee.

I shook my head, surprised and yet not. "Uh... how did you get a key to my house?"

She shrugged. Even early in the morning on a rainy day, she looked perfect. Her blonde hair was curled, framing her face, and her jeans and sweater put my pajamas to shame. "Jasper left me a key a few weeks ago when I had to drop something off for you, so I made a copy."

Mollie, to a T. I wasn't even upset. I grabbed a couple of bags that were precariously balanced in her arms, and she gave me a grateful smile. "Mol, what is all this stuff?"

She dropped the rest of the bags on the floor and handed me one of the large coffee cups. "This is caffeine, which you will need because the rest of these bags are supplies to make centrepieces for your reception."

"Centrepieces?" I groaned. "Can't we just throw a bottle of wine in the middle of the table and call it a day?"

Mollie glared at me, carefully sipping at her coffee so as to not smudge her perfectly applied lipstick. "No, Ava, we cannot just throw booze in the middle of the table. This is supposed to be a classy event!"

"I didn't realize werewolves were classy," I muttered, earning myself another death stare from my best friend. "Sorry! Sorry. Bad joke."

Mollie ignored me, getting to work setting up a mini assembly line of all the supplies she had brought. It looked like way too many pieces for my jumbled mess of a mind to make sense of. "I know what you're thinking, Ava Green, and yes, this is all necessary. What would people think if they showed up to a reception and there weren't any centrepieces?"

I gratefully sipped at the coffee, wrapping both hands around the warm cardboard. "Umm... that Jasper and I love each other so much we forgot about decorations?"

"Wrong answer." Mollie put her fists on her hips, giving me a stern look. She shook her head, pulling out a fluffy white flower. "We're making hydrangea arrangements. They mean unity, and I thought that was fitting given all our backgrounds. Unfortunately it is not the season for hydrangeas, and we don't live in a place that grows them well anyways, so we're using artificial. No matter, they'll still look great."

Mollie walked me through her vision, which involved several hydrangeas, a tall glass vase, some weird fluffy things, and some sticks that I was sure I could've found outside. Not like I would mention that to her. With only a few days to go before the wedding, Mollie was on a rampage. We worked in comfortable silence, Mollie doing most of the arranging while I tossed the sticks in, and texted Jasper. When the doorbell rang, I shot out of my seat, eager for the small break it offered. "That must be the washing machine repairman! Don't get up. I'll let him in." I hid my smile as I walked to the door, leaving Mollie grumbling about my ungratefulness as I passed her. She loved doing this kind of stuff, and knew I was useless at it, so it was all just a front.

I opened the front door with a grin to two guys in dark cargos and coats. "You must be here to fix the washing machine. Thank God, I'm not sure how much longer I could've survived without clean clothes."

The shorter man returned my smile. "Of course. We'll get it fixed for you right away. Can you show me to the laundry room?"

"Follow me." I held the door open and waited for them to come inside. Mollie offered a small wave, and then immediately turned back to her vases. "It's right through here."

"Great." The shorter man gave me another smile. "It shouldn't take us too long based on what your husband said was the problem."

"Fiancé," I corrected. "I'll leave you to it!"

I left them in the laundry room, coming to sit next to Mollie on the floor once more. Mollie continued arranging her flowers as she spoke quietly to me. "I'm surprised Jasp let strange guys come in the house while he was out, just with all this stuff going on with the other pack."

I rolled my eyes. Mollie had always been overly protective of me. "They're just here to fix the washing machine, Mol. Then they'll be on their way."

She shrugged, and I stuck sticks into her vase with a bit more force than was necessary. Now Mollie's words had gotten to me, making me nervous. "I'm going to get a glass of water. Do you want one?"

"I'm good." She shook her head.

I passed by the laundry room on my way to the kitchen, hearing the two men speak quietly. "It has to be the dark-haired one. She let us in."

"She said fiancé, not mate or husband though. We have to be sure."

What the hell? Mollie had really gotten into my head, making me paranoid. It was the only explanation for the way the hair on the back of my neck was standing tall, and the way my skin crawled. I pressed my back outside the laundry room, trying to hear more to ease my mind. My blades were in the bedroom, because I hadn't thought they were necessary for a morning with Mollie. No. They were just repairmen. This was ridiculous.

"We'll just take both of them."

Fuck. Who the hell had I let into my house? I stepped forward into the laundry room, ready to attack, just before the taller man rushed past me toward Mollie in the living room.

The shorter one reached behind the door, slapping a sweet-smelling rag over my nose. "Too little, too late, sweetheart," he muttered. The last thing I remembered seeing was Mollie's unconscious body being dragged out my front door. And then the world went black.

Chapter 4

I was cold, and it was dark. Where the hell was I? I couldn't remember anything other than Mollie and I arranging those Goddamn centrepieces, and the repairmen coming over, and then...

The Goddamn repairmen. How could I have been so stupid? Especially with everything else going on. I should've been more cautious, checked their credentials, *something*. Anything. Shit. Now I was kicking myself. What would Jasper think when he came home and I wasn't there? And with only three days to the wedding. *I knew the fucking wedding wasn't a good idea.*

I felt around next to me. The floor was cool to the touch, and damp. It felt like a basement of sorts, especially with how black it was. I had no idea how long I had been out for, or how far they would've transported us. The darkness was disorienting, making it hard to breathe in its thickness. But I couldn't focus on that. I needed to figure out where I was, and how to get out. My brain felt foggy, still not functioning from whatever they had dosed me with.

A quiet groan sounded from next to me. "Ava?"

"Mollie?" I whispered. I got up onto my hands and knees, making my way slowly to where the groaning was coming from. "Mollie, say my name again so I can find you."

"I'm here, Ava. Where... where are we?" Mollie's words were slurred, her voice quiet, but just loud enough I could crawl to her. "What the... hell happened?"

"The repairmen weren't repairmen," I muttered. Even crawling I was unsteady, swaying from side to side. "It's my fault for not thinking."

"Can't... blame yourself."

Mollie's words were closer, and sure enough with the next shuffle of my body, my hands landed on something soft and warm. *Mollie.* "Are you okay? Does anything hurt?" I started to pat her body down. I wouldn't be able to see blood in the darkness, but hopefully I'd be able to feel wetness and go from there.

"Not hurt... but my head... so fuzzy." Mollie sounded like she was about to fall back into unconsciousness, but I needed her to stay awake in case there was a chance we could get out of here. She was tiny, but I wouldn't be quick if I was having to carry her.

"Mol, I need you to stay with me, okay?" Whatever they had given us was hitting her a lot harder than me. "We need to get out of here before Jasper and Merrick lose their minds."

"Merrick..." Mollie murmured. "Where's Merrick?"

"He's looking for us, I promise, Mol. I'm gonna try and contact Jasp now, okay? Just stay with me." *Shit*. I had to focus on connecting with Jasper down the mate bond, but I wasn't comfortable not keeping Mollie awake. I had to though, if we were going to be found.

Jasp... Jasp! Can you hear me? But the only thing echoing back at me was my own voice. My thoughts were going nowhere, no matter how hard I tried to project them. Either they had done something to this room, or whatever they had dosed me with was limiting my ability to connect with Jasper. *Jasper!* But it was useless. I knew he couldn't hear me, no matter how much effort I put behind the words, behind the force of my projection. Mollie and I were on our own. In the dark, with no weapons, no idea who had taken us, and no clue where we were. I rubbed my hand down Mollie's back. "You with me?" I whispered.

"Yeah. I'm... here. I can't think... straight." She moaned softly. "Jasper?"

I shook my head, which I quickly realized was a useless action in the dark. "No luck. They're blocking me somehow."

"Me... too. No magic." In the shadows, a brief flicker of flame appeared, illuminating Mollie's palm before it faded to nothing. *Okay, so no magic either.*

I sat down, pressing my back against Mollie's so that I didn't lose track of where she was. Cradling my head in my hands, I tried to think logically about the whole situation. We didn't know who had taken us, but they had some knowledge of the supernatural. It would be safe to assume these were Merrick's pack, come to take me. But why me, and not Mollie? At least that was the who. But the why? I was at a loss. Did they hate interspecies mates that much that they would throw us in this basement? Or were their intentions more sinister?

"Okay, Mol. Are you listening?" I lifted my head up, willing my eyes to adjust to the pitch black around them. It was futile, because no amount of focusing made it any brighter. Jasper would be able to see in here, no problem. But Mollie and myself? Wasn't happening.

"Yeah." Mollie's breath was laboured, but her voice sounded more focused than a moment before.

"I don't think they're going to hurt us. Not yet at least. We're both relatively unharmed, and the fact they're keeping us in here means they need something. So, reasonably, at some point, they'll have to bring food in." I nodded to myself, satisfied with my explanation.

Mollie was quiet, her breath the only sound. "Makes... sense."

"I'm going to feel around for the door so I know where it is when they come in. When they come in to feed us the first time, I'll try and get a bearing for where we are. Then we can make a plan. Hopefully with some food in your stomach, the drugs won't affect you as much..." I trailed off, knowing my plan relied on a lot of contingencies. But it was better than nothing, and nothing was the alternative. "When they feed us, we'll sneak out of here based on how many of them come in, and how much I can see out the door." I had a feeling this room had some kind of ward on it that dimmed Mollie's magic and was blocking my connection with Jasper. If we could at least get out of this room, or this basement, or whatever we were, I might be able to get in touch with him. But until then, we were on our own and needed to rely on each other.

"Okay." Mollie's voice was definitely getting stronger. Thank God. I couldn't do this on my own.

"I'm gonna crawl and try and find the door now. Don't

move too much and keep talking to me so I know you're awake." I patted Mollie's shoulder, and then turned in what I hoped was the direction of a door. If I found a wall, I could just follow it around. But I didn't need to smash my face into anything either. My brain was cloudy enough as is. I crawled slowly, reaching my hand out in front of me every few feet to see if I could touch anything, but the room was bigger than I had initially thought. "You doing okay, Mol?"

"Yeah. Doing fine. You find the door yet?"

"Not yet." I frowned. "I have to be getting close to a wall though." My hand dropped into something wet, and I grimaced, not wanting to know what I had just touched. Hopefully just water. *Ugh.* But the next time I put my hands out in front of me, my fingertips scraped something solid. *The wall?* "Mol, I think I found the wall!"

"Thank God," Mollie muttered. "Unless they dropped us in from the ceiling, the door has to be somewhere."

I rolled my eyes. "Can we think positively please? I'm sure there's a door somewhere." I loved Mollie to death but being trapped in a pitch-black room with her for the rest of my life did *not* sound like the most appealing option. I slid my hand along the wall as I crawled. There was nothing but the uneven feel of the cold walls, bumpy and gritty under my fingers. Until… there. Was that a door frame? I curled my hand around the raised ledge, excited to find something distinctly metal under my touch.

"Mollie, I think I have the door!" I raised myself up so I was standing on my knees, patting the metal surface with both hands. Definitely a door. "I'm going to stay right outside the frame, so when they come in next, I'm ready."

Mollie's scoff echoed in the darkness. "*If* they come in."

When. I wasn't offended at Mollie's lack of optimism, but I wasn't taking anything else as an option. They had to come in, at least to feed us. Or to make sure we weren't dead. And I was going to be ready. I sat with my back to the wall, one hand curled awkwardly against the doorframe to remind myself it was still there.

I wasn't sure how long we sat there for. It could've been

minutes, or it could've been hours. There was no time to judge time in the dark. It was thick and heavy, suffocating me the longer we waited. Occasionally Mollie and I would talk from across the distance, but sometimes she would fall back asleep without me right next to her to keep her awake. From a distance, I heard it. *Footsteps.* "Mol, are you awake? I think someone's coming!"

Somewhere in the dark, Mollie shifted, her clothes rustling as she moved. "You sure?"

"Pretty sure I hear footsteps." I took my hand away from the frame, not wanting to lose a finger if the door swung open and pressed my ear closer. Footsteps, coming our way. "Let's hope they're coming to us."

I held my breath. I hoped the footsteps would come nearer. Before I could track the footsteps any longer, the door swung open and flooded the room with light. I blinked, trying to get my eyes to adjust to the brightness so I could see what was behind the door. I could just make out the outline of a person in the door, silhouetted in the shadows. "Wakey, wakey." The voice was deep and rough, leading me to believe a man had opened the door. "I hope your accommodations are to your liking."

His face finally came into focus, and I recognized one of the men who I had mistaken for my repairmen. He wasn't paying attention to me at the side, so I tried to look around him and get a feel for where we were. The hallway behind him was bright, and there was a window not far, so our room wasn't in a basement. It definitely looked like a warehouse of sorts. Didn't help me with the *where* but at least knowing the kind of building we were in would help. The man caught me staring, giving a kick to my calf. "Don't even think about it. We doped you both with belladonna. Not enough to kill you, but whichever one of you is the witch will be pretty damn useless for awhile. And this room was constructed with silver, so you can't contact your little *mates* either."

The way he said mates made me cringe, but I needed to see Mollie now that I knew what they had given her. The room we were in was created entirely out of concrete, not a window in sight. Mollie sat in the middle of the room. Her face was pale in the new light, dark purple bruises under her eyes. But she caught my eye, and gave me a small smile, and I knew she was okay for now. I whipped my head back around to our captor. "Why the hell are you doing this? You know we both have mates. They'll know we're missing eventually, and they'll come for us."

The man laughed, an awful sound that sent a chill down my back. "Honey, we're counting on it. It was bad enough when we heard the pack around here was letting wolves mate with humans, but when one of our own pack left us for a *witch*? Well that just won't stand." He sneered down at me. "We let them know where you are, and exactly what we're expecting. They'll have a choice. We can't let the matings continue, so once we figure out which one of you is the storm summoner, and which one is the witch, we figure out a more... suitable use for both of you. They can choose to renounce the matings themselves, or we can do it for them. And one day, when you're all smiling in your new roles in our pack, you'll see how right I was all along. How much happier you'll be for it."

There was that name again. *Storm summoner...* I was absolutely horrified, and across the room Mollie was silent. I could only imagine the thoughts running through her head. This was not the kind of problem you were supposed to be dealing with days away from your wedding. Flowers. Dresses. Those were the kind of problems I expected. Not kidnappings from angry werewolves who didn't approve of who I loved. And how badly would it hurt to break a mate bond? Jasper had said it could be done, but had never gone into detail. I couldn't let that happen. "They'll never go for that. Not in a million years."

"We can be quite... persuasive when we need to be." He shrugged. "Besides, Sage has already laid claim on the handsome dark-haired one. Surely that's a consolation prize worth winning."

Fucking Sage. I was fuming. I should've known she

would've played a part in this. "So what's your plan then? Leave us locked up in this room until our mates show up, and agree to break one of the most powerful kinds of bonds? Sounds like a pretty poor plan to me."

He crouched down so his face was at eye level with mine. I could see the wolf prowling behind his green eyes, the temper he was doing nothing to hide. "The way I see it, I've got a witch with no access to her powers, and a Venator with no access to weapons. I don't think I'm doing too poorly here."

I narrowed my eyes and bared my teeth. "You underestimate us if you think that's the only thing we have going for us."

"We'll see." He stood, brushing off the knees of his pants. He reached into his coat pocket and pulled out a crumpled tin foil package, tossing it toward Mollie. "Lunch. Eat up, ladies. I wouldn't want you passing out before the excitement starts." With that he turned and slammed the heavy metal door behind him.

Shit. Once again we were cloaked in darkness. I crawled toward Mollie, using the same slow deliberate method I had used to find the door. Once I was sitting next to her, she patted my body until she found my hand, putting what felt like half a sandwich into it. "I think it's peanut butter," she whispered.

"What if it's drugged?" I asked. But my stomach was already growling, not remembering the last meal it had.

I felt Mollie sigh before I heard it. "Does it matter? You heard him. They've drugged me with belladonna, and you can't get a hold of Jasper. I don't think we're breaking out of here without someone opening that door first."

I took a bite of the sandwich. Definitely peanut butter, and definitely stale. "It's not over yet. We have a few things going for us that I don't think they're expecting."

"Like what?"

I chewed thoughtfully, thinking about the interaction with our captor. *Storm summoner* he had called me, same as Orcus. But I couldn't dwell too hard on that right now, not if

I wanted to focus on getting out of here. "For one, they still don't know which one of us is the witch and which one is the Venator. We can use that to our advantage next time one of them comes in. Catch them off guard. Even if I can get out to the hallway I might be able to communicate with Jasper and warn him."

Mollie leant against me, resting her head on my shoulder. "True."

"And the most important thing is they don't seem to understand that Jasper and Merrick will never give up on us. Not *ever*. So I hope they're ready for a fight if they do show up."

"I hope they'll be okay." Mollie fell back into silence.

I stroked her hair. This reversal of roles was strange. For years it had been Mollie acting as my protector. Defending me, standing up for me. Making sure I was okay. But without her magic, she seemed like a shell of herself. This time, I'd protect her. "They will be. And we will be too. I'm not going to let anything happen."

I nodded, hoping if I sounded sure enough, I might even convince myself.

Chapter 5

Mollie and I sat with our backs resting against each other, in the cold, dark room. Sometimes we talked, telling stories and jokes to keep our spirits up. Sometimes we were quiet, lost in our own thoughts. No one had come back in the room since the fake repairman had brought us the sandwich. When we got tired, one of us would sleep while the other stayed awake. Then we'd swap. Eventually someone would have to come back. Wouldn't they?

Every so often I'd try to reach Jasper through the bond, throwing my thoughts as far as I could, but it made no difference. Nothing was leaving this room. I wasn't as defenceless as they thought I would be without my blades, but it didn't matter while we were locked in this room.

"Do you ever wonder what your life would be like if you hadn't met Jasper?" Mollie murmured.

I had thought she was asleep, and her quiet voice startled me. I considered her question. Had I? Definitely. Would I change anything? Not for a minute. "I've thought about it, sure. But I can tell you right now that even though it might be safer, and calmer, it wouldn't be my life. I wouldn't be *me*."

"Yeah." She sighed, her back pressing against mine. "Life would've been a lot simpler without Merrick. Without people against our relationship. Against *us*. I took for granted how easy I had it with Ben. Even hiding being a witch was straightforward -- you just don't talk about it."

"Do you regret it? Leaving Ben for Merrick?" I asked. We had never really discussed it, her broken engagement with Ben. It all happened so suddenly. One moment she was with Ben, and the next she was mated to Merrick. Such a change surely had to have an impact on her life.

Ben was steady, reliable. But a mate... a mate was different. It took away a lot of your supposed free will, and Mollie was right -- being with a shifter wasn't straightforward. It came with a lot of responsibilities and uncertainties.

"Not for a minute." She was silent for a moment, and when she spoke again her voice was tired. "I don't think I could imagine my life any other way, now. I always thought I'd have control over my life, that mate bonds were more a suggestion than anything."

"I don't think there was ever a future where we didn't end up here," I mused, running my hands through my tangle of hair. Had I missed my own wedding yet? Was Jasper looking for me? Missing the wedding wouldn't be the worst thing in the world. Maybe we could elope instead if we got out of here. *When* we got out of here.

"In a dirty, dark room?" Mollie laughed, but it was without humour.

I bumped her shoulder with mine. "No, you goof. Here. All our cards on the table. No more secrets. But you sound exhausted. You should try and get some more rest. I'm sure they'll be coming back in soon, and I'll wake you up if I hear someone."

Mollie yawned, the warmth of her back dropping away as she curled up onto the floor. She had been using her sweater as a pillow. "Just a few minutes. I'm sure I just need a few minutes and then those drugs will finally be out of my system."

I sat next to her, waiting for her breathing to even out. I wasn't so sure about the drug thing, but it wasn't like I could do anything about it here. I wasn't an expert. I needed to get her to the pack hospital, where they knew about the effects of drugs on supernaturals. Once I was sure she was asleep, I got back onto my hands and knees, ready to crawl to the door and wait for our captors to arrive again.

It was easier this time, now that I had some idea of distance and space. Didn't make it any more pleasant, but easier was nice. Soon enough my hand bumped into the cool wall, and I followed it around to the doorframe. I sat next to the door, my back pressed against the wall, and my knees pulled into my chest. They had to come give us some food soon. Or check in on us. They obviously wanted us for something -- *me* for something, even though they obviously knew more about this storm summoner shit than I did.

Jasp... I couldn't help myself from trying to reach Jasper through the mate bond while I waited in the pitch black. I gently touched the healed mark on my neck, feeling better to just sense some part of him with me, even if I couldn't hear him. *I miss you, Jasp.*

I sat like that for a while, listening to Mollie's quiet snores, tapping my toes on the cool ground. Eventually, another sound joined in... footsteps? Definitely footsteps. I jumped to my feet, getting into a defensive crouch next to the door. "Mollie," I whispered. "Mollie, wake up."

Mollie groaned behind me, and I pressed my lips together. I was on my own thanks to the Goddamn drugs they had given her. It was fine. I could handle this. One wolf, two at most. I had handled worse, and now I at least had an idea of who was keeping us and why. I'd make them all sorry.

The doorknob twisted, and I crouched lower, bringing my fists up to my face. As the door swung open, I darted toward the small entrance, determined on taking down whichever wolf stood at the door before they could even enter. I rushed the body in the crack of light, wrapping my arms around their hips before I felt their arms close in around me. *No. Not happening.*

"Whoa! Whoa! Baby, what the hell?" I knew that voice. I knew this smell. I froze in my attack, peeking up under my arm at the face of the man I was about to take down in my race to freedom.

"Jasper?" I whispered. What the hell? How was he here?

He smiled at me, pressing a finger to his lips as he stepped deeper into the dank room, now filled with light from the hallway. "Yeah, baby, it's me."

"Oh thank fuck, Jasp." I fell into his open arms, and he embraced me tightly. At this moment, I didn't care how he had gotten here, or how he knew where to find us. All that mattered was he was here, and my soul felt like it was rebuilding itself one cell at a time. Being apart from your mate was a feeling I wasn't sure I'd ever get used to.

"I was so fucking worried," he whispered into my hair. "So fucking worried." He held me at arm's length, looking me over carefully.

I shook my head. "I'm fine. Really. Starving, but they've basically just kept us locked down here." I looked up into his warm caramel eyes, so grateful I was seeing him again in the flesh. "How the hell did you find us anyways? They gave us belladonna, and apparently this room is laced with silver. I couldn't hear you. I kept trying the mate bond, but nothing worked."

"Your new best friend wasn't exactly discreet about where he was holding you two. I'm not quite as stupid as they think I am, so Merrick and the boys are out front distracting them. There's only so many rooms in here, so I just kept trying doors until I found you." Jasper pulled back, putting his hands on either side of my face. "Fuck, Ava, you scared the shit out of me."

I let my body sink into his touch, our heart beats synchronizing once again. "It's my fault, Jasp. It's all my fault. If I hadn't been an idiot and let the guy in, we wouldn't even be in this situation."

Jasper frowned, his grip tightening ever so slightly. "Do *not* think that. Not for a moment. Do I wish this hadn't happened? Absolutely. But how were you supposed to act any different when I tell you a repairman is supposed to show up? I probably would've done the same. Besides. This pack would've weaseled their way into our life one way or another."

"They wanted you both to renounce us as mates." My heart ached even for me to say the words, displeased with the idea we might be separated from our mate for good.

"Good luck with that one," Jasper muttered, rolling his eyes. "Do you know how difficult it is to get a wolf to renounce their mate?"

I chewed my lip. "Umm... I'm hoping pretty hard. Especially because it was Sage who wanted to claim you next."

Jasper scoffed, mumbling something about Sage under his breath as he looked around the barren room. Mollie was laying weakly on the ground where I had left her. She had briefly opened her eyes when Jasper had entered the room, but when she realized it was Jasper and not the other wolves, she had drifted back to sleep. It made me nervous how much she was sleeping, and how hard I had to work to get her to stay awake. She needed help -- and fast. I frowned, shaking my head. "The belladonna they gave us hit her a lot harder than it hit me. Apparently, it'll weaken witches. She doesn't have access to her magic, and I don't think she'll be able to walk out of here -- if I even manage to wake her up. We'll have to carry her." I paused. "If we can figure out a way out of here."

He frowned. "Don't talk like that. There's always a way out. I got in, didn't I?"

"True. But you also had extra help. We're kinda on our own until we get outside with the rest of the guys." I knew we were in a warehouse, and I knew there were at least two wolves guarding us, but that was about it. Other than that, I was flying blind, and I wasn't sure how much Jasper would've been able to take note of while he was sneaking back here. "Were you able to see how many wolves are out there?"

"I kept to the sides, so I could only see a few. I think I counted four inside. There were two more outside with the guys when I left. But there could be more I missed. We're in some kind of machine warehouse, so there's lots of places to hide."

Well that was both good and bad. Four inside. *Maybe.* Four we could handle, even with a lethargic Mollie. But if there were more, and they were hiding, we were screwed. "Did you bring my blades?"

Jasper smiled, the crooked grin that sent waves of desire straight through me. "Who do you think I am, baby?" He reached behind him, where he must have been wearing straps, and pulled out my makhairas.

I reached for them, immediately feeling complete with

the curved knives resting in my hands. "Not that I wouldn't kick their asses without them, but it feels damn good to have them back on me."

Jasper laughed, quietly, so as not to alert anyone to our presence. "I know you'd kick their asses with or without them. Wouldn't be the woman I'm marrying otherwise."

The wedding. Shit. I'd have to ask him if we missed it after we got out of here. Jasper walked over to Mollie, crouching next to her. "Hey, Mol. It's me, Jasper. We're gonna get you out of here, okay? I just need you to stand up and lean against me. We'll take it nice and easy."

Mollie blinked her eyes, trying to stay conscious, and nodded. "Merrick?" she whispered.

"He's waiting for you outside," Jasper responded. Mollie smiled up at him and wobbled to her feet. I tucked both blades in one hand so I could support her other side.

"Which way do we go when we leave the room?" I asked. Mollie was shaking between us, and the sooner we could get her to a doctor, the better.

"Left." Jasper tipped his head in the direction of the window at the end of the hall I had noticed previously.

It took us a minute to adjust to moving with Mollie's weight, but by the time we stepped out into the hallway, we were experts. I was feeling surprisingly hopeful. We *would* get out of here. Mollie *would* get some help. I *would* get married. Except... one thing was nagging at me, chewing away at my mind. Maybe Jasper would have more insight.

"They called me the storm summoner, Jasp," I whispered. I didn't want to mention about the dreams that had woken me up. Not now. Not with everything else going on.

He whipped his head to the side so he could look at me. "Isn't that what... that thing called you?"

"Yeah."

"What does it mean?" His caramel eyes were filled with concern, and I couldn't be certain if it was about the kidnapping situation or about the whole *storm summoner* situation.

"I don't know." I sighed. "But I have a feeling we're going to find out."

Chapter 6

The hallway was eerily quiet as we stumbled through. Having been heavily drugged when they brought me in here, I was entirely reliant on Jasper's directions to get us out. The idea didn't make me comfortable. Since becoming a Venator I was used to have some amount of control over situations I found myself in but walking blind through a building I had been trapped in was the complete opposite of control.

"I can feel your nerves, baby," Jasper murmured. We still weren't able to communicate down the mate bond, but I guessed our feelings were transferring now. Small miracles. Maybe the words would come back once we got ourselves outside. "We're coming up to the warehouse door here. Keep to the left side when we get in there. There're more boxes to hide behind. If we're lucky, we won't have any interference until we get to the front doors."

"If we're lucky," I repeated under my breath. I had heard that phrase way too often, usually out of Jasper's mouth. Just ahead of us was a doorway covered in a plastic curtain, dividing the stark white hallway from what I assumed was the main warehouse.

"Keep to the left," Jasper reminded me. "Keep to the left, follow my lead, and keep your blades ready. If things get too heated, I'll shift quickly so make sure you've got a handle on Mollie."

We parted the thick curtain silently, creeping our way into the large room. It was colder in here, filled with large machines covered in plastic tarps, and skids piled high with boxes. The solid walls were grey concrete, and a large greenhouse roof covered the ceiling. I could see why Jasper had problems seeing how many wolves were here with so many places to hide. What was in our favour was also going to work against us. We moved to the left side, keeping behind the skids. I could hear people talking, but with the echo of the large room, I couldn't figure out how many, or where they were coming from. Jasper pressed a finger to his lips, and left Mollie and I behind a huge tractor, pointing to the next row of skids. I nodded my assent, letting Mollie rest more of her body weight against me as we sank to the floor. I kept my eyes on Jasper, and our gazes locked when we realized how close one of the wolves was to us.

"Did you hear that?" I didn't recognize the voice, so he wasn't one of the ones who had kidnapped us originally. Jasper shook his head at me, warning me not to join him at the next set of boxes where he crouched.

Another voice I didn't know responded. "No. Are you losing it? That's the third time today you thought you heard something. Leo and Cass have a handle on the assholes at the front, and there's enough of us in here even if there *was* something to worry about."

"Seriously, man. I promise I heard something." Another set of footsteps joined the voices, and I was certain my heart was going to pound out of my chest. Beside me, Mollie trembled against my side. So there were at least three wolves in the warehouse. Another two outside. The odds weren't looking great. I assumed the assholes they were talking about at the front were the guys, and hoped they weren't running their mouths too much.

"What are you two fuckheads arguing over now?" *That* voice I recognized. One of the men who had come to my house and come to visit us in the room. I tightened my grip on my makhairas, eager to make him and his snobby attitude pay. "When was the last time someone checked on the girls instead of worrying about a stupid rat in the warehouse?"

Girls. His voice was so belittling I wanted to punch him in his stupid face. I'd show him what a *girl* could do. But I couldn't blow our cover. Not when we had no idea how many of them were actually out there.

"I'll go," the first voice sighed, and his footsteps trailed out of hearing.

The other two voices faded, and Jasper gave me a quick nod. I got Mollie to her feet, and we hobbled over to join Jasper. No sooner had we dropped down next to Jasper before we all froze. "They're gone!" The man who had presumably gone to check on us was running, heavy footsteps thundering on the concrete floors. "The door was open, and they were fucking *gone*."

A growl echoed throughout the entire warehouse, shaking the plastic walls where we tried to make ourselves as small as possible. I caught Jasper's eye over Mollie's head as another growl joined the first, and then another. One more. Two more. Three. The sounds of a dozen wolves surrounded us and my eyes widened. That was a lot more than three. "Our new friends outside have obviously played a nice little trick on us!" our kidnapper was shouting, seemingly in charge of the setup going on here. "Bane, let the guards at the front know not to let them leave. Everyone else, shift and split up. There's only one way out of here, so those girls have to be in here somewhere."

I cursed under my breath, listening to the cracking of bones and shredding of skin as wolves shifted all around us. *Shit.* What were we going to do now? I clutched my blades tightly. I could handle a wolf, even two or three without a problem. But ten? Eleven? I wasn't sure my skills stretched that far. And if Jasper shifted it would be noticeable.

Jasper tipped his head to the right. I followed his gaze to where a small tractor was draped with a heavy blue tarp, also partially covering the skids of boxes next to it. It made a small cave, offering more protection than the one-sided hiding place we had now. "Run," he mouthed.

There were wolves nearby, but I couldn't tell from what direction. Jasper was right. That hiding spot might be our only chance to get out of here. A growl sounded from close by, shaking me to my core. Wolves didn't scare me anymore. Being unprepared in a warehouse full of angry wolves? That scared me. I nodded, getting Mollie unsteadily to her feet again, basically dragging her across the concrete to our tarped hidey-hole. I caught the tail of one wolf as he darted behind a piece of machinery, and there, at the front, was the door. So close, and yet so damn far. I practically tossed Mollie into safety, diving in myself just before another wolf prowled too near for comfort. I said thanks to whoever was listening that the belladonna weakened our scent, as much as it weakened Mollie's powers. I looked behind me, but Jasper was nowhere to be found. *Shit.* One day, I was going to kick his stubborn ass.

"Jasp," I hissed, trying to get his attention to no avail. I cursed my still weak bond, blocking me from being able to communicate telepathically. The tarp that kept us safe was also blocking my vantage point. Goddamnit. "Jasp!" Finally he ducked underneath the tarp, crawling behind the skid of boxes to crouch next to me. "What the hell do you think you're doing?"

"Getting out of here? Preferably alive," he whispered, giving me a weird look like he had no idea what I was saying.

I rolled my eyes, exasperated. "There's an entire pack of them, and there's three of us. How do you propose we get out of here alive, let alone in one piece?"

He was quiet for a moment, rolling his lip between his teeth. Next to me, Mollie bounced her leg, making me even more nervous than I already was. "There's only three of us, but you're the storm summoner, baby. That's gotta count for something."

My chest tightened, my heart pounding loud enough I was sure it would give us away. I could hear the wolves prowling the other side of the warehouse, their footsteps keeping time with each other. "I don't even know what that means, Jasp!" My whisper was frantic.

Jasper smiled, pressing a kiss to my forehead. "I have complete faith you'll figure it out. I'm going to shift and distract them. You and Mollie head right for the door. Do *not* stop for any reason, you hear me?"

"Jasp, no. You'll be outnumbered." I shook my head, frowning at the idea of leaving Jasper behind. My heart hurt at the concept. I knew these wolves wouldn't want to kill another wolf, but could I really be sure? They'd sense an enemy wolf as soon as he shifted. "I can't lose you."

"You're not going to lose me. But our options are

fighting together and leaving Mollie to fend for herself, or you getting Mollie out of her while I hopefully keep them occupied." We both looked down at Mollie, still drifting in and out of consciousness. "We both know the right thing to do here."

I sighed. "I know. But I don't like it." I looked up at him, staring deeply into his eyes. "Promise me you'll be right behind us."

"I promise." He tugged his shirt over his head and started to unbutton his pants. "Wait for my howl and remember what I said. Run for the door and don't turn back. For anything. Will you be able to support her weight?"

I chewed on the inside of my cheek. "If she can hold a bit of her weight herself, I'll be fine. It's just a short distance at this point, right?" I could picture the door as I had seen it before we had taken cover, probably 150 feet away at most. Short enough, relatively speaking.

"I'll be fine," Mollie piped up at this point, fury sparking her eyes fully alive for the first time. "We're getting out of here. All of us."

I nodded to Jasper. "Go. We'll be ready." He jogged off, disappearing behind another skid of machinery. The sounds of his shift followed, and the wolves that had been sniffing around our hiding place faded away. They had already sensed another wolf shifting in their presence. Turning to Mollie, I gave her a fierce glare. "Do *not* push yourself. I know you want to get out here, but I don't need you collapsing five feet from the door either."

She held up her hands, stained and dirty from our time in the room. "I promise."

I offered Mollie my hand, getting her arm wrapped around my shoulder as we both crouched under the tarp. I wanted to be ready. If Jasper was doing this for us, then I needed to make him proud. And on the other side of our skid, Jasper's howl echoed through the warehouse. "That's our cue. Let's go."

I could either dart through the skids and machines like we had been doing, which offered more cover, or I could make a straight shot up the centre aisle which would be a hell of a lot quicker. Balancing Mollie's weight, quicker seemed to be the better option, if not necessarily the safer one.

We shuffled the best we could toward the front doors I had seen earlier. Growling wolves were growing closer, filling our ears with the sounds of animals who did *not* want to see us escape. I gave Mollie a quick sideways glance, and her face was set in determination. She slung her arm over my neck a bit more securely, and we continued our awkward run to freedom. The door was growing closer, and I could barely feel Mollie's weight as we ran. I was just so desperate to taste the fresh air.

And then right before the front door, a large black wolf stepped out into our path, ready to pounce. *Fuck.* I gripped my blades tightly, ready to get out of here at all costs. I didn't want to kill anyone, but I couldn't stay here. And then another wolf joined him from the other side, blocking the door. Damnit. No matter. I could handle it.

A third wolf joined the pack closer to us, and I cursed the mate bond that meant Jasper couldn't warn me. Still, we trudged toward the door, ready to fight our way to freedom. The fourth and fifth wolf made me pause. The sixth had me stumbling over my toes, barely catching Mollie before she flew face first onto the ground.

I struggled to get her back over my shoulder, and when I looked back up, we were surrounded. The wolves had stalked closer, forming a tight circle around us, and were pacing nearer by the second. I had no idea where Jasper was, but I had to hope he was alive. He just wasn't here. I set Mollie down at my feet, taking a makhaira in each hand. I brandished my blades toward the wolves, snarling the best I could. They didn't care, stepping towards me.

"You might be able to kill one or two of them before they get to you. But six? I don't think so." I looked up to see the face of our kidnapper, smirking at us from across the warehouse. "We're not letting our new weapons go that easily."

Weapons? Fuck that shit. I gritted my teeth together, ready to leave a trail of bodies if that's what it took to get out of here.

"And if six won't do it, there's more." Another few wolves popped out from behind skids. Still no Jasper, and our odds were looking slimmer and slimmer by the minute. Mollie clung to my legs, pressing her back against me. The circle that surrounded us was getting smaller, and I felt like I couldn't breathe. Where was the fucking air? Spots flashed in front of my eyes as I tried to stay focused on the wolves. *I'm sorry*, I thought down the useless mate bond. *I'm sorry*. I had failed Jasper. Failed Mollie. I could make a stand here, but I was fooling myself if I thought I'd make it out. The spots blended into one another, making it so I could only see black. I closed my eyes against the onslaught, desperately trying to stay calm.

And then the thunder sounded. Quietly at first, like it was in the distance. And then louder. Wind howled, whistling past my ears. An enormous tearing sound engulfed my senses, a shredding that was too close for me to feel safe. And then it was gone. But was that... a raindrop that hit my face? We were inside. Rain was impossible. I cautiously opened my eyes, and the first thing I noticed was the greenhouse cover that acted as the roof to the warehouse was gone, torn away by the wind and leaving us exposed to the elements. The wolves looked shocked, stopping their advances.

"Don't be fucking babies! Get them!" our kidnapper howled. But even he looked thrown off by what was happening, as the thunder grew closer together, and the rain turned from a drizzle to a downpour. Where there had been clear sky before, there was now a wild storm. And I was pretty sure *I* had created it. And in the distance, Jasper rounded a corner. *Finally*. The wolves shook themselves out of their daze and continued to make their way toward us. Jasper and I wouldn't be able to take them all on. But I was the storm summoner, and I had brought a Goddamn storm here. I wasn't going to take this lying down. I closed my eyes, and a loud boom of thunder accompanied a crack of lightning that felt like it sizzled right next to my face. When I opened my eyes, the wolves were out cold. *What the hell*? I hadn't actually expected that to work. I knew one thing though, and it was that the coldness flooding my veins wasn't from the cool rain. No, there was something inherently dark about the storm. About *me*, and it made me want to scrub my skin until it burned.

Jasper looked up at me in shock, too far to make it to my side, and all I could do was look back with the same expression. I had no idea what happened. All I knew was there was a thunderstorm rolling around us, and the wolves that had surrounded us only moments ago were unconscious on the ground.

The only one still standing in the storm I had created was our kidnapper, standing with his back turned to us. He was human, facing Jasper who was still in his wolf form. "You really want to go through all of this for a fucking human? For a Venator that's no better than a weapon?"

Jasper growled. He was pissed.

"We would've forgiven your first mate debacle with some well-placed loyalty, like handing over the storm summoner. You could've had it all, Jasper. A place of prominence in our pack. A *real* mate. A pack with the storm summoner and a witch. You might not have liked it at first, but eventually all of you would've seen it our way. The Alpha would've had no choice but to listen to me, listen to us then. I wouldn't sound crazy anymore, not with new weapons and wolves in hand. Power. Glory. No one would dare fight us. We could've had it all!" He threw his hands up in air, smiling at the rain that poured down on him. Was he insane? He had to be. I wasn't sure I could hit him with lightning at this distance, having no idea how my new power worked. If I could get closer...

Jasper met my eyes, giving his big wolf head a quick shake. He knew what I was thinking. He was right. I needed to get Mollie out of here. I turned back toward the front door, ready to run.

Our kidnapper laughed. "Oh well. I really didn't want to kill you, but at this point you aren't really a wolf, are you?" The sounds of his shift made me pause, Mollie clinging to my neck.

Go, baby! Don't turn back! At the last moment, the mate bond fell back into place with Jasper's command. I pressed my lips together, took more of Mollie's weight on my shoulder, and moved as fast as my legs could carry the both of us. I had to trust Jasper would be okay. The bond would keep me informed. The doors were so close, only a few feet away, and I could only barely hear the sounds of Jasper and our kidnapper fighting over the raging storm. Jasper would win. It was the only option I allowed myself to believe.

Mollie and I burst through the front doors together. In the pouring rain in front of us were the two guards Jasper had mentioned. Adrian, Beau, and Merrick stood on the other side, shock and surprise evident in their faces. The first guard darted toward us, and without thinking I shot a bolt of lightning in his direction -- not close enough to kill, but close enough to knock him out cold. My body thrummed with power, and a need for more. I needed to shut that feeling down, and quick. I was so focused on getting my emotions under control, I didn't see the second guard shift and bound in my direction. My makhairas were nowhere to be found, abandoned somewhere in the warehouse, so I crouched as tightly as I could, wrapping my body around Mollie. The guard growled, thick with menace, and I shut my eyes. But the impact never came, and when I opened my eyes, Beau had blocked the path of the other guard, knocking him to the ground but not without sustaining a nasty bite on his shoulder. "Don't even fucking *think* about getting back up, fucker. Backup is already on the way." He shot me a cocky grin. "Duke stayed behind to wait for our signal. Apparently, Sage and the other women who were involved with this little coup had holed up nearby -- the cops already apprehended them. The number one rule of wolves is to not fuck with other wolves' mates. The majority of this pack is gonna end up disbanded or in jail."

I stifled a groan. I wasn't surprised Sage was a part of this whole thing. I didn't have much time to dwell on it, because sure enough, the engine of a car was pulling into the wooded lot where we stood, and then another. *Our pack.* I loosened my grip on Mollie, and Merrick immediately enveloped her in his arms. I still couldn't see Jasper, but I could feel him. He was okay. *We* were okay.

"Oh my fucking God, I've never been so happy to see your goofy ass face in my life." I ran up to Beau, wrapping my arms around his neck, both of us soaking wet from the rain that still poured. "But what the hell do you think you were doing? I had it handled!"

Beau laughed and put me back down on the ground, holding his arm where it bled. I knew the bleeding would stop with his quick healing soon enough, but he had been lucky. He could've been hurt a lot worse. "Jasper would've had my ass if I had let anything happen to you, baby girl."

"He's right. I would've." Jasper's voice hit me before his arms wrapped around my shoulders, pulling me against his chest. I whirled around in his tight grasp, running my hands over his dripping face. I knew he was okay but knowing and seeing were two different things. Above us, thunder rumbled and lightning cracked. "I'm fine. I'm fine, baby. I had to put him down, but I'm okay, I swear. Besides, I knew I was safe in the hands of my fiancée, the storm summoner."

I laughed nervously, shaking my head. "Don't call me that. I don't like how it felt. How it made me feel, I mean. The storm… it didn't come from a good place."

Merrick and Mollie appeared at our side, attached at the hip. Mollie looked ready to pass out, and I knew Merrick would get her to the pack hospital as soon as she'd let him. But you didn't argue with the look in Mollie's eyes right now. "Your mom could summon storms too," Mollie murmured. "I had always thought it was some dark magic my parents had given her, but the fact you could do it too ruins that idea. It must be some kind of Venator thing, only passed down through certain bloodlines. I could always look into it more… but how did they know about it?"

I held up my hand, giving her a soft smile. "Even if it isn't dark magic, I'm not interested in using that power again. Ever. It's too close to Monica's shadows for me. And I could care less how they knew, because it's over. Chapter closed. Now can you *please* focus on yourself and get to the damn hospital?" I really did have no interest in using the power again, and as for how the other pack knew… I was tired of digging into dark secrets. I wanted to focus on the here and now. For a little while, at least.

"Great idea, Ava. I'll take this one to the pack lands," Merrick agreed, already scooping up a protesting Mollie and carrying her across the wooded lot to his car.

Jasper pressed a kiss on the top of my head. "And we have a wedding to plan."

Adrian burst out laughing at the expression on my face. "We didn't miss the wedding?" I asked.

"Nope. It's tomorrow, and now that you're safe it's still a go." Jasper sounded way too happy for just escaping a warehouse filled with wolves. I looked up to the sky, where bits of dark purple cloud were breaking way to sunlight hiding beneath. The storm was nearly over. "And if it's okay with you, baby, I'd really like to get home and get some rest. After I run back inside and grab my clothes and your blades."

I finally took in Jasper's appearance, naked from when he had shifted, and laughed. "I guess that's a reasonable request."

He smiled and darted inside the building, while we waited outside, letting the chaos pass us by. Eventually Jasper reappeared, fully clothed, and my blades in hand. The four of us walked together to the car, passing by wolves from our pack, and some local police allies who were flooding the warehouse. The other pack wouldn't get away with their actions. Beau unlocked the doors to his truck, and we all piled in. I slid in close to Jasper, unable to take my eyes off his face. "Promise me you won't ever fucking scare me like that again."

Beau pulled the truck out of the lot, heading back to the main road, and Jasper laughed, wrapping his arm around my shoulder. "I'll do you one better, baby. I'll vow it."

I smiled, settling back against Jasper's chest. Comfortable. Safe. At peace. "Till death do us part."

His laugh shook me where I laid. "Now you're getting it."

Chapter 7

I took a deep breath in. And then another. And then one more -- just for luck. I had battled wolves, demons, and even my own parents. I could do this. Right?

A warm hand rubbed my back, and I was grateful for the small touch. "You good, girl?" Mollie whispered. A night in the pack hospital and some rapid detoxing I had no hope of understanding had gotten Mollie back to normal in no time at all.

I smiled. "I'm good." For the first time in two weeks, hell, for the first time in months my mind felt clear. Nothing stood in between myself and Jasper, and I wasn't going to let anything come between us ever again. The new Ava, the one who was wearing the perfectly imperfect dress and was staring back at me in the mirror, wouldn't let that happen. We were forever, Jasper and I. Marked, bound together in this life and the next.

"You better be, because it's almost time." Mollie smiled at me. Her blonde hair done up in an elaborate updo, and her deep red dress was almost the same colour as her lipstick. As my only "bridesmaid" -- and my unofficial wedding planner -- I had let her choose whatever she wanted for her dress. Needless to say, I wasn't surprised it was perfect. The late afternoon fall light filled my kitchen with warmth. "You remember, right? I'll go down first, you wait for the music cue, and then you and Merrick will walk down together."

I rolled my eyes, taking one last look at myself in the mirror. My hair was down in soft waves, the shift dress anything but white. No, the dress Mollie and I had chosen was black, an elegant silk number that draped over my hips and gave me a shape where previously there had only been muscle. And the best part? Nothing could stain black. "I remember, Mollie. We've only been over it about a thousand times now."

"Shush," she muttered, giving me a glare. But I knew how excited she was, and the glare was all for show. Her bouquet was a smaller version of mine -- all white, the flowers she had called hydrangeas mixed together with roses, and other flowers I would never be able to identify. Whatever they were, they were beautiful. "And for heaven's sake, do *not* run down the aisle. Take your time, please!"

"Hon, I think we've got this," Merrick interrupted Mollie, pressing a kiss to her lips. Even with the heels I knew her dress hid, he still towered over her. "I promise, we won't do anything to embarrass you." Merrick had been thrilled when I asked him to walk me down the aisle. But honestly, I couldn't imagine it being anyone else. Beau and Adrian would be standing next to Jasper as his groomsmen, and Duke would be playing his violin (who knew?) for our ceremony music.

As if I had conjured it, the soft strands of music began to play outside my backdoor. It had seemed weird to get married anywhere other than outside, even if there was a chance the weather wouldn't play nice. So Mollie and I had gotten ready in my bedroom, and I had yet to see the setup she had spent all morning getting ready. Caterers and other random workers had been in and out all day. Was my washing machine fixed? Absolutely not. I wasn't sure it was ever going to be fixed. But at least we'd have a beautiful twilight wedding. Leave it to my best friend to be kidnapped one day and planning a perfect wedding the next. "Go, Mol. Merrick is right. We won't embarrass you."

Mollie pursed her lips and began to walk out the kitchen door.

"We won't embarrass you... much," I whispered. Merrick stifled a laugh, and Mollie turned to look at me with concern written all over her face. "Go, Mollie! I'm just kidding. It'll be perfect."

With one last worried glance over her shoulder, Mollie stepped outside into the sunset filled backyard. I caught a glimpse of benches lining a petal draped aisle before the door closed. I tapped my foot, waiting for the music cue Mollie had mentioned before.

"You guys are already bonded for life," Merrick

murmured. "This is just show for the rest of the world."

I looked up at him with a smile. "I know. I'm just excited to see him."

"That I can understand." Merrick grinned back at me, linking his arm with mine. The music shifted tempo slightly, and my heart did the same. "I believe that's our cue."

Jasper's voice popped into my head. *I love you. I bet you look absolutely stunning.*

No peeking. Merrick was opening the door, and we were stepping outside into the lush, magical garden Mollie had transformed my backyard into. Jasper stood at the end of the aisle, with his back still toward me.

I would never.

I took a step off the patio, my bare foot coming to rest on a blanket of flower petals. Around me, our friends and family stood, smiling at Merrick and myself as we slowly made our way toward the massive green arch at the end of the aisle. *Liar*, I teased.

You're right. At the same moment his words hit me, he turned around. I couldn't believe I had ever doubted this wedding. Jasper's warm eyes were filled with nothing but undying love for me, flooding our mate bond with feelings that only amplified my own. Merrick was right. This wedding was just show, because what I was feeling right now could never change. It was forever, just like Jasper and I. *You're beautiful.*

You're not too bad yourself. Merrick and I were halfway down the aisle, and I couldn't stop the ridiculous grin from spreading across my face. Jasper was striking in his black suit, his muscles straining against the rich fabric, and his hair pushed away from his face. His tall figure was framed by the extensive green arch Mollie had obsessed about for weeks, and now seeing it in person, I couldn't complain. It was perfect. Next to him, Beau and Adrian smiled at me wearing matching black suits of their own. No tuxes here -- not for the wolves. That was just asking for trouble. Not that it mattered. I'd marry Jasper if he was wearing a paper bag. The music began to slow, and I caught Duke's eyes over his violin. I wasn't sure his and Jasper's relationship would ever go back to the way it was before, but it was funny how weddings changed people. He gave me a soft nod, something I took as his blessing, and my heart wanted to explode from the love I felt in the moment.

Finally, we were at the front. Merrick pressed a quick kiss to my cheek, and then disappeared to take his seat. I reached my hands out, and Jasper clasped them so tightly in his own I was surprised my bones didn't break in his touch. "I love you," I murmured.

A thousand emotions rolled behind Jasper's caramel eyes. "I love you more than I could ever put into words."

I knew he spoke nothing but the truth.

The ceremony was quiet and quick, the sun setting behind us as we stood together and spoke the words that would bind us together legally. Jasper even vowed not to scare me ever again. Words that, when it came down to it, meant very little. Our love was unbreakable, undefinable by simple vows. But professing our love for our friends was the important part. After everything we had gone through, we deserved that much. The minister was a wolf from the pack, and when he proclaimed us husband and wife his smile was that of a doting father.

Jasper and I hadn't even finished our first kiss before Beau was whooping beside us. "It's party time, bitches!"

"Beau!" Mollie snapped. "At least save it for the reception."

I smiled against Jasper's lips, enjoying the feeling of my husband's arms wrapped around me. Beau and Mollie were oil and water, but hopefully with a bit of tequila in them, everyone would loosen up.

Eventually we all found our way to the white tent Mollie had arranged to be erected in the yard. Inside, she had transformed the space into even more of an enchantment than the rest of my garden. In fact, I wouldn't be surprised if she had used actual magic to make it as beautiful as it was. Round tables surrounded a wooden dance floor, and everywhere you looked there were flowers,

flowers, and more flowers. Greenery draped from the ceiling, and chandeliers made up for the quickly setting sun. I even had to admit that the centrepieces Mollie had forced me to slave over were perfect. A bottle of wine just wouldn't have done her vision justice.

Arms wrapped me in a hug from behind. "I'm just so happy for you both."

I turned around to smile at Lucy, embracing her warmly. "I'm so glad you were able to make it." Lucy's turn with the Orcus had only amplified her anxieties, and while she was working through them, social gatherings were not her favourite place to be.

"I wouldn't have missed it for the world." She grinned brightly. "It was so beautiful. I didn't know you were so artistic!"

I laughed and pointed at Mollie who was twirling on the dancefloor with Merrick. "I'm definitely not the artistic one. It was all her. If it was up to me, we would've eloped at the courthouse." Duke came up behind Lucy with a quiet smile on his face, placing a gentle hand on his mate's shoulder. "Duke, I can't thank you enough for playing at the ceremony. I had no idea you could play that beautifully."

He shook his head, looking in the direction of Adrian and Beau who were downing shots at the bar. "If you had friends like them, would you really make a big deal out of playing the violin either?"

I pursed my lips, trying not to laugh. "Probably not."

Duke reached around Lucy, clasping my hand in his. "You'll take care of him, won't you? He acts like he doesn't need help, but he does sometimes."

"I'll protect him with my life." Duke and I looked at each other, and I knew then we both had Jasper's best interests at heart. He gave me a quick smile, and then led his mate to one of the tables at the edge of the dancefloor.

The reception was a whirlwind, and if it wasn't for Mollie shoving plates of food in my face, I'm sure I would've forgotten to eat. If my glass was ever empty, someone was there to refill it. Wolves and old family friends from town alike were constantly surrounding me, asking me to dance, congratulating me. It wasn't until I had finally sat down at the table for what felt like the first time all day, that I realized I hadn't seen Jasper since God knows when. Someone tapped me on my shoulder, and my instinct was to turn around and tell Beau I was too tired to dance. He had spun me so much on the dance floor I was surprised the world still wasn't spinning.

Instead, I found Jasper's smiling face. "Can I have this dance?"

I grinned, taking his hand and getting to my feet. "Do you even need to ask?" I linked my arms around Jasper's neck as we swayed lazily on the dancefloor. Words were unnecessary, as comfortable as we were in each other's presence. I rested my head on his shoulder, as one dance turned into two, and the night slipped deeper into darkness. The world faded away, until there was nothing other than Jasper and myself, rocking back and forth to a quiet melody.

Jasper pulled me closer against his body, pushing my hair back so he could press his mouth against my ear. "Let's get the hell out of here."

I smiled, my body already burning with desire for him. "We can't exactly skip out on our own reception."

"Sure we can," he argued, sweeping his finger along the neckline of my dress. "It's our wedding. We can do whatever the hell we want. Besides, everyone is drunk anyways."

He had me there. A few too many rounds of shots had everyone feeling good. No one would remember much of anything in the morning. "Let's go."

Jasper pulled me out of the tent, his hand dipping lower and lower on the silk covering my back. His touch drove me wild, and he gripped me tighter as we found our way into our bedroom. He closed the door softly behind us and twirled me around to face him. An evening of dancing, and a few drinks gave his tanned skin a flushed glow, and his bright smile was one to rival the sun.

"Mrs. Knight," Jasper breathed, dragging his finger

down my neck. "I believe you're mine now, in every sense of the word. And in return, I give you my soul. Be careful with it."

"I promise to guard it with my life," I murmured, placing a hand on each of his warm cheeks.

He smiled wider, dipping his head forward to kiss me. I slid my hands around the back of his head, tugging on his dark hair, and Jasper ran his tongue along the seam of my lips. I moaned, my body bending to his will, and my mouth opening for his touch. He moved his hands to the back of my dress as we kissed, feeling for the zipper. One smooth tug of his hands, and the black silk laid in a pile at my feet. Jasper paused, pulling away from my face to take me in fully. His eyes darkened slightly, and he licked his lips.

I shrugged as casually as I could manage. "The dress was too backless for a bra and panties."

Jasper shook his head. "If I had known you were naked under this dress, I would've left the party hours ago." And then his hands were trailing every inch of my skin, his mouth dominating mine. I tugged at the buttons of his shirt impatiently, desperate for him to be just as bare as I was. He shrugged off his now unbuttoned shirt, breaking our kiss for a moment so he could strip off his pants. He scooped me up under my ass and brought me to the bed, parting my legs with his hips as he fit the thick head of his cock at my entrance. "Hard or slow, baby?"

"Both," I whispered. He offered me his crooked grin, pinned my hands over my head with one of his, and then slowly pushed his way inside me. My back arched off the bed, desperate to reach more of him, and his moan tangled with mine. His thrusts were slow and methodical, driving both of us crazy, but deep enough I felt him everywhere. Even as my breathing picked up, and my body caved to the pleasure building within me, he still didn't change his pace.

"Come for me, Ava," Jasper commanded, his eyes finally giving way to the animal inside -- the animal I loved as I loved him.

I was never able to deny him when he was this way. I

whispered his name as I came around his cock, Jasper rocking into me with the same level of love and desire he had that first time we had sex. I was still tumbling down from my orgasm when he cried out his own release, growling my name as he shook inside me. We laid like that, like we always had. One soul, together.

The moon glowed in the dark, softly illuminating the bedroom where Jasper and I lay tangled together. The moon that had tied us together from the moment we met, watching over us as we fought and loved. Protected our family and defended our relationship. The moon had seen it all, a silent spectator of our lives. Could it have warned me against such a life of danger and turmoil if I had listened? Maybe. But I also knew from the moment Jasper walked into that coffee shop all those months ago that something in my life had shifted for the better, and I was never letting go of that feeling. So maybe the moon knew what it was doing after all. Maybe it had watched us and smiled, knowing our lives were falling into place. A soft smile crept across my face, and I whispered my thanks to the night.

Epilogue

Three Years Later

I shaded my eyes from the bright sun with my hand, and then looked down at my watch. "Okay, guys, that was awesome. Let's try it one more time and then call it a day. It's too hot to be out here."

A mix of groans and cheers followed my announcement. I looked to my side at Jasper, still as handsome as the first day I had met him and smiled. He pressed a quick kiss to my cheek and grinned back. "Can't please them all, baby."

We were on the pack lands, in the middle of the field, surrounded by a dozen or so young wolves. Some of them hadn't even shifted for the first time yet, but Jasper and I had pegged them for having potential, and their parents were more than thrilled for the active kids to have an outlet. Training wolves to be Venators was *not* where I saw my life going, but I couldn't say I was upset about it in the slightest. The kids were eager to learn, and their wolf abilities made them naturals in both hand-to-hand combat, and weapons. It had taken some convincing on our part, to talk Alpha Dean into letting us recruit and train new Venators from wolves in the pack, but eventually he saw things our way. Besides, we had lots of new blood after the remains of Merrick's pack had eventually merged with ours. Turns out, it had only been a small group of them who were stuck in the old ways. The rest of them were more than accepting of Venators and witches integrating with wolves.

Being a Venator was something that usually got passed down from parent to child, with the exception of my parents. But with modern times, more and more families were choosing to not have children, and the Venators were slowly dying out. After the wedding, I had been called more than once to other local packs to help them with some supernatural problem or another. Turns out, the next closest Venator was in Texas. Jasper and I had no plans for children at the moment ourselves, so we came up with the idea of branching out from Venators being only human. If you really thought about it, the advantage a supernatural Venator would have on its enemies would be enormous. And maybe -- just maybe -- it would prevent some of the prejudices Jasper and I had to go through.

I loved the kids. They worked hard and were eager to make us proud. For some reason, my awkwardness resonated with the young Venators, and they really listened to what I had to say. I had one rule. We only taught them self-defence skills. I still wasn't really sure what had brought on my ability to summon storms, besides my intense fear, but I knew it wasn't a side of being a Venator I wanted to explore. I wanted to pass down a legacy I could be proud of, not one I couldn't be certain didn't involve dark magic. Occasionally, I still would feel the thunder rolling in my veins, and the urge to shift those bruised clouds overhead. I could see how my mother would be tempted by that side, be drawn to the darkness that thrummed within. But it wasn't something I wanted for myself. I wanted to be strong, not powerful, so I let the feelings drift over me and then wash away.

Not that anyone minded our training was purely combat. Parents were excited when we approached them. Merrick was eager for his own child to join, even if said child was still cooking in Mollie's body. Mollie was less than certain, and I couldn't say I blamed her. Their life had fallen into a comfortable rhythm after the wedding, with their own marriage taking place only a few months after. She didn't want to upset the status quo. Merrick wanted his family to be prepared. It was always the way, wasn't it? The pull between safety and excitement. Knowledge to keep things the same, or to make things better.

I watched the groups as they sparred with bokken -- the same tools Jasper had used to train me all those moons ago. They would do just fine, even if no trouble came their way. And if it did, they'd be ready. I whistled loudly, calling their attention to me, and dismissed them for the day. It was the dead of summer, and the heat was killer. Myself, I couldn't wait for a cold shower and the air conditioning that called to me from our apartment.

Jasper and I collected the strewn equipment, tossing it into the oversized gear bag we carried back and forth. "I think that went well today. They're really getting a handle on the bokken. We might be able to start with actual weapons next month," I mused.

Jasper zipped up the bag, tossing it easily over one shoulder. "I wouldn't be surprised." He reached for my hand, and together we walked back to my car in the parking lot. "Do you ever think about it being your kid?"

I wrinkled my nose. "All fourteen of them? Are we building a bunkhouse?"

Jasper laughed. "No. Just one. Maybe two."

"I don't know." I had thought about it, sure. An adorable chubby cheeked toddler running around with Jasper's dark hair. But was it really what I wanted from my life? "I guess I had always assumed I would have kids, but I'm not sure if it's because it was what I was told I needed to do, or because it was something I truly wanted."

"I think I'm the same way," Jasper murmured. "I love the kids we train. But our life is so uncertain, is it really fair to bring a child into that?"

"And is our life really missing anything without a child?"

We both sighed, getting into the car. "But we would make cute kids," he argued.

"The cutest," I agreed, starting the engine. I looked at him as I pulled out of the parking lot, and we both started laughing. A few miles passed with a comfortable silence between us. The drive between the pack lands and our apartments was short anyways. "It's not to say we have to make any decisions right now."

"No. We definitely don't." Jasper squeezed my thigh as we pulled into the complex. "But that doesn't mean we can't practice." His voice dropped suggestively. I knew *exactly* what he meant.

"Jasp, I'm all sweaty." I laughed, parking the car in its

usual spot.

"Like that's ever mattered to me before, Mrs. Knight." We got out of the car, and Jasper left the gear bag in the trunk as he came around to walk next to me.

I cocked my head and raised my eyebrow at him. "And just how were you thinking we'd practice, Mr. Knight?"

"I have a few ideas."

Before I had a chance to respond, Jasper had swooped me up into his arms, racing for the front door. "Jasp! Put me down!" But I couldn't stop the laughter from escaping. He kicked the door shut behind us, kissing my face as he walked us into the bedroom. Placing me on the bed, he straddled my hips and stripped his shirt off. Years of being together had done nothing to put a damper on the impressiveness of Jasper's body. His stomach was still carved into hard abs, his toned skin a few shades darker in the summer. I never lost the urge to reach out and make sure he was real.

"Lay back, baby," he whispered. I hadn't realized I was resting forward on my elbows, examining him closer than I needed to. Shit, he was beautiful.

I fell back onto the bed, pushing away blankets and pillows so there would be no barriers between us. Jasper leaned forward, tugging my shirt and sports bra over my head, and tossed them onto the floor. The *messy* floor, because some things never changed. I shuffled pushing my pants over my hips as Jasper kicked his own off. This *practice* as he was calling it today was fairly standard for us after a good training session. Sex and fighting forever intertwined.

"You're beautiful," he murmured, dragging his finger down my face, and gliding it along my collarbone. He was one to talk, his dark hair perfectly tousled, and his caramel eyes shifting toward the black of his wolf's. "More and more beautiful every damn day." He didn't stop sliding his hand down my body, across my hips and coming to cup the wet heat between my legs.

I moaned softly, my body already aching for him in a way I could never control. "Will you still think I'm beautiful when I'm 80 and covered in wrinkles?"

Jasper smiled, kissing me deeply. "Even then. Especially beautiful then, because you'll have spent your entire life loving me, and being loved by me."

I tipped my head to the side, giving him better access to my neck as he dropped to kiss and lick the light scar of his mark. Less visible now, for sure, but still just as sensitive. As his tongue ran over the scar, I shivered, and he sank a finger between my wet folds. "Shit, Jasp."

"So wet for me, baby. Always so ready for me and my body. Will you ever get enough?" He curled his finger inside my pussy, his words reverberating against my neck.

"I don't...think so..." I stammered. I closed my eyes, focusing on Jasper's motions turning me on in a way no one else ever could. My husband. *My mate.*

"Do you want to come on my fingers?" Jasper pushed the palm of his hand onto my clit, and I cried out. "Or do you want me to fuck you to release?" His tongue lazily swirled on my neck, his fingers fucking me with a much more aggressive rhythm. Pleasure was building, a tidal wave I knew I wouldn't be able to control.

"Fuck me."

He grinned against my neck and pushed my legs further apart with his knee. His cock nudged my opening, demanding my complete compliance. I gripped his shoulders, and he eased inside me. Both of us moaned in relief, our bodies feeling whole once more. It would never be enough, and we both knew it. Despite his fervor in getting me into bed, and the desperate rhythm his fingers had played, Jasper took his time as he thrust in and out of me, making sure I felt every last inch of him. He raised himself up on his elbows, kissing me deeply as he fucked me slowly. I rolled my hips against him, the friction immediately pushing me closer to the edge of oblivion. "You gonna come for me, baby?" Jasper murmured against my lips.

He slowed his pace even more, torturing me as he ground his body against my clit. I was definitely going to come for him. I'd come for him a thousand times if he'd let me. My orgasm rushed through my body as I cried out Jasper's name, his cock rocking me through my release. It only took a few more thrusts before Jasper was calling out my own name, his body shaking with his own orgasm. "Fuck," I whispered.

"I love you so damn much." He brushed a kiss against my forehead, and the curled up beside me, resting his head on my chest. I knew he'd be asleep in moments, and I ran my hands through his hair. Eventually I'd get up and shower, maybe attempt to make some dinner. But right now I was content.

"I love you too," I whispered. He mumbled something incoherent back, already half asleep.

I thought about our day, our conversation, our *lives*. It really didn't matter. Kids, no kids, money, no money. I had no control over these things, so I didn't want to stress over them. *No*, I thought, stroking Jasper's hair where he laid on my chest, snoring softly. I had spent so much of my life trying to control the uncontrollable. It had gotten me nowhere. But right now, in this moment, I was happy. And if it meant going with the flow to stay this happy, I would gladly let the current carry me along.

Torri Heat

Torri Heat has always loved control. Her mind was blown when she discovered she could control entire worlds through story writing. Throw some steamy romance in there, and it was pretty close to perfection. Torri loves dark heroes who ride off into the sunset on their motorcycles, fierce heroines who can fend for themselves, and a sprinkle of the paranormal to keep things interesting. When she's not creating alternate realities you can find her managing her three ring circus of kids and animals.

Torri at Changeling: changelingpress.com/torri-heat-a-217

Changeling Press E-Books

More Sci-Fi, Fantasy, Paranormal, and BDSM adventures available in e-book format for immediate download at ChangelingPress.com -- Werewolves, Vampires, Dragons, Shapeshifters and more -- Erotic Tales from the edge of your imagination.

What are E-Books?

E-books, or electronic books, are books designed to be read in digital format -- on your desktop or laptop computer, notebook, tablet, Smart Phone, or any electronic e-book reader.

Where can I get Changeling Press E-Books?

Changeling Press e-books are available at ChangelingPress.com, Amazon, Apple Books, Barnes & Noble, and Kobo/Walmart.

ChangelingPress.com